LOVE'S ENCROACHMENT

LOVE BELVIN

MKT PUBLISHING, LLC

by Love Belvin

MKT Publishing, LLC

 This book is a work of fiction. Names, characters, places, and incidences are fictitious and a product of the author's imagination.

ISBN: 978-1-950014-50-7 (Paperback)
ISBN: 978-1-950014-49-1 (eBook)

MKT Publishing, LLC
First print edition 2021 in U.S.A.

Cover design by **Visual Luxe**

~

Prologue

THE MOMENT I MAKE IT TO THE SIDE OF THE HOUSE, I TURN BACK TO WAVE *him off. I can't see his face but can make out his body's incline to pull the gear knob of his pickup before taking off down the quiet block.*

My heart's racing, but not because I'm about to sneak inside the window of my parents' home at close to three in the morning: I've done this a thousand times over the past seven months. It's because this is the first time I allowed him to drop me off in front of my house, and it's making me want to jump right back into his F150 and just drive until the gas runs out.

But there's no time for that. I want to be asleep by the time my father gets home from work. I grab the crate I keep at the back of the small cottage house before creeping back to the side. Stepping onto the crate, I quietly detach the screen then lift the unlocked window. Reaching inside, I pat air in the dark room for the dresser that sits to the immediate left of the frame. I place the screen there before lifting my body to climb inside.

I could be quieter if I were a robber, but my family sleeps heavy when Gunnery Sergeant Preston Taylor isn't home. It's like our bodies subconsciously know when his shift is over at four am; our sleep turns restless around that hour. When my feet are on the floor, I turn to attach the screen back to the frame, locking it into place. Next, I slowly pull the window down. Once shut, I sigh, turning the lever to lock it.

The sucky thing about sneaking back into the house at this hour is not being able to wash sex off. Not that I want his scent off of me, just my stickiness. But there's no time for that luxury. I head toward the door of my mother's tiny sewing room, my body feeling heavy every step of the way. It isn't until I'm a few feet from the hardwood flooring of the hallway that I see his shadow.

Fuck!

My heart drops and bladder chugs.

My father's in a robe and slippers, stretched, it seems from one wall of the hall to the other with his fat fists planted into his waist.

"Young lady, you can think whatever you please about ya mother. But you must think I'm a fool." His lips tighten into a ball. "What did I tell you about a lie?"

My mother creeps out of their bedroom and into the hallway behind him. The usual sketch of fear is lining her face. I could see my sister, Jenise's, head craning from the doorway of our bedroom, too.

I swallow hard, switching the weight on my shaking legs. "It always catches up to you."

"So you think sneaking out every night, at all crazy hours of the night wasn't gonna catch up with you, Nyedeera Taylor?" Before I can think of a response, he warns, "And I'd be careful with my truth if I were you. You know I know everything."

Shaking my head, I want to disappear. I want this to be over with; waking up three days from now and having this all forgotten about.

"I—I..." I swallow unintentionally. Nervously. "I haven't been able to sleep at night."

"All week?" he shouts, taking a step toward me. "You haven't been able to sleep, so you've been sneaking out?" His eyes narrow to a squint. I'm partially relieved at his inaccuracy. He only believes it's been this week, and I'll continue to allow him to. "You been out with a boy, Nyedeera?" My eyes damn near pop out of my head. I think before I answer, the way he's taught us to. Fear. It pumps through the veins of this family, bowing at his feet. My knees are quaking, mouth is super slimy and sour. "Never mind." He grabs my arm and yanks me near the open bathroom.

My entire body tenses.

"Hey, now, Preston!" my mother cries with a compromised bite.

You can hear the protective momma bear in her croak and the pleading in her cry at the same time. "Please."

Daddy's neck jerks, face swings her way as his eyes widen and brows hike in warning. He pulls a box from the pocket of his robe. "You just make sure she pees on these right. I only got three."

My knees buckle as my mother gathers the pregnancy test boxes at her chest. Tears pool her eyes as she looks at me with pity. She understands what I do: there's no negotiating or compromising with Gunnery Sergeant Preston Taylor of the United States Marine Corps.

My mother toddles into the bathroom, face filled with apologies. I understand but don't respect it as I follow her inside.

Waiting outside the bathroom while my father stands over the pregnancy kits is torture. It's useless: I've always been smart. Things have been different with Launz, but we've been safe. He's the first guy I've been super comfortable with. Still, we've been responsible these past three months. My sister, Jenise, inches closer to me, her small act of support. She, too, has been here. Any sign of insubordination in this family calls for extreme and imminent punishment. I'm sure this brings a torrent of bad memories for her.

Her eyes are heavy as she quietly crawls her left palm against the wooden panel walls using her fingers to reach my right one. It's balled into a fist, and I can't hear anything over the blood rushing through my head.

She squeezes my hand and mouths, "It's going to be okay. Alright?"

I nod. Not being pregnant is the only place my confidence lies right now. It's the punishment for sneaking out that's making me nervous as hell. He doesn't know about my job, but I already know I'll have to quit. I've lied to them, too. It is what is. He'll probably make me call him every hour on the hour after school to make sure I'm home, though all he really has to do is check with my mother. But that isn't good enough for Gunnery Sergeant Preston Taylor. It's the fear and control he needs to execute. The thing I hate about him.

I try taking a deep breath. Either way, I'll be fine. I've been surviving my father's tirade all these years. I'm almost an adult, with mere weeks to go.

Then he won't hear from me again...

A cry rips from my mother's belly in the bathroom. Next, I hear a bang, then my father's heavy steps. Before I can process it all, he storms out, rushing toward me.

"You know, out of you and your sister, I never thought it would be you to be the biggest dummy ever!"

"Why?" slips from my mouth, my eyes wild with fear.

"Don't matter!" he shouts. "One dummy, two dummies, now there's about to be three!"

"Thra—three?" My eyes dart around him for my mother.

Why is he so close to me? What's going on?

"How long you been pregnant, Nyedeera?"

"That's a lie—"

My head swings back, hitting the wooden wall. He hit me. *My hand shot to my mouth. Crimson liquid smeared on my fingers.*

"You hit me? Over something I didn't—"

WACK!

"Preston!*" my mother cries closer this time as I drop to the floor.*

"You wanna be around here acting like a slut? Bring babies into the world for me to take care of!" WACK! *"You think whoring around is an expense I gotta pay? You think I raised you to be a momma for a bum that ain't gone do nothing but ask into ya pants again?"* WACK! *His open palm across my shoulder, arm, and hip feels like flashes of fire, burning in trails.*

"Preston!" my mother screams. "That's enough! Please!" She sobs, "Pleeeeease!"

I lay there as he hit me over and over, stunned. The pain. The audacity. This had to be a bad dream. There was no way I was pregnant.

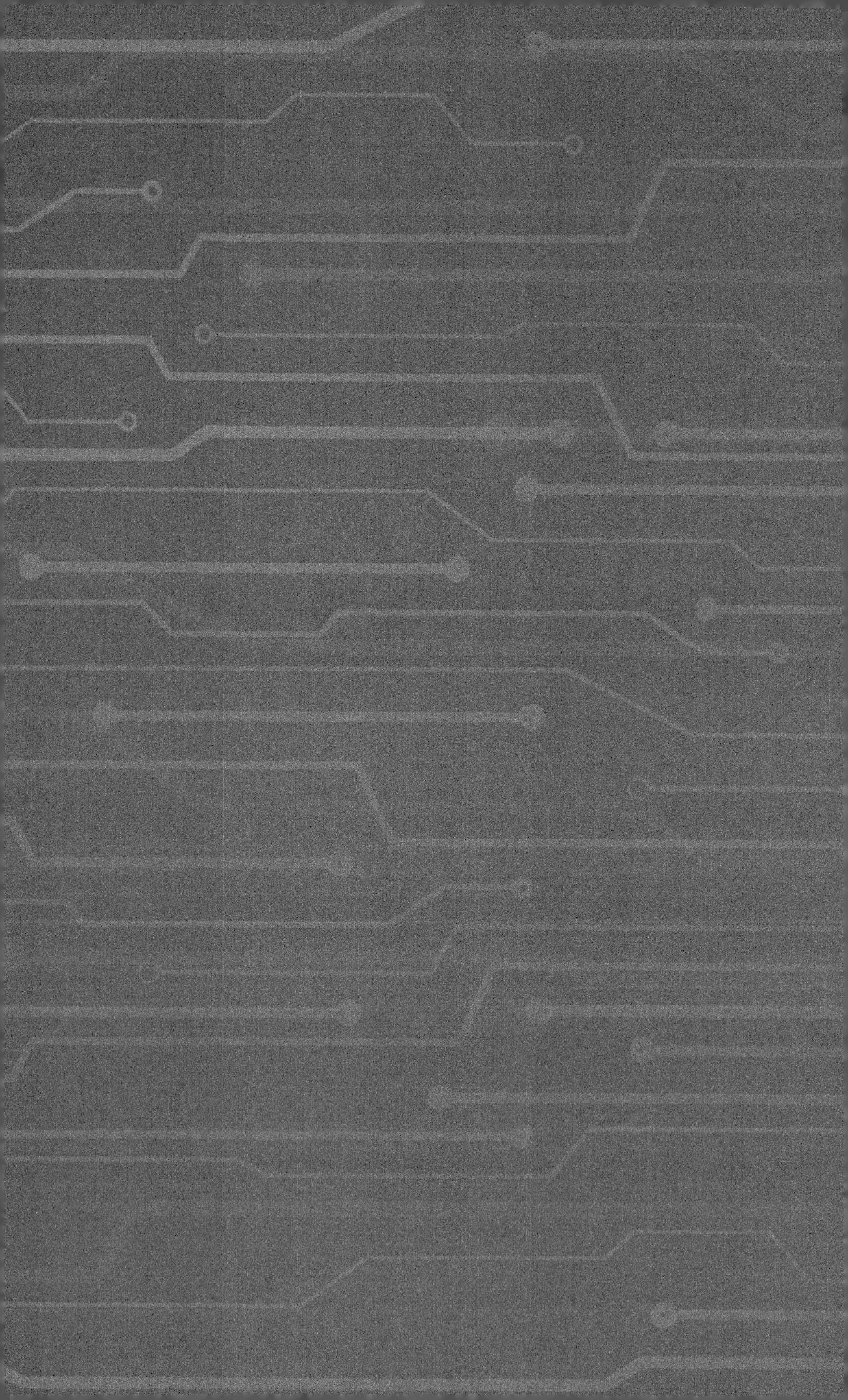

~ONE

PRESENT DAY

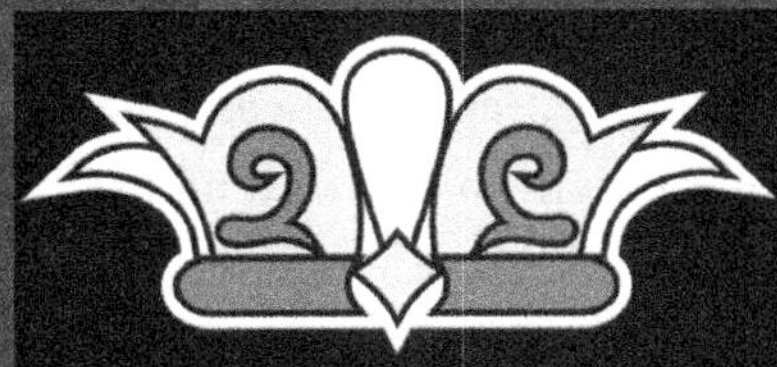

STEPPING OUT OF ONE OF THE DOORS OF THE festive banquet room at the *Hotel La Maison de L'amour*, I was relieved to find a bar across the gold, marble flooring. The band's rendition of Volo's *"T'es Belle"* flowed into the gallery. I strolled over, needing a break from the romantic celebratory vibrations.

I took a seat at an empty barstool, wondering why in the hell I flew out to Paris for a wedding. Deep down inside, I knew. My boy and fellow-musician, René, was marrying the mother of his children. It seemed ridiculous to me. Why get married after fucking the same woman for thirteen years and having three children with her? They didn't even live together until two years ago. For years, René swore he wouldn't. That was until Stephanie broke it off with him and began dating. Her relationship lasted mere weeks because René moved in with his family after that incident and brought an engagement ring with him.

"Qu'est ce que je peux vous servir?" the lone bartender asked, tossing his chin my way.

I didn't know French, but understood there could only be one thing he'd ask me at the bar.

"Uh… *Château Blevin*?" I'd been on a spree with it all day, no need to switch it up.

"*Château Blevin*. Oui." He spun around for a wine glass.

I pulled out my phone, accepting I was here alone with no one to hold a meaningful conversation with. René and I met ten years ago while working on one of Ragee's albums. His new bride was an assistant executive editor at *Time Magazine*. And I guessed they had to get married *all* the way out here.

I scrolled through my phone. A *TMZ* headline caught my attention.

Timothy Jameson demands $10 million in back-pay for what he describes as being his daughter's "emotional support system" over the years. He claims Tori "The Banger" McNabb promised to financially take care of him indefinitely in exchange. He said his daughter reneged on the deal around the time her engagement to Connecticut Kings' running back and special teams player, Deon Johnson, ended. Jameson suspects his daughter's estrangement is due to the heavyweight, world champion's new husband, Ashton Spencer, CEO of fast-food conglomerate, B-Way Burger. The two wed and produced a child together rather quickly.

My damn head tossed back and I hollered into the high coffered ceiling. This shit was wild. I knew Spence had to be heated as hell over having their names in the headlines again. It was usually him putting others' names in there from his journalism. Now, the tables had turned. In fact, his wedding to Tori was the last I'd attended. Theirs was a lot more simplistic than this affair, yet with the same touch of elegance.

As my wine was being delivered to me, a text came through. It was my mother, causing me to snicker this time.

Joanne Pierce: *Son I know you're away but could you carve out some time to visit your old man and old lady when you get back?*

"So my old man can belittle me for not having a wife and kids?" I murmured to myself. Twirling the wine around in the glass by the stem, I scoffed, "I'll wait."

I knew I had to visit my parents soon, especially because they lived less than an hour from me. But if being a man to my father meant me spending money just to have to fuss, fuck, and fight until the day I die, I'd continue to limit my time in that man's house.

Monica: *Did you remember to pack the Dunlop kit?*

Shit!

My sister's text reminded me I didn't.

Me: Fuck

I took a deep pull from the wine, my eyes going to the set of doors to the banquet hall where the reception was in full swing. Three women walked out, heels clacking the shiny marble floor and hips on the two of them swinging generously.

Monica: *In case you're looking for me in the next hour I'll be out looking for a guitar cleaning kit because my nest-brained imbecilic brother didn't bring everything needed for this Parisian trip. You want to play with your friend tomorrow but can't remember to bring all your tools!*

My head reclined and eyes ballooned. She'd been testy over the past few days.

Me: Your boss.

I had to fuck with her. Monica had been well-compensated as my personal assistant over the years. She somehow couldn't suspend her role as my sister while on the clock, though. My thumb kept tapping until I ended up checking my stocks via a customized app. That was until a text notification, then another and another popped up at the top of my screen.

Jamal Hillard: *You're in. Kings. 2 yrs. $7.3M annual with $750K in incentives for Playoffs, Super Bowl, and/or make coach of the year. Congrats.*

I pulled in too much air, causing me to swallow some of it. Jamal, my agent, had gotten them to come up from six point six—

Wait!

I got the job. *Holy shit!* Blinking successively, I tried processing that I'd gotten the job.

Thank you, God…

Monica: ***Congrats! Hillard just hit me!***

ADJ: ***Congratulations, my G.***

My head swirled as my phone kept pinging. I'd gotten the job.

"How is it that a good ass looking man like you is at a celebration of unity, but you're solo?" A gruff feminine tone floated over me.

To my right was a leggy, almond-complected woman with dark, long wavy hair falling over her tantalizing cleavage. Her strapless, tulip-top mini dress displayed her small frame tastefully: not too tight, but certainly stating her bad bitch status.

I pulled the wine glass to my mouth and asked, "Solo where?" before taking a sip.

She smiled, naturally tightly-slitted eyes slanting even more. She was a Black woman for sure, definitely mixed with something. Her pitch black narrowed eyes, soft curly edges of her hair, and golden skin confused me. I was a colorist man, preferring darker women to lighter for some time now—even their pussies felt different.

She made a show of glancing around me. I followed her actions, realizing her two girlfriends stood a few feet away, behind me on the left. They were whispering as they watched us—watched me. The twinkle in one's eyes couldn't be ignored. It was cute, actually. I scoffed with the glass to my mouth as I turned back to golden legs to my right.

"I'm with them."

Her smile deepened, then she shook her head as her eyes fell to the floor. "They're with me. I saw you at the wedding. You sat alone. You did at the reception, too." Her chin jerked in the air as she gestured to her girls that I now recalled leaving the banquet room a few minutes ago. "They're seeing if I can go along with my desires."

"And what're they?"

"Puis-je vous obtenir quelque chose, mademoiselle?" the bartender asked her.

As I slid my phone into the pocket of my suit jacket, she seemed stuck, his language lost upon her. "He's asking for your order," I assisted

"Oh!" She shifted her weight onto her white toes. "I'll have whatever he's having, but to-go—" She hesitated, closing her eyes briefly. "I mean, I'm hoping to take my drink and him with me, up to my room."

The girls behind me broke into sputters of laughter.

I turned back to the nervous, yet apparently forward young woman. "How old are you?"

Her dark eyes rolled down to me from the bartender, then they fell to the floor again as she bit into her peach-stained lips. "Grown." Those darkly-lined eyes rose to me again. "Over thirty."

Damn…

She was grown, indeed, but still too flashy in style for my tendencies. Flashy was equivalent to youth in my book. At forty-three, youthfulness was desired in a very surface, rather superficial level only. Mental acuity, substance, and aggressive life-experience were a must.

Still, I nodded. The inebriation from the wine I'd been drinking all afternoon and recent announcement of my new employment had my judgment suddenly loosening.

"What's your name?"

Soberly, she answered, "Ty."

"What's up, Ty." I nodded. "My name is—"

"Alaunzo," she interjected. "I know. I saw your nameplate in there. And you had no plus one, except for this wine you've been making me want to ménage with." She took to the seat next to me just as her *Château Blevin* was being served.

The bartender waited until she twirled the glass and took her tester taste. I watched her throat work the red wine down. Her beauty couldn't be denied.

Placing the glass down, she paid the server a nod. "That's good." Her tone was breathy. "Thank you."

He walked off.

She pretended to not see me closely inspecting her. "Do I know you?" She began to ring vaguely familiar.

"Maybe," she quickly answered, not looking at me while going for her glass for a gulp. Then Ty turned to me. "I'm American like you. We're at the same wedding for Americans. So, it's possible you've seen me."

That logic didn't sit well with me. It was too vague. But it was also too late: I was intrigued. Light skinned or not, I'd already envisioned pinning her legs over her head. My dick was stiffening.

"Okay. Let's be clear, Ty." I turned to face her, opening my body. "What do you want?"

Shyly, her eyes rolled up to me. "You."

"How?"

"Naked. With me. Doing the things Stephanie and René'll be doing tonight in Paris, but the American way."

I tossed my thumb over my shoulder. "With them?" I needed clarity, to know what I'd be getting myself into.

She shook her head. "I don't do that. I'm barely doing *this* right."

Ty stood, questioning me. She was warmed up, more confident about her desire. "I have a suite here."

After paying a few seconds of consideration, I stood, grabbed my drink, and followed Ty to the elevator.

I hate gospel music—

Sighing internally, I didn't mean that exactly. It's just that listening to it over the past thirty-eight years of my life had too often reminded me of death. Like now, sitting here in a room built for the last hours of peoples' lives, floating in the stale, clinical air was the ending of The Rance Allen Group's *"Ain't No Need of Crying."* When I walked in a few minutes ago, the Mississippi Mass Choir's *"Near the Cross."* Songs supposedly created to inspire depressed me.

"You…listening, young…lady?" my father wheezed.

His head and body looked so tiny in the small hospice bed. Gray hairs soft as a baby's.

My eyes blinked his way just as the depressing playlist transitioned into John P. Kee's *"Standing in the Need of Prayer."*

"Hmmm?"

"Did you…hear…what I said?"

I thought for a second. "That you were proud of me. Yeah."

His thin lips quivered. "It's…more than…that," he struggled for a cadence. "I…need you to know…something—"

"Sir." I shook my head, twisting in my chair to turn toward his bed. "It's okay. I just want you to be at peace now."

"I'm tryna…speak, child." Gunnery Sergeant Preston Taylor was present in the room. Weakly, even at thirty-eight, a part of me curled in fear. "Zo." I cringed. "I know what…I had you to do. I…know you didn't like it at first…but you obeyed. You were *all*—always the sassy, independent one. I…know it was a hard…time for you. I just…hope now you see…what a good *yun*—young…man he is that your old daddy…here had your best *in*—interest at…heart." I felt empty staring at him.

"Zo's grown…now. In college…into the football…thing. He made it in life…to a place many *yun*—young Black men don't without strong *pay*—patriarchal *guy*—guidance. You helped me do that for him. *Tha*—thank you for letting…your old man do what *wa*—was best for this family. *Yu*—you've been a great…mother. Now, *yu*—you can go about…your life and try to find a special *yun*—young man for…*ya* —yourself." His veiny hand extended to mine. It was cold and shaky over my arm. "*Yu*—you have my blessings."

My face fell even more, if it were even possible.

"Sir, I'm not young anymore. My youth is gone. I'm only what I've done. A mother and a lawyer."

I'd given my youth to my father's direction. And now, he was about to be gone. His life had been fulfilled, legacy extended and on his deathbed, he gave his blessing for me to find a man? Where? How? No. The prospect wasn't impossible, but his blessing held no power. It was ineffective now. I'd be forty soon, my goals for companionship hadn't been traditional since my child was a young boy. It was the sacrifice I'd made.

He shifted his head to face the ceiling again. With a cold pat on the back of my hand, my father assured, "*Yu*—you still have...many days ahead...of you. Plenty of time...to get it...right, Nyedeera. *Puh*—please tell Zo to...come in."

I was floored. The doctor predicted my father had four to forty-eight hours to live and still, with that grim prospect, he couldn't drop the sergeant act. It was in him. Ingrained in his flesh, carved in his bones. No amount of words would change who Gunnery Sergeant Preston Taylor was. And I, for one, refused to waste any efforts trying to get my father to see himself in his last hours.

Standing from the chair, I leaned over his bed and pushed my lips into his cold, hollow, spikey cheek. "I've always respected you, Daddy."

He didn't respond and as I ambled out of the room decorated with crosses, fresh flowers, and depressing gospel music, I didn't expect much else from the man who gave me life and taught me how to fear.

Just across the hall, sitting on the sofas in the waiting area, my mother and son's heads shot up. My sister, Jenise, turned my way, trying to read my face.

I turned back to my son. "He's ready for you, Zo."

Zo stood and sauntered inside, grief heavy on his shoulders and an impending broken heart slowing his stride. Once inside, Zo closed the door behind.

"I'm going to run to the ladies' room," my mother grunted, pushing herself up from the low sofa chair.

I nodded, going to my purse. My hands shook as I tapped into the note app and tapped to highlight the number I'd had stored in there for months. Then I selected the option to call before placing the phone to my ear. With a pounding heart and dry mouth, I paced over to the corner window as the line rang.

"Hello?"

My tongue was thick and dry and my voice trembled. "Hi, I'm looking for Alaunzo."

"Yes," the woman confirmed. "Who's calling?"

I blinked, left hand going to my forehead. "Uhhh... Nye." I cleared my throat. "Nyedeera Taylor."

There was a spell of silence followed by a new briskness in her tone. "Okay. Is he expecting your call?"

I cleared my throat, prepared for this. "No, actually. Umm... He hasn't heard from me in over twenty years."

"Then what can I say is the nature of this call?"

When I sensed someone close to me, I whipped around and found Jenise crowding me, her face screwed. I felt trapped between two energies but refused to recoil. But fear was an emotion I'd been too converse with, thanks to the man lying on his deathbed. Courage had been my new prospect I'd been seducing.

"I need to tell him about his son."

"His son?" the woman demanded.

"Yes. I'm the mother of his child, and I'd like for him to know."

In front of me, Jenise's eyes went wild and mouth tightened as she growled. *"Are you fucking kidding me, Nye? Have you been plotting this? The man isn't even dead yet and you're defying him."*

Ignoring my sister, I turned to the window. "Hello?"

"Yeah." The woman sighed. "I'm here. Just stuck on this one. Never got one of these before." She exhaled again. "I'm his assistant. Can I have a number for someone to contact you about this?"

My brows raised and I shifted my weight onto one hip. "Someone?"

"Yes. Someone. You don't expect to make a crazy claim like this directly to him, do you? I can have someone get back to you regarding this far-fetched, deranged claim."

"Far-fetched, maybe. But there's nothing deranged about me or my truth."

"Well, I've known the man all his life and can tell you with clarity, this shit is a farce, but first, I'mma let you play a little. Your number please, Billie Jean."

My head jerked back, begging her damn pardon.

Determined knocks had my face shooting up from the pillow. I gazed around the suite, stuck. My mouth was dry and head throbbing from dehydration. Then a thought struck.

She did leave, didn't she?

By the sounds of the urgent knocks out front, it was obvious I was here alone. *Good.* I lifted myself from the mattress, still smelling her. Rubbing my dry eyes, I sauntered out of the bedroom, bypassing the dining room. When I finally made it to the door, the next round of knocks was more like bangs.

I swung the door open to find a seething Monica. Ignoring her tight facial expression, I retreated to the kitchen.

"Why in the hell weren't you answering your phone?" she bitched. "I've been trying to call you all morning!"

After pulling out a glass pitcher, I drank the orange juice straight from it. The coldness trailed down into my empty stomach, sweetness exploding on my tongue.

"*Launz—*" Her rant was disrupted by her phone. "Hi." She sighed, answering. "Yeah, Jeffrey, I was calling to tell you, unfortunately, Launz won't be able to make it to the session today." I damn near choked, dropping my torso to avoid spilling the cold shit down my bare chest. "Yeah, I know," she sympathized with him. "He's disappointed, too. An emergency's come up at home. We're about to leave for the airport now. If you want, you can send the tracks over once you guys are done and we can have the engineer add Launz's strings like the last time."

As Monica listened in on the call, I looked at her like she was crazy.

"Okay. Let me know either way. I can make it happen. Yeah. Thanks." She nodded before again expressing, "Thanks. I appreciate that."

When she dropped the phone from her ear, I demanded through gritted teeth, "What the fuck, Nick?"

"You would know if you would've answered your damn phone!"

Knocks rattled on the front door interrupted her again. Huffing, Monica turned to leave the kitchen. As I drained the juice, I heard feminine voices in the distance. Placing the pitcher down, I left the kitchen, immediately spotting Ty in the dining room. Her body language seemed uncomfortable, which wasn't a far cry from when I met her last night. She didn't warm up until I had her naked and admiring my body. Then, she went crazy on my wood, impressing me.

"Hi there."

"Hey," she murmured, unable to look at me now, though I wore only my boxer briefs.

Now, her cheeks were warm, head down, and eyes smiling softly as she inspected beneath the table. My inspection shot over to my sister, standing in the middle of the living room, her head swinging from Ty and her friend, who was standing near the door waiting. It was comical. Monica could be intimidating when she wanted. Add that to Ty here doing her morning walk of shame. She looked different this morning. A different kind of familiar.

"Did you forget something?" I asked gently, having no time to follow my curious thoughts.

Ty's head popped back up and she lifted a piece of jewelry in the air. "Yeah. My earring must've fallen out of my purse—or never made it in when I tried slipping them in there...*last night—or this morning*." Her voice dipped at the last few words.

I nodded and Ty did an about-face, turning on her heel.

"Safe travels," I bade in her wake.

"Thanks," she replied sheepishly, appearing to be fighting a giggle.

Like Monica, Ty's friend waiting on her didn't smile. Her regard remained on my hovering sister. With her head low, Ty left my suite for the second time today, only she was showered and fully re-dressed from our fucking.

The door closed and I faced Monica again. "Now, why are we busting up in my suite hours before my session and then canceling said session with Jeff without my direction?"

With her neck twisted and forehead strained, Monica blinked several times. "You know her?"

I shrugged with my lips. "Marginally." But I didn't have time to explain myself: I was partially hungover, thanks to unspecified amounts of *Château Blevin* I consumed most of yesterday. Plus, my session had just gotten canceled. "What's going on, Nick?"

"No, no, no, no, no, no..." she murmured successively before taking off for the door to lock it. She returned, bypassing the living room and meeting me in the dining room. "This is too damn much."

"That's why I'm trying to find out what the fuck's going on!" Monica scoffed, eyes shooting around as though she was processing a thought. This shit further irritated me. "Listen, either you tell me—"

"Not even you can be this dense! You don't know who she is? Do you even know her name?"

"Yeah!" I barked back, matching her tone. "Ty."

"Yeah. As in Tynisha." Her chin dipped when she correctly perceived my eyes glazing over. "As in '*Taking Tips from Tynisha*'," she tried again.

My head swung, needing more than the crumbs she was dropping. "Okay."

"You've never watched that show?"

My face tightened. "It sounds familiar."

"It's only been on the air for almost fifteen years!"

I closed my eyes, taking a deep breath. "Get to the point, Nick."

"Okay. How about this? Does Tynisha Lang or Tynisha Alston ring a bell?" My eyes opened and rolled to the side because that did sound familiar, though I didn't know how or why exactly. "Okay. Try this shit on for size: Alton Alston."

Al—

"Fuck."

My eyes closed in shame. Alton and StentRo used to train at *Moorestown Creek Country Club* back in the day. That place wasn't too far from my crib. As a member of the club, I'd run into them there and shoot the shits. We weren't boys, but definitely had respect for each other.

"Ain't they separated or divorced?"

Monica rolled her eyes. "Every other month, but nothing ever gets filed."

Shit…

It began coming back to me. Al stayed in the media behind his shit, but I had no idea his wife was on her bullshit, too. Ty's plan last night was to get me to her suite. That was until we got onto the elevator and I hit my floor first. No way was I going anywhere with a chick I didn't know, not to mention, her girls were still with us. They walked her to my door. That's when I had to tell them good night. Unless they wanted to voyage into something erotic, I wasn't with the voyeurism shits.

Is that why she was so mousy in her approach? Because she's creeping on her husband?

Quickly deciding to deal with that at another time, I asked, "Let's get back to you canceling with Jeff."

Taking a dramatic deep breath while casting her eyes toward the ceiling, Monica backed into one of the four pillars outlining the dining room. Yeah. Her rather large frame of six feet even and close to three hundred pounds made it that melodramatic. "I hate that this is even necessary."

"What?" I snapped.

Monica rolled her eyes again. "I got a call last night from a woman claiming to be the mother of your child." My head jerked back and face folded. "Yeah. Random. I know. But following good protocol, I called Chesney. I told him how Billie Jean, the fool, demanded to speak to you right away. When I gave her Chesney's number, she said that wasn't good enough; she wanted to speak to you. So, I called Chesney myself and he suggested that she call his office, but that I'd get you back home to settle this."

"What's the rush to settling something that's nothing? This shit sounds ridiculous!"

"I know, but you just got hired with the *Kings*. Right now ain't the time for Billie Jeans to start popping up with baseless ass accusations."

My fists went to my waist and I rolled my head around my shoulders. This all seemed foreign to me: the damn fuzziness in my brain, my empty stomach, my sister in here basing at me, finding out the Ty girl is Alston's wife, and someone thinking I'm their baby's damn daddy.

"Nick, you know me. C'mon." It sounded crazy. I scoffed, "A baby?"

Monica shook her head. "No. This is no baby." Her eyes rolled again. "It's a grown ass twenty-one-year-old man."

Twenty—

"I was just out of college twenty-one years ago! Who the hell is this woman?"

Monica went for her purse hanging from her shoulder. "Some strange shit." She pulled out another phone, squeezing her eyes into the screen. "Some Taylor chick," she murmured as I strolled off for the kitchen again. *Taylor?* That didn't sound familiar. I wasn't even fucking like that in college. I hadn't really gained my stride. It was all about football and a long breakup with my music—that technically never happened. Nope. No Taylor. "Nye. Nyedeera Taylor."

That's when my legs froze. My forehead strained and eyes raced left to right against the cabinets above the counters.

"How do you spell that?"

"Weird," she snorted. "N-Y-E-*D*—"

My damn lip hit the floor. "Fuck..."

~TWO

22 YEARS AGO| NEW JERSEY

WE WERE CLOSING WITH "GROOVE WITH YOU" BY the Isley Brothers. Coran's riffs were different tonight than any other time we'd performed this number. I strummed the strings with precision, anticipating the curves in his notes. A smirk cracked my face when he rolled his abs, giving more passion than an empty room required. The last guest was crossing the threshold of the entrance door. Still, we played well over four minutes more.

"And it's a wrap!" Henry, the bass player, called.

"Damn, Coran!" Chez, the keyboardist, complained. "You started too high. I had to find a spot to transition the note, making me sound like an ass for a minute."

"Nah." Coran adjusted the mic stand. "Yo ass started too low and then dropped the note, fucking me up."

Disconnecting the cord from my axe, I mentally tuned them out.

Denny, the drummer, jumped off stage. "Damn, they cleaned up fast tonight." Then he whispered to me as I boxed my guitar up. "Oh, look. They got her closing by herself tonight. She probably happy as hell to have more time in the room with you."

I scoffed, hopping off stage myself. "Whatever, man."

"Lemme go back here and get this money." Denny headed to the kitchen door of the restaurant. "Be right back."

I slowed my stride, gazing around the spot. Corey's was a soul food restaurant in Trenton. A jazzy spot, the restaurant had an excellent reputation for its genuine southern recipes and musical ambiance. It was still official enough for locals to get dressed when dining in and had even attracted political tourism in the state's capital.

Denny's aunt owned the spot with her husband. The aunt, Cheryl, was the face of the restaurant as a Black woman, and her husband, Dan, a white man, only came out for public relations, if then. Ms. Cheryl paid us regularly, though it wasn't much. It wasn't about the money for me. Playing the strings had been a therapeutic break from football. It balanced the machismo of the sport and the overbearing expectations of it, too. Tonight, though, I was pushing it too close. I had an early start the next morning that I needed my sleep for. And after one in the morning with a forty-minute drive up to New Brunswick, each second was precious at this point.

"I don't bite, you know?" My head swung up to the girl...well, she was waitressing again tonight. Behind the bar, she cracked a smile, making me feel awkward, for some strange reason. She had been since one of the guys pointed her out to me a few days ago. The girl swirled around, widening her grin. "Unless you do. Then this would be a different conversation."

Finding my damn wits, I swiped my jaw. "Why're we talking about biting? I ain't caught up with my shots yet."

"Lucky for the both of us, I am." She patted the bar, instructing me to have a seat. "You played well tonight."

As she went about stacking glasses, my face turned tight. "Tonight?" I scoffed.

"Mmmhmmm." She nodded, little arms working fast. "You were off a couple of times last week."

"Shit..." I found myself chuckling, looking behind me for one of the guys.

This chick just played me. "Didn't know I was being assessed by a master. You play?"

"Only with hearts, not instruments." She winked. "Can I get a ride?"

My head reared and forehead tightened. "I 'on't even know your name and you asking me for a ride? You don't even know which way I'm going."

"I know your name, Launz. And I know you can spare a twenty-minute drive."

"Twenty minutes where?"

Her eyes disappeared. "Down by Fort Dix."

"Fort Dix? That's more than twenty minutes out of my way. I'm going in the opposite direction." The girl was crazy.

"Here ya go, boy," Denny appeared at my shoulder, counting out bills. "Don't spend that all in one place."

"You've got gas money, and I'm finally done." The girl winked and smiled as she wiped her hands on the apron tied to her slim waist. "I'll go get my things and meet you by the door."

"Yo," I yawped after her. "You don't even know me. I can be a serial murderer, rapist, or something wild like that. What if you don't even make it home?"

She patted my hand over the bar. "You just got paid. You kind of work here. If I don't make it home tonight, everyone here knows who I left with." She winked again and took off.

"Oh, shit!" Denny snickered.

"Daaaaamn," Coran, just joining us, clowned.

"What is your name even?" I called after her.

She twirled around to face me without breaking her pace. "Nye!" She rolled her eyes, grinning. "Duh!"

The guys laughed, nudging my shoulder.

"I 'on't even know this chick." Tired as hell from a crazy day, I damn sure didn't want to give her a ride.

"I'll take her." Chez grinned.

"Shit," Coran sucked in a breath. "She'd have to compensate me upfront. And by upfront, I mean out in the parking lot."

The guys laughed. I was fucking irritated.

"Is she even a waitress?" Chez asked. "She's only been in the front for about a week now."

"She's a wash girl in the back. Supposed to be filling in for Lisa," Denny explained. "But Lisa still locked up in the county for that credit card fraud shit."

"A'ight." Chez lifted his hand in the air for dap. "I'm out."

They all filed out together, leaving me alone. Before I could think about ghosting ol' girl, she was right back at the bar. She ditched her heels for Converses.

"Ready to blow this joint?" She winked.

TWO WEEKS LATER

"Hey. Why haven't I seen you do homework?"

Nye turned to me, then her expression melted into a Cheshire smile. "Because I'm smarter than you." She rolled over to her side on my dorm bed to face me.

"How?" I asked, sitting at my desk, typing the introduction to my Global Management and Strategy class. It was taking longer than I thought to write two paragraphs.

"Because my classes at BCCC are fashioned the same way my classes were in high school and middle school. I'm there from eight to three, and when I'm done with my last class, I take an hour or so to complete everything I can there on campus."

"And that makes you smarter than me?"

"Yup. Because you're here on a Monday night, working. And look at me." She sat up and stretched her arms out. "Chillin'!" She did a shimmy on my bed.

I rolled my eyes back to my desktop. Why did I have this girl in my dorm? Why had I been spending time with her at all? I dropped her off on a corner —because she didn't want me to see where she lived—two weeks ago for the first time, and I'd seen her just about every day since. We'd eaten fast food in my truck, gone to the mall, and she even came to one of my games. Tonight was the second time Nye had been in my dorm.

"What're you studying at BCCC?"

"I haven't declared yet. Still deciding."

"Well, what do you wanna do?"

Nye shrugged, eyes cutting to the side. A rare act of shyness from her. "I don't know."

"I'm sure you've thrown around some shit in your head a time or two. We all have. You said you got an older sister?"

"Jenise, yeah."

"She's in college, right?" Nye nodded. "What's she studying?"

"English lit or some boring bullshit like that." She scratched her scalp through her braids, closing her eyes while doing it.

"I like your braids."

"Really?" She winked. "What about them?"

I shrugged mentally. "They're natural. I like natural women."

She placed her chin on her clasped hands. "What else do you like about women? Light? Dark? Short? Skinny?"

"Dark." I shook my head. We were getting off track. "You like to read and write?"

Nye's eyes snapped open, realizing my inquiry. "I am not about to study English lit, Launz. I'm my own person. I don't follow behind my sister or anyone. I march to the beat of my own drum."

That made mad sense to me. "Which is why I know you've got an idea of what you wanna be, girl." The muscles in her face fell and Nye looked away. I shifted in my chair. "If you don't wanna tell me then just say that."

I never took her for a shy person. Matter of fact, Nye was the opposite of shy. She behaved like an only child. Very assertive, confident, aware of her own magic. I picked up on all of that in these past two weeks. For shits sakes, she'd been hanging around me like we'd known each other from middle school.

"Counselor at law."

My head whipped to face her. "What's that?" Then I thought. "A lawyer?"

She nodded, still not looking at me. "It's not something I talk about—with anyone."

"Then why are you at the community college? Shouldn't you be looking at a four year?"

Her cheeks lifted and eyes narrowed, softening. Nye clapped her hands, swinging them in the air. "Soon!" she singsonged. "Not everybody comes from a well-to-do home with their father being a big-time farmer for all the local healthy grocery stores across half the Garden State and a mother who's a bigwig in banking."

"Whatever. My parents do well, but we've never been rich. And you said your dad is a high-ranking officer in the Marines, right? They make bank."

She shrugged. "We've never been poor, but with my sister in college first, I tried to be reasonable."

"Where would you go if you could transfer tomorrow?"

She took a deep breath, eyes sweeping around my tiny dorm. "Rutgers seems cool to me."

I turned away, going back to my paper. "Right," I murmured. Nye was being slick again. It was what she did often. I didn't talk a lot, but when I did, I had no time for sarcasm.

For the next twenty minutes, I focused on the two paragraphs, going between the keyboard, textbooks, and my notes from class. When my alarm sounded, I was down to my last part. I'd have to finish it later tonight or early tomorrow morning because I had to go. Coach called a team meeting tonight at eight. But before that, Nye had to get home, and I was her driver. Rarely did I get a quiet moment to do school work. Between practices, training, classes, and giggin' when I could, there wasn't much time for anything.

"Ut!" I hit save and pushed back from my desk. "Time to get you home."

Nye hopped off the bed, looking around for her coat. I wondered what she got out of coming over today. Last night, when I dropped her off after Corey's closed, Nye asked if she could come hang out on campus. I told her sure, but I had a paper to start after class today. She found her way up to my New Brunswick campus and I treated her to lunch before we came back to my room.

"Did you see my hat?" she asked as I reached for my keys on the dresser,

only they were covered by her hat. I plopped it on her head as she giggled. Then I tossed the keys in the air. "Let's bounce."

I'd only managed one foot toward the door when half my body was yanked back by her little hand.

The fu—

I turned to Nye for an answer, only to be met by her smokey eyes and taut lips reaching in the air. "One last thing." She pulled me nearer as she stepped into me. My body acted on its own accord, leaning down into her. When her palm flexed at the back of my head, my dick lurched, scaring the fuck out of me. But it was too late. Nye's soft and warm lips were on me. She smelled like Big Red gum over mild vanilla.

I'd never been this close to her to feel, hear, and taste the rhythm of her breaths. I honestly didn't know experiencing it was a thing before now. And for once, Nye's fiery nature was unsound and a new feature of her persona had denuded. Desire. As her lips caressed mine with the intent to please, her tongue attempted to seduce me. I hadn't been with a lot of chicks, but I'd slept with enough to know this was different. It definitely was not what I was expecting from Nye.

She liked it. Nye liked kissing me. I knew this by how she pushed into me even more. Carrying her weight was a small price to pay against the shock of this shit going down. Was this her vibe? Did Nye come all the way up here from Central Jersey to fuck around?

When she pulled back, I froze. She ended the mouth wrestling with a sucking pull from my bottom lip. Nye's eyes searched my face as she grinned seductively as hell.

"When were you going to finally do that?"

"I—I..." I ain't know what to say. My dick was pounding so hard, my ears felt hot.

When I felt the soft and determined touch of her hand grasp my dick, I sucked in a harsh breath I regretted right away.

Staring me straight in the eyes, she remarked with confidence, "You're so shy, Launz." Nye rubbed from the root of my cock to the head, back and forth three times. "I don't know if that's a good thing or bad for me."

Then Nye moved aside me and opened the door. As she walked out so coolly, I was stuck, trying to figure out what the hell had just happened.

PRESENT DAY

"Thinking about Gramps?"

Seeing nothing but white pillows, I turned away from the window. "Not exactly." My face melted into a smile at his beautiful face. The tiny piece of joy I gave birth to was now a grown man in more ways than one. It was a realization I still struggled with as a mother. "You thinking about Gena?"

Zo scoffed, rolling his eyes. "I'm thinking about how I'm leaving Arizona for New Jersey two days after my grandfather died to meet my father. Gena isn't even in the equation."

"At the moment," I countered. Zo faced me again. "Don't forget you're about to transfer to a new school."

He took a deep breath. "True that."

And I knew that single fact was what I'd been stressing over since my son decided to pursue a football career. For years, we thought it would be baseball, but he dropped a bomb on us last summer, stating the desire to transfer out of his college program to a Division I school for a better football program. Zo and I had never been separated.

Like my parents and siblings, Zo and I had traveled a lot, but mostly together and never alone. Now, with my father gone, cutting the leash on Zo felt more and more like a daunting inevitability.

I'm not ready…

"You never answered me." Zo's graveled voice snapped my attention.

"What?"

"What're you thinking about? You're over there brooding. Don't try and say you're not."

I shrugged. "Maybe about where I fit in at in New Jersey."

His head snapped back. "You? New Jersey?"

My head bobbed left to right, forehead stretched. "You'll be here. Your father—"

"Pause." Zo shook his head. "Let's not allow those titles to get ahead of the meeting. The guy likely thinks you're crazy—*I* lowkey think you're crazy about this. And who's to say we'd hit it off or care to have a relationship? I'm grown, Ma. I've been raised by a strong figure. A man I just lost."

"Zo, your grandfather caused lots of damage with his controlling ways."

He rolled his eyes, turning away while exhaling. "I don't wanna go there. Not today. He's not even in the ground, Ma. I get your hang-ups with Gramps. I really do. But when it comes to my father, I've been without dude this long, and I'm turning out quite well."

I heard the resentment in his tone. "Alaunzo is just as much a victim in this as you, you know." Zo turned away from me again, eyes cast into the window view he had across the aisle of the aircraft. "Yes, it's hard to have no one to blame but the people you love, but we have to keep that in mind."

"Is that why you're flying out here? To rekindle some childhood love?"

My head snapped and neck twisted. "First of all, check your tone. Second of all, the only guy I've ever been in love with is the one I birthed. Know that!" I gritted through tight lips. "I was a kid when I met Alaunzo. A child, much younger than you. That wasn't love, that was an encounter. So whatever motives you think I have other than what's best for you, you can cancel each and every one of them."

Instead of responding, Zo pulled his headphones over his ear, powered on his music via the phone, and attempted to zone out. I was grateful. That could have been ugly had we not been on a plane. As much as I tried remembering his feelings throughout this process, I had my doubts, too. What I was doing was past crazy. It was a crisis possibly too late to repair. And I was alone on it.

22 Years ago| New Jersey

The theater was dark and loud from a movie I had no interest in seeing in the first place. Annoyed by the rhythm of my legs bouncing from my toes, I stood to leave, not being able to take it anymore. This boredom is for the birds. *I excused myself, brushing against people's knees as I made my way to the aisle. Charging up the walkway to the door, I pushed it open and hiked it out to the lobby. Finally, I was able to breathe when I made it outside.*

But not for long.

"Yo, man!" he cried. "What're you doing?"

Rolling my eyes while bent over with my palms planted on my knees, I gritted. "That flick is fucking boring."

"Boring? Taye Diggs, Morris Chestnut, Nia Long—this all Black cast is the hottest ticket out right now! What's boring about that?"

"You! You're boring! Why are we at the movies anyway?"

"Didn't you tell me yesterday after Corey's you wanted to hang out tonight?"

"Yeah, but I meant the two of us, not coming to a crowded theater."

"Girl, do you know what that movie is in there? If this ain't us hanging out, tell me what you had in mind."

"Something that required privacy." I dumped my back on the stone wall of

the building, not caring about the pain shooting down to my toes. I was frustrated. "Something requiring our privates."

I caught Launz's mouth drop open. He glanced over his shoulder briefly then looked my way again. "I don't even know you."

"How much do you need to know to want to touch me?"

"Aren't you eighteen, Nye?"

I blinked hard. "No. Nineteen. I'll be twenty in May. And you're twenty-two, which ain't a big difference."

"It's kind of big to me. You're fresh out of high school."

"You calling me a kid? I know you ain't doing that. If I was so much of a kid, Launz, why have we been hanging out for the past three weeks together, almost every day?"

"We both kinda work at Cor—"

"And why did you kiss me back in your dorm last week?"

"That was—"

"And don't try and say that was all me because your dick like...vibrated in my damn hand. I felt how hard your balls were—"

"Fuck, Nye!" he whispered hard as he leaped around in the air to see if anyone had heard.

"Do you have a girlfriend?"

"No!" he barked, and I kind of felt bad having him come out of character.

Launz was sweet, laidback, and sort of shy. That shyness is what drove me crazy, turning me on something feverish because of this guy!

"Then what the hell's keeping you from wanting me? And don't say because I'm nineteen. Your dick goes hard for me, an adult. If I'm cool enough to hang around, why am I not attractive enough for you to want?"

His face screwed. "You wanna be my girlfriend—"

"No!"

"Then what're we talking about, girl?"

"Adult shit. Aren't we friends? I've never even seen your room at home."

He scoffed. "Coming from the girl who doesn't let me drop her off in front of her doorstep at night."

"I told you. It's because my father still treats me like a damn kid, something you're making me feel like right now."

Launz took a deep breath, covering his face with his palms. Then he exhaled. "My bad, man."

"Woman." I made clear. "I'm a woman, Launz."

"Oh, I know." He nodded, hands shooting into his pocket. "I knew that since the first time I saw you at Corey's. You didn't need the short skirt and high heels you wear now to convince me you're a woman." Heat shot through my core. Rolling his eyes, Launz turned away again and rubbed his face. When he returned to me, his eyes were to the ground. "I've been stressed out. That's all."

"About what?"

"School, football. Everything." Launz reclined on the building next to me. "My pop's been on my ass about what I wanna do with my life."

"After you graduate in May?"

"Yeah. Now, too. He hates that I wanna do music, and hates me possibly being able to go pro a little less."

"So, he wants you to go pro?"

He shook his head. "He wants me to do something that feels right to him."

"Like go into the farming business with him?"

Launz shrugged. "He's never invited me to, but I'm sure if I took a management or desk job at some no-name company, he'd feel like I'm doing 'man things,' whatever that means."

I snorted, "He sounds controlling, like my dad."

"Controlling," he murmured, pretending to try it on for size. We both chuckled. "Mel Pierce is the biggest know-it-all I've ever seen." Launz laughed to himself.

"Does he scare you?"

He turned to me. "Dad? Nah. Just the fear of disappointing him does every day." I nodded, allowing a few seconds to pass between us. "Does your dad scare you?"

Shitless...

Bumping his shoulder with mine, I collected a soft smile. "Do I look like the bullyable type?" His head rocked left to right, buying it. "Now, let me ask you this. Are you always this slow about sex?"

"You always this straightforward about sex?

Not at all...

I shrugged with my lips and shoulders. "I'm a feminist. I know what I want and pursue it. Shoot me."

"Your sister the same way?"

Jenise? I shook my head. "She's got her own vibe and I've got mine."

Taking a deep breath, Launz nodded. "I can respect that. Well, I got my own, too. I know one year doesn't feel like much, but I thought you were eighteen. You said you graduated high school last June."

"And?" I demanded.

"And that was only a few months ago. Girl, I'm a senior in college."

I pushed up from the wall and got close to his face. "Because of my father's job, I told you we move like every three years. I got left back one year in a snooty district. Sue me."

Scratching his brow, Launz murmured, "I'm not trying to judge you, Nye. I'm just keeping it real with you. We're good." His face tightened. "How long have you guys been in Jersey? You know when he's going to be reassigned?"

I couldn't help my smile. "Will the right answer make you wanna do me sooner than later?"

"Nah."

My soul deflated and I sulked. "Then come on. Let's finish the movie." I started my way toward the doors. "I gotta make curfew or my dad'll go ape shit crazy."

This waiting for sex thing is for the birds...

"Nye..."

I jumped around and yelped, "Yeah!"

"I ain't no sucker. You ain't gotta be thirsty for me to hit."

I rolled my eyes and continued for the lobby. "And you ain't gotta be so dry, Launz."

Even though it's what drives me crazy about you...

PRESENT DAY

"They're ready for you now, Ms. Taylor." A leggy woman with a long, silky chestnut ponytail and matching glasses gave a neck bow as she clutched a portfolio to her chest.

Exhaling softly, I immediately became annoyed by how frantically nervous I became in the three seconds it took for her to make that short announcement. I followed her from the waiting area of *Chesney's Law* and down a long hall. Passing mounted portraits of Thurgood Marshall, John Adams, Belva Lockwood, and Johnnie Cochran made me regret my style of dress for this. Typically, I'd suit up in heels and an *Asè Garb* briefcase, which was my typical work uniform as an attorney myself. But I didn't want that energy. I wanted to be as practical as possible about this. It was what the Launz I remembered deserved.

The woman pushed open one of the two doors of a conference room. "Ms. Taylor is here."

Right away, I noticed Edward Chesney. He looked just as polished as he did on his website and the videos I'd googled of him, preparing for today. He was a lengthy white man with smart spectacles and well-behaved blond hair. The expensive Italian suit he donned could cover a couple of monthly mortgage payments, and his shoes were likely worth more than the average monthly rent for an apartment in the U.S.

As Chesney stood from the head of the table, there were two people on either side of him, whispering in haste. Ignoring them, he inspected me from top to bottom, then pointed to a chair to the right of him. "Esquire Taylor, I wasn't expecting a lone ranger." He cleared his throat, then gestured with his head. "Have a seat."

Of course, he knew I was a lawyer, but the observation about me coming alone was a slight. It made me suddenly regret the blue skinny jeans, white *BSU* tee, black cropped blazer, and black *Converses* I'd decided to go with in the name of a peaceful "reunion." I'd forgotten about the brutal temperatures of the East Coast winter until Zo and I landed a few days ago. My needed winter coat was collected in the reception area and I'd decided to forego a purse, seeing I would be in New York City today. Now, I felt bare.

I rounded the table, summonsing all the courage I could possess, hating the weakness in my knees and heart at the moment. I was not that woman; had never been.

"Is he behind you?" Chesney, still standing, asked. I peered toward the door I'd just come through. Launz's head was still low, in a whispering session, pouring over paperwork with the two people aside him. "Your son, Ms. Taylor."

That's when Launz's head popped up across the table from me, and I saw him for the first time in over twenty years, and my... He more than looked familiar. I saw Zo in Launz. It was a mature version of my son. The baked tortilla complexion; impossibly dark, thick brows; incredibly dark curly lashes; high cheekbones; and lower thicker lip. It was a feature I'd rarely seen in people. Something I'd first recognized in this man. I wondered if his hair was still curly beneath the bucket hat he wore today. This was more than I bargained for. I didn't expect the nostalgia of a brief, long-ago friend.

"*Nu—*" I swallowed, unable to take my eyes from Zo's twin. "No," I corrected myself. "It's just me for this."

"Why?" Launz asked, brow line tight.

I licked my lips, trying to snap into the here and now. "He's uhhh... He's back on campus. Ummmm...taking a meeting."

"A meeting more important than this one?" The drop in Chesney's inflection had me turn his way.

That's when it felt like I had the room—in the absolute wrong way. All eyes of judgment were cast upon me.

"Understand this," I began. "as much of a quandary as I've created with all of this, my son's juggling a lot. We've got a lot going on in our world."

Chesney followed with, "What he has going on back in Arizona is more important than a paternity discovery?"

"He's not in Arizona."

"Then where is Mr. Taylor, *Ms.* Taylor?"

"He's at school In New Brunswick."

Chesney's regard jumped to Launz, who appeared just as confused. I could explain everything. I was looking forward to finally talking to him, which was why I was okay when Zo said he'd sit today out. I knew it was because of his doubts, though he claimed today was one he couldn't miss with his coordinators on campus.

"I see." Then Chesney's eyes fell. "Well, Mr. Pierce nor I was aware of Mr. Taylor being a resident—*be it temporarily*—of the state." He turned to his associate. "*Whallus, be sure to make note of that.*"

"Why?"

"It is of no legal business of your own. This meeting, with all of its brevity, is over, Ms. Taylor." Chesney stood, and so did Launz.

"What do you mean?" I peered around, seeing two men appear at the door of the room.

"This meeting was to discuss an arrears payment arrangement."

Wait... "I thought this was a meeting to discuss confirmation of paternity."

Chesney, now at the center of the room, stopped and snorted my way. "Ms. Taylor, as an esquire yourself, *though not litigating*, I'm sure you know if the subject in question was not within a ninety-nine point nine, *nine*, nine, *nine* percent probability of paternity confirmation, you would *not* have the pleasure of visiting my office today, nor that of breathing the same air as my client, Mr. Pierce."

I blinked, shrinking in my chair.

Whoa...

I knew without a shred of doubt Zo belonged to Launz, but hearing it from a complete stranger struck me emotionally. Beyond that, it had been becoming very clear that there would be no conversation between Launz and me. There was so much I had to share with him, to explain. Dude was giving icy vibes. Granted: it had been years, but I didn't recall this energy from him. Disappointment rained over me instantly.

What the hell?

"Are you sure that's all you thought it would have been?" Chesney posed.

I caught eyes with a woman across the table. She looked familiar and she didn't. Locked in determination, I found Launz at the door with the two men vying for his attention.

"Launz, I was hoping we could talk."

His head rolled over and the words of his expression could kill. Launz snorted, "Apparently we've had something to talk about for over twenty years, but *now*—today—is the day you're hoping to?" His eyes went lazy, which was dangerously deceptive for me. He scoffed, shook his head softly, then stepped off.

Launz left.

"Kindly have Mr. Taylor contact my office to reschedule," Chesney requested in a tone expressing indifference. "I'll be across the country for a couple of weeks starting next week. I'd like to get this settled before then."

Then he, too, was out.

Slamming into the seat, I closed my eyes while letting go of a painful breath.

A skitter of laughter pushed from across the table. "This so did not go as planned, I see."

I rolled my eyes behind my lids before opening them. "You know, while I understand being at the root of this quagmire, the last thing I expected was that." I referred to Launz leaving moments ago. "Apparently, he's done well for himself over the years, but he wasn't that cold back when."

"That wasn't frigidity. It was balancing."

Again, the woman looked familiar, but I was sure I didn't know her. Her voice sounded like something I'd heard recently, too.

"Well, I knew him years ago when he was practically my son's age, and he was never that steely."

"And I've known him all his life and can tell you, you and your son aren't the only ones with a lot going on aside from this 'quagmire' you've caused." She gestured toward the door, referencing Launz, too. "So does he."

My head fell to the side. "Do I know you?"

The woman stood from the table, shaking her head while controlling her smile. She reached across the table for a handshake. "Under normal circumstances, seeing who my employer is, I'd be icy toward you myself. However, seeing as your son is family, I'll try for civility. But if you try me the way you're trying my employer, I will skin your light skinned ass proper." Her beam deepened. "Monica."

It took me a moment to recover from that bomb of news blended with a threat. I didn't move to meet her palm.

"You never answered if I knew you."

Her eyes lit with recollection. "Oh, no. Other than when you made that magical call to my brother to start this 'quagmire' that's inconveniencing us all, including you and your son. Seems he had more pressing events to tend to today."

My eyes lobbed between her hand and face.

~THREE

PRESENT DAY

"YEAH," HE MURMURED INTO THE PHONE, standing in front of me, attention halfway into the television screen. His hand was stuffed into his basketball shorts, reminding me of his middle school years. Except now, he was a twenty-one-year-old adult. "I know. Yeah, Gena. You know I do." His voice was subdued and if his girlfriend from back home in Arizona, on the line, knew like I did, she knew his attention was in his second love: sports. I liked to think I was his first. "You need to stop acting like that."

Rolling my eyes internally, I fixed my gaze to the television his tall frame nearly covered. Wil Cunningham had just hit the screen on the *WAWG* network. I didn't follow sports, but Wil's name was bigger than what she did for work. She was an icon and role model for Black girls and young women. So, my spirit brightened whenever seeing her do her thing.

"Yeah." Zo finally moved, turning toward me. "But, Gena, baby, I gotta go. I told you when you called the queen was here." He may have acknowledged me, but I could see and hear the disappointment in his voice. Zo was angry with me, even if he took it easy on his old lady. His jaw twitched, confirming what I felt. "I'm gonna hit you back as soon as I leave the cafe tonight, I swear." He listened as she spoke. "Alright, baby girl. Bye for now."

Zo held a tight smile until he dropped the phone. After taking a deep breath, he flashed me the phoniest beam before asking, "So, you say you have no idea why my 'father' and his legal team were brisk with you, queen mother Nye?" My head pushed back. "Well, wake up and smell the coffee."

He turned to face the television I'd purchased him. It quickly reminded me of how larger his living space was than what his father had over twenty years ago on this same campus. Admittedly, it was quite creepy when I learned one of the three schools my son considered transferring to, to further his football career was the one his father had attended.

Within seconds, he moved aside, giving me full view of the television screen. Zo increased the volume as Wil Cunningham reported, "...the *Connecticut Kings* just announced the hiring of its new head coach, Alaunzo Pierce. Pierce, the former offensive coordinator of the—"

Then Zo added, "And then there's this..."

He turned the channel again to *ESPN* where Stephen A. Smith and his cohosts were in the middle of a discussion.

"I believe Pierce is the ideal guy to turn this team around," Stephen claimed. "The former, and long term, head coach Lou left them on bad terms. We've all heard whispers of his drama. Even saw a post on IG from quarterback, Trent Bailey, denouncing him in coded words, saying something about 'when leaders drop the ball' almost two years ago. But let's see how he gels with Alaunzo Pierce, seeing how Pierce ain't as vintage as we've seen in the *Kings'* head coaching camp in recent years—"

When Zo muted the volume, my bottom lip was to the floor.

"Your baby daddy, Ma, ain't the same regular-smegular guy you once knew from some unheard band at some hole-in-the-wall soul food restaurant back in the nineties. Your boo is a whole ass head coach in the major leagues."

He tossed the remote on the other end of the sofa before taking off, leaving me with my dubious circumstances.

"What is a King?
Sit down, let me tell you while you polish this crown.
Dedication, leadership, skills, and no fear!
We prowl the field, slay a panther, and devour bears..."

I bobbed my head as the front office staff and a handful of players chanted the *Connecticut Kings'* song. Chests were pounded, feet stomped, and air punches thrown with pride. The damn floor vibrated with the conviction of the team's dedication. All thirty or so in the room held their drinks in the air.

When they were done, Eli Richardson, the owner of the team, boasted, "Welcome to *Kings* Nation, Alaunzo Pierce!"

The room roared with applause. "Hear, hear!" one shouted.

"Hell yeah!" another yelped.

We all air-toasted and gulped a bit of our drinks.

Eli, a *Mauve* man, swallowed back the brandy and gave pause for the burn to descend his throat. He chuckled. "That fucking ADJ is brilliant at branding. Generous, too." He raised his glass in the air again, saluting his buddy.

Though he was, thankfully, absent, Azmir Jacobs' presence was in the room in the form of his spirits. He provided the brandy, champagne, and even my favorite wine, which were all from his brand. *Château Blevin* was my shit and he made sure to have it stocked for today, the official day I signed on to be the head coach of the team.

My day had begun with a rough start in Chesney's office, but being here in the room filled with positivity, I could *almost* forget I was the father of an adult child.

That damn girl…

"I was hoping to have a chance to work with you," I shared with Jordan Johnson, who'd almost walked past me on his way to the door. "It was one of my motivations for applying for the gig."

Johnson snorted, half a smile on his face. "Time to move on."

"I see. Sad to see an immense talent like yours go. I haven't heard about your retirement outside of this office. Give me a year." I was only half-joking.

"Nah. I gave the game my feet and arms for years. Now, it's time for me to give my everything to my wife, kids, and grandkids. Ya dig?" With a nod, I relented. "I'mma go grab this meeting down the hall with the big homie." Johnson headed for the door with the same half-hearted grin.

The room was full of festive energy around us, people talking spiritedly. Then he turned back to face me. "With all due respect, don't fuck this up." Those words confirmed the ill energy I'd been picking up from him since he moseyed into the room. "We've been through a lot of dudes thinking they could do the job. Head coaching isn't an overnight type of success situation. It's something the coach, coordinators, and players have to grow into. It ain't about what you can bring to the table. It's about what you can bring out of the team." He shook his head. "Don't fuck it up, bro."

Trying to mentally process all he'd just said, I nodded. Johnson took off, leaving me in the fumes of his wake. That could have put a damper on what should be a celebratory event, but I got it. I understood. The *Kings* had been through two head coaches in the past three years. The former one, Lou, had been with them for years, and his days of fucking young girls had finally caught him and stained the *Kings'* brand.

The latter head coach, Jeff Nealson, couldn't shrink his ego to understand he wasn't the star of the team. He wanted to compete with the franchise players for shine instead of playing the background like any decent coach would. Hell, I'd even heard about him flirting with the wives and girlfriends of the players *and* allegedly sleeping with a baby's mother.

So, out of fifty-three players, having only four here at my orientation, told me what time it was. My addition to the team wasn't met with much expectation by the players. The morale was low in *Kings* nation.

A slap on my shoulders broke my thoughts. "Okay! I have another event down the hall. That one a separation, unlike this welcome party." Eli chuckled. "Now, Pierce has to visit his new office, the practice field, *Hotep*—and I…" He scratched his chin and furrowed his brows. "…believe housing."

I nodded. Housing was a part of my package. I had an option of a condo in a development the *Kings* owned or a standalone, one-family house. I didn't need the space of a full house, so I was looking forward to the condo.

"So, he'll be needing to get along," Eli continued. "And so do I." Then he turned to me and we moved for the door. "Rose, our President of Operations, will be taking over from here."

Rose was waiting outside in the hallway. She'd just greeted Trent Bailey, who casually strolled past, nodding in a form of a greeting. That was accompanied by a hard staredown from toe to head, then he stuffed a lollipop back into his mouth as he continued down the hallway.

Eli cleared his throat while scratching his brow. "*Uhhhh…*" His hand whipped the air. "You will have your opportunity to address your players soon enough."

Jumping in with the assist, Rose smiled deeply. "Very soon. But for right now, let's go check out the facilities, huhn?" She nodded, inviting me to follow her.

As we strolled out of one of the available units, I glanced around. The area was pretty quiet, well-manicured lawns and trees even at the start of winter.

"So, what do you think?" the property manager asked.

"It's definitely enough space."

"Yeah," she remarked quickly. "It will be just you, you said. But do you have any children? Are you married?"

That simple question about having children hit different today. My once standard answer of no was a complicated yes now.

"Just me," I murmured as I noticed a petite woman and a kid as tall as her come out of a unit across the way.

She carried a filled laundry basket as he dragged a garbage bag behind.

"Hey, Jade," I could hear Rose greet once the two made it to the ground level.

That snapped me into gear and I hopped down the stairs. "I can help with that." I extended my arm, requesting the basket.

"Jade, this is—" Rose attempted.

"I know who he is, Ms. Hitchens," she made clear while eyeing me with deep suspicion.

Jade Bailey may have been thinking I was like Nealson and wanted her ass. While that was furthest from the truth, I couldn't back down now.

"Good, then you should know I'm working to be a part of your family." My eyes skirted over to their son. "Hey, Kyree. You mind if I help you, too?"

Kyree eyed his mother wearily. While peering at me, Jade ordered, "Go get that last box. Call Trent and tell him we're on our way."

Kyree handed me the garbage bag and sprinted back toward their unit.

"Moving day?"

"I'm used to it," she replied as I recovered the basket from her arm, then moved aside for her to lead the way.

I winked at Rose the moment Jade began for the parking lot, telling her it was okay.

"Any plans for the winter?" I was sure to walk aside her.

"Still deciding."

"Well, whatever you decide, I hope it's just what you need for restoration."

Jade snorted, giving me a cursory glance. "Why? So you can whip this team into tip-top condition to win the next *Super Bowl?*"

"Nah. So that you guys can recover from transitioning yet again to another regime. I understand it's hard."

"Do you?" she grunted.

"I do. I've been the player and the coach: I've seen it from both sides."

"Yeah, and why did you leave Seattle a year ago?"

She knew my resume.

"To take care of my parents. Dad had a stroke. Found him on his crop sprayer in ninety-two degrees. He'd been out there cooking inside and out. Needed to see him to good health, support my mother, and get his business affairs in order."

She tossed her chin toward the right. "That bag goes in the dumpster." We headed that way. "And you think you're ready to lead the all-mighty *Kings* back to their royalty status?"

"I know I'm ready to be a part of the family."

"I see you've brought Kaleece Williams—a woman—with you." Jade nodded, possibly impressed. "Miles Brown, too." She lifted the lid of the dumpster.

I tossed the bag inside. "The talent's already here. I thought to bring a few tools to assist."

Her long lashes were touching as she kept her gaze and volume low. "Trent said that's the one plus of you coming along."

Oh, did he?

"Really?"

Jade's head whipped my way. "Look. We're all looking for a silver lining here. This team deserves better than what they've had."

"And I agree." We'd made it to her *Bentley* truck. "I just wanted to introduce myself to the first lady of the *Kings*. I understand it's going to take some working, but I'm willing to do what's necessary to earn the trust of my franchise QB."

With the command of a fob, the carriage door opened. Jade's little arm reached up and leaned on it. She motioned for me to put the basket in with the other boxes packed away in the trunk. "Then be prepared to do the work."

I found a space for the basket. Having no more to say, I gave a final neck bow. "Looking forward to getting to know you guys—in the family sense," I was sure to make clear.

On my way back to Rose and the parked limo, I saw Kyree closing the door to what I now knew was Trent Bailey's unit. I found that to be interesting.

"Coach Pierce," Jade called after me. With one fist on her hip and her head to the side, she warned, "My husband is a good man. A team player and preserver. He takes command well, and he believes in the game like a second religion. The problem is, he loves too hard when it comes to this team. Attached to his big heart are expectations. He expects good in everyone. In every coach. What I don't think Mr. Richardson, Ms. Hitchens over there, or Paul LeGrier remembers is Trent's weakness."

"What's that? If you don't mind me asking."

"He was a fatherless child and is now a fatherless man. The only patriarchal figure he knew was his uncle, who's gone. Trent's logical, but there's still a hole in his heart that he assigns to the seat you're about to sit in. He's looking for honesty and leadership. He doesn't want your dirty predilections, like Lou. And he definitely doesn't want you trying to fuck me or any other wife, girlfriend, or baby's mother on the team. He wants those tools you mentioned bringing." She poked her lips, eyes blinked successively and chin rose. "If you can make good on that, you'll have the favor of Trent Bailey for life. And trust me, there's none like it."

Damn…

I nodded, understanding the olive branch she'd just thrown my way. The insight was gold. But Jade didn't need my gratitude for her being so vulnerable. She needed me to do right by her man. And as I turned to head for the limo, I silently pledged just that.

"Mrs. TB, huhn?" Rose beamed as I approached her, leaning against the limo.

"I believe it was."

"Okay." She stood straight. "So, will it be the condo? These are our largest units." She wiggled her head playfully.

I'd told her, as I did everyone else, I'd be more interested in a condo. That was until I learned I'd be living so close to the one player most valuable to me. That wouldn't be a healthy situation.

"I think the ranch would be a better fit for me."

Rose gasped, "Oh, really! I was really off with this one." She laughed, opening the door to the limo.

I took a deep breath and murmured, "Yup."

So was I…

"Alright. Let's get you to the airport. I know it's been a long one for you."

As the jet floated over the clouds, escaping the sun, exhaustion began to kick in. It had been a long day. More things had happened in the past eight hours than I could process. The most pressing matter on my mind was my team. Both Jordan Johnson and Trent Bailey had a lack of interest or desire for my coming aboard. No, Johnson would no longer be on the *Kings'* roster, but his reaction to seeing me spoke to how severe Bailey's take on my installation was.

Did I care? Hell yeah. Not gelling with the players was a sure way of this run in Connecticut only lasting one year. I didn't want that stain on my record. If given a fair shot, I could work with the organization and turn their team around. But I had to start at the top. I'd read about Trent Bailey: his rise to fame and fall from grace, all to regain what he'd lost and more. TB had the reputation of being religiously disciplined. His views were only in black and white. His dedication to the game was unparalleled, and his ability to be coached was evident on the scoreboard. My handling and engagement of him was something I had to consider.

My phone rang, reminding me I was on a private flight. The *Kings* were sure to roll out the red carpet today.

"Yeah..."

"How's it going?" my sister, Monica, asked.

I yawned, sitting back in the plush leather seat. "It's been a long one."

"And it doesn't stop."

My eyes burst open wide. "Whatchu mean?"

"I finally got ahold of your son— *Damn*. That felt weird."

"Sounded it, too." I chewed on my lip.

"Well, anyway, I spoke to him to try and schedule a time to meet about the arrears payment."

"And?"

"And he doesn't feel it's necessary. He doesn't want money."

What?

"And does his mother agree with that?"

I was by no means a wealthy man, but my needs were met. I had a couple of mortgages and helped my parents, sister, and nephew out when necessary, but the timing of learning I had a kid and being signed to the *Kings* were superb. As much as I'd been skeptical about Nye, since having her torpedo her way back into my life, even she couldn't have known about my career pursuits.

Monica reminded me, "Well, as we know, she's no longer a party of matter. He's an adult." Things went quiet and my eyes got locked into the clouds in the air. It brought the word *ghost* to mind. How you can see something or someone and encounter them, all to find there's nothing or no one there. "So, what do you think? We drop it?"

Like Trent Bailey's father...

I didn't recall his name because he was a fucking nobody, but I'd heard about his father trying to tap his pockets a few years ago. Suddenly, the vague details began to populate. I'd heard through mutual friends how after never showing up for the kid, he reached out for help with a sick son. *A sick son!* What a weak bastard. Black men didn't need to be abandoned in America. Only death was a suitable excuse for not molding your own to survive in this jungle.

As easy as it would be—

I dropped my head in my palm. "Nah. Set up a meeting with us. ASAP."

"But he doesn't—"

"Just for me to introduce myself. I'll let him tell me what's what."

If something as simple as an introductory conversation could save me from being Trent's irresponsible ass father, it would be the least I'd do.

Monica took a deep breath. "Okay. I'll get on it. See you in the morning."

"Later."

My attention returned to the purple sky. I had no idea what I was doing. But I knew it damn sure had to be something.

21 Years ago| New Jersey

"Oh, fuck," he grunted in a whisper, body jerking beneath me.

His swollen breastplate was dewy with dark, tight curls of hair sprouted all the way down to his jerking abs. Eyes squeezed so tight as I rolled over him, tightening my walls against his throbbing dick. Those tightly curled lashes formed into deep black slits and his messy brows formed one line high on his head.

I'd finally gotten Launz to have sex with me. Three times. This was our third time and I was undeniably addicted. It wasn't about the sex—something I'd been grateful for. But it was about this unnamed need to strip him raw. He was too vacant—so he led others to believe by not speaking much. Launz was cool, hardly ever getting roused except by me when I pushed too hard about us hanging out more or doing this.

The guy made me wait four months!

His hard breathing slowing told me his orgasm was done. Slowly, his jet-black lashes fluttered open. My eyes widened wildly, nervous about what he was about to say. Launz made me feel like a damn hoe for wanting him this way.

"You ain't..." he heaved. My face tightened. "You never..." I watched his Adam's apple bob, nervous with anticipation. "You didn't..."

"Ain't what?" I snapped.

His eyes burst wide, shocked by my impatience. "Cum." Launz swallowed again. "You've never done that—with me."

Oh...

I shook my head.

"Why? You've never had an orgasm?"

"Yeah." I lifted from his pelvis and reared to unplug myself from him. Flinching from the tenderness created by rubber friction, I swung my leg over and flipped to the side of the small dormitory bed. "I can. It's just gotta be a certain way."

"How?"

I glanced his way. "With your mouth."

With the same inflection, Launz asked again, "How?"

Shrugging with one shoulder meeting my chin, nervousness gripped me again. "I'd have to show you." I swung my legs, hopping off the floor. "It's late. I gotta get home."

As I took the exit off of the New Jersey Turnpike, curiosity trumped my comfort preference of silence.

"So, you been in the area long?"

I felt Nye's eyes shoot over to me, and it took a few seconds before she answered. "No." I caught the soft shaking of her head in the dark truck lit by headlights and street lamps.

"How long you been living out this way?"

"About three years now."

"Oh." My forehead stretched with revelation. "So you had to transfer mid-high school. Crazy."

"I'm used to it."

"How?"

"I've lived in about five cities and three countries."

I did a double-take. "How?"

There was a beat before she answered, "My father's in the military. Remember? He's a specialized trainer, one of like five in the world who has his specialty and mastery, so..." She shrugged. "He's in demand. Gets the assignment, we move, he does his thing, finishes... Rinse and repeat."

"That why he's hard on you concerning guys?"

"What do you mean?"

"You don't want me to drop you off in front of your house." When she didn't answer, I couldn't help my nosiness. "Did you have a lot of boyfriends?"

Nye laughed. Her head fell into her hands as she shook it. "Are you serious?"

"As a muthafucka."

She continued giggling. "No. In fact, I've never had a boyfriend."

"You're nineteen and as pretty and...friendly as you are, you've never had a boyfriend?"

"So, pretty and friendly is how you describe me?" Her head bobbed up and down. "Interesting."

I couldn't articulate myself in the moment. Nye was a lot. In the past four months, she attached herself to me with little wiggle room. Before her, my life was football, music, and school. Lately, it had been those same things with Nye snuggled in between football and music. We hung out everywhere in public and private, alone and with the guys from Corey's band outfit. It was weird. We weren't dating, but definitely fucking now.

It was inevitable: Nye had this je ne sais quoi about her that most could feel. I'd seen it. It was evident in the way people would respond to her presence and even mere words. Nye had quickly become one of the most popular waitresses at the restaurant, and she wasn't really a waitress. No one knew when she'd go back to the kitchen. This was bold and charming and disarming. That was how she got me: neutralizing my tendency to say no. And she got me to fuck a nineteen-year-old. Yes, she was grown but fresh out of high school. It was something Nye made me forget with her conversation alone.

"Nah. Smart, too. You seem street smart." Without a doubt.

"I think I can see what you mean. I'm worldly."

"Yeah. I guess that's natural for a military brat."

Nye sighed, "I guess so."

"But never having a boyfriend?"

Her head whipped my way. "How many girlfriends have you had?"

I thought for a few seconds. "Maybe three."

"Three? And you're how old? Twenty-two?" Then her head dropped to the side. "And you're going to tell me you've only fucked three girls, too?"

"No. I'm not." I shook my head. "Because that piece of my life is none of your business, just like me asking you about your dick count."

She nodded as we neared her "drop off spot." "Touché, Mr. Pierce. Anything else you want to know before I leave you for the night?"

"Yeah. Does your sister get dropped off here or another neighborhood?"

"I honestly don't know. She does her thing and I do mine. That's how we roll as a family."

"Sounds sad." I pulled the truck to a stop at the curve in front of a house.

"Depressing really, but we're good at it." Her tone was cheery and her shoulders reached her ears in a shrug, but I didn't believe Nye.

I tried digging deep. "What's your favorite thing to do?"

She shrugged. "Lots."

"Okay." I thought for a moment. "What's your favorite thing to do to relax?"

"Oh, that's easy. The same thing I do when I'm stressed and need to think my way out of trouble."

"Which is?"

"Pick my nose."

My face tightened, nose lifted. "For what?"

"What do you think? Boogers. It's the most relaxing and satisfying thing to do. I do it when alone and can zone out and think my problems through. Discovering new boogers, then rolling them in my hand until they drop on the napkin or tissue is my favorite pastime."

What in the hell?

"Who are you, Nye—" I hesitated. "What's your last name?"

She turned to me with low eyes and a shy grin. "Taylor."

"Taylor." I parroted, trying it out for size.

"Yup." She nodded, popping her lips. "And I am everything. And I mean that." Her gaze cast out into the night. "My brother says I'm like air, I stay with a flow."

"Oh, you have a brother?"

She nodded. "Mmmhmm. Junior. He's younger. I'm the middle child."

"Oh." I'd heard my mom and her friends talk about the middle child syndrome before. I never knew it was a thing. Nye describing herself may have possibly permanently defined it for me.

"I want to know everything...wanna be everywhere. I want to experience life. Want to know all there is to know. Odd facts about random cultures' nutritional habits, God's purpose for creating every insect that exists—how does New York Times curate its best sellers' lists."

My head popped back and I scoffed. "That's random as hell."

"That's me." Nye patted her chest. "Nyedeera is synonymous with random."

"Nyedeera," I tried it on for size. The sudden knowledge of her full first name made her even more mystifying to me. "Nyedeera Taylor," I murmured.

"Yup." She pulled in a deep breath. "And there's that." She opened the door. "Thanks for the sex and ride home, Alaunzo Pierce."

Of course, she knew my full name, having been in my dorm, and even my parents' home.

"Wait up." She paused at my voice before closing the door. "I won't be at Corey's tomorrow. I got this thing with a friend of mine."

Her brows met. "Are you trying to ghost me before Valentine's Day?"

My face balled tightly once I understood her question. "Why? I'm not your man, Nye."

"Okay. So long as you know tricks are for kids." Her head dropped to the side. "Only treats for Nye." She closed the door and began for the corner.

As I did a gazillion times since meeting her four months ago, I waited. For what, I didn't know. Nye disappeared around a corner and I'd remain for minutes long with my engine off to listen for a scream, scuffle, or something on a regular ass middle-class neighborhood block.

When I felt I'd been sitting there like a square long enough, I sparked the engine and drove damn near forty-five minutes back to campus. I wanted to say it was the price I paid for her pussy, but even I knew that was a joke. Nye was more than a piece of ass. What exactly was she? I had yet to discover.

~FOUR

PRESENT DAY

INSTINCTIVELY, I GLANCED UP FROM MY tablet and saw when he sauntered inside the lobby.

Damn…

I stood to my feet, placing the device on the coffee table next to me. When his eyes landed my way, I waved him over. I felt like I was seeing my ghost. The kid was my spitting image in high school. Light skinned as hell and lanky without the weight. Mine came second year in college. So what was he waiting on to fill out? Did I walk like that back then? Now?

When just inches away, he offered his hand and I did the same.

"Zo," I greeted.

He nodded with a mild smile. "Pierce." Quickly, he blinked and nervously, I froze then snorted. "Alaunzo Pierce." He chuckled dryly. "Weird. I know."

"No. It's just strange having a son whose name is Alaunzo Pierce, but he isn't a junior." I swung my arm toward the leather single sofa across from me. "Please. Have a seat."

He did as asked. "Please don't tell me you named your son Alaunzo Pierce Junior." He shook his head and—oh, my fucking god—rolling his eyes into the air as he chuckled. "Because that would make this shit more awkward than it already is."

"Nah, man." I snorted. "I didn't."

"Whew!" he sighed, and I wondered how authentic it was.

Nervously, I motioned for the attention of the bartender. The place was empty enough to do from a distance. "What can I get you?" I offered.

"Oh, nah. I'm good." He sat up in his chair. "Maybe water."

"H2O," I called over to Marty.

"This is…" His eyes brushed around the lounge. "Cool."

Sucking in a breath, I replied, following his line of sight. "Yeah. It's the only place I could think of us meeting that wasn't exactly *Rutgers* territory."

His eyes burst wide, startling the shit out of me. The kid resembled me incredibly. "Oh, right! Congrats on the new gig, by the way."

I bowed at the neck, patting my chest. "Appreciate it."

"The announcement hit the coaches' office my second day on campus. The staff went a little loco. Heard you used to coach here."

"Yeah." I grabbed my wine. "Ten years ago, this would have been Jerry Springer-worthy."

"Who?"

I tried again. "Maury Povich?"

Zo laughed. "I'm just messing with you. My mom and aunt watched all that horrible television back in the day."

That made me laugh at myself. "Well, it's good to know you have a sense of humor."

"You've got to, man. Life's crazy. Short, too." Marty was at his shoulder, delivering a bottle of *FIJI* and a glass with ice. "Thanks." His attention returned to me. "I know this shit must be crazy to you, too. The timing is bizarre as hell."

I nodded, taking a sip of my *Château Blevin*. "It is."

"I heard Wil Cunningham say you had your orientation up in Connecticut. Was it the same day of the paternity result meeting?"

"Yup."

"Wow!" He sat back in his seat. "The same day you found out you had a son, you had to go introduce yourself to Trent Bailey and Jordan Johnson. What a day, bro."

I chuckled, scratching my brow. The shit sounded bizarre, alright. "Something like that, yeah. But I'd already known about the results for a day or so before the meeting, which is why my plan, that day, was to go over my missed responsibilities for you." This shit was an out-of-body experience. For real.

I was talking to someone who looked like yester-year me about catching up child support payments. What had I done in life to deserve this shit?

"Yeah." He rubbed his chin. "About that: I've kicked it with my mother. Told her I didn't think it was fair for you to be left holding the bag. She put us in this situation. I know her heart is good. She's not looking for a payday at all. In fact—" He shook his head. "Never mind. The bottom line is I'm good." Those last two words nipped at me. "Didn't grow up rich, but I've never known poverty. My Gramps took good care of us. Then when Mom finished school, she was able to carry the load by herself." He sat up in his seat again and wiped his mouth. "My family ain't perfect, but we've avoided Jerry Springer. This situation's…" He rocked on the ball of his feet. "Fucked up, but…"

When he stalled again, I pushed. "How are you feeling having just learned who your father is? Did you think I was dead?"

"Nah, man," he breathed, unable to look at me. "I just figured you ain't give a shit, which was cool with me because my Gramps made sure I was solid. We did a lot of shit together. He made all my games, dances, proms, and graduations. He took me on fishing trips, bought my first car, taught me how to knot a tie, polish my shoes." He scoffed. "The man even tried teaching me a little game for the ladies." His eyes hit me again. "So, I was good…until a month or so ago when my mother told me she knew where you were and that you didn't know I existed."

I shook my head, throat a damn rock. "I didn't."

"See," he spoke up. "That's where it gets gray for me. It would be a hell of a lot easier if I could hate you…begrudge you…believe you're a deadbeat." His head shook as his eyes landed below. "Then I'd have a target for the anger that snowballed the night I learned about you."

You do.

Your mother.

"But!" He inhaled deeply before releasing it. "No need to waste emotions, especially when my Gramps' health took a turn for the worst. Losing him was the toughest thing I've ever had to survive. No disrespect, but I'd take being fatherless any day over not having that man around." Zo tossed his head in a shrug. "So, we're good."

That's when I realized his "I'm good" phrase was a blow each time he said it. It was the phrase I developed once his mother up and disappeared. It had turned into my motto for women since. I didn't ask for much from them, neither did I take much. I preferred a variety of transactional relationships with minimal emotions and expectations involved.

Perhaps it's been my shield?

And surprisingly, that shit cut something deep. I remembered Nye's father. He was a decorated tyrant. At least, that's how she'd described him to me all those years ago. I remembered her showing up to *Corey's* one night with a bruised and sore arm because he'd shoved her to the floor while in a rage about her not sweeping just beneath the refrigerator and stove. So, how was he father of the year to his grandchild?

"I see you just turned twenty-one on January third. What made you transfer to *Rutgers*?"

He shrugged. "Wanted to start taking my football career seriously. Plus, they were one of three D-1 schools willing to welcome me. I was at a JUCO back home. The coaches and team as a whole were cool, and I actually had another year of eligibility to play because of a medical redshirt my freshman year. Even though I was a couple of classes away from finishing my Associate's degree, I felt I was ready to expand my talents, so I put in for a transfer."

Transferred from a junior college...

"What position do you play?"

"Now? Running back."

"Half or full?"

"Half. I was one of the top running back prospects my senior year of high school, but didn't take my classes serious." His head rocked forward and lips pouted with humility. "As a result, my grades took a hit, so I ended up signing with a JUCO team."

"Hmmm." I picked up my glass for a nip. Sounded like someone was full of excuses, but I had to know. "How good are you?"

He snorted, eyes falling away as though caught off guard by the question. "Well, let's see. Like I mentioned earlier, I was one of the top running backs in the country my senior year of high school. Last year, I averaged a little over sixty-three yards per game." He swung his head side to side, eyes toward the ceiling, recalling his numbers. "A little over four yards per carry, but that was because I was sharing time with three other backs in the rotation. I'll see how Coach decides to use me, seeing that I wasn't able to participate in spring ball."

I nodded again. This was supposed to be a brief meeting where I'd try to convince him to take money in lieu of my absence for twenty-one years. But taken by his fascinating personality, I didn't want to lose a second of his time. So, I continued asking questions...about football, school, the instruments his mother made sure he played, and the travel he did with his grandfather and family. I even discovered he had a girlfriend he'd left behind in Arizona, a small town just outside of Glendale where his grandfather settled his career in the *Marine Corps*.

He asked me about football, mostly. Zo also had questions about my parents and sister, but many of his questions were fashioned around my career in the *League*. He never asked about my personal life or if I'd had kids, ironically. And I played the conversation at his pace. We talked so much, I'd lost time. That was until his phone chirped.

"Ah, man." Zo regarded me apologetically. Then he chuckled, eyes rolling toward the ceiling. "I forgot I had this thing." He stood. "I guess I got lost, kicking it with…" He tried motioning with his hands.

I hopped to my feet and pulled out my phone. "Listen, I enjoyed this. It wasn't my intent to hold you this long, but I can't lie and say I regret it. It may not help that I feel like I'm looking in the damn mirror."

"Yeah. That." Zo laughed, swiping the lower half of his face. "Mom said you were shy, so I ain't think this would go long either."

"I'd like to chat again. We never made it to the support payments."

"I told you, man." Zo gently dismissed my offer with a wave of his hand. "I'm good." *Fuck*. "It's cool to know you're not some asshole, you know?"

I took a deep breath, gaping at him. "I'd like for you to know more. My pops would be thrilled to show you the farm." I explained to him what my father did for a living and having to rent out his farm after getting sick. Apparently, Zo was flirting with the idea of studying biotechnology. "Fair warning, though: he'd take up more of your time than I have today. And my mother would feed you until your damn belly bursts."

Zo found that funny and I was grateful, hoping he didn't think I was thirsty for wanting more of his time.

"That's cool."

"Give me your number and I'll set it up."

"Cool." After reciting his number to me, I sent him over a text. "I know you're crazy busy with Connecticut and all. So, I'll understand if…" He tried continuing with his hands. "Well, you know. If it takes you some time to explain all of this to them."

I extended my hand to him. "Looking forward to kicking it with you again. Thanks for this, Zo."

"You're welcome, sir." He met my shake.

Then I watched my "son" gait out of the lounge, feeling a sadness unlike any other.

"Damn, those Pierce genes are strong," Marty shouted across the lounge while wiping down the bar. "Your nephew? Cousin?"

I snorted silently, rocking onto the balls of my feet and watching Zo head to his car from the floor-to-ceiling window.

I was shaking as he pulled open the door and dropped inside the rental.

"That was long."

Zo started the car, and just when I thought he'd ignore my burning unspoken question, he turned to me, brows knitted. "Are you sure you two weren't together, together? Like... I mean, I would understand: Gena and I are about the same college age as you two when all that went down. Look how caught up we are. So, if you were—"

"Alaunzo Pierce!" I grated. "If I were in love, I'd have no problem sharing it. We weren't even a couple like you and Gena. We were just young—I was young. And dumb as hell. That's it! What's got you wound tight like this?"

He rolled his eyes heavenward, the way his father used to when agitated or embarrassed. "Because in that whole hour or more-long conversation, he had lots of questions about me growing up. Nothing inappropriate or unusual. But not one was about you. And for the two of you to have this significant thing called a whole ass child in common, him not even acknowledging... That sounds like pain to me. Either pain or total assholeness happening in there. Possibly a sociopath, which would explain his reputation as a top-tier coach. You described him as shy, and maybe you're right because he's got this weird way of making you feel he's in the conversation with you without using many words. But whatever his weird guy thing is, he's not an asshole."

Wide nostrils narrowed and decompressed with each heavy breath coming in and out. Zo was angry. I turned away, gazing blindly outside of the car. The same disregard to me Zo was describing of Launz felt similar to the chill I felt in Edward Chesney's office last week. And right now, my problem was I didn't know *that* Launz. Who had he become? Did I expect him to be the same shy guy I met in the late nineties? Hell no. But I did imagine some resemblance.

"I'm sorry this was a bad experience for you, Zo." I truly was and had no one to blame but myself.

I heard his bitter scoff, though I couldn't see his face. "That wasn't a bad experience. It was an awkward one, for sure. But what makes it awkward is he isn't a bad guy, and neither am I. The man wants to give me money even though I don't want it. What do I do with this, Ma? How do I act?" I shook my head, pained by his apparent confusion. My list of questions to myself surpassed his by volumes. "He wants me to meet his family."

I froze, not expecting that invitation.

"His family? As in his wife and kids?"

Zo shrugged, turned toward his window, and rolled his eyes again. "I don't know about all of that. All I know is he doesn't have a son named Alaunzo Pierce Jr."

What?

I wanted to ask, but decided to drop it. It wasn't my business and Zo was irritated, so I left it there.

"I'm running close to my flight." I sighed, rubbing my forehead. "We should go."

Without another word, my son flicked on the ignition and we pulled out of the parking lot.

"Come on, Daddy!" Monica shouted from the kitchen. "We been waiting!"

My mother snickered, understanding only Monica could get away with speaking to our father that way. Had it been me, he'd taken a bat to my ass.

Seconds later, my father swept into the kitchen, clearing his throat, brows knit tightly. "I was just talking to my buddy in there. He's watching the next set of videos?"

"*Bugs Bunny*?" Mom asked.

"Mmmmhmmm." My father took the only available seat at my parents' kitchen table.

"He's addicted to that show now," Monica noted. "Don't matter how old it is."

"It don't," Pops remarked defensively because he was a *Bugs Bunny* head.

He'd been watching that and reruns of *I Love Lucy* since I could remember. It was a strange facet of his persona still at sixty-nine years old. "Okay. What's so important that we need to meet as a family?"

"What more important thing do you have to do, Melvin?" My mother questioned.

She, too, could put pressure on my father. Everyone could in the Pierce household except for me.

"Nap."

Monica burst into laughter at my father's honest clapback. I snorted myself as my father rubbed his eyes, unbothered.

"We know about the new job," my father mumbled, hand still working over his face. "…given the proper congratulations and all."

"Well…yeah." I sat up in my seat, clearing my throat. "That's part of it. I accepted the job…flew up to Connecticut for the orientation and decided on housing."

"So, you're about to move up there?"

I let go of a deep breath as I processed her question. "Well, no. The season's technically still happening. *Super Bowl*'s in a week, although the *Kings* didn't make it."

"Tuh!" My father sucked his teeth. "Ain't come close. Tearing that poor kid, Johnson, up and jerkin' around Amare." He shook his head as though annoyed.

My father's team was the *Philadelphia Eagles*. Why was he arguing, and seemingly passionately, about another team?

"Yeah, but a new sheriff's in town," Monica announced. "Launz is about to right the wrongs." Her head bounced with a single affirmative nod.

My older sister could be my biggest fan when she sensed adversity, and my father had always been my greatest adversary.

"Beyond that," I tried reeling them in. "there's a new and extraordinary matter on the horizon." My mother's head fell to the side. Monica's eyes bounced between both parents. "I don't know how else to share besides to just do it."

"Yes." Monica pushed me.

My mother's face tightened. "What's wrong?"

"I recently learned I have a son."

My father's head swung my way so fast, he knocked into the table. "What's so wrong with that? Who's the mother?"

My head rocked up and down, lips pursed as I tried calling on the right words to explain. "Well, that's the thing. You guys have never met her, really. Her name is Nye—Nyedeera—"

"I don't know no Nyedeera."

"That's what he said, Daddy," Monica cried.

"Nick," I admonished her. Now wasn't the time to be argumentative.

This shit was heavy enough. Monica rolled her eyes away. My mother leaned her head to the opposite side. "What is going on here, Alaunzo Pierce?"

"I'm trying to explain, Mom. Back at *Rutgers*, when I used to gig at

Corey's, I dated one of the waitresses. Her name was Nye. I only knew her for about eight months. Saw her a lot—"

"Hell, that's obvious!" my father hissed.

"But then it was over. And that was that, until a couple of weeks ago when I was in Paris. Monica got a call from Nye—"

"Nooooo!" my mother droned deeply. "Oh, no! She had the nerve to wait over twenty years later to call you? What she want? Money? How do we even know he's yours?"

I closed my eyes as I nodded my understanding of her alarm. This shit was wild, nothing I thought I'd ever have to explain to my family.

"So far, not about money."

"Then what is it about?" my mother demanded.

That's when it dawned on me. I hadn't spoken to Nye to ask. "I don't know, really."

"What has the girl said?" my father now expressed his questions. "And how old is the boy?"

I shook my head. "I haven't spoken to Nye. Zo is his name and he just turned twenty-one a few weeks ago."

"Zo?" my father parroted.

"Yup." Monica annunciated the P sharply. "Alaunzo Pierce Taylor."

"Pierce Taylor?" my father yelped. "She gave that boy somebody else last name?"

I thought about that. "Nye was a Taylor."

"Was?" my mother asked. "Is she married now?"

Frustrated this soon into the conversation, I snorted, "I really don't know, Ma." Didn't even care to know. "What I'm trying to explain is the spring semester of my senior year, she disappeared. I tried calling her. Even went to the house after a while to find it empty. I haven't heard from her in twenty years."

"Where she from?"

"She isn't. Her father was in the military. He was assigned here in Jersey, which was how she landed at *Corey's*. She went to *Burlington Community*." Was a freshman, I recalled. "I even went there to see if I could find her, but nobody knew her."

"*Burlington County Community College* is *Rowan College* now," my mother clarified.

"Not back then, Momma," Monica corrected.

"Oh, I know!" my mother chirped, leaping in her seat. "I'm sixty-eight years old, been living in this county longer than you been alive: Don't you think I know, Monica?"

Closing her eyes, Monica expelled a puff of air with her palm in the air. "Excuse me, Momma."

This was growing out of control. *That damn Nye!* She was wild and confounding back in the day, and now she was casting a spell of drama from confusion on my family.

"Hang on, Pierces." I splayed my fists in the air. "We're being presented with a quandary here—I am, I mean. I'm sorry for the drama that is me having had a child for more than two decades and not knowing. But I've met him—"

"When?" my father was quick to demand.

"Yesterday."

"Yesterday? And you're just telling us today?"

"Ma, I had to process it all myself. Still am, if I can be honest."

Every one of us at this table was over forty. Hell, I was the baby at forty-three years old. It was hard as hell bringing this juvenile shit to my parents, especially because of my father's failed expectations of me. He'd wanted nothing more than for me to be settled in a nine-to-five with benefits, married, and with children. I knew he didn't respect my life choices. On some days, I wondered if he respected me at all.

We were all past the juvenile age where drama like this was likely to take place. Not the closest family, but definitely a connected one with pretty mild lifestyles. I never imagined making an announcement like this to my parents.

"Again, I'm sorry about this." I tried. "And I'm trying to think it through to see what's best for everyone involved."

"So, what do we do now?" My mother clamored for some sort of insight.

"Well, Momma," Monica interjected, trying to assist. "We wait until Zo breaks and gives an indication of how much he's seeking."

"Money?" my mother shrilled.

When Monica nodded, I felt compelled to reroute the discourse. "I think you should meet him."

"His mother, too?" Dad asked.

Without a second thought, I shook my head. "Just Zo. I'd like for him to meet you guys and for you to see for yourselves who he is."

Monica began massaging her temples. "I can't believe we're here. You think he's ready for that?"

"I do." My head bobbed up and down.

The table rattled. "Then let's go ahead and do what needs to be done for your mother." My father escaped from the table as fast as he could. "I don't like seeing my girl like this," he mumbled, headed toward the door. "Monica, make the arrangements. Next week is good. I got a couple of doctor appointments, though. So work around them. I'mma go watch the program with my buddy in there."

His buddy was my nephew, Monica's son, Andrew. As innocent as my father's "casual" mention of him was, it was a twisting of the dagger for me. Andrew was all of our best bud. At almost twenty-four years old, my nephew was an invalid. He was diagnosed with Cerebral Palsy at just a few months old. As a nonverbal, his condition consumed our family. It had been all hands on deck with his care since his mother, Monica, brought him home, announcing his birth and sharing his diagnosis.

Dad was out and my attention returned to my mother. Her eyes cast down to the table were glossy. I was sure this felt like déjà vu to her in many ways.

Monica likely agreed by the way she stood with heavy shoulders. "I'm going to grab my phone to give Zo a call," she mumbled much like my father as he left us seconds ago.

I reached for my mother's curled hand as she hung her head. "I swear, I'm sorry for this. I'm going to try to salvage as much as I can. I swear it."

As my mother peered down at our joined hands, she nodded. I was thankful she couldn't see the soft shaking of my head as I rolled my eyes.

That damn Nye…

"Yeah," I grunted into my cell, nestled between my head and shoulder as I balanced the heavy box in my hands down the last of the steps. "I look forward to hearing back from him."

The receptionist bade, "Goodbye, Ms. Taylor."

"Ummhmm—bye." I managed the box onto my mother's coffee table. "Wooo!" I chirped, out of breath. "What's in there? A slab of steel?"

My mother chuckled, tossing loose pictures from one box to another. "You're young. Ain't got no reason to be outta breath, child."

"Momma, I carried that box and the three before it down from the attic: I got a reason to be out of breath." I tossed myself on an available couch. Since I arrived back in Arizona two days ago, she'd had the living room cluttered with boxes, claiming to be purging. "I need to get over to my place to do exactly what you're doing here."

"You've only had that place a little while and with just you and Zo. How much cleaning you got to do?"

"They always say you underestimate how much you've accumulated until it's time to pack up and move."

"So, you're moving to New Jersey?"

I shrugged, eyes locked in an empty space on the wall near the front door. "I don't know where I'll end up, but now that Zo's gone, I don't have to be here." Then my head rolled to face her. "Except to check in on you."

"Hmmm..." She chuckled dryly. "That was the realtor?"

"His office. Yup!" I exhaled. "They're going to try and schedule a day next week to come and see the place and talk about my asking price."

"I remember when you bought that place. It was before your father's retirement dinner." Her head tossed back and she laughed. "Child, the man announced his retirement one day then the next day, you were on that computer, looking for houses."

I cringed at that memory. We moved to Arizona from North Dakota. I was grown, but Zo was barely ten and while I could have left my parents, who followed my father's military career all my life, I didn't want to take away the sense of family from Zo. He and my parents were so close. It was so evident that, even though I had my own apartment in North Dakota, Zo had his own bedroom at my parents' and it was just as functional as the one he'd had at my place.

They did everything together. When my parents' children were grown and didn't want to vacation anymore, Zo was there to cover their need of dependents. He brought to them a youthful energy my mom and dad lost when my siblings and I had enough of...my father. So, hell yeah: when my father finally announced to the family his impending retirement after we'd settled here, I bought a house instead of renting like I had done so many times before. It was a needed investment.

"Your cousin, Lenora's, wedding invitation came two days ago." I froze at my mother's announcement. "She sent yours and Zo's here, too."

I had no interest in that wedding. Lenora was one of my least favorite people. She was the daughter my father made clear he never had and always wanted. His affection for her all these years strained our relationship. That, and the way Lenora chewed it up and spit it in the faces of my sister and me. I couldn't commit to that right now—didn't want to go anyway. I decided to ignore the announcement.

"So, now what?" I asked to the air.

"That's what I wanna know. How long are you going to be on that leave of absence from work? The funeral is done. Your daddy's buried in the ground. When's life going back to normal for you?"

I murmured toward the ceiling, "Life will never be normal for me. I don't know what normal is anymore. Haven't felt normal for twenty-one years."

I could hear the pause in her movements. She didn't speak for a while.

Then I heard, "How are you going to survive, taking these flights back and forth…staying in all those hotel rooms in New Jersey?"

My shoulders shrugged against the padded sofa. I could still smell the burnt tobacco from my father's cigar pipe. "Dunno, but I'll figure it out."

She chuckled. "You know, Preston used to say you were the toughest girl he ever knew. Remember that time we moved to that camp in Japan and that soldier tried to jump bad with your daddy, not knowing his commanding officer had just flown in on an assignment? That man ain't know English and you ain't know Japanese, but he understood every word you said when you told him you'd kick his pink ass if he didn't get his finger out yo daddy's face." She tittered on, finding that hilarious.

"Or that one time you had that stray dog living with us in Puerto Rico for two months before anybody knew. I was wondering why you started asking for extra meat all of a sudden." She shrugged. "Figured it was a growth spurt."

That made me snort. The dog was cute; mixed breed who left me once he got healthy and strong.

User…

"I remember when I was in the hospital for my fibroids and you snuck up to that hospital every day, even after Preston whooped your butt for cutting school to do it." Her tittering was good-hearted. "You was so small, too, Nye."

"I hated not having you home," I confessed. "Jenise and Junior were so annoying, and Daddy didn't make it any better."

"That one time you kept getting suspended for taking up for the boy getting bullied, your daddy said he ain't know what to do with you. He said beating you never changed you, it only kept him consistent."

"He beat us too much," I hissed. "And I got it more than anybody."

That ended the laughing spell for my mother. Seconds later, she lay a photo album on her lap. "Sell the house. Go make sure Zo's settling in, in New Jersey." She nodded decidedly. "Go do what you need until you have a reason to pick up the pieces, Nye."

The moment I opened my mouth to argue I hadn't been fragmented in the first place by my father's passing, my phone rang.

"Zo?"

"Yeah, Ma. How you doing?"

I sat up, placing my feet on the floor. "I'm good."

"How's Grams?"

My eyes raced over to my mother. "She's good. Here purging—her word."

He laughed, calming me right away. "That's good. Tell her not to do too much. Save whatever she needs for my spring break. She know I got her."

"Of course, she does. What's going on in Jersey?"

"Nothing much. I just got off the phone with your light skinned ass baby daddy's sister—"

"Whoa!" I yelped. "Alaunzo!"

"Yup," he sighed. "That's his name, too. Anyway, they want me over for dinner."

"Dinner?" I trilled. "Who? When?"

I wasn't there. I was here in Arizona.

"Yup. To grub and see their light skinned ass, long lost family member."

I rubbed my forehead with a heavy hand. "Let's chill on the language, Zo."

He laughed. "Nah. I'm just having fun with you. He really is light skinned, though."

"I know," I droned, hand moving to rub the back of my neck.

"I bet you do." He laughed. Everyone found humor at my expense, it seemed. "They invited me over on Saturday."

"I'll be back Saturday morning. What time?"

"They only invited me, Ma." I blinked deeply, feeling my mother's gaze on me. That hurt. "It's all good. I doubt the head coach of the *Connecticut Kings* is going to invite me over to his parents just to butcher me up."

"That's not funny, Zo."

Chuckling, he argued, "It actually is. All of this is pretty comical to me, Ma."

"Zo—"

"I'm good. Give Grams a kiss for me. Tell her to send me some double chocolate cookies, too. I gotta go."

Sighing, I relented. "Bye, babe."

"Bye."

When I saw the call had ended, I turned to my mother and immediately identified the pity in her eyes.

"You're young, Nye. A full life ahead of you no different from your son. Go be you. Go figure out life for yourself. Not for Zo, but for you, dear." Her eyes skirted around the cluttered living room. "Go fill some boxes. Make memories… for you."

Why did that sound like such a scary ass feat? I had degrees, a career, owned a home, and raised a child to go to college. I was single, healthy, free, and lost. Being lost made me afraid. Being afraid was a far cry from that little girl my father surprisingly thought I was.

~FIVE

PRESENT DAY

ZO WHISTLED HIS AMAZEMENT AS WE NEARED the driveway. "This all you guys?"

I nodded. "That and then some that can't be seen from the road. He's got more property about four miles east of here, too. It's a bit larger than these nine acres."

"Wow…" He pushed up on his legs in the passenger seat, peering around me at the snowy lot of my parents' property.

"How are you dealing with the snow? It's dumped twice in the past few weeks," I noted, pulling into the long driveway leading to my parents' home. "It's been more than we've gotten in years."

"We get snow. It's a cakewalk compared to North Dakota."

"North Dakota?"

"Yeah. We moved to Arizona when I was nine, almost ten. My

Gramps got transferred out there. Even though I was little, I remember all that snow and the cold winter temps. It was crazy."

So, Nye took my son to North Dakota? I wanted to ask where he was before then, track his whereabouts since she went ghost on me, but thought not to. After meeting Zo last week, I realized I liked the kid and decided I wanted him to like me, too. Badgering him with questions about his mother's recklessness wouldn't aid in us building a relationship. I needed to be smart and play this thing safe.

I beeped the horn once we were close enough to the house to park.

When we stepped out, Zo observed the vehicles parked around the garages. "Expecting company?"

His smile made me laugh. It was strange as hell, walking into my parents' home with a spitting image of myself. "C'mon. They're excited to meet you."

We trekked up the stairs of the front porch and I opened the screen door to let him in. Monica was the first to greet him.

"Hey, nephew!" She hesitated before physically approaching him. "Is that okay? Can I hug you?"

"Oh, sure!" Zo extended his arms. "Don't look to be no cooties going on in this beautiful home."

That lightened the mood, even had my dad standing to his feet from the sofa. Approaching Zo, he rocked the goofiest smirk I'd seen in years.

"Well, I'll be." Dad inspected him expressively from head to toe. "You almost taller than ya daddy over there. What're you? Six even? He only six-one."

"I flirt with five-eleven," Zo replied. "You must be my young, cool uncle." His smile was charming, familiar.

My father's expression dropped, clearly taken by Zo's wit. "I see why you're in *Rutgers*. You smart. Real smart, young man!"

"Well, I may now know where I get a lot of my intellectual capacity from," Zo shared. "At least, I now know where my environmental interests come from. I hear you're a fellow agrarian—or at least, I'm considering it. I've also been told you have another farm slightly larger than this not too far away. I'd like to see it one day…learn a thing or two."

The embrace my father wrapped him into had a pang of jealousy lashing through my belly. Good-heartedly, Zo laughed while returning my father's silent expression of amazement.

When they broke apart, I gestured to the side of him. "Zo, this is probably the one with the most anticipation for this day." My mother clutched one fist over the other, lips pursed together with her cheekbones high. She was tensed from head to toe, looking to be on the precipice of tears. "Oh, wow," I mumbled. "You've never been this emotional at any of my graduations, proms, or any accomplishments I've garnered over the years."

"Nothing tops bringing home a twenty-one-year-old baby, Launz," my sister, Monica, playfully chided me. "How many mothers have this experience?"

Ignoring her, I gestured toward my mother. "Zo, meet the greatest woman I've ever met, Mrs. Joanne Pierce."

"Wow!" Zo blinked hard and successively. "I feel like I stole some of your face." It was true. Zo resembled my mother considerably. Growing up, people often commented on how many of her features I had. Monica was my father's twin. "It's a pleasure to meet you."

When Zo reached for her hand, my mother tugged him into her personal space. "Uhn-uhn," she grunted. "Don't deny me this." My mother's grip on the kid was so strong.

I watched her rock him from side to side. When she finally decided to let Zo go, she dabbed at her eyes, trying to hide her face. "Sorry. I told your…father I wouldn't embarrass you or him, but…"

"It's cool." Zo nodded. "Completely. There's no script for today. I told my mom I would just flow with it."

My father sucked in a breath. "Ya momma know you're here?"

"Yes, sir, she does. I spoke with her this morning."

"Where's she?" He was being unapologetically nosy.

"She's staying at a hotel in Princeton." Zo waved off the fact.

"Oh, that's just thirty minutes, or so, up the road." My mother seemed to have directed that statement to me. "I wish she would have come."

"Well, I was the only one invited," Zo scoffed. "And seeing she's already had her time with big Launz *be it long ago*, I figured I'd come alone." Monica burst into laughter and I choked on my spit. Zo found his joke—or my reaction—funny himself and patted me on the back. "Who's this fella?"

I felt when his hand left my back and Zo crossed the room.

"Oh, dear," my mother trilled, perking up. "This is my oldest grandbaby and superhero, Andrew."

Zo dropped to his haunches and gaped at Andrew with an open mouth. This was a tense moment for us all. We were a protective family and didn't expose Andrew to strangers. In fact, none of us wanted him in a facility to be possibly taken advantage of by strangers. I worked my ass off to provide in-home care. And now, watching my "son" gawk at him made me feel uneasy.

"Who put this awful jersey on you, bud?"

"What's wrong with the Eagles, son?" my father croaked.

Pretending to ignore him, Zo softly promised Andrew, "If I'm invited back again, dude, I'll bring you gear from a real champion team."

My father begged his pardon. "And who's that?"

Zo stood, placing his hand on the headrest of Andrew's wheelchair and smirking. "Apparently, they were smart enough to hire my father." He winked.

Where do I know that wink from?

Monica and my mother laughed. My father's head fell toward a shoulder. I felt the muscles in my face tighten.

Damn...

I felt like I'd seen his energy someplace before.

"The *Kings*?" my father shouted. "No." He shook his head. "Ain't no grandson of mine gone be no *Kings* fan. *Kings* nothing unless they're paying you like they are ya daddy here. That's the only way!" Shaking his head, my father sauntered out of the living room.

Sobering his expression, Zo asked softly, "What's his condition?" His hand went to Andrew's shoulder.

I watched my nephew's neck swing in the opposite direction, eyes rolled to the back of his head.

"Andrew's my son," Monica spoke up. "He has cerebral palsy."

"Ahh!" Zo's attention went down to his first cousin. *This is wild...* "Hey, man!" Zo called out gently, engaging Andrew. "I have another cousin like you. You guys are true rock stars." Monica's expressive eyes swept over to me as Zo leaned over to get eye-level with Andrew. "Just know you're seen and heard by me. You're real. You're special." Zo's head lifted and he regarded us. "And apparently well-loved. Much respect." He gently fist-bumped Andrew's partially closed hand.

"Your cousin has cerebral palsy?" Monica's emotions were bundled in her throat.

"I'd have to ask my mom to confirm. I haven't seen him in like almost a year. He's a few years older than me, too. He's in a home in D.C. My mom takes me to visit him regularly—until I got to college and football consumed so much of my time. But she still goes, sometimes by herself."

"Your first cousin?" Mom asked.

"Does your mom have other children?" Monica wanted to know.

"Yeah. My first cousin. His name is Leon." His gaze met mine. "Mom has an older sister and younger brother. No." He shook his head. "Mom only has me."

My mother must have caught that not so subtle action, too, because she followed his line of sight to me with narrowed eyes.

I vaguely recalled Nye's siblings, but knew she wasn't an only child like Zo here.

"Young man, come on in here!" Dad shouted from the kitchen. "I got a cold beer for ya. You twenty-one; you can handle it while I tell you about them *Eagles*!"

Zo's shoulders lifted as he tittered silently. I caught his squeeze of Andrew's shoulder before moving toward the sound of my father's voice.

Mom shook her head. "I hope you're hungry."

"Starving," Zo assured as we ambled out of the living room.

Monica stayed behind with Andrew.

"I'm sad to see you leave." The moue on my mother's face saddened me. As we all stood in her kitchen, I felt responsible for it in some indirect way. "Please say you'll come again."

"Oh, he'll be back now," my father assured with a grunt. "We got stuff to do. Don't we, son?"

Zo smiled cheerily, beam so free, unlike mine had rarely been. "I'm honored to be welcomed back." He reached in his pocket for a pinging phone. "My mom would be proud."

His attention fell into his cell as mom gasped, "I'd like to meet her. Please tell her she's welcome any time!"

He glanced my way and sniggered. It was an act of communication I was a little delayed in catching. The moment had fleeted and Zo turned back to my mother. "I'll be sure to let her know."

The unmistakable expression of joy on her face melted my heart. She handed him a brown paper shopping bag. "This is for you. I don't know what you'll do with it all, but in case you have a refrigerator in your dorm, you can have something to snack on."

"Snack?" my father jeered. "That can feed a few of his hungry teammates. "If they ain't around it'll all go to waste, Joanne!"

"Oh, no. Trust me when I say it won't. This'll be dinner tonight and lunch for tomorrow," Zo explained.

"Breakfast?" mom chirped, eyes swinging my way. "You don't have a meal plan?"

I wanted to roll my eyes at her obvious affection turning her naïve. "Mommy!" Monica chided. "The boy is enrolled in a Division I sports program; of course, he has a meal plan."

"And he's gonna need some wheels," my father added. "I told you, that *Explorer* just be sitting out there. You can put a few miles on it."

"Thanks for the offer, and I'll keep it in mind." Zo patted his chest and performed a humble neck bow. "And thanks for the food today. I needed something home-cooked. That's one thing I miss about being close to home. There's no love in the cafeteria and restaurant foods. At least, not the ones I can afford."

"Well, as you can see, your grandparents here will always welcome you with an empty belly," Monica remarked. "Wait. Is that okay? Can we call you grandson and nephew?"

"Sure," Zo agreed. "Apparently, it's who I am. And if you guys are going to be spoiling me like this, I'll be back each and every time I'm invited."

"Please do," my mother begged.

"Alright, alright." I waved them off. "Gotta get the kid back to campus so he can get back to people his age."

"Oh, no, you didn't!" My mother's brows lifted.

Zo chuckled.

"We don't want to overwhelm him just yet." He'd eaten the biggest feast I'd seen my mother make in years. My father had taken him out back and to the other farm. The two were gone for over an hour. "He won't come back."

I directed Zo in front of me and we headed to the front door.

"Good meeting you, Drew," Zo gently acknowledged my nephew then tapped his knee.

The nurse tending to Andrew today smiled at the compassionate act. I was stunned frozen. He gave him a nickname. What a compassionate thing to do. I watched my mom and sister hug Zo goodbye, Mom's being the one that lingered. Zo smiled through the entire ordeal. My father ended it all with a proper handshake before we finally left out of the door.

Zo gave a final wave after placing his food in the backseat and closing the door. He slipped inside, immediately checking his chirping phone. Quickly, Zo placed the phone in his pocket.

I was prepared to put the car in reverse, but instead I steeled, spine curled over. "If I'd known." My throat closed up in senseless regret. I'd been quietly observing him all day. I didn't know this kid, but felt inherently akin to him. He was a walking Alaunzo with the personality of Nye. The unlikely combination was a powerful dynamic, shaking my fucking core. Slowly, I turned to him to further explain—or try to. "If I had known she was pregnant…" I kept fucking up.

"Bro!" he shook his head while yelping spiritedly. "Let's not go—if we go there then I'd have a beef with my mom. And I can't do that. She's my best friend. I've been trying fucking hard, bro, not to give into the anger I've been holding onto all these years for you not being around. I can't go there about her." He shook his head.

Taking another deep breath, I tried again. "I would have never asked for an abortion. I would have supported her on anything. I would have been your father."

For seconds long, we locked eyes. I could see the storming anguish in his. The cool, witty, charismatic kid in my parents' home was hiding pain and anger. I wanted to cut through it all and give him my heart, but understood it wasn't that simple. That brewing storm was twenty-one years in the making. Only time, patience, and wisdom could conquer it.

"My life's been fucked up since November when my Gramps' health took a dive. Then just before Christmas, my mother tells me about you. Gramps dies right after the New Year. Like… We brought in the New Year in hospice. Then…" He shook his head, tormented gaze outside near my mother's shrubs. "This has been a lot." He turned to face me again. "And that's why I can't talk to you about my mother. I learned the anger I'd been quietly building for you isn't for you at all, but it's still here and I don't know what to do with it. You're a fellow victim in this paternity bullshit and she's the culprit. But the culprit is my best friend and has been my ride or die all my life. So…" He shrugged.

Wordlessly, I nodded, processing it.

"You haven't asked about her."

My head reared and eyes found his. "Who?"

"My ride or die."

"No?" My forehead tightened.

Zo chuckled, gazing around outside. "No."

"Oh."

His chuckle deepened. "It's all good, man. I appreciate you bringing me to meet your family. They pushed that fast forward button on making me feel a part."

I gave a single nod. "I'm glad to hear that."

Blinking hard, I finally put the car in reverse and backed out of the parking space. We took off down the long driveway as the sun set over our heads.

"Sounds good, Devin. Thanks." I typed my password into my laptop with the cellphone wedged between my head and shoulder.

"No problem at all, Nye. We'll get your home sold. I don't foresee it being on the market long."

"Exactly what I want to hear. I'll start looking into moving and storage companies."

"Sounds like a plan. Please let me know if you need any assistance. My office can forward you a list of them."

"Thanks, Devin. Chat soon."

"Bye."

When the call disconnected, I realized I hadn't heard Zo's voice in a while. I craned my neck to look out of the bedroom door, into the living room of my hotel suite. He was there, sitting on the arm of the couch, watching the television screen. Just as I'd left him to take the call from my realtor telling me he was sending over a listing agreement, Zo was on the phone with Gena.

I rolled my eyes, standing from the desk. "Is that the new dating vibe?" I sighed. "Being glued to the phone although you're not saying anything?"

I liked Zo's girlfriend, Gena. They'd been dating since high school. Sweet, well-mannered girl with personality, but since he'd been out here, Gena seemed clingy. She was always calling and, it seemed, Zo had been doing lots of pacifying. He wasn't the type of kid who played with hearts. Zo was pretty much a loyal, one-chick at a time type of guy. I hoped little Miss Gena didn't think that would change just because he moved out East.

Zo tossed me a cursory glance before going back to the screen. "Nah." He snorted. "The new vibe is having your baby daddy on primetime television, being interviewed on a red carpet, though."

My regard swept up to the mounted television where Launz was suited and looking rather urbane in a two-piece suit. His outgrown hair I observed at Chesney's office last month was wild and kinky, shape up sharp, and full beard dark as his thick brows. He stood with one hand in his pocket and the other at his thigh balled into a loose fist as he spoke. I could tell the woman speaking to him on the red carpet was smitten by the gleam in her eyes as he leaned down slightly to hear her.

"It's good to see you out this year, and congratulations on the move to Connecticut!"

"Thanks," Launz bowed at the neck. "Exciting times."

"Have you moved in yet, so to speak?"

"Well, yes and no. I've been getting the lay of the land. I've met with the team of coaches and coordinators and visited all the facilities —even met some of the players. I'm excited to develop our chemistry so we can dive into work."

"Oh! Exciting!" She mimicked, throwing her fists in the air to express that. "It's too bad the *League*—and the *Kings*—are losing a phenomenal wide receiver in Jordan Johnson." She pushed the mic toward Launz for a remark.

"Oh, for sure. I was fortunate enough to run into him in the front office during my orientation. Glad I was able to express my disappointment in missing the opportunity to make history with him, but was sure to express my congratulations. He's young, bright, and has a full life ahead of him."

"Trent Bailey," the woman began. "There are rumors floating about his desire to move on before the season begins. As we all know, he signed a four-year contract and we're at the end of it. It's been said he's fed up with the front office over the poor choices they've made in head coaches these past three seasons—you possibly being the final straw. What do you have to say about that?"

I had no idea what was going on with Trent Bailey, but whatever it was didn't sound good.

Launz was composed and didn't flinch as he replied, "Trent Bailey's one of the best quarterbacks the *League* has seen. He's certainly top three in the game right now, despite his adversities. I'm blessed to have a chance at working with him. He has a strong family behind him at home and with the *Kings*."

"What's going on with the *Kings* and Trent Bailey?" I asked. "And what do they have to do with Launz?"

I didn't realize Gena was on speaker until I heard her breathy laughter.

Zo shook his head. "TB's now a free agent. And you forgot your baby daddy was hired as the head coach?"

The baby daddy mention threw me askew at first. Oh, how I hated that role placed on me. I was no one's baby anything. That label was ghetto. Ghetto, Nye was not. I was a mother: single and completely independent. At least, that's what I believed until about a month ago when I opened Pandora's box with my son's paternity reveal.

"Oh, right." My eyes squeezed closed as I shook my head. "I guess I have to remember Launz is in the big *League* now."

"Now?" Zo's forehead wrinkled, reminding me just how much he resembled the man of discussion. "Been. This is his second coaching gig in the *League*."

"Wasn't his last job an offensive coordinator for the *Seahawks*?" Gena asked.

"Yup. Started off as the assistant O.C.," Zo qualified.

"Ms. Nye, did you know he was the head coach of *Washington, USC*, and... *Arizona State*?"

Arizona? Launz had been in the same state as Zo and didn't know he existed? I felt like shit.

Delayed, I chirped, "Yeah. Kinda."

I knew Launz was coaching football from my research on him on and off over the years, but I guess I never caught on to which level because I knew he played football in college. Looking him up to finally gather the balls to tell him about Zo over the years had never been about money, so I never actually paid attention to the fanfare, only the title.

"Boo, let me call you back. I need to kick it with my mom."

"Okay. I'm gonna run to *B-Way Burger* with Charlotte. I'm taking my phone."

I rolled my eyes. *Why wouldn't you take your cell phone with you to run an errand, Gena? What twenty-year-old leaves a room without their mobile phone, much less their home?*

Zo rolled his eyes, probably annoyed by the clinginess I'd been catching of her lately. "I got you, booboo."

That had me rolling my eyes again. When I knew the call had disconnected, I sighed, "What's up with that girl?"

"Nothing." He dropped himself onto the sofa then rubbed his eyes. "It's been a rough time."

"That will only get rougher. This is a four year program. Even with the credits being transferred, you're looking at, at least, two and a half years, depending on which major you take on."

"Mom," he droned, still rubbing his eyes.

"Don't *mom* me. I don't want you getting caught up in growing pains, Zo. You're still so young."

"I need a favor."

"What?" I was halfway happy he changed the subject.

"You're flying back home when?"

"Devin just said he'll be taking pictures of the place the day after tomorrow. He'll likely start showing the house this weekend. So I'll probably check in next week and start to pack up for a few days before coming back."

"Can Gena come back with you?"

My head bounced back. "Why?"

"Because I wanna see her."

"And who's paying for her flight?"

He sat up, face melting into a cheap expression. "I can help with some of it."

"Some of it? Zo, where is she supposed to stay?"

"At the hotel with you? You seem to like this place. She can sleep on the couch."

"And do what else while you're on campus being the productive college student *she* should be? How long will she stay? I don't know how long I'll be out here."

"*Why* are you out here?" His brows narrowed.

The potentially rude question would have stumped me if I wasn't already unnerved by sounding like a...mother for not wanting Gena out here so soon into his time at *Rutgers*. But I was ready.

"Because my only child is across the country, out here alone. You're getting to know your father's family, people I don't know to trust you with—"

"Ma, stop it." His mild chuckle was dismissive. "I've been to see those people twice in the past ten days. I'm not sure how much harm they can do at this point. They're cool—and speaking of which, I'm going to take Pop Pierce up on his offer to take his truck."

"You're not!"

"Why?"

"You don't know that man. You even call him by his last name."

"Because we're still getting to know each other."

"I'll figure out your transportation."

"Via what? *Uber*? Those costs have to be draining your pockets. This hotel is draining your pockets. The flights back and forth, too."

"Zo, I am not a struggling mother. I'm a working professional, who does quite well, in case you forgot."

He stood to his feet. "But you're on leave from the firm. Unpaid."

I shook my head. "No. I actually took bereavement."

"That was a month ago when Gramps first passed. Your leave of absence is without pay."

"And I'm not without a savings, Zo." Although he was correct about the expenses, Zo didn't know how much I had this all planned out—for months.

"Listen, I appreciate you looking out for me, but from this point, I've got to figure things out for myself."

"And I'm not letting you? I've never balked at your visits with Launz's family. I'm okay with that and even if I wasn't, you're grown."

"But you're here, wasting money to play big brother instead of moving on with your life."

"Alaunzo Pierce, you just lost your grandfather—"

"Who was your father. And yeah, I know you guys didn't get along, but he was still your dad and I know it was a loss for you, too."

With wide nostrils and rubbing lips, I dropped down onto the sofa. I couldn't tell my son how I had not been grieving, and not because I wanted my father to die, but because I'd been too preoccupied with correcting the worst mistake of my life. Flying back and forth since last month had been a distraction from the reality of not having Gunnery Sergeant Preston Taylor living on earth anymore. The fierce, iron-fist ruler of our family was gone, leaving me the sole responsibility of looking out for my only child.

"Why can't Gena wait till spring break?"

Exhaling deeply, he moved for the door. "Don't worry about it. I'll figure it out."

"Wait." I stood facing him. "How did this go from you asking me for this favor to you telling me I'm smothering you out here?"

"I didn't say that, Ma."

"Then what's going on here?"

"I'm trying to figure out the same thing. And at the same time, I'd like to see my girlfriend. Just like you don't want to leave me out here, it's not reasonable to think she wants to see me, too?"

"I'm your mother."

"And I'm an adult."

I blinked hard, readjusting my head over my shoulders, surprised by his comment. But before I could respond, Zo left out. The broke kid who wanted to dramatically end this conversation was the same one who was using my Uber account right now to get back to campus.

Rolling my eyes hard, my regard fell to my lower body. I was still wearing my workout gear from my yoga workout just as Zo arrived earlier. I needed to shower and get ready for a *Zoom* call with a law firm in Manhattan. Turning on my heel on a huff, I thought to myself, I had zero interest in working in New York City.

Why did I apply for a job out there?

I had no answers to why anymore. Lately, I'd been in a race against the wind. Sadly, I had no destination.

~SIX

21 YEARS AGO| NEW JERSEY

She hit play on the portable stereo she'd asked me to bring tonight. After the synthesizer runs ended during the intro of the song, the rhythmic organ chords began. Then I felt her pounce onto the bed.

"Shit!" My body tensed. "You okay?"

Nye giggled. "I'm fine. Stop it."

"Do you have to be so dramatic—"

"Shhhh! I'm trying to hear the guitar feature."

I felt her walking around me, on top of the mattress. Once again, I let this girl have her way. I was blindfolded and mostly naked on a hotel bed in Somerset. Fucking around with Nye, I was somehow spending Valentine's Day with her even though we weren't "celebrating" it.

"And this is Prince?"

"The Beautiful Ones." *I nodded, not being able to see shit. "Yup."*

"You like the guitar in this we can't even hear?"

I laughed quietly. "That's because you don't know instrumentation."

"But I do know something—well, two things."

"What's that?" My head bobbed to the song.

The genius in that man had always inspired me.

"That Bridgette likes you."

My face wrinkled, and I hated not being able to see right now. "Who's that?"

"The hostess they just hired."

"How you know that?"

"A few of us were on break on Tuesday and she said it. She said she wants to suck your dick." I laughed as Nye continued to walk around me. "You find that funny?"

"I do."

"Why?"

"I shouldn't say 'funny.' I actually find it cute."

"What's so cute about it?"

"That she tells a bunch of coworkers she wants to suck my dick, but don't tell me. It's cute." Childish as hell, too.

"You're still laughing, though."

"My bad. You sound mad."

"I'm not. But you're gonna find this hilarious." I waited—blindly. "I told her she can't suck your dick."

I did find that funny. "Why not?"

"Because you're gay and prefer stronger jaw muscles than hers."

At first, my whole body froze. Then I remembered who I was talking to. Nye always hit that shock factor. You never knew what was coming out of her mouth from one moment to the next. She was a crowd favorite at Corey's. The customers had begun to ask to be seated in her section. She was killing in tips. Even offered to pay for dinner tonight—funny selection, but she paid.

"Anyway." I pretended to be bored with her slander. "What's the other thing you know?"

Then she dropped down closer to my ear. "How you can make me cum."

My dick lurched in my boxers at that, a flash of warmth hit my lower belly. I swallowed saliva that had collected at the back of my throat out of nowhere. "How's that?"

"First, answer are you down?"

"Down for what?"

"To make me cum."

What was she getting at? We were here, at a hotel, for sex. Why wouldn't I want her to cum? She made me cum all the time. I didn't think I'd ever made a girl cum except for my neighbor at my parents', Qionna. It seemed one-sided and unfair.

"I'm down."

"You sure?"

"Nye!"

"I just want to be sure you're sure."

"Damn! I'm sure, girl."

"Okay. Stay still and react accordingly. When you want me to stop just say it and I'll stop."

"Nye—"

I felt her steps over my head. Then I felt her little hands at the waist of my boxers. My abs jerked when she pulled my dick out of my boxers. She'd handled my cock before, but this felt different. Nye caressed me in her hands, warming me all over. I felt her on and around me, but her concentration was in her hands. She stroked me with full palms, giving me a hand job for a while. I didn't get it, but didn't mind. My brain was tickled with her berry scent and body pre-occupied by her boldness.

When I felt her hands lubricating and her strokes getting looser, a croak escaped from my nostrils. I wasn't a moaner with sex, but this I couldn't help. My hands drew into tight fists, I didn't know where to put them. This was Nye's show. Then her long breaths hit my wet dick, swelling it even more. My hips begin to move. If this was what Nye wanted, I was down.

I felt her shift beneath my arms, her body somehow extending to reach over my shoulders. That's when I smelled it. Her pussy. It didn't have the berry scent her titties and mostly everywhere else on her body had, but it wasn't foul either.

Damn...

Were we really doing this?

Was I going to?

When the lips of her pussy reached those on my face, I didn't have a chance to consult my mind. I kissed her. Nye's hips swayed. Then I reached up and kissed her deeper. I had no clue what I was doing, but wanted to try it out. Her instructions to react accordingly came back to mind then my tongue slipped out and up. I lifted my head to go deeper and tasted a thin layer of gel. It was unusual and definitely not food. Again, it wasn't nasty and, oddly, made my cock twitch in her hands.

So I swiped between her lips again, this time with more confidence. The texture was different, and I wanted to taste everything. The hairs on her lips provided landmarks for parameters and I explored. Nye rocked her hips over my face, not always moving in my intended direction. Once my tongue slipped inside her. That was weird, but so curious, I lifted my head and grabbed her butt cheeks, reaching deeper.

A heavy breath hit my cock again and I could have sworn I heard her moan. I couldn't be sure with her thighs against my ears. She rocked over me for a while as I tasted the depths of her pussy. When I felt her warm mouth on my cock, the back of my head hit the mattress. Nye's technique was like mine: timid, yet determined. She wasn't the self-assured, confident savant. She was new to this, like me. I liked this *Nye.*

Needing to get back in the game, I pulled her pussy closer to me again and roved my tongue over the swollen bump between her lips I guessed was her clit. Girls liked that being played with, I knew from fingering them. So I licked there. Damn, it felt bigger against my tongue than I remembered it looked. When Nye's ass moved wild over me as I licked with my full tongue, I took that to mean it felt good. The problem was she was doing a number on my dick, too. She said this would make her cum. No damn way I'd blow before her. I wasn't weak like that. So I went crazy on her clit and started sucking it like I'd seen in porn. I swear, eating pussy was something I'd been saying I'd do for a while now, but never had the girl I felt I wanted to go there with. Nye wasn't that girl for me either, but since she felt otherwise, I was here, eating her juicy pussy.

I didn't think I'd ever been so turned on in my life. Her hair or wetness didn't faze me at this point. Making her feel good was my goal. I just hoped I was.

"Launz..." she whispered over my dick, telling me I was on to something.

So, I stayed there, sucking. I gathered all of her clit between my top lip and tongue and sucked. Nye's moans grew uncontrolled, turning me the fuck on. I couldn't hear the music. All I could do was feel and taste. Feeling greedy, I wrapped my arms around the small of her back, holding her to me as I sucked on her lollipop. Her suction on my cock tightened, mouth moved faster. I somehow found myself doing the same with my head until her hips began to buck and back arched at the same time.

Nye rocked into my face, her mouth working harder if that was possible. This wasn't looking good. I wouldn't last. Her ass twerking in my hands and over my face drove me wild. I'd never had this sensation before.

"I'm cumming!" she quickly cried in a voice I'd never heard before.

Quickly, she went back to my cock as I held her ass cheeks captive to my head and her pussy to my mouth greedily. My balls warmed and I knew it was over, and had no idea how to stop my orgasm. I came so hard, harder than I ever had before her. As Nye's hips slowed, she jerked my shit in her hands as she licked me over and over. My toes curled and palms squeezed her cheeks.

Nye hopped up, causing a rush of air to hit my soaked face. I didn't realize how much I needed oxygen. My chest heaved as I tried catching my breath. Nye climbed from over me and turned on the mattress to lay on her side, head-to-head next to me. She slid the mask from my eyes, the light momentarily blinding me.

"How did I do?" she asked with a goofy smile on her face. "I watched enough porn videos to prepare for tonight."

That snapped me out of my fuzziness and I spit out a hard laugh. I grabbed her by the natural curls on her head and ruffled them. "You're on your way, kid."

Nye giggled. "You ain't too bad yourself, greedy."

I cracked up, rubbing her wetness from my face.

One thing was for certain. I liked that shit. It was by far the most erotic thing I'd ever experienced in my life.

PRESENT DAY

"Okay. This tentative plan sounds promising," his rasp pushed through the speakerphone.

"Yeah." Raj, standing across from me, agreed. "So, we'll do the live recording that week in May and then the following week, I should have the studio booked out."

My sister, Monica, wrote quickly in her portfolio at the kitchen table. This was an informal meeting. Rhythm and Blues chart-topper, Ragee, stopped by this evening. He was in the area and wanted to lock me down to record his next album. Usually, this matter would be handled by way of our staff—in my case, my sister, Monica, and his people. However, this situation was unique. Raj and I had a special friend in common.

Although irregular in my in-person attendance, I considered myself a member of *Redeeming Souls for Abundant Living in Christ Family Worship Center* in Harlem, New York. Raj was the one who put me on nearly ten years ago, but I could never be a traditional member, chasing my career. I'd coached for several college teams on the West Coast and even got hired in the *League*.

But when I returned home to care for my father, I needed spiritual support and guidance and found myself in Harlem more often. I lightweight played for the church's band here and there. They were an unparalleled group of musicians. It was truly an honor. It was at *Redeeming Souls* that I surmised pastors with a keen interest and/or talent in music assembled superior musicians to ensure a thorough worship experience. And Bishop Ezra Carmichael was meticulous with his selection of musicians.

"That'll work for the band, too," Dwayne, the music director at *Redeeming Souls,* agreed. He was on a three-way call as well as Bishop. "We can have the rest of the guys reserve that week and the week before for rehearsals. You good for rehearsals?"

Monica grunted across the room, expressing her frustrations. She had to make my schedule work for my needs, which had been increasing lately. When I looked to her for an answer, she nodded without giving me the benefit of her eyes.

"A'ight." Raj tapped rhythmically on the countertop, a quick tune before informing into the speaker, "Launz is working it into his schedule. I only need to be there one night for rehearsal for the one single. Right?"

"Yeah, man," Dwayne confirmed. "So, I should be getting those lyrics and reference over to you in a couple weeks."

"True that," Ragee agreed. "Now, I can have my guitarist the following week all to myself." He winked.

Bishop and Dwayne laughed into the line.

"Hang on, now, there," Bishop warned. "I believe it is safe to say, once you've had Pierce's axe in your ensemble, he belongs to you. You may have been the intercessor, but we're all on the same side of the fan barrier."

I snorted as the doorbell sounded. Monica pushed the chair back from the table, scraping the floor. She went to answer the door.

"Now unto Him that is able to keep you from falling, and to present you faultless before the presence of His glory with exceeding joy," Dwayne began spitting out quickly. "To the only wise God our Saviour, be glory and majesty, dominion and power, both now and ever. Because, brothers, Lucy's pulling out them dishes, finna fix my plate!" he added with hilarious dramatics.

"Amen," Raj conceded.

I followed. "Amen."

"Peace and blessings," Ezra rasped before I lifted the handpiece to end the call.

"A'ight, man," Raj exhaled. "Let me get these dates to Wynter so they can populate on my calendar."

That reminded me. "You still haven't found an assistant?"

"I did, but he didn't work out," Raj explained. "Dude kept showing up late."

"Later than you?"

His head dipped low before retracting. "Yes! And I can't have that in my camp."

"I feel you."

Good assistants were hard to come by; competent and professional ones were a rare find.

"We out, Matt!" Raj shouted out into the dining room to his adopted son. I went to address a notification on my phone. Seconds later, Matthew whisked into the kitchen.

"Mr. Launz, your old *Atari* game is amazing!"

"Thanks, man!" I hi-fived him. "Next time, I have to battle you." I ruffled his hair. As my gaze lifted, Zo's figure that had been becoming more familiar was entering the kitchen. "Oh, hey, man!" I lifted my hand as he approached for some dap.

Monica was right behind him, sauntering to resume her seat at the table.

"What it do?" he greeted, then glanced around the room. He did a double take at Raj, who'd just lowered his phone. "*I*—I" Zo stumbled over his words. "I didn't know you had company."

"Nah, man," Raj smiled. "We were just leaving."

"Yeah. I'm hungry." Matthew announced, patting his belly. His innocuous, cheap smirk had Raj and me snickering.

"Then let me get you out of here. I don't want to hear Blue's mouth." Raj tossed his chin at Zo. "Yo, do I know you?"

Monica snorted behind us. That snapped Zo out of the confounded state he seemed to have been cast into.

"Nah. I doubt it," I interjected. "This is..." That's when I became stuck. How did I introduce Zo? I didn't want to overstep or offend him. "Zo Taylor. Zo, this is a buddy of mine, Raj."

Raj proffered his palm. "Nice to meet—" His eyes bounced back and forth. "Aye, man. Y'all..."

"We know." I nodded. "It's freaky. We're getting used to it."

"Nice to meet you, bro." Zo finally snapped out of it. "I have all your music. My mom loves you. I took her to see you in—" Zo shook his head, cutting himself off. "My bad, bro. Just nice to meet you."

"The pleasure is all mine." With his brows furrowed, Raj murmured, "Until the next time, Coach Strings."

"Yeah, man!" I moved to give him dap. "Later, Matt!"

"Bye, Mr. Launz," Matthew returned, trailing behind Raj. "Next time."

I chuckled, watching Monica see them out.

Zo pointed to the door the father/son duo had just exited. "My bad about that, man."

"Nah." I waved off the notion. "It's all good. We still have rules of engagement to establish. I didn't know what to say."

"Oh." His head bounced. "Okay. Nah. It's all good. Awkward, but all good."

"What brings you down to Moorestown, New Jersey?"

Zo texted me earlier, asking if I was in town. When I told him I was, he asked if he could stop by, he needed to talk to me.

He rubbed his chin. "I...ugh..." Zo hesitated. "I need a favor."

My face tightened as I moved to lean against the counter. "Anything." Had he finally decided to have the conversation about my child support owed to him?

"So, my girl...Gena. She...*uhhh*—we want to see each other. So, we got her a flight out for a couple of days, but..."

"Is this a Valentine's Day visit?"

"Nah. Like Thursday."

The day after tomorrow...

"Okay. What can I do?"

Monica returned to the room, resuming her seat.

"Well, she can't stay in my dorm. Plus, it's like…small. So, I thought about when you had me over a few days ago and figured you had the space. So…"

When he hesitated, I tried helping him out again. "You want her to stay here?"

"Well…" He rubbed his chin. "Yeah."

While my mind ran a lap, Monica interjected, "Is your mom still in town?"

Zo turned to her. "She is."

When Monica's face tightened into an expression I felt and understood, I was also compelled to neutralize possible negative vibes.

"Zo, if you need a place for your girlfriend to stay, I'm cool with it being at my home. I just want to be sure I'm not missing something here."

"Like what?"

"Like your momma," Monica quipped. "Why wouldn't your mother want to spend time with…"

"Gena."

"Yeah." Monica's head rolled. "Gena. What're you leaving out?"

Zo's head lifted slowly as he inhaled deeply, then his chin met his chest. "Okay. So great segue."

"Then let's keep it coming then?" Monica's head bobbed.

"First, yes." Zo turned to me and my regard swept from my sister to him. "What you're sensing is me trying to do something independent of Nyedeera Taylor, the great. I tried getting her to let Gena stay with her first. It'll only be a couple of nights, but Queen Taylor believes it's too soon since I left her back at home." *Hmmm…* "What she doesn't understand is that we're going through a hard time now and things are pretty serious. It's difficult for me to focus on my classes with things as up in the air as they are now. I just need a few days to show her that I'm good on campus…she wants to meet all of you, and—we just need to talk face-to-face, not *FaceTime*."

"How serious are these things that are 'up in the air' with you two—"

"Nick…" I warned my sister, channeling her breaks with my eyes. Yes, Zo's answer was vague as hell, but I understood as a man, not all of our shit could be explained. Zo needed to see his girl for a few short days and I'd make that happen for him without the third degree his mother had obviously wanted to put him through to help. "She can stay here. I'll be in and out, but'll have a room put together for her. Is that all you need? I know you said the flight's been taken care of. What about transportation?"

"I can take care of that."

"Okay. Cool. Say no more."

"One more thing. About my mom." Zo stalled.

"What about her?"

"You haven't exactly acknowledged her yet."

My forehead wrinkled. "What do you mean? I've only seen her once, last month in the City."

"Right." Zo nodded. "I heard you barely looked her way." My head fell to the side. I was missing something. "You realize you haven't asked me about her, much less reached out to her yourself about the *conversation?*"

"What conversation?"

Zo's eyes lit up and he scoffed, "About how the hell I got here and you and I are just finding out about each other."

Ahhhh…

My head bobbed.

"Look, man, I don't know what went on between you and her back in the day. I don't even know how you met or why she waited so long to tell us about one another, but that aside: communication has to be had. I mean. I'm here." He gestured my home. "I wanna be here. I want to get to know you and my family. I'm giving this a go. But she's a part of my life, too. Aside from keeping my damn father from me for twenty-one years, my mother's solid. She's strong, protective, and loyal as hell to me. So damn loyal, I can't get her to go back home and stay there." When I didn't reply, Zo's palms slashed the air. "All I'm saying is talk to her. She wants to talk, too, but Nye Taylor is so much like Gunnery Sergeant Preston Taylor, she would rather die a slow death than to show weakness."

What in the hell would I possibly have to say to Nye? I couldn't think of anything fruitful we could exchange ever again in life. But for the greater good, which was Zo, I wouldn't express that.

Taking a deep breath, I tossed my chin toward Monica across the room, conspicuously observing every word. "Find time in my schedule for a sit-down with her. Maybe dinner with the three of us?"

Zo scoffed and I turned to him with wide eyes. He was an adult now and was the very root of my only connection with her, so why wouldn't he be there?

I raised my hand to him for a dap. "I look you out, you look me out."

Receiving me, he challenged, "Oh, that's what this is."

The sound of his laughter loosened the muscles in my chest. It made me curious about what his juvenile chortle was like. I'd missed so much of his life.

"Damn right, it is."

"We're revolutionizing the royal family," I reiterated to the boxes of fifteen attentive faces on my computer monitor. "I'm very much aware of the abuse of trust the *Kings* family's endured with previous head coaches, and I'm willing to work for my grace. And quite frankly, I need your help to do it."

I observed the nods of understanding or simple courtesy before Sloane Brooks motioned to speak.

"Brooks," I announced, inviting the wide receiver coach to unmute herself.

I watched her take the task. "Yes. I'm sure it's been expressed a lot on the call earlier, but congratulations." My head bobbed in acknowledgment. "As you know, I just lost a franchise receiver and, of course, have been working hard on brainstorming development plans for what I have now. What potential receivers are you looking at for the draft?"

"Well, to start, I sympathize with the absence of Johnson in the upcoming season. He was a true champion and dedicated to the game. His commitment to his QB as well as coaches and coordinators helped gel the team. So, shit." I exhaled, emptying my lungs. "My bad on that. As far as the prospects: I've been poring over the most updated list of eligible draftees and free agents for a few weeks now. I'm, of course, waiting to hear about those who are adding to the draft and eligibility pool as they come in as well." I shrugged with my lips. "Nonetheless, we have talent here we need to cultivate and maximize on.

"In all transparency, I'm most excited about that. I'm eager to work with the skill we have here that's not quite fostered, yet very much at our fingertips. As I mentioned earlier, working with this nutritional firm to incorporate new dietary plans at each player's individual level will be key. Brooks, the yoga regimen you began almost three years ago with your receivers has been on that revolutionary level I'm pledging to apply across the board."

Sloane's head rocked up and down. "Thanks."

"Yeah. I've read your notes on the advantages of yoga. Last night, I read the progression report, too. Good stuff. It's great that I don't have to utilize too much time convincing my coaching team of the benefits of holistic health. In addition to that, at this stage in science, there's no doubt that nutrition is a significant component of athleticism. It can also be a method of bonding for the first and second-string players. Hate it or love it, they'll be in that rough adjustment period together."

"The trenches," Kaleece murmured her understanding and agreement.

"But, Brooks," I thought to add, "If you need a franchise receiver in Johnson's wake—"

"I *have* a franchise receiver." Her forehead wrinkled at the one-word emphasis. Then Sloane shook her head, catching her temper. "Amare is a franchise player. He's been under the tutelage of myself and Johnson for two seasons now. He's studied, humble, coachable, and dedicated to becoming one of the best receivers the *League* has seen." Then arrogance widened the lower half of her face. "We're good over here with what we have, but if you want to send more unbridled —*or bridled*—talent my way for grooming, I wouldn't be disappointed."

For a spell of time, I didn't speak. It was good to see her express confidence in her players, but I understood it for what it was. I knew of Sloane Brooks' affinity toward Rut Amare, third season wide receiver for the *Connecticut Kings*. Their turbulent pairing a few years ago when they were both new to the organization was one for all the gossip fodder. Whispers of their dramatic tête-à-têtes hit the media their entire first season together. In the inner circles of the *League*, it was known that Amare was teetering on the edge of termination for his sexist views of having a female coach. But Brooks was built in a manner to stay and play rather than to dismiss "unbridled" potential.

So, I let her sit in it—dramatically—before concluding the meeting.

"Good to know, Brooks." Nodding, I emphasized. "Good to know." I sat up in the leather desk chair of my home office. "Well, unless there are more questions, I won't belabor your patience any further. Again, I'll be in Connecticut in a couple of days. Some of you, I have meetings with already, however, you all know how to reach me if needed. Clear?"

A barrage of affirmations hit at once with them unmuting simultaneously. Once most had disconnected from the videoconference, I ended the meeting completely. I was thirsty and my back was locking up on me from sitting for so damn long. The walk to my kitchen was short, but it felt good to be on my feet. Sludging toward the refrigerator, a reminder of my schedule flashed in my brain. I had less than fifteen minutes to suit up for my afternoon run. That was between my mundane afternoon and me getting some ass tonight.

Affectionate murmurs had me pausing while pulling a bottle of water from the fridge.

"I swear, I'm good with whatever you choose. I just don't want your choice to be based on my current lifestyle. I can be whatever you need for me to be when you need me to be it. I'm here for you, baby. I swear it—"

"I know," a soft, dramatic cry erupted. "I know you are, but it seems so unfair because…" Zo's girlfriend, Gena, who arrived yesterday, tried catching a breath. At least it sounded like it, based on the deep, audible gasp that was louder than her words. "I'm only in junior college, but you're here doing bigger things. It seems so unfair to disrupt your—"

"Shhhhhhh!" Zo hushed her. Though they were around the wall on the other side of the kitchen, I could tell he was embracing her. Their voices that intimately low. "I got you, girl. I'm here either way you wanna go."

My first thought while hearing her smothered sobs was there had never been a girl or woman I'd *ever* been into like that to have me an emotional whispering mess. Then my following one was a question.

How many things in life could have these young people so vexed?

Closing the door of the refrigerator, I decided to quickly skate out of the kitchen, returning to them their privacy.

~SEVEN

PRESENT DAY

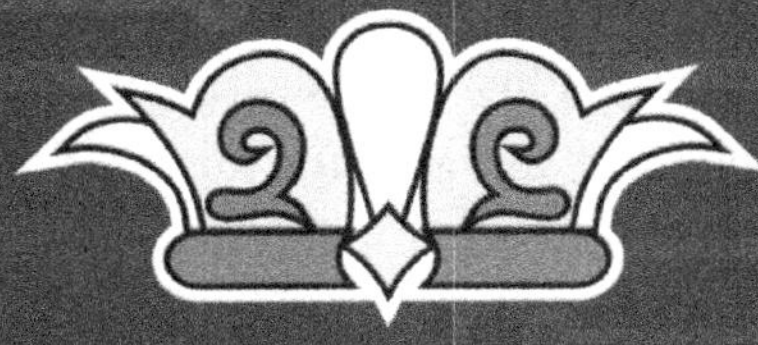

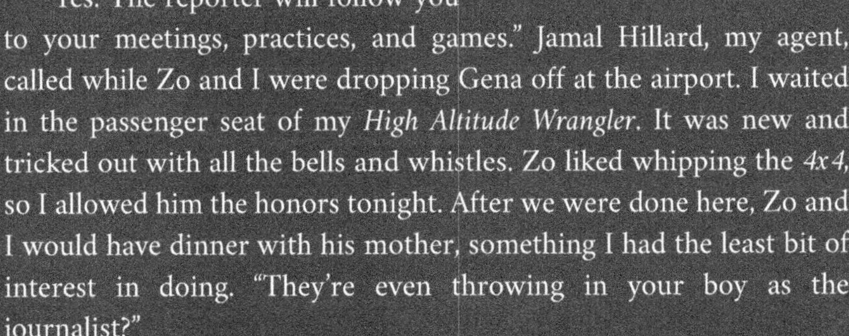

"They're saying an eight-month coverage period—"

"Coverage?" I asked. "As in shadowing?"

"Yes. The reporter will follow you to your meetings, practices, and games." Jamal Hillard, my agent, called while Zo and I were dropping Gena off at the airport. I waited in the passenger seat of my *High Altitude Wrangler*. It was new and tricked out with all the bells and whistles. Zo liked whipping the *4x4*, so I allowed him the honors tonight. After we were done here, Zo and I would have dinner with his mother, something I had the least bit of interest in doing. "They're even throwing in your boy as the journalist?"

My regard swiped from Zo, preparing to kiss his girl to the dashboard ahead. "*Who*—what?"

"Ashton Spencer."

I chuckled. "Spence doesn't do sports. And predictably, you're going to say…"

"He just did that big piece on Tori McNabb. Last I checked, boxing was a sport reported on in *Sports Illustrated*."

"Yup. And that assignment for him was totally out of his norm. Anyway…" I shook my head, sitting up. "I can't do press now. Not until I earned the trust of my players and team. Remember, that's what got Nealson's ass tripped up with them. He wanted the highlight reel alongside his players. Plus, I ain't with the cameras, man. I ain't one for attention. Spotlight shit ain't for me, bruh. You know this."

Knowing we were in a no-stop zone at the terminal, my eyes drifted back to the kids. I blinked and squinted my eyes in the shadow of the night, just outside the glass doors of the terminal when Zo rubbed the flat belly of his girl. It wasn't just an intimate gesture, it was one of symbolism.

Shit…

The girl was pregnant.

I fucking knew it!

What the entire fuck, Zo?

Was that really why he wanted her to stay with me? His words to her yesterday in my family room replayed in my mind.

"I swear, I'm good with whatever you choose. I just don't want your choice to be based on my current lifestyle."

Had they decided, since that conversation, to have the baby? Did his mother know? So many questions ran through my mind while, concurrently, an undeniable warmth permeated my chest. Drips of joy infused my heart. A damn grandfather. I'd just been made aware of being a father! This was some crazy shit.

"Did you hear me, bruh?" Jamal's tenor broke my stream of thoughts.

I blinked again. "Huhn?"

"I said think about it. Yeah, I know your reserved nature, but I also know your genius. The world needs to learn of it, too."

When I saw Zo heading for the truck, I needed to dead this

conversation. "Hey, Hillard, I gotta go. I'll hit you in the morning about the meeting with the front office."

Jamal played it off with a light titter. "A'ight, man, I'mma let you go."

"Cool." I hung up as Zo dropped into the driver's seat.

Needing something to do with my hands, I mindlessly scrolled through my notifications on *Twitter*. Zo set the navigation to the address of *DiFillippo's* in Hackensack. My mind ran with worry and possibility as he pulled off and drove for a few minutes.

"I know you and my mom have been, been..." He waffled again at a time I hoped he wouldn't start an emotional circumlocution. I couldn't handle that right now. I was still getting to know my son. "...a real thing, but..." Zo attempted to forge ahead while weaving onto U.S. 1/9 North, his head swinging between the rear and side-view mirrors. "Have you ever been on the escarpment of a decision that would mark the course of the rest of your life? Like..." His head swung left and right, focusing on weekday, evening rush-hour traffic. "...something that could change everything you are for better or for worse?"

Air sandbagged through my lungs as my head whipped to my window. There was nothing to see but evening travelers. He was right: I'd never made it to anything official with his mother. But the realness of what he'd just said was my lack of experience at ever having something genuine. So, like an idiot, my reply belied my truth.

"Like *what*?"

That was the dumbest shit I'd ever asked.

"Like..." My twin's head bobbed left and right. "The time you were in love when you were a youngin' like me."

My hips propelled upward and shoulders squeezed tight. I rolled my eyes to my right, out of the window. "Can I keep it real with you?"

After a beat, Zo acceded to, "Please."

I realized in that moment just how much this surreal opportunity at being a father meant to me and just went for it. "I've never...had the opportunity to be in anything exclusive with a woman."

His head whipped to face me. "All them chicks you got? You're shitting me!"

"Nah." I shook my head. "I don't have 'all them chicks.' And I'm not."

"How?" Zo had trouble understanding it.

It was my fault. Since he'd been at my place with Gena, at least three of my lady friends stopped by for one reason or another. I didn't typically keep a heavy flow of traffic through my home with women but, of course, the one time my son was there, several had reasons to drop by. I enjoyed women—unapologetically—but being in love hadn't been a pocket I'd ever been caught in.

I shrugged, feeling apologetic—not because of how I chose to remain single, but not being a resource he clearly needed at the time. "I don't know. I guess it's a matter of me simply not having come across a woman who appealed to me on an emotional level like that." Needing to move the conversation along, I asked, "Have you asked your mother?"

"What?"

"About this thing you're facing. Maybe it's something she can provide insight to." For some odd reason, I'd rather it be Nye than her father. Him raising my kid still didn't sit well with me. At all.

Zo scoffed. "Nah. Not this. Not yet, at least." Then he tossed me a cursory glance. "You ready for this?"

My eyes widened and I blew out a breath. "As ready as I'll ever be."

Zo laughed, turning up the volume to Young Lord's latest single, "*I Ain't a Killa...But.*"

"Private room?" Zo noted out loud, waggling his brows as we followed the hostess to the back of the restaurant. "Swanky."

I asked Monica to book us a private room because it would be my first time talking with Nye and I had no damn clue where the "conversation" would lead us. When I left home, I had a list of topics I would allow and a longer one of what I wouldn't discuss at all. Now, there was only one thing I hoped we would discuss and that was supporting Zo and his girlfriend, Gena, with this baby—alleged, of course.

"I can take that for you?" the host offered while I removed my coat before taking a seat at the table.

"Sure. And can you have the waiter bring a glass of *Mauve*? Neat, please."

He took my coat. Zo thought to keep his in the trunk. "Very well, sir. Anything I can have sent back for you, sir?"

Zo looked my way. "This is going to sound strange because I am twenty-one, but you're footing the *DiFillippo's* bill. You mind if I have a beer?"

My face tightened. "What would your mom say?"

Zo's eyes lit with humor, then his face followed. "I don't know, but I'm so happy you're finally about to talk to her so you can ask her questions like that." His attention went to the host. "Anything you have on tap, please."

"Absolutely. I'll get that in and Marcia will be right with you two."

When the host left, I had to ask again. "You sure your mom ain't about to come in here, see you drinking a beer with me, and cuss my ass out?" He chuckled. "I'm dead ass, Zo."

"I just sent my lady off, across the country while we're in a sensitive state. I can actually use a stiff *Mauve* myself. Actually," he scoffed. "I can wait until I get back on campus and have a half a pint of *Paul Masson* and be just as nice off of it as you can with that expensive brown juice." My head shot back, disputing that lie. "But instead, I just want to have a beer or two." He blinked. "With you." A sudden frown settled on his face. "I actually like hanging out with you and my mom —when she's not trippin'."

I was stunned into silence by his confession. Zo, a twenty-one-year-old kid, liked hanging out with me?

He'd been over for the past few days since his girl was in town. We shared meals together and I had even driven them to Philly so Gena could take pictures at the *Liberty Bell*, the steps Rocky ran at the *Museum of Art*, and the *Love Park* before ending our time in the city at

Geno's—all in between taking calls for work. That afternoon and into the evening, I played the chauffeur and photographer. But even before his girl arrived, I'd had dinner with Zo after his last class that day, and we'd been to visit my parents again, too. Hearing that he enjoyed spending time with me hit a tender bone.

I was caught in a trance when the waiter arrived at the table, placing our drinks before us while another lay menus aside us.

"We're expecting a third party, correct?"

"Yes," Zo answered. "We are."

"Okay. I'll leave these and return in a few minutes, unless I can get you something else."

Irritated, I wiggled my fingers. "That'll be all for now."

"Okay."

As I sensed them walk off, I asked Zo, "So, whatever this is that has you so stressed about your girl, will you discuss it with your mother tonight?"

Zo swallowed back a gulp of his beer and picked up his chirping phone from the table. "Like here, at swanky *DiFillippo's*?" That charming titter sprinkled the air again. "Nah. Tonight's for you two to talk. Talk about anything. Just exchange words over a meal." His regard dropped to his phone below, on his lap. "This shit I'm dealing with, I guess I'll have to figure it out." Then he took a deep breath, bringing the phone to the table again. That was Gena. She's boarded."

I wanted to ask how she was emotionally, but didn't understand why I cared in the first place. Was I sure she was pregnant? Had she eaten before I put her back on a flight across the country?

Shit…

I should have upgraded her to first-class. Was she in first-class to begin with? Who were her parents?

Am I overthinking this shit?

"I need a job," Zo murmured after swallowing back more of his beer. He pushed his lips into his gums.

"You're owed money. What do you need? I can cut a check or make a transfer first thing in the morning."

"Yeah," he sighed. "But what I need, I need to earn, not inherit. You were in college when my mother conceived me—I mean, you two—conceived me. Right?"

I thought for a minute. "Right."

"Well, if you knew then what you know now about who I am as a person, would you have dropped out?"

"Your party's here awaiting you, ma'am." The host pointed into the private dining room of posh *DiFillippo's*.

He was the first thing arresting my attention. His eyes were big as he pulled the tumbler to his mouth and swallowed back a deep swig while peering at my son. I didn't pay the time needed to really look at him last month in his lawyer's conference room, but tonight, even under the soft lights of the quaint room, his striking presence wouldn't allow me to skip over his countenance. Launz, in just a hoodie, a shadowy beard, and wild, kinky twist out-styled hair, was a mature version of the boy I birthed. Both had russet skinned, sculpted cheekbones, and incredibly unfair dark and long eyelashes.

"Ma'am?" the host startled me from my reverie.

I sauntered over to Zo, though his back was turned to me. "Oh," I chirped. "Beer? On a weeknight?" Leaning over, I kissed his cheek.

With pursed lips and a tight, closed-eye beam, Zo reached behind to find my cheek, returning my embrace. "Mommy."

I found my way to the empty seat, nervously clearing my throat as the host pushed in my chair. At first, I couldn't look at him.

That was until his subterranean deep cords implored, "Nyedeera." My eyes swept up from the menu. "It's good to see you."

Really?

My eyes skirted over to Zo, gulping down his beer. "Oh. Well, I guess it's nice to be seen."

"Apparently, both of my parents have meticulous palates. Pops likes to chow at *DiFillippo's*, too," Zo commented, eyes bright with humor. "I really got big shoes to fill in terms of class. Maybe I'll drop out and become one of your assistants." He snapped his finger. "My bad. Your sister is yours already," he told Launz.

Launz's face fell, an emotion crying out behind the mask of his face.

"Can I get you something to drink or do you need time?" The waiter had arrived, replacing the host.

"Oh." I blinked, trying to think. "I—uhhhhh..." My eyes skirted over the leather menu portfolio. "Vodka—top shelf—a shot of lemon juice and two slices of lemon on the rocks."

He bowed at the neck. "Very well, ma'am."

"So, what do you do for a living, Nye?" Launz had me damn near falling from my seat when he asked. "Catch me up on your life over the past twenty-one years—if you don't mind."

"Oh, my!" I chirped, fingering my neck. I didn't think the man wanted to share the same air as me, much less catch up on my life. "I'll let you go first." I tossed him a wink as I pulled my purse to my lap to search for my hand sanitizer.

Launz shrugged with his lips. "Well, I've been around, I guess."

"Technically, not," Zo murmured, interjecting as he grabbed his beer. "You've been around the country coaching."

"Yeah and no. I've never left Jersey, only checked out for work. I entered the *League* as a free agent. Played my first season in Miami and—"

He was drafted when I left?

"You got drafted?" Zo's wild eyes exacted my feelings to the T.

"No," Launz murmured. "I got called after the draft. I wasn't a focused player in college. I was there, regarding talent, and committing to the team, but never expressed that on the field. My coaches told me from my second year in the *Scarlet Knights* program, I was a better coach than I was a player. It was a running joke, until one of them proved it by recommending me to the QB coach for the *Dolphins*."

Launz shrugged with his palms around his tumbler. "I got the call for third-string as an undrafted free agent. Anyway, I played for a few months then fucked up my body and confidence too much to be on the field anymore. Cracked ribs, concussion, and banged up my shoulder pretty bad. Was laid up for months."

"Then you came back home?" Zo asked, clearly beguiled by this story. "I mean, I know you told me you played ball in Florida, but I didn't know that meant the *League*."

Launz tossed back his brandy, then nodded as he swallowed, an act so mundane felt so manly in the moment. "Came home and ended up with three jobs. I worked as a substitute teacher and helped coach the school's football team. On weekends, I'd help my dad on the farms. And I did that for about two years before another one of my former *Scarlet Knights* coaches recommended me for an assistant coaching gig in Camden. That job got me the one coaching at your New Brunswick campus, which we know is *Rutgers'* only D1 football program."

"Oh, right," Zo nodded.

"Well, I performed well because the opportunities kept coming. I was young and without a family so when an opportunity opened on the West Coast—"

"*Washington, USC,* and *Arizona State.*"

"Yup." The waiter approached, interrupting Launz. Interrupting us. "I'll take the eggplant parm with penne pasta and a house salad," he ordered. "Oh, and the caviar and chips."

"I'm gonna do..." Zo hesitated while opening and perusing the menu. "Damn. This is a fancy selection. Mom, what are you having?" He peered my way.

That was an easy choice for me. "I'll have the Panzanella salad with a side of cold water oysters."

As I handed off the menu, Zo murmured, "I have no idea what none of that is so I'll just take the lasagna."

"Excellent choices made by all," the waiter added while collecting Zo's menu. "I'll put these selections in right away. *Ahhhh!*" He smiled. "And here's your drink, madam."

My cocktail was placed in front of me and the waiter lingered until I sampled it. After a nod of approval, he left.

"Can I get you another?" the second waiter quizzed Zo.

"Nah. No thank you."

"And how about you, sir?" he asked Launz.

Launz peered down at his glass as I took a full sip of my drink, enjoying it. "Yes, please."

"Make that two," Zo confidently requested. My brows met. *This boy wants brandy? Mauve* no less? Inherently, he faces me. "I wanna see what the talk is all about. Plus, I'm celebrating my parents having a civil conversation for the first time since I was born."

That stung. Zo was a light-hearted and witty kid, so I knew he meant no harm, but having my transgressions thrown in my face like that was no fun. I wouldn't shrink, though. I never did.

But if I could...

I pulled in a deep breath through my nostrils while grabbing my cocktail. As I gathered my feelings, my gaze met Launz, whose eyes bounced between my son and me. "You were saying?"

Caught off guard, he stumbled visibly then recalled. "Oh. Me! Well, yeah." He scratched his brow. "College coaching led me to my first *League* gig. And that's when I landed in Seattle for a few years, until my dad got sick."

My forehead rolled back. *Oh...*

I watched Launz take the last bite of his blini topped with crème fraiche, and caviar. His eyes were on me.

"So, after law school, I went to work for a small firm—"

"Three blocks from my school." Zo stuffed a whole blini into his mouth and chewed. "These are good as hell!"

I rolled my eyes internally. Zo had been allowed to speak freely around me for close to six years now. In his teenage years, I needed to earn his trust fully. And for me, that meant providing the illusion of a friendship. Friends speak candidly around friends. They're allowed to express themselves without condemnation. But Zo's lips had been loose for the past twenty minutes or so, since his little *Mauve*.

Launz's wide eyes swung from Zo to me. "Yeah. One of my favorite treats. Say, Zo…" He reached for his napkin and wiped his mouth. "…now that you have the two of us together, should we talk about my arrears payout for you? Do you have any specific financial goals or anything?"

Zo smirked as the waiters gaited into the room, carrying trays topped with food.

"Not really." Zo shrugged his lips. "Not yet anyway."

Our food was being served to us. My salad looked great and oysters amazing.

"A bottle of *Armand de Brignac* for the lady's oysters, please," Launz ordered.

"Very well." The waiter nodded before taking off.

"Yes!" Zo pumped his fist in the air. "First beer, then *Mauve*, and now *Ace of Spades*? This day didn't turn to shits after all."

"Zo!" Embarrassment peaked, I'd had enough. "You've been rude since I've gotten here. What's going on with you?"

His mouth and eyes were open and wide. Regret colored his face, reminding me of my baby, rather than a young version of his father. "My bad, Ma!" Zo's eyes squeezed closed. "I may be over the top. It's just…" He shook his head. "It's weird and exciting having a meal with both my parents." His hand reached over to find mine. "I'm happy, don't get me wrong. I think I'm just a little too hyped. I'll watch my mouth."

Again, Launz's regard, alarmed and concerned, bounced between the two of us. "It's all good, man." Then he gestured toward me. "So, Nyedeera the esquire."

Oh…

I nodded. "Yup."

"What kind of lawyer?"

"Constitutional law."

"Really? What does that entail exactly?"

I lifted my index, asking for a moment to quietly pray over my food. When I was done, I peered up to see Launz and Zo doing the same.

I waited until they were done to resume the conversation. "Constitutional law is the matter of interpreting the U.S. Constitution and that of its states and articulating them in a manner of justice for a needed party."

Launz chewed and licked his lips. "Who needs that argued?" He flickered his fork in the air, emphasizing his confusion.

"Many people. Organizations, individual people." I began with my salad.

"Like who?"

Zo was into his phone at this point in the conversation.

"People like you. A celebrity who has been recorded expressing a strong opinion in this cancel culture society. You may express your views on the Catholic church encouraging sexual abuse by..."—I waved my hands in the air, thinking fast—"...the mere fact that they don't publicly shame priests who have been found guilty of assault—or have a process by which they effectively investigate, convict, and condemn the offenders. They may attempt to sue you and your employer for false allegations of them encouraging sexual assault. Well, the *Kings* quickly decide to separate from you to absolve themselves of any culpability.

"That's when you come in and say the *Kings* violated your First Amendment Rights of free speech."

Launz nodded and chewed. "But I'm not a celebrity."

"You're a public figure: you're a celebrity." I forked more of the salad as the bottle of champagne was being brought in.

As the waiter made work of uncorking it, much to Zo's entertainment, Launz asked, "Why does that lawsuit seem familiar to me?"

"Because something similar happened to Ellis Erceg," Zo answered, eyes still on the champagne now being poured for me just in time for my oysters. "She made the comment about noticing most of the shoes on the black market from Ericka's footwear line were due to Asian bootleggers. Then the network for *"Envying the Ercegs"* tried to cancel the show."

Launz's head rolled back in recognition. "Ahhh..."

"Mom helped out on that case."

"Really?" Launz's head bounced back.

"Just as a consultant," I explained while traveling the first oyster to my mouth. "My firm farmed me out." I pulled the half shell to my mouth for a tilt, wanting the aerodynamic experience then slurped down the pearl.

Delicious...

I went for my glass of champagne and when I brought it to my mouth, I noticed Launz's eyes on my neck. They slowly raked up to my eyes, stopping at my mouth. Quickly, I swung my attention over to my son. That's when I damn near choked.

"Zo, when did you get that?"

Zo dropped his flute. "Huhn?"

"So, what cases have you worked on lately?" Launz interjected, clearly attempting to change the subject.

I decided to let it ride. I'd get Zo's ass right later tonight or in the morning.

"Mostly dry matters: constitutionally challenging judicial appointments...assisting with court-ordered deadlines." I shrugged, returning to my salad. "Nothing fun like that one case."

"So, you're in court a lot," Launz surmised as I peered over to Zo.

"Not really." I shook my head. "I don't prefer to be."

"How does that work?"

"Easily. I work for a rather large firm. I'm with a research team—"

"The head of the research department." Zo pointed to the ceiling with his brows plucked, cementing that insignificant fact.

"Anyway. I've gone into court plenty of times, but that's not my typical workspace and I've preferred that."

"So you're the brain of the operation? Preparing all the ammunition to be fired off in court?" Launz accurately depicted.

"I prefer the title of artillery specialist. Arguing is a specialty in and of itself. We have associates who are better skilled in that area of our work than I am." I shrugged, loosening the pearl in a shell. "I'm best at thinking, not performing."

When I tilted my head and swigged back the oyster, my thoughts raced to Launz. Eating oysters around him now felt awkward. There was an art to them I decided to not pursue with the ones I had left.

When we were done eating, the leftover food was cleared, and the bill generously paid by Launz, Zo stood and swayed immediately over his seat.

"Whoa there, partner!" I went to aid him.

"I'm good, Ma," he argued immediately. "Just a little tipsy."

"And irresponsible," I challenged.

"I had a few drinks for the first time with my parents. I don't know how much more responsible I could have been tonight."

Anger began surging my veins and gripping my skull.

"Zo, what's going on with you? Is this how you decide to represent me in front of your father? Is this the impression of you, you want him to have?"

"Mom, chill," he pleaded. "I'm good."

"You sure, man?" Launz asked. "I can tell something shifted for you earlier today. If there's anything you need to talk about—need from me—just say the word."

My head flew to face Launz. "What in the hell happened earlier?"

"Ma! Chill," Zo repeated. "I *do* want something from you, though." His regard swung over to me. "From you, too."

"Just say the word," Launz invited him.

"My momma needs a place to stay—"

"Alaunzo!" I was so embarrassed.

"No, Mom!" He shook his head dramatically. "You've been staying in and out of that hotel, wasting money. You're also on leave from work, which means you're not getting paid."

"Boy, that is my business and no one else's. I'm not hurting for nothing. My grown ass can take care of myself!"

"I know you can," Zo argued. "I'm not saying you can't. You're the strongest person I know on earth. My point is, your plan is expensive as hell. I'm good here in Jersey, but if you need more time to make sure of that, at least make it more economical."

"By staying in a stranger's house?"

"Whoa!" Launz blinked, affronted.

Zo fell into tears, laughing. "I think it's high time for you to cop to this man being your baby's daddy. Staying at his house temporarily is pretty harmless compared to the nasty stuff you two've done once upon a time."

Oh, hell no!

"That's it—"

"Zo, too far!" Launz growled in a way foreign to me, yet so natural.

"My bad!" Zo cried. "I'm really bent right now!"

Launz shook his head. "Not too bent to apologize to your mother."

Zo sniffled dramatically. I didn't know if it was an act of humility or his inebriation. "I'm sorry, Momma! I keep messing up. But I really need this. I need *you* to do this. I've been getting to know the guy and he's cool. I've been checking him out. He's not as shy as you said, just laid back and in his head a lot. But he's a good dude."

My eyes went wild. "Zo!"

"It ain't like I'm asking you to share a room with him. Dude got six bedrooms and four bathrooms. There's more than enough space there. Plus, he's back and forth to work in Connecticut anyway."

"Alaunzo Pierce, do you know how incredibly leeching you're being now? First, you go behind my back and arrange for Gena to stay with him and now this? You're supposed to be getting to know your father, not using the man!"

"Hang on," Launz resumed an ounce of tranquility to his tone. "I wouldn't call it that, Nye. He's a kid—"

"He's a grown man, who's acting like a male child right now!"

"Ma!" Zo's face screwed. "I told you I'm a little tipsy right now."

"A little tipsy?" My chin dropped. I was past the point of seething. "Zo, you don't even drink, and certainly nothing more than beer! I'm about to take off one of these heels and beat your ass for embarrassing me like this!"

"That's not necessary," Launz once again interjected. "The point of you making this grandioso announcement of my paternity to us was for us to get to know each other. Right?"

What?

"It damn sure wasn't for your money. I'm far from broke!"

"That wasn't my sentiment. I'm saying your words to him are making me feel like a damn interloper, allegedly the opposite of what you wanted between my son and me. Correct?"

I took a breath, trying to gain a hold of my temper before I cussed his light skinned ass the fuck out and beat the shit out of his light skinned ass twin on the other side of me.

"She's a boss feminist, man." Zo shook his head. "We ain't winning nothing tonight. I screwed this up, big time."

"No." Launz faced me. "Tell me, Nye. What is it that you want? Really?"

"Oh, you're finally asking?"

His arm swung across the table toward Zo. "Apparently, my son left me no choice tonight. Your welfare is obviously something stressing him out. If I can help, I will!"

"Your help isn't needed. I'm perfectly fine!" I had a solid savings in the six digits and was expecting two payouts relatively soon, the sale of my house being one of them. "And who's to say I'll keep flying out here anyway?"

"Ma, you're about to sell the townhouse and you've been applying for jobs out here."

I could have slapped his face off for telling my damn business.

And from that, I had two eerily identical eyes stapled to me in doubt. Utterly speechless from embarrassment, I could think of nothing to say.

Launz pivoted slightly toward the door, where a waiter inconspicuously waited for our "family" feud to end so they could clean up behind us. "Look." He exhaled. The muscles around his eyes turned slack when he registered the agitation on my son's face. "Zo's right. I'll be back and forth to Connecticut, setting up a home and office there. Other than my sister and housekeeper dropping in sporadically, the place will be vacant a lot. I can have a set of keys made for you tomorrow. It's not a big deal. I believe him when he says you're an independent woman who enjoys taking care of herself."

"Fine!" Zo clapped his hands and turned for the door. "Then it's settled. Ma, you're moving in tomorrow. Check out of the hotel when you get back there tonight."

And then he was gone.

Dizzy with irritation, I turned to Launz. "I'm truly sorry about this. I know I did this all wrong. I don't know if you have a family or are working on one. I didn't mean to drop this on your lap." I rubbed my forehead, frustrated with myself—and that Zo! "I see you're still a solid guy, and I appreciate you extending your generosity to me."

Launz shook his head. "This ain't got shit to do with you and everything to do with this kid."

A flash of pain lanced through my belly as he turned and left the room behind my drunken son.

~EIGHT

22 YEARS AGO| NEW JERSEY

LAUNZ

"Those snares are done," Denny, the drummer, moaned.

Coran, the lead singer, scoffed, "Told you to tell your aunt."

"I did. She keep saying soon, but the sound is fuckin' with me."

"Me, too," Coran mumbled at the table. His eyes then grew wide as he peered over my head. "Aye, look it here!" he piped up, smiling wildly. "If it ain't the top earner of the week for the third time in a row! You killing them, girl!"

I turned and found Nye coming out of the kitchen, carrying a big ass bucket of clean glasses.

"Pito, you can go now," she called across the room to the busboy cleaning the tables. "I got it from here."

My heart literally began to beat faster at the sight of her. It had been happening for a little while now. In fact, I wanted to get up and help her, but that went against the norm. She did her job and I did mine here at Corey's.

Pito glanced up. "You sure?"

"Yeah." Nye waved him off. "It's just those two up front. I got them. I know you gotta catch that bus."

Pito dropped his towel and gave her a nod before stepping off. "Gracias, Nye."

"Whatchu gone do with all that tip money, Nye?" Coran, teasing, asked her.

Nye's head swung up and eyes squinted against the ceiling. "Good question."

"You ain't gonna spend it on your man, are you?"

Nye winked. "Maybe. Either my boyfriend or yours."

The guys laughed, expecting a witty comeback from her. It was what she was good at.

"Oh, yeah?" Denny pushed. "Why haven't I seen him around, picking you up from work at night?"

"Because the last time he was here, he got a bad migraine from hearing you play that raggedy snare."

Even I hung my head to laugh at that.

"She got you, man!" Coran cracked up, too.

"Yeah, yeah." Denny shook his head. "I'm outta here. I'll get up with y'all tomorrow."

Chez and Coran stood, and I followed suit. As they exchanged their final words, I trailed behind them. Stupidly, I paid a final look to Nye, who had been eyeing me already. She winked, then shook her head before going back to work.

From the time she turned the corner, I watched her through my rearview mirror. When she made it to the truck, I fired up the engine.

"Hey," she greeted. "Long time no see."

"I thought you'd be longer." I peered through the side-view mirror before pulling out of the parking space.

"Why?"

"Because you offered to finish Pito's job."

Nye laughed, buckling her seatbelt. "He was practically done anyway. Besides, I know how it feels to have to walk like eight blocks out because of missing that last two-eighty-seven bus. It's stupid that they kill the route so early."

I'd been driving Nye home every night I played at Corey's, and even some I didn't for so long, I'd forgotten how she'd gotten there before me.

Then I hit her with a question I'd been preparing for since this morning when I woke up and realized we'd both be working tonight. "You think you can stay with me tonight on campus?"

Nye turned to me, eyes calculating my request. I wanted her in my bed all night and when I woke up in the morning, just like she was on Valentine's Day, the only time we'd spent the full night together.

"You know I want to."

"But?" I asked, though I already knew the answer.

"You roll your eyes and I think it's cute, you know? I thought guys rolling their eyes were effeminate."

"That charm ain't getting me what I want." I didn't want to change the subject.

Nye groaned, finally expressing the frustration I felt. "I know what you want. And I'm going to give you most of it tonight. Just not overnight." She reached over and kissed me.

That wasn't good enough. "So where to? I can 'sneak' us into my room at my parents'." I didn't want to and she knew it.

When I was sixteen, my mother got tired of hearing my guitar and moved me into their partially finished basement. It had its own door in the back, so I could come and go without disturbing them much. Yes, I could have girls in my room, but I technically didn't live there anymore. Also, I didn't have a girlfriend for it to be cool for me to bring some girl home just to "use my bedroom." My parents would see right through that shit and call me out on it. Nye and I had been together in my room at my parents' quite a few times, but when they weren't home or they thought I was spending the weekend there.

"Let's go to that hotel in Westhampton again."

"The Marriott?" I groaned, trying to stay composed while weaving in and out of traffic.

"Yeah."

"I'm low on cash today."

"Who says you're paying this time?" She waved a wad of cash in front of me.

Then a question occurred. "What're you doing with your money? If you'd let me take you to my dorm, you wouldn't have to waste it on a room for just a few hours. If you'd stand up to your father, you wouldn't—"

"To move."

I stopped at a light and met her gaze in the darkness of the truck. "What?"

Nye nodded, eyes cast out the window. "I'm saving for my own place."

"Where?"

She shrugged. "Maybe I'll get a room somewhere. Or—" She turned to me. "—maybe I'll be your roommate after you graduate next month. Are you going back home?"

I thought about that. And at this point, I knew I wouldn't get an invite to the draft for the League. I'd likely have to go another route to get in. Even though she was fucking with me, the thought of living with Nye didn't turn my stomach. She was...fun. Smart, tough, thoughtful—Nye was all those things and more. She was the first girl I actually liked hanging out with. It wasn't the sex either. Nye was...everything. Nothing like the girls I'd dealt with. Not needy, just carefree and spontaneous as hell.

"The goal is not to."

The light turned green and I let up off the brake.

"Good. Then we need to talk about your savings, bruh. I ain't gonna be paying all the bills." My snort was interrupted by the abrupt sound of her clicking out of her seatbelt and stretching across the bench to me. She put her tongue in my ear and my dick swelled immediately. "Unless you wanna work out an arrangement of you getting it up every morning before I go to work and every night when I get home." Then Nye snatched her body away. "Wait. Can you even cook, my guy?"

My head tossed back and I cracked the hell up. "If you don't put your seatbelt back on!"

"Launz."

My face was wide from laughter. "Huhn?"

"You ever got head while behind the wheel?" Her tiny hand was on my thigh in search of my waist.

I sucked in a breath. "No!" I croaked, scared as hell. "Hell no, Nye!"

The girl was crazy as shit!

PRESENT DAY

"Right in here." She pointed into an open door.

Immediately, I saw it was his home office. Trent Bailey was in his chair with a toddler girl, I presumed to be his daughter, on his lap behind the desk. As she played with the chains on his neck, he chewed his bottom lip while paying me a cursory glance. Deep inside, I fortified myself for what could be an abrasive introductory meeting.

"Thanks, Ms. April." I gave the woman a neck bow.

Her eyes grew wild. "Miss? You the coach! Ain't you just a couple of years younger than me?"

I smirked at Trent's aunt, per her introduction to me when I arrived at the Bailey estate in Alpine. "I wouldn't know what to guess with a Black woman. I assure you, my reference is not based on your appearance. At first sight"—I stretched the truth—"I never would have taken you for his senior. So, forgive me for just being polite."

April eyed me warily while chewing on her gum. As a patient man, I waited. "Oh!" was all she returned.

Then I heard another feminine voice. "Don't forget the gel for the heating pads."

"Damn," Trent murmured. That's when I realized he was on a call via speakerphone. "You didn't pack those, either?"

"I was rushing out and got everything in the drawer but that. And don't let Ky bring that *PS5*. This is a family vacation. He already has his phone and laptop."

"You doing too much now, Jade."

Sharply, she returned, "You heard what I said, Trent."

His eyes landed on me in enmity. "I gotta go. Company just arrived."

"C'mon, Ava Nese," April ordered to the baby girl. "Let your dad take his company."

Trent kissed his daughter and let her down onto the floor. Her little legs worked out of rhythm as she ran into April's arms. The two took off down the hall.

"Before you go, did you remember to pay Leo? I told him you would before we leave."

"Jade!" he barked, but without an ounce of testosterone.

"Pay him," was her response. "Bye for now."

Trent hit a button, ending the call before standing. I met him in the middle of the office that was, by far, larger than mine. It would make sense for it to be; Trent Bailey had a mansion.

"Thanks for coming."

"It's a pleasure to be here." Trent pointed to one of the chairs across the office in a sitting area. I followed his invitation and crossed the room for the sofa. "Or should I say, it's good to know the good ol' pastor."

"It helps," Trent agreed, sitting across from me. "But only Jesus saves."

Ahhhh…

Trent was confirming I needed saving for his good graces.

"Then let's get right to the point, shall we?"

He flung his fingers, inviting me to. "I knew what this was when you asked for it."

"I'm not the type of coach to beg for leadership and respect. I haven't done that shit since high school ball. At this point in my career, I'm far more conversant with grown men who have a voice and a perspective." With pouted lips, Trent nodded as though he agreed. "I understand you and the rest of the players have both. And I'm here to receive both. I feel the need to make that clear."

"With all due respect, you can't believe you're the first to make that claim."

Fucking Jeff Nealson…

"I can't speak for what others have said or done. I just know I have my own endeavors for the *Kings* that include football—exclusively."

Trent waggled his finger. "And that can be problematic, too. It's never just about football and should never be. As the captain of this team for more years than I can count, it's always been about modeling good leadership, integrity, compassion, and dignity. It's not just about the field for me to work effectively. It's about my walk. It's about me making sure all fifty-two players are seen by me. I divide my attention by giving priority to the first and second tier-ers, but everyone gets the best of me from May to January, and sometimes February.

"It's learning their temperament, overlooking their bullshit. It's giving tough love, going to funerals of people I never met but understand they were valued. It's being big bruh to an egotistical Rut Amare, to hugging it out with a bloody Terrance Grant after quietly, yet violently whooping his ass for trying to holla at my pregnant lady in the locker room after practice because I know I have to work with him on that green. It's about knowing the names of grandmothers and god-kids and their stories. It's about fuckin' caring, man."

Stunned by his lack of acknowledgment, I exhaled and blinked hard. "Again, TB, this ain't my first rodeo."

"Yeah, but it'll be your first ride with me." After a long stare, Trent's head bounced back for emphasis. "Bruh, I'm tired. You and me ain't the same age, but you ain't too far from me to get how fucked up my burnout is."

"So, we're about to make this about my age now?"

Ignoring that challenge, Trent continued, "You did your research on me," he referred to me reaching out to Ezra Carmichael to get some of Trent's off-season time today. "You know both Lou and Nealson were in their sixties—hell, Coach Lou was damn near seventy when that shit came crashing down about those prostitutes. Both them dudes couldn't show integrity when it came to women. Do you know how bad it would've been for the franchise if Nealson tried some shit with *my* wife? Bruh, you gotta understand all of our perspectives here. The front office keeps dropping the damn ball, that last time risking our households."

Last week, I'd heard Nealson, the previous head coach, had actually gotten one of the linebackers' baby's mother pregnant and strong-armed her into an abortion. Of course, I understood how unethical that was.

"Look, man: he was out of pocket—both of them were. Neither Brown nor Nealson showed an ounce of moral discipline or respect for themselves, not just the organization and the players."

"Yeah. So, my question to you, Pierce, is: how do you think your walk with us would be different? I've done my research, too! You're only forty-three, never been married, and have no kids? You can't even relate to me or my teammates."

"I can relate professionally, which is why I got the job, Trent." I felt my fucking temper flaring, which was a bad sign. "Look, I'm not gonna sit here and make any promises or try to pledge to some moral conduct. But since you wanna challenge my personal life, I'll tell you yes, I am happily single. Although I'm a product of two committed, married parents, this lifestyle's been kind to me. I don't fuck prostitutes: never have. I don't need to pay for ass. And to keep it a buck, I'm a practiced private person. I'm not ruled by the chase of ass."

"Good to hear."

Hear…

I scoffed, looking away. This shit with Trent Bailey would be a marathon, I then understood.

"Look, man, I gotta pack up to get the family on the road. I'm not even supposed to be speaking with you right now."

"Why not?"

"Because this here," he pointed toward the floor, "is Jade's time, and she ain't about sharing it with the *League* who can't give her a trustworthy head coach."

I scratched the back of my head, confused and offended. "It was Jade who arranged it."

"At your request—or should I say, at Pastor Ezra's."

"Trent, I'm trying here." All I could do was stare at him.

I could tell he was warring with something inside. I knew it had to do with the low morale of the organization due to my predecessors, but I didn't understand the stubbornness. I was not Brown or Nealson, neither would I start my time here kissing ass. That was a far cry from me simply proving myself. There was a distinct difference.

Trent hung his head, exhaling. "When the shit popped off with Coach Nealson and Richardson, Williams, and LeGrier came to me about their next selection for a head coach, I told them to bring me someone who could relate to me. That's it. Let that man understand what it's like walking in Jade Bailey's shoes from May until January. Make sure he knows how she runs this place like a tight team itself. How she only sees me maybe three to four days a week. How most of those days, she allows me to come home to minimal noise in the house.

"How that woman strategically manages my time with the kids, our side businesses, and hers. How she only gets *Bye Week* with me during the season, and that's only parts of me because my head is still in the game. How she has to raise our kids practically without me. The next coach governing over such a significant portion of *my* life needs to know when she miscarried our baby a while back, I only had one day to hold her and promise it wasn't her fault, assure her that her body was perfect, and that I'd give her another one whenever she was ready. They needed to know I use my agent to help romance her when I'm focused in the season because my stupid ass don't know how to woo her materialistically.

"I asked them to know how much that woman starves in those, sometimes, six months from my absence and considers it a privilege. And let's not mention my off-season training, because, bruh," he referred to his body, "this shit don't happen by working six months out of twelve. This incoming man had to understand how exhausting it is for me to give my all for flaky ass football fans one half of the year then spend the last half fighting to prove to my wife why I'm worthy of her starvation—her year-round commitment." Trent shook his head. "So, if you think just because we know the game of football well and how you've been granted some of Jade Bailey's time, that I owe you something right here and right now, you've just wasted pastor's and mine."

Defeated, I stood, rubbing my lips together. "Thanks for having me over." I proffered my palm.

With turmoil weighing his face, too, Trent accepted my shake. "Thanks for coming by," he graveled.

"I'll see myself out."

Doing so wasn't a difficult feat, seeing his office wasn't much of a distance from the front door. Once there, a grounds worker, based on his soiled uniform, held it open for me. I thanked him with a nod and left out for my car. When I drove off the Bailey estate, I admired the professional upkeep of the landscape. It made me think about the picture Trent just painted to me about the struggle of his and his wife's marriage as a *League* couple, and how many didn't know it was what all the players in *committed* relationships experienced. But to the world at large, their lives were as perfect as the manicured land I passed through to get to the main road.

It was similar to how Trent assumed I didn't know about his lifestyle, as though I hadn't coached for years and had to serve as a therapist to my players and their families at times. As though I didn't have my own now that Zo was in my life…and now his mother.

Nye "moved" in a couple of days ago. I hadn't seen much of her because I'd been mostly in Connecticut. Today, I was returning home, but had stopped to visit my QB before heading down the *Turnpike*. And as a result, a tight grip began at the back of my skull.

My telephone rang through the Bluetooth, suspending the music.

"Hey," I answered, eager to hear from her.

"I hope you're not going to flake on me."

"Not on your life, shortie. I'm ready for you." I damn sure was.

"Good," she purred, or at least that's what my dick heard. "I bought two bottles of this expensive ass *Blevin* wine."

"Awwww…" I cooed teasingly. "*Château Blevin* tastes better on you than it does in a glass any day."

She sputtered a laugh and I knew I had her. "Boy, get your ass over here."

Pressing down on the accelerator, I pledged, "You got it."

Thoughts of being in the presence of a woman tonight temporarily aided the stress of not having yet connected with my franchise player. I'd have to table that accomplishment for now.

Lying on my back and legs, I tried breathing in through my nose and exhaled from my mouth while feeling the stretch in my hips and abdomen. Pulling in air and slowly releasing it, I could feel my lungs expand as I gradually lifted my chin to roll onto the top of my head. The "Fish Out of Hero" yoga pose seemed so simple in sight, but the execution of it was hell. My body misted all over. As my head tilted back, I took note of the high ceilings in his family room. The long, drop ceiling fan centering the space. The man had an impressive home. I closed my eyes to elongate my spine, spread my hips, and roll to the top of my head—or try.

A thud sounded, causing my eyes to burst wide. A collection of massive muscles coated in honey golden flesh slid into the archway of the room, the only cotton on him were socks and boxer briefs. My eyes bulged at the realization of Launz's alarmed presence. Possibly too quickly, I lowered my chin and pushed from the floor into a W position, whipping my head back to meet his seething scowl.

Then it hit me.

Oh, my god!

I scurried up and over to the remote control on the end table to power off the stereo.

Turning to him, I tried to explain, "I didn't know you were back in town."

Unbiddenly, my appreciations trailed down his bare, heaving chest and swollen, grilled abs—his narrowed waist, then bulging thighs.

When did he get cut like this?

Wordlessly, Launz dropped his face into his hand, eyes closed. Then he turned to take off. I honestly didn't know he was here. I'd been staying at his place for less than a week now and, as Zo explained, Launz had been back and forth to Connecticut. We'd only see each other in passing. The same with his sister, Monica, who had a room here, though she hadn't stayed the night since I'd been around.

I scurried upstairs to the room I'd been staying in and armed into a kimono then grabbed a towel. When I made it back down to the kitchen, I was happy to see Launz working the *Keurig*.

"Hey," I greeted, patting my neck dry. "I'm really sorry about that."

He lifted one arm, waving off my regret. "S'all good."

I tried again, hoping for my chance to finally talk to him. "It's good to see you here. Your home is lovely. You've done well for yourself."

"I can't complain." He drew water from the faucet into a glass to toss back a few pills.

"No." I opened the fridge door for a bottle of water. "I guess not. I feel...grateful that Zo can see you in this light." That felt stupid and nebulous...incoherent. It was confirmed when Launz didn't reply. He stood over the coffeemaker, peering out the window with one hand planted on the countertop. The posture curved his broad back now clad in a thin fitted t-shirt, glutes hidden behind lounge pants. "Thanks for being so welcoming to him."

"He's my son," he murmured. "What choice did I have?"

"What I mean is, I'm grateful that Zo can see you well and thriving."

Swiftly, he gazed my way. "Were you expecting anything less?"

My eyes dropped and chest rose. "Yeah. The worst."

"Which is?"

I shrugged. "A gamut of scenarios: homelessness, drunkenness, psychosis, one tooth left?"

He snorted genuinely, yet regrettably. "Well, damn."

"So, you did get into the *League*?" I recalled our conversation at *DiFillippo's* a few nights ago. "I don't know why I find that so fascinating." He'd mentioned it the night I randomly suggested we become roommates. Back then, Launz didn't speak of one sure profession. He was stuck between music and football, something I recalled his father despising. "I know you said it wasn't for long, but again, I see you've done well." I gestured to the grand kitchen with my eyes.

Launz squinted, clearly expressing pain in his head. "Sorry. Major headache."

Ahhh...

"And I'm sure my music didn't help. I listen sometimes when doing yoga."

"I see." He struggled through a smile. "Nah. This pain is a familiar foe. Stress headache. But to address this...my home. Don't be overly impressed. Yeah, I'm in Moorestown, but I cheated my way in here. Bought it in twenty-eleven during the mortgage crisis. It was a foreclosed property I was fortunate enough to move on."

I nodded. "But still. You were able to have something in place to acquire it. Zo told me about you having to save your parents' estate. I read a few articles about it, too."

His brows lifted, as did one side of his face. "You researching me?"

Swallowing hard, I fortified my guts for honesty. "I've looked you up several times over the years: personally and hired a professional."

I waited for a response to that. Launz's eyes widened then he squinted, reminding me of the headache. "Nah. Well, I bought this first. Was able to stack a little with my first couple of college coaching gigs. My father got sick a few years later. By then, I was in the *League*: pay was more generous, so I did what I had to do."

Pushing my lips into the air, I nodded. Launz's coffee was pouring into a mug and I decided to swig down water. My mouth grew dry at the start of this "conversation." He sniffed the bean brew with need. Then I watched Launz blow into the mug before attempting a sip. Frustrated, he groaned.

"I think you did well. You had a kid and managed college, a law degree, a career, and buying a home."

"I had lots of help from my family. Even my sister chipped in a lot with Zo when visiting. My parents were amazing."

Launz's eyes locked onto mine, holding me captive. It felt like he was channeling something in me or giving me time to tell him more.

"Zo said his grandfather was instrumental in his life."

My eyes fell as I nodded. "He was." He blew into his coffee again. That one dismissive act reminded me that I was in Alaunzo Pierce's home. As familiar as I once was with him, I was now a stranger to the man. There was so much between us, beyond time. I owed him answers and had been eager to serve them up, but hadn't been given the opportunity. Until now. "Look, Launz—"

The doorbell rang and Launz's brows plucked with curiosity. He carried his mug out of the kitchen and less than a minute later, he returned with Zo on his heels, animated and loquacious.

On a Friday morning...

"Look," Zo demanded. "I need help."

I asked, "With what?"

"I need to get my own place off campus…and a job. I need a job to help me pay for that."

"Why do you need a place to stay?" Launz asked. "You're in a football program. I wouldn't advise that: most of your teammates live on campus."

"Then I can stay, but I'll still need the apartment."

"For what?" I practically screamed.

"For Gena. She's moving to Jersey."

I blinked. "No the hell she's not, Zo! Gena needs to get a grip or move on."

I'd already been juggling too many things with this boy and his father. The last thing I needed was to be concerned about Gena out here and so far away from her parents. These kids had lost their minds!

Zo rubbed his chin, nostrils flared wide. "Mom, I mean no disrespect here, but I'm grown and so is she. We can make these types of decisions without your permission."

My head spun and before I knew it, I was racing toward his little ass.

"Excuse me?"

My forceful rush was intercepted by a strong arm and virile-fragranced body. "Whoa! Whoa! Whoa!"

~NINE

PRESENT DAY

"Okay." I tossed both of them hard gazes. "Let's start this from the top, in an orderly fashion, leaving out any disruptions." My glare lingered on Nye. Then I turned back to Zo. "Why the urgency?"

His shoulders lifted. "Because she's my girl. We're committed to each other and decided we don't want the long distance relationship thing. We want to be together."

"Okay. So what're you going to do to make that happen?" Nye challenged.

"I can find her a decent apartment in New Brunswick. I did a little digging. A one, maybe two-bedroom apartment will do."

"You get her the apartment and what?" His mother pushed.

He shrugged again. "She can get a job, I guess."

"You guess?" Nye's head popped back.

"We can figure out how to get her a job," I added. "I have a few connects if she doesn't have a trade."

"Please don't entertain this," Nye grated. "It's insane. They're kids."

"Adults," Zo corrected. "And what's insane about two people who want to be together?"

"The fact that you two are too young to want to make such a rash and expensive decision. You're saying you won't even live with her. So what's the point, or what will be next is you dropping out of the program because the distance is still too much?"

"Mom—"

"Mom my ass, Zo. You think you have all of this figured out, but you don't. She's going to need a car to get around. Hell, even I'm still renting one."

"I can get you a car," I spoke up, thankful for finally having a place to cut in. "I have one in my garage. An *Audi* that's a few years old, but with only a few miles on it."

Nye croaked her disbelief as her head popped back again. Then she blinked, shaking her head. "I'll deal with you later. I refuse to lose it right now." Then she blazed out of the room.

Zo slammed himself into a seat at the table. Feeling the ache in my head subside, just slightly, I pulled out a chair across from him.

"Keep it a bean with me."

"I just did," he grumbled. "And apparently, I'm too young to want anything."

I shook my head. "Nah. What's really going on between you and Gena?"

"I told y'all—"

I shook my head again, palm lifted from the table. "I'm calling my lawyer and accountant this morning, and I'm gonna cut you a check for six damn figures: the least you can do is tell me what it'll be spent on."

I'd decided. I wouldn't keep waiting for Zo to grant me permission to take care of my obligations as a man. With him came inherent patience. Until now.

Zo's glossed eyes went lazy as he tried to focus them on me. "She's pregnant." He swallowed. "And I'm going to do right by her…and the baby."

I nodded, eyes bouncing all over at what this meant for me. A grandfather. A forty-three-year-old grandfather. Did they even make those yet? I skipped being a dad and went right into being a damn PopPop. And I'd be okay with that. If this is what Zo wanted to do, I wouldn't skip this part of his life.

I reached across the table for his hand. "I'm gonna stand with you."

Needing nothing further, I left the table and picked up my coffee. After my run, I'd start making a round of calls.

Grandfather…

"Hey…" he called out for me as I was almost out of the kitchen. I turned to Zo. "Don't tell my Mom. Please. She's going through a lot and I gotta wait until she's ready."

Although I didn't feel good about it, I gave him a nod before taking off.

My thumb plucked the strings of my *Fender* telecaster against a track as my stomach growled. I knew it was time for me to eat something, but there was a painful annoyance at not getting this particular sequence down. It was something I knew Raj would go mad for on his upcoming LP. I'd been at it for close to three hours when I sensed the change in sound and knew it had to be from the door opening.

Nye craned her neck into the room. "Hey there!" She smiled deeply. I noticed her darkly lined eyes, straightened hair flowing down to her chest, and black, silk blouse.

I reached over to cut the track. When I turned back to her, I peeped her checking me out from head to toe—literally, as I was only wearing jeans. Her face sobered from the cheery smile and Nye stepped further into the room.

"We really gotta talk about your body."

My gaze dropped from my chest down to my toes as I held the *Fender* upright from the floor. "I like it just fine."

Nye's head bounced back and lips pursed. "Well, that's not what I mean, but it's good that you do. It's a good body."

"Then what's there to talk about?"

Breaking our determined gazes, Nye's regard swept to the plaques stacked on the floor, against the wall. She ambled over, then fell on her haunches and looked through them.

"Holy shit, Launz," she murmured. "This is your work? These are all platinum tracks!" When she finished shuffling through the Billboard plaques and I didn't reply, Nye stood to her feet and I noticed her all black business attire. She must've just gotten in. "You're still at it."

"Music?"

"Yeah."

"Always."

This felt awkward. Having her here, a total stranger I once knew stood in my makeshift studio and had also been staying in my home for close to a week. I grabbed my shirt, knowing neutralizing the sudden tension needed to happen ASAP.

"I think that's great. I really do!" Her smile dimmer now. "Well, anyway. I'm glad I found you. I thought of something on my way home from a meeting. Are you too busy right now?"

"Nah. I was actually telling myself to finally break for a bite to eat before I head out for dinner later."

"Perfect! Follow me!"

Placing my guitar on its respective rack, I paced behind Nye out of the room and down the hall. The sounds of her heels clacking against the hardwood flooring felt different. In a moment of absent-mindedness, I wondered where her man was and if he knew she was staying in my home.

Has to…

We passed by the kitchen and sauntered into the dining room. Before I realized this was our destination, Nye sang, "Happy Valentine's Day!"

On the long glass table were Spanish prayer candles, wine, vodka, glasses, and…

B-Way Burger?

My gaze met her silly expression and Nye snickered. "Tell me you remember."

Hungry, I stepped closer toward the food and grabbed a fry. I eyed her while chewing and Nye flogged her arms in the air, emphasizing her anticipation of an answer.

I murmured while chewing, "I can't believe you bought religious continental candles to a hotel on Valentine's Day."

She curled over, cracking the hell up.

"So you're a cocktail girl?" he observed out loud, biting into a *B-Way Classic* with cheese.

I couldn't remember what the man ate twenty-two years ago. I didn't even know if Launz ate red meat, seeing how cut up he was. But I did recall this afternoon when leaving a job interview up in Bergen County that the only Valentine's Day we spent together, not as a couple, I brought *B-Way Burger* to the hotel room we got, and that was our dinner before we…did the nasty things kids our age did.

"More like a vodka one. I'm not sure if I like cocktails. I don't like sugary ones. I prefer vodka, lemon juice, and ice. That makes me a happy girl." I smiled. After a spell of silence, Launz took a sip of the wine I'd taken notice of his preference for. I noted, "*Château Blevin.*" His brows lifted. "*Very* good. But not for the faint of pockets."

"Ha."

I smiled despite myself, not knowing what that meant. "I buy it for birthday celebrations of bourgeois friends and colleagues."

"Then you're a good gifter. Do you like it yourself?"

"I do. I better for the price of it." We laughed. After another lengthy silence, I continued for conversation, remembering how reticent Launz could be. "That '*Freedom*' track by Brielle won a Grammy. And the Pixie album you have a plaque for… What's the name?" I snapped my fingers, willing it back to memory. "'*Mirrors and Makeup*.' That's it! That won a Grammy for album of the year a while back." Those plaques in his studio were just stacked to the side but were monumental. "Ragee's '*Pixels*' won a Grammy, too." Launz nodded. "Where are your trophies?"

"In the basement."

"Basement?"

He shrugged with his lips and sported a cheap grin I was grateful for. Wiping his hands, Launz shared, "I've been saying for years, I'd hire someone to decorate my living room in a manner fitting them as décor. It's something I never got around to."

"Oh, my god, Launz! You're a Grammy award-winning guitarist." He nodded. "Does Zo know this?"

His eyes rolled up to the ceiling, considering that. "I haven't."

"Why?"

"Because…" He was at a loss for words. "I'm getting to know the kid. I guess it's not something I lead with when getting to know people."

"Then what the hell do you say when meeting people?"

His face tightened and Launz grinned. "I start with my name."

"Then what?"

"Maybe that I coach?"

"For the *League*?"

He shook his head, grinning. "Maybe not."

"Then what?"

Launz chuckled. "I really don't know. I don't meet new people I'm interested in getting to know often."

"Do you date—" My eyes fell. That question wasn't intended verbally or in thought. "I know I shouldn't *hav—*"

"I perform…tricks."

Shit…

My brows furrowed. "What're tricks?"

He reclined in the high back chair, now done with his burger. "Something I reserve for women I want to keep in my company."

Damn.

What did that mean?

"My house was officially sold today."

"By the judge of that faint smile, I take it you're not happy?"

Shaking my head, my eyes wandered to the corner of the room. "I really don't know how I feel. Can I be honest?"

"Of course." There was something so virilely confident about the delivery of those two words.

"I don't feel very secure right now." The transparency in which those words were shared scared me. "I've always been known to be the forceful go-getter—and I think I have."

"That's what I remember of you. Spirited and spontaneous."

That didn't make me feel good at all. My attention fell to my pewter nails. In all the craze of my stay in Jersey, I did find a nail salon near Zo's campus that was decent. Now that I was here, I'd likely have to find another. Or would I? How long would I be here?

"Spirited and spontaneous," I murmured. "One adjective I haven't felt in months and the other I want nothing to do with. I am completely a fish out of water right now."

"You've been interviewing for jobs."

"A job I'm not sure I want."

"You don't like being an attorney?"

"Most of my time is spent reading and writing in an office, which I was good with until…" My head rocked left to right as I tried to find the words.

"Until your family was uprooted?"

Without looking at him, I nodded. "Until my father died, I made the biggest decision of my life, *and* my son packs up and moves across the country."

"It is wild how he landed here near me."

"Very!" My head bounced up and down before I went for my drink. "I could only imagine how this would have gone down had the boy settled back on the West Coast or in the south."

"Then where would you have been?"

"Wherever that boy landed."

"You're a devoted mother."

"He's all I have. All I've ever had."

"Damn." His brows raised, rim of the glass near his glistening lips from a recent lick. "I'm so behind the curve on that type of bond."

"And it's my fault." I swallowed painfully.

After an awkward stretch, Launz cleared his throat. "This is going to be…odd, but I've committed myself to Zo. You're his mother. Stay as long as you need."

Grace I didn't deserve. But I took Launz at his every word. This was for Zo, not me. He'd given Zo a monstrous payout for past child support just yesterday. I had no idea what my son had planned to do with it, but I had to be sure whatever it was would be a lasting benefit for him. That meant I had to give the kid a stern talking to soon. He'd been so out of character lately, I didn't want this tension between us to tarry.

"Thanks, Launz," my voice box cracked at that. I wasn't an emotional woman, but just like back when I met him, Launz's aura neutralized me. This was a familiar sign of his compassion that I knew long ago. "I'll figure something out while appeasing my determined son. I won't stay long."

"Nah," He pushed back from the table and stood, "you won't or else I'll start charging you rent. You just sold your own crib. You got it."

I scoffed. As he collected our discarded wrappings and fry and onion ring cups, I thought to ask, "Are you going back to practicing?"

"I'm actually done for the night. I've got to go over a few offensive formations I've been writing up for my coordinators and coaches to prepare for my time up there this week. Then I'm slipping out for a bit tonight."

Oh...

It *was* Valentine's Day.

"I won't be disturbing your groove around here, will I?"

"What do you mean?"

"Your... You know... Tricks."

Launz shook his head. "No, Nye. You won't interfere with any of that."

As he sauntered into the kitchen, holding an arm and handful of trash, I believed him.

"This was so good," Jenise groaned across the table from me. She licked her lips out of palate appreciation and necessity. "I've eaten at countless five-star establishments across the country—the world, thanks to Daddy—but here is the only place I've never had a less than gratifying meal. I've met the guy who owns these restaurants."

I learned since my sister returned from undergrad to decipher her claims for truth. But her words about this restaurant intrigued me.

My patting of the corners of my mouth slowed. "*DiFillippo's* isn't a franchise business?"

She shook her head before going for her champagne. "Chain, and has expanded since he bought it from first-generation Italians."

"Wow..."

"Yeah. Both times I was in a room with him, I tried throwing him an eye and the second time, even introducing myself to him, trying to shake his hand."

"What did he do?"

"He spoke, but didn't receive my hand at all. Bastard."

I reached for my beloved vodka and lemon juice on the rocks, internally asking myself, '*Is it a cocktail*?' remembering Launz's question a few nights ago before preparing for a Valentine's date. Damn, did he look urbane in all black—jeans, collared shirt, and a blazer—when passing into the hall leading to the garage to leave.

"Is he married?"

"Yeah, but such a minor detail for a wealthy Black man like him. They need an extra set of pussy lips like they need more hours in the day."

I rolled my eyes. "You want dessert?"

"Sure do. How's my nephew?"

"On one." I rolled my eyes again.

"How?"

"His lil' love life. He's switching up on me out here."

"Well, maybe he needs his space from you. Perchance him dating like a young man his age out here is what he needs to help cope with losing Gunnery Sergeant Preston Taylor."

I murmured, low key annoyed by her assumptions. "Zo's still dating Gena and, apparently, that's all he wants. Doesn't sound like it has anything to do with Gunnery Sergeant Preston Taylor."

The place was almost packed. Soft music flowing from the hidden speakers at a volume not interfering with the chatter in the place. Beautiful white lights gave the room a warm feel, and the delicious scent of garlic topped off the ambiance. We weren't in the private room Zo, Launz, and I dined in last week, but the restaurant's elegance filled the building.

"He's still with that child? I would've thought he made a clean break when coming out here."

My head fell to the side. "What's wrong with Gena? She's sweet, smart…a good girl."

"Nothing, other than a local girl. My nephew is no longer limited to his hometown. He's in a Division I program now." She sat back in her seat. "What's Mommy saying?"

I shrugged. "I haven't talked to her about it."

"The woman's lost her husband of more than forty-five years and you haven't been in touch with her?"

"I didn't say that. At all. When I was home over a week ago, I was with her. Every time I go home, I'm with Mommy. Can you say the same?"

Jenise rolled her eyes. "I have a career and I'm all over the place."

"And I have a son and a career, Nisey. But I make time for her."

"All I'm saying is she should know what's going on with you."

"Does she know what's going on with you? Junior?"

Jenise laughed. "Do we ever know what's going on with Junior?"

She was right: we didn't. Our brother didn't keep in touch with the family. He wisely shot our father the middle finger once he turned eighteen and left out on his own. Junior was sweet, strong, and smart, but wrong for basically cutting us all off when he left. While I understood his anger, his decision left our mother broken-hearted and Jenise and me isolated. Our father convinced me he didn't care. And Jenise and I simply accepted his absence.

My eyes skirted around the room before I whispered, "Do you think I stayed too long?"

Jenise's head pulled up from her phone. After a long gaze, she asked, "Home? Did you stay too long with Mommy?"

My regard fell.

She sat up in her seat, exhaling. "Look, Nye, he wasn't perfect by any stretch, but I never judged you for sticking it out with him until… The end."

"Then why do I feel so damn weak for doing it?"

It was something I'd been thinking about a lot, especially this past week, staying at Launz's place. It had been quiet around his rather large home. His place in Moorestown had been a great oasis for meditation and even prayer. I'd prayed more since my father took ill than I had in my entire life—and those prayers were not for my father. They had been for Zo and me, and lately more me than Zo because he seemed to be fine. It was me who I could no longer identify; life had changed for me so much. The big secret I'd held for over twenty years no longer had a hiding place. Zo now knew his father.

"You're not weak," she grated, rolling her eyes. "You're no such thing. It's just that Gunnery Sergeant Preston Taylor grew up with an abusive father. He was poor and homeless before being an adult. He had it hard those few years in the Mississippi streets until joining the *Marines*."

"But he did too much."

"Yeah," she agreed, though with doubt in her tone. "But it was all he knew."

"And I stayed."

"Because of Zo."

I shook my head, giving my attention to the corner. "That was a cop-out."

"Okay. Then let's talk something real." Jenise tossed her napkin onto the table. "Because you were stronger than Junior and me." That brought my regard back to her. "You stayed because he could never break you."

"I raised my son around him—with him!" I whispered hard.

"He loved Zo more than he did us, it felt. That was not a failed decision, Nye."

I shook my head. "It was a weak one. I should have stepped out on my own, like you and Junior. And just like then, now that he's gone and Zo is here, figuring out his adult life, I feel lost."

Jenise sputtered a laugh. "You? Nyedeera Taylor lost? That's the most asinine shit I've ever heard. You've never been weak or lost. I don't know anyone who's stood their ground more than you. Never met a person to look a monster in its eyes. Nye, you've always been sure of yourself and showed up for the occasion. You've ripped heads off of girls my age for making fun of my clothes. You even taught Junior how to get his eighth-grade bully on the ground. Weak? Lost? I don't think so. You're the one who inspired me to go to law school!"

But I was. It wasn't something I'd argue with her because no one seemed to believe I wasn't as strong as I appeared.

"You're finally admitting that?" I glanced at my wristwatch for the time. "You mind if we skip dessert? I got a long drive ahead of me."

Jenise's brows met. "New Brunswick is only about forty-five minutes from here. You're still at the *Cranebridge Hotel*?"

I shook my head while going through my purse for my wallet. "I've been in Moorestown."

"Morristown? Isn't that even closer?"

"No. Moorestown. South Jersey."

"What are you doing all the way down there?"

"Excuse me, ladies," the waitress interjected. "I see you're done with dinner. Would you like to see our dessert menu?"

"I would," Jenise swiftly replied. "I don't need the menu, actually. The tiramisu to-go, please."

"Alrighty then. And for you?" The waitress' attention was on me.

Typically, I'd enjoy the crème brûlée, but I was preoccupied on the hour-and-half commute down the *New Jersey Turnpike.*

I smiled. "I'll pass tonight. But you can take this." I handed her my card to cover our meal.

"Very well. I'll settle this and be back with your receipt and the tiramisu."

"Thanks."

"Now, answer my question."

I blinked confused. "I'm sorry. What was that?"

"Why are you staying in Moorestown?"

Oh, right. That...

Taking a deep breath, I fortified myself, remembering how distant Jenise and I were. We'd always been decent sisters, but not the best of friends. We hadn't been confidants since my father's overbearing dominant persona turned Jenise into an entirely different being. She exuded a false confidence that made her a know-it-all and highly judgmental. While over the years, I managed to get her to tone it down with me, it was still who Jenise chose to be. So I'd stopped sharing such personal matters with her years ago. She was surprised that I confided last fall how I was planning to reach out to Zo's father and have them meet.

"I'm staying with Launz."

Her face tightened so hard that her eyes disappeared. "Who is Launz, and why are you staying with him? You hate staying with people. You didn't even like staying with Mommy and Dad after having Zo."

"Launz is Zo's father. I'm staying at his place because Zo pushed for it."

Jenise blinked hard. "The hell? You don't even know this man."

I shook my head. "I don't."

"Then why do you trust him to stay in his home?"

I have no idea how I've done it. But it's turned out not being bad at all.

"I don't know." I was cowering. Even threw the weakest excuse. "He's hardly ever there. He works in Connecticut, seasonally now."

"Work in Connecticut? What type of day-laboring foolishness is going on with my nephew's father?"

I scoffed at her ignorance. "It's not that at all. Launz is far from unemployed. He's a football coach." When Jenise still seemed pressed by the way she peered at me nonplussed, I amended, "In the *League*."

She quizzed, "What kind of coach?"

I shrugged, "Head coach."

"Of what team?"

"The *Kings*?"

"As in the *Connecticut Kings*?"

Confused, I murmured, "Those are the only ones in the *League* I know of."

Her eyes bounced around the room as Jenise calculated the information I'd just given her. "How old is he?"

I rolled my eyes. "Why?"

"Because any man who could be Zo's daddy is too young to be a head coach in the *League*."

"Zo said the youngest one there is in his mid-thirties."

"Oh," was her only utterance. "I don't know when they started doing that. First, there was a shortage of Black coaches on the screen every Monday, Thursday, and Sunday —still is."

"But the *Kings* is Black-owned."

"A rarity." She shook her head. "Anyway, I still don't understand why you're staying at that man's place. You sure he's not going to off you one night for keeping his son from him?"

"He could, I guess." I don't think I'd mind the right *offing*—

Shit...

Did I really say that?

"What's his name?"

"Huhn?"

"Zo's father. You said Launz?"

I licked my lips, unreasonably fluttered by sharing his name. "Alaunzo Pierce."

Jenise's eyes burst wide and head jolted backward. "That's my *neph* —" So shocked, she couldn't even finish. "You named Zo after that man?" I nodded. "And you didn't tell any of us?"

That wasn't true. I told my mother as I filled out the paperwork at the hospital. My father was at work, giving me the peace of mind to do what was right.

The receipt and Jenise's dessert were delivered and my card was returned to the table.

"Thanks," I offered with a smile.

"Thank you, Ms. Taylor. Please come back and dine with us at *DiFillippo's* again."

My attention returned to my sister across the table. "Jenise, I told you months ago, this thing with Zo's father didn't sit well with me."

"You actually told me several times over the years, but now I feel you've plotted a lot behind Gunnery Sergeant Preston Taylor's back."

I shook my head. "I would've done this if he were still alive and well. I couldn't take it anymore."

"Holy shit," she whispered. "You have changed. No. I don't believe you're weak, but maybe you think you're lost because I've never known you to be..." She flipped her palms up to me. "this! You do seem off. And my advice to you, dear, is not to let him sense this vulnerability you're giving off. You're fucking Nyedeera Taylor, daughter of Gunnery Sergeant Preston Taylor. The only person I know to ever go toe to toe with that impossible man. Don't let this

Alaunzo Pierce confuse your strength. So, whatever shit you've got going on, figure it out."

I couldn't recall the last time Jenise had given me a pep talk. In fact, I never knew she thought so highly of me.

To avoid my eyes watering any further, I asked, "And you'll call Mommy?"

She rolled her eyes, then began gathering her things. "Maybe after I look up Mr. Pierce's salary. He owes you and my nephew money."

He didn't, but if Jenise was off her bullshit just for the night, I wouldn't say anything to rattle her cage.

I stood, grabbing just my purse. "I need the ladies' room before hitting the road."

"You, too? I swear, aging is for the damn birds."

"I'm pretty sure having carried a child has a lot to do with our weakened bladders, too."

Yeah. I knew I said I wouldn't push her peaceful state too far, but I hated that Jenise would forget she, too, had a child. A child who, though older, needed her far more than Zo needed me at this point in his life.

~TEN

PRESENT DAY

THE HOUSE WAS QUIET, BUT LIT COMFORTABLY low. I wondered if anyone had been here since I left for another interview this morning—one I didn't know if I wanted to critically pursue. Wandering down the stairs and toward the kitchen, it was a little after nine at night and I was restless. On my way down to Moorestown, I spoke to Zo and had even called to check in on my mother. Right now, I was all talked out, yet still pensive.

Launz's home was beautiful. It was spacious and with traditional charm. It boasted high ceilings, arched doorways, a closed kitchen design, step-up family room, and step-down living room. The stairway curved up to the third floor where two of the six bedrooms were. This was a meaty house, built to be a home to a large family. It had struck me as strange that Launz lived here alone. His sister, Monica, had a bedroom on the main floor, but was never here.

Another odd fact was there were only four televisions in the house: Launz's master suite, Monica's room, the family room, and in the basement. I'd been watching lots of *YouTube* if I didn't want to be in the family room.

After closing the door on an uneventful refrigerator, I moseyed on into the dining room and poured myself the leftover *Château Blevin* I'd gotten for Luanz on Valentine's Day. I took the first sip and hummed appreciatively when my phone rang.

I rolled my eyes while answering, "Tod, what can I do for you."

"Nyedeera Taylor. Well, hot damn. I was able to track down the ranger."

"Oh, let's not be so dramatic. You called, I answered. It was as simple as one plus one equals two."

"More like chances of flopping a flush, Ms. Taylor."

I took a small sip of wine. "Oh, I don't play poker."

"And yet you understood the reference. Such a stark reminder of your mental brilliance, hence my exhaustive search."

"More like an APB. Definitely a warrant."

"Oh, darling. And here I thought you enjoyed your work here at a *Klein and Schmitts.*"

I smiled tightly, though he couldn't see me. "Get to the point, Tod. I'm in the middle of something."

With that, I decided to bring the entire bottle with me back upstairs as there was about another glass left.

"With pleasure. Are you leaving?"

"Why would you ask me something like that?" I played along.

"Damn it, Nyedeera: whispers are sounding off from across the damn country."

"About what?"

"About these informal interviews you've been taking at firms in New York and New Jersey. Are you leaving us?"

"Tod, you know as a current employee of *Klein and Schmitts,* that is an inappropriate question to ask." I began the stairs.

"But I thought we were friends."

"What did I tell you about having friends at the practice when you were first hired and I trained you?"

After an abbreviated pause, he exhaled, "They're non-existent."

"And if there were ever a time where you and I had a chance at being anything resembling friends, it ended when you were promoted to Randall Schmitts' watchman."

"Excuse me. I'm the vice president of operations."

"You're a practicing attorney doing the work of human resources and a dedicated personal assistant."

Tod sighed, "Is this about the pay thing again?"

I scoffed, "You've got to be kidding."

"Me getting hired years after you and being given twenty-five percent over your salary was not my call."

"And neither is this call. So what's it for again?"

"Taylor, just be honest. Are you leaving the firm?"

"Again, that's not for you to ask. Have I made an announcement to leave?"

"No, but first it was bereavement for your father. Then, it was vacation time, and now it's leave."

"And?" I stood at the top of the steps on the second floor. Instead of going left to my assigned bedroom, I dithered with my regard to the right on the open set of French doors.

"And." He groaned frustrated. "Marian stopped by your place to drop off a sympathy gift and saw a for sale sign on your lawn."

Quietly exhaling, I rested against the banister. Although Launz was generous enough to put me on the same floor as him, the two rooms really felt worlds apart, possibly because he was never home.

I cursed the mental and emotional space I was in. Never in a million years did I believe I'd be...stuck. The truth of the matter was I hadn't fully decided to leave my firm. However, I had no desire to go back in the near future. My father was dead and my son was grown, and no longer dependent on me financially. I wasn't old enough to be in a mid-life crisis, but too young to feel like I'd completed the major accomplishments of a lifetime. I had an extensive education and work tenure and was the mother to an adult child. Where to go?

My eyes instinctively crawled to the right again. With renewed—albeit temporary—inspiration, I spoke up. "So, I guess Murphy didn't share the completed report I sent to him on the Adams case?"

"The case you began just before Christmas?"

"That would be the one, Tod. Also, I've begun the Levin report."

"On leave?"

"I understand the importance of continuity. I'm not sure when I'll be prepared to resume my office hours or full caseload, but will be in touch with HR regarding my options. Whatever I decide will be communicated to them first. In the meantime, stop sending your wife to my place under the guise of sympathy. You whipeepole are so damn nosy!"

I stepped into Launz's grand, carpeted bedroom. It smelled of him—the current day him. I had no memory of his scent from over twenty years ago.

"Oh, no you didn't, woman."

"I did!" I couldn't help my grin. It was partially from Tod, and the other half a sense of familiarity of myself. "Now, bye."

"Bye, Taylor."

I placed the bottle on his nightstand as my regard swept the room. Next, I removed my phone from the crook of my neck. It took a few seconds to locate the remote control. I sipped the wine as I made my way to his mammoth-sized bed. My knee hit the mattress first and I tapped the power button. The channels out here were different than what I was used to, but I learned my favorites over the past few days and stuck to them. I started with *MSNBC* to catch up on the world of politics.

Over an hour later, I was stretched back on his mountainous, decorative pillows rolling boogers on a paper towel I grabbed at some point. It was my comfort space when I was able to relax while thinking.

Find a job here in Jersey…

Go back to Arizona and resume work at *Klein and Schmitts*…

Leave Launz's and figure all this shit out at the hotel…

Return home and move in with Mommy…

Get an apartment here and let Gena move in until she—or Zo—grow out of this damn puppy love phase...

The sound of a car door being slammed had me jolting up and out of sleep. My head swung left and right.

Damn it!

I'd fallen asleep in his room.

The television was at a low volume and now, I couldn't hear what had awakened me. Thankful for not having been caught in here, I gathered the wine glass and bottle and my dirty napkin to leave. On my way to the door, I froze, then turned to place everything down to smooth the comforter and fluff the pillows.

After dumping my companions of last night in the bedroom I'd been staying in, I trudged into the bathroom to relieve myself. While washing up, I thought of my audacity to even step a toe in there. I didn't know the man!

After brushing my teeth, an exchange between two women had my head pop up from the towel I used to dry my face. I couldn't make out what they were saying exactly, but their voices were clear and flowing into the bathroom window. I dropped the towel and pumped a facial moisturizer into my hand before making my way out into the hallway. The inside of the house sounded empty as I traveled to the main level. I knew the bathroom was in the rear of the house, so I went toward the kitchen. The voices grew louder and coherent as I stepped outside, tightening my robe.

Monica turned to me after the woman she was speaking to discovered my presence and gaped at me like she'd seen the second-coming.

"Oh," Monica chirped. "I hope we didn't wake you."

I would have answered, but couldn't extract myself from the gripping surveillance the curious visitor had me under. The woman was short—shorter than me—in a brown long down coat and boots. It was hard to say much more about her appearance because of how tightly drawn up her face was.

"I'm fine," I replied to Monica, further tightening my robe.

That's when she caught on and Monica turned back. "I forgot to tell you and apparently Launz did, too. This is Camay, Nye. I'm so glad I decided to stop here before heading up to Connecticut. Otherwise, she wouldn't have been able to get in for her tools. Camay's been doing the gardening around here—"

"I'm Launz's friend who helps out with the aesthetics of the place," Camay corrected. "I've been telling him for years, he needs to beautify the outside of this house as he's done the inside."

I lifted my brows and nodded.

"Right," Monica exhaled. "Anyway, I guess she's doing her work out here today."

"Okay." I tore my eyes away from Camay, though hers burned my face. "I'll leave her to it. I'm meeting Zo for breakfast before his first class today."

"Awww!" Monica beamed. "Okay."

As I turned for the door, Camay quickly observed, "I caught the name, but you never said how she's related."

My brows furrowed as I tripped over my feet on the step inside.

Monica must have caught the underhanded demand in that low key question as well because she tarried in her response. "Oh. I guess Nye is a relative. She's my nephew's mother."

"Nephew?"

"Yes. His name is Zo." Monica's chin lifted. "I guess he hasn't told you?"

Camay's lashes smacked and a false smile widened her face. "Tell me what?"

Aww, hell!

I dropped down the steps and proffered my hand. "Nyedeera Taylor. I'm the mother of Launz's only child." Hesitantly, she took my hand for a shake that was just as half-hearted as her false beam. "He's generously allowed me to stay here for a short term while our son gets acclimated to his new campus. I hope that isn't a problem for you two."

Her mouth fell open and Camay appeared shocked by my transparency. "Well... *I*—I... I don't see how it would."

"Okay. Great." I turned back for the house. "Monica, you have a package that was delivered yesterday. I placed it at your bedroom door."

"*Uh*—okay," Monica uttered before I closed the door.

Inside the toasty kitchen, I murmured to myself, "So you *do* have a girlfriend with whom you've not shared the news of your son—and his mother staying at your place." Then I stopped and my neck snapped. "*Aaand* you don't give her the keys to your place?"

Interesting...

Whitaker rocketed the ball into the air as Amare cut the wind against its speed. Within seconds, I knew the pass would be an incompletion. I also knew why. Amare's speed was built for Go routes, and Whitaker didn't have a handle working one-on-one with this particular wide receiver yet.

"Damn!" He grunted, twisting his body with clenched fists.

Miles Brown, the quarterback's coach, glanced my way.

Ignoring him, I shouted, "Grant!"

Right away, the tight end ran to his position on the practice field, and I gave Whitaker the cue to begin. He did, taking the snap from the center and throwing the ball into the air. Grant missed the pass by mere seconds.

Disappointment washed over Grant's face until he sprang onto his toes. "One more try, coach! One more!"

Craig Jackson, the defensive coordinator, murmured in advisement, "Kid's hungry. Got a monster on his back."

It was what he'd shared with me about the tight end built more like a big receiver who'd come close to being cut by the previous head coach. Apparently, Grant had something to prove this season and was expressing that today.

After deciding, I requested, "Fuck the Go route. Let's try a Comeback!" I blew the whistle and Grant jogged back into position. This area of the practice field was quiet while other players and coaches were carrying out different drills. I stepped closer to Jermaine Whitaker, a four-year vet in the *League*. He'd been second-string to Trent Bailey for three seasons now. His nostrils were wide as heated air pushed from them forcefully. "You don't know their patterns."

"What you mean?"

"You need to practice as many routes as you can with them so you can count the drum of their runs."

"I 'on't get it."

"You're throwing like TB."

"He's first string!"

"He's also seasoned with these guys. He had to study the receivers' patterns, speeds, habits, and their tendencies. When Amare runs, stops, turns, and assesses, there's a pattern to his moves with each route. Focus on their patterns as you're practicing with them. Study them and that's when the connection comes naturally. Not only mental synchronization happens, the physical form will take place, too. That ball will meet their palms. This game's not just about physicality; there's a science to it."

I understood Whitaker was being given more responsibility today than usual, but I needed him to pick up something new, and from me, if he was going to be my ace in the hole this season.

It was the third week in April and I was hosting a few days of voluntary practice for the team. For most of my staff, this was mandatory. However, the players had to make the decision if they'd step up or not during their off-season. About a third of them did. Some who didn't were still vacationing, or they simply had no interest in working during their time off, like my franchise QB.

Invitations had gone out to him. It wasn't until the third that we received a response of "no thanks." It frustrated the hell out of me. No, it wasn't fair to ask him to break from his vacation or time off. Yet, I knew none of these men and women on the field enjoyed being losers for the past four years either. So, yes, I made a big request. It was for the greater good.

All this week had been a chance for me to see the team at play, coaches and players alike. It was also an opportunity for them to get a feel for me, too. They could start to learn my field temperament. I'd been able to talk to most of the players and have sidebar conversations with my staff on the field. This had been good, but only for those who cared to show up.

"Let's go!" I blew my whistle.

Whitaker sent the ball down the field and Grant performed a stop and go, going deep. The ball fumbled from the tips of Grant's fingers, but it was a cleaner attempt than previous ones.

"Coach, you see this shit?" Kaleece Williams, my offensive coordinator, jogged over to me with her device.

Simultaneously, my assistant, Russell, called out to me. "A minute of your time, coach!"

They both met me, virtually at the same time. "TB's fucking kidding me."

"You saw it, too?" Russell asked Williams, figuring they were informing me of the same thing.

She tapped to have the video play. *TMZ* had caught Trent coming out of a restaurant and asked him if the rumors of him requesting a trade were true, to which he answered, "I'll say this. Respect is an esteem that should be paid both ways. When it isn't mutual or there's no reciprocity, it's good to be reminded that you have options." Then he dipped inside a waiting SUV.

"Yo, TB's wild for that. Usually, he keeps shit to the chest," Russell informed, and I believed him as he was a tenured staff here in *Kings* nation.

Williams issued me a gawk of concern. She, like me, was new to this organization. We had high hopes which included Trent Bailey. As they gaped at me for direction, I noticed more of the staff on the field peering up from their phones, then eventually my way. My frontal lobe lightened twice, then was succeeded by a throb growing up the back of my skull.

Shit...

"I'll let the front office deal with this," I murmured, attempting to end the huddle.

My phone vibrated in my pocket. I pulled it out and saw Monica's name across the screen.

"Yeah."

"Jamal is asking for your final answer on the *Sports Illustrated* interview."

I thought about it for a few seconds. "I said no. Definitively!"

The timing was bad. I'd already made it clear to my agent I had no interest in promoting my role here in Connecticut. I understood he had a job to do, but dammit, so did I. And if I were with the shits of exploiting my new job, I wouldn't be any better than the immoral coaches Bailey assumed I was akin to.

Again, bad timing for this confirmation.

"*Okaaaay* then..." she sang. "George Wright called about the back yard. Are you ready to begin construction?"

We'd talked about this, too. "I am if he's okay with not having access to the house when no one's home."

"I think that's why I'm revisiting this. I'm thinking between the three of us, someone should be here enough to get it done."

I scratched my head. "The three of us—" Then it hit me. "Oh."

Nye...

"Get me now?" Monica sounded irritated, likely because I'd snapped on her about Jamal.

"Yeah. I guess."

"Last thing. Camay's being promoted on her job." My eyes closed on that reminder. "How do you want to celebrate her?"

I needed to get back to what was going on, on the field. "Flowers?" grated.

"Not after she learned about Zo from his robed mother, clearly staying in your home!"

Taking a deep breath, my eyes scanned the busy field. There were about close to thirty of us here today. I had to get back to work.

"I'll leave this to your discretion."

"I don't have a baby's mother and a wanna-be girlfriend."

"But you have a baby's daddy."

"That I barely know!"

"Nick, I'm in the middle of practice!"

"But her ceremony's tonight and I'm trying to prepare you for it."

My face fell. "Tonight?" *It is…* "Shit!"

"You forgot you were returning to Jersey tonight?"

"No, but I guess I didn't remember what for." I was looking forward to being home. Maybe plucking my strings tomorrow.

"Let me guess," she sighed. "You're not going."

"I'm in Connecticut."

"You won't be tonight." Monica sensed the lie conjuring.

"I will be when you call her in a few minutes to break the news."

"Damn, Launz. And right after she finds out you have a kid from said kid's mother."

"That was a couple of weeks ago." I'd forgotten all about Camay running into Nye at my place, which I didn't know why. Camay called me right away, demanding answers while appropriately controlling her emotions. We were not exclusive. Hell, I'd never been exclusive.

"But you know she's still reeling from it."

"Water under the bridge."

"Yeah, because you weren't there. You didn't see how aggressive your baby's mother was introducing herself." I rolled my eyes. "She said, 'I'm the mother of Launz's *only* child.' *Only,* Launz? I don't know Nye, but there was a power play with the usage of that singly, possessive word."

"Yeah," I exhaled, removing my hat to scratch my head, all with my free hand. "Nye's no novice. But I gotta get back to this. Use your discretion and fill me in when I call on my way home tonight."

"Bye, Launz." The irritation in her tone couldn't be missed.

I wished I could offer her more energy on the topic, but the truth of the matter was, the Nye I knew was hella manipulative, socially forward, and deceptively charismatic. I couldn't focus on that. What I'd been low key stressing over was the realization of having a son and not just a mentee hanging around that I actually liked. I was a father and knew shit about being one.

All thanks to the manipulating, socially forward, and deceptively charismatic Nyedeera.

"Alright, Whitaker!" I shouted. "Let's try that Comeback with Amare again!"

And just like that, Camay and Nye were forgotten about.

But not that damn Trent Bailey…

The first thing I realized when walking into the house from the garage was the alarm hadn't been activated. Quickly, I realized it wasn't a big deal seeing the *Audi* I'd loaned Nye was in its usual place. I couldn't recall if Zo told me she'd returned from Arizona yet. But clearly, she had. Didn't matter to me at all. I headed straight up to my bedroom to drop off my luggage. Feeling the weight of my two duffle bags, one thing was for sure, laundry couldn't be avoided tomorrow. Maybe I'd grill some steaks while enduring the task.

Perhaps I'll invite Zo to come through—

"Shit!" I whispered, startled by the sinuous movements of a caramel trunk and bare legs in my bed.

Ass!

That was definitely a round ass beneath polka dot panties.

In my damn bed!

"Oh, my god!" she tweeted, frightened her damn self, pulling the sheet over her breasts that were obviously nude, unlike her ass.

Instead of making an already gauche moment more awkward, I turned around and left. It had already been my sole agenda to go out back and have a smoke anyway. My stomach was empty and head screaming, and the only cure on my horizon was a cigar. I grabbed my smoke coat from the closet near the back door then an *Arturo Fuente Hemingway*, a *Macanudo Gold - Lord Nelson*, a cutter, and lighter.

Stepping out onto the deck off the family room, the air was stiff and temperature brisk. Smoke blew from my nostrils from simply breathing. I dropped down the stairs and sauntered toward the firepit to turn on the gas switch then flicked the lighter gun, sparking a flame. Stretching back onto the lounge chair, I exhaled amid the relentless ache in my skull. As the fire grew, I inspected the illuminating area. My yard was big as hell, grossly unkempt and underutilized. I'd been saying for years I would invest in landscaping back here, but had been distracted each time the opportunity came. Finally, I'd have this place up and running in just a few months.

I cut an *Arturo* then took my time lighting up. The woodsy scent calmed me immediately. Sitting back further, I pulled on her to get started while tapping into my phone for some sounds. The last in my *Tidal* account would do. Ernie Isley's guitar lead in *"Voyage to Atlantis"* was the perfect soundscape for this frosty night breeze. The sessions I had with Raj and *RSfALC* next month came to mind. Seconds later, one of the French doors opened and out came a thin figure I was still unaccustomed to having in my space.

Nye hopped down the stairs, wearing a thick winter coat. She'd slipped on sweats and slide-in boots, and grabbed a hat and gloves, too, as she carried a bowl, leaving steam in its wake. Incredibly naturally, as though she'd done it countless times before, she pulled a chair up to the pit and sat across from me.

She blew the spoon after scooping whatever she had in the bowl, eyes captivated by the blazes dancing from the pit. "You spoke to Zo?"

Nodding because I'd spoken to him on my way home, I returned, "'Bout an hour ago."

"Did he go out with the guys on the football team or track?"

Zo told me he wasn't in the mood to go out, but didn't want to stay in his room tonight. He said he'd much preferred coming back over to my crib to chill, but knew I'd be tired after the long day I'd had today and the late hour I returned. He shared how a few guys from the track team had been inviting him out and did so again tonight. Zo said it would have been rude for him to decline again. Odd thing was, a few of the players on his team expressed wanting to chill with them as well. So, either way, he had to go out tonight.

"Track."

Nye sputtered, giggling. "Leave it to my child to have so many options as the new kid on campus. I told him he should hang out with the football team. Get to know them in the off-season so when it's time to practice and play, their chemistry would be established."

"He'll have plenty of time to do that." The season had just ended.

She ate more before scoffing. "Even out here, he attracts people. Everybody loves that Zo. He's a magnet."

It was similar to what I thought of her all those years ago. At *Corey's,* people were drawn to Nye. "Reminds me of someone I met twenty-something years ago."

When my eyes lifted from the pit, I found a sad smirk on her face.

"Hey..." There was a pregnant pause before she continued. "There's no television in your guest bedrooms. I know there's one in the family room, but I fall asleep to the television. I just figured since you're away so often, I..."

My regard rolled from her to the fire. I'd known she'd been sleeping in my bed. Figured it out last week when I found a scrunchie against my sheet when I stretched out in the middle of the night. I didn't like it, but didn't speak on it either. This shit was too complicated. My life had been flipped over three times like a vehicle after hard impact. The first was learning about Zo, possibly becoming a grandfather, then having this bizarre being I thought I'd never see again staying in my home.

The shit was unreal.

"Anyway, I thought you'd be back tomorrow. I guess I was so tired after being in the air or an airport all day from my flight being delayed, I didn't think."

"You flew in too, today?"

She nodded. "Got in around four. Picked up beans on my way here after Zo mentioned bean soup when I spoke with him earlier between flights. Didn't have a chance to soak them, but made it work. He came by, ate, and talked before he left to go hang out with...now I know the track guys." She scoffed. "I showered and told myself I'd watch a bit of the news before crashing. I guess the news ended up watching me."

It was bullshit, but I let it fly.

The song was coming to an end, and once it did, the dead silent air contradicted the natural vibe out here. My headache hadn't subsided much either. I preferred smoking alone or with another smoker. So, it wasn't easy for me to think of something to warm the cold air between us.

"I trust your mother's okay?"

"Oh!" Nye chirped. "Yeah." She nodded. "Yeah. The doc confirmed what I thought. Her gout is acting up again. She don't have Gunnery Sergeant Preston Taylor of the *United States Marine Corps* around to keep her on track with her diet. That *and* she's never been consistent with taking her meds *because* he was so good at helping her keep up with her health."

"Who?"

"Oh." She blinked hard, sitting back. "My father. Before he passed, he was always a disciplinarian in just about every area of his life—and others—and would keep them on a cocktail of vitamins, a healthy diet, and would even make sure she walked around the neighborhood daily for exercise. Now that he's..." She spooned more of the beans. "Anyway." Nye chewed and swallowed. "She's good for now. I'll be back out there soon to check in on her. How's the new job going?"

At that question, I rubbed my throbbing head. "Still early yet, is what I keep reminding myself."

"Zo mentioned how competitive those roles are in the *League*."

"Especially for a Black man."

"Tell me about it. The same with law. He told me about Trent Bailey not being happy with the *Kings*."

Nodding, I amended, "He's the type of man who drowns in passion. Whatever he values, he commits to. I'm trying to get an opportunity at him."

"So you haven't spoken to him?"

I nodded, pulling from the stogie. Blowing out the smoke, I shared, "I went to visit him last month."

"Up in Connecticut?"

"Nah. Here in Jersey. He lives in Alpine. I stopped through there on my way home from Connecticut."

"Didn't go well?"

"What he values, he commits to," I repeated.

"He'll come around. You're a good man and good karma follows you."

That confidence was striking. "How do you know I'm a good man?"

Nye's attention dropped to her bowl. "I've only known you to be."

"You didn't know me then and you don't know me now."

She pushed her soup around in the bowl using the spoon and murmured, "You've accepted my son. That confirms a lot of what I knew and know."

I laughed. "Accepted? I'm not sure I'd use that word to describe how used I feel."

Nye's head shot up. "Used?"

"The kid shows up looking like he stole my damn DNA, Nye. A few weeks ago, I cut one of the biggest checks of my life, and here you are, the most deceptive and manipulative person I've ever known, staying in my house."

"Launz—"

"The last time I saw you, you lied to me. Remember that?"

"Launz, we still haven't talked yet."

"And yet, you're here…in my home, introducing yourself to my friend as the mother of my only child." Chuckling, I sat up to dump ashes. "You know, I don't think you knew or know me, but I damn sure know you. You're untrustworthy."

Her eyes grew wide. "Untrustworthy? That's patently untrue."

I tossed my head back and laughed despite the painful tension in my skull. "You gotta be fucking kidding me. You just lied to me about sleeping in my bed."

"How do you figure?"

"You only went into my room tonight to watch the news? But when I find you, you're only in your panties. So you watch the news in your panties on strangers' beds?"

Irritation lanced my chest at discovering my *Arturo Fuente* was losing flame. For a couple of minutes, I sat there deciding to re-light and continue to play nice and naïve for the sake of Zo, or to just call this day a stressful one and sleep it off.

The latter felt best. I hit pause on my phone, then gathered my shit and walked off.

Passing her, Nye uttered, "I'd really like to talk about what happened whenever you're ready."

I ignored her ass.

Talk?

I'd gone beyond talking since she showed up in my life. I wrote a fucking mortgage-size check!

~ELEVEN

PRESENT DAY

I ROLLED OVER TO MY SIDE, SLIDING MY ARM beneath the pillow. My dick twitching snapped me out of my sleep. A soft flowery scent invaded my nostrils and I lifted from the pillow, warily glancing around my dim room. Wintery air pushed through a curtain bringing with it a beam from the bright morning sun.

Fucking Nye!

Annoyed as hell and still tired, I pulled myself from the bed and moped into the bathroom to take a leak and wash up. When I returned to my room to gather laundry, I smelled cooked food. Carrying two hampers downstairs, I could hear voices in the kitchen. It didn't take long for me to recognize Zo's. I dropped the hampers in the hall and sauntered inside.

Nye was zipping around, plating food in one of her yoga outfits.

Her hair was pulled into a ponytail on top of her head. I'd learned in this short time of her staying here that she practiced yoga regularly, and typically in the morning. Zo was at the table, tapping on his phone.

"Grand risings, sir!" he greeted, beam so bright it seemed unnatural.

It also got me each time. Nah, I didn't feel like a father, but oddly enough, I couldn't deny the kid was my son. His personality was of his mother, but his shell was undeniably from me.

"Grand indeed." I met him in the air for a dap. "Didn't know you were coming by today."

"Yeah, man. I told you I wanted to check in with you last night, but you got in so late."

Oh, shit…

He did.

I sat down at the table across from him. "Yeah. I'll be here a few days before going back up."

Nye put a plate of food in front of me, causing my spine to recline in the chair. I wasn't expecting food. Scrambled eggs and crispy bacon. It smelled amazing.

When I peered up at her, Nye's expression was hard, eyes squinting. "That headache gone?"

Licking my lips, I was stunned. My eyes skirted over to Zo, who observed expectantly. The vibe was set and it was clear wherever I left it last night, Nye didn't bring it here this morning.

And how did she know I'd be down here anytime soon?

"I guess I was able to sleep it off," I murmured. "Thanks." She took off thankfully and I quickly returned my attention to Zo, or else I'd follow her ass cheeks across the room. "How did it go last night? Good to see you're not recovering."

Nye giggled, causing me to look her way. She was carrying a plate of flapjacks and a bowl back to the table. "The boy doesn't drink, and certainly not hard. I tried telling you that last month."

Zo's expression turned cheap. "Yeah. I'm really not an all-nighter type of guy. I'm more like the drink-nurser and designated driver who makes you leave early because I'm so damn tired."

As I chuckled, amused and surprised, Nye served me the pancakes and grits.

"I hope you eat all of this. My first morning in here, I noticed you had pork and beef products and the grits were in your pantry. The pancakes, I made from scratch for the boy." She winked at Zo before taking off.

When I gazed his way, Zo shrugged, brows hiked.

"You ate already?"

"Nah. The man of the house or company gets served first."

"Oh."

A wide beam opened on his face as he peered up to the oncoming traffic. Nye was serving his plate. Zo had everything I was given, except for grits.

"You got something against grits?"

"I don't eat anything porridge-y." He turned his nose up, then bowed his head for a silent expression of grace.

That snapped me into action to do the same.

Before I was done, Zo had picked up his fork to dig in and asked, "Speaking of serving the man first: Ma, you been in touch with Ernest? How's he managing you being out here so much?"

Nye was over the kitchen sink gazing out the large bay windows, overseeing the rose garden Camay had been working on for a while for me. The view, even out of bloom season, was captivating and one of the selling points of this place for me over ten years ago.

"This view is so peace-provoking," she mused much to herself. Then Nye's volume hiked, "I spoke with him last night. Not much he can do but sit tight as I take care of my son. I'm a single parent. He's always known this."

Nye had a man?

I wouldn't ask, partially because I didn't care.

Chewing, Zo swung his head left to right. "Non, ma mère. You say that's changed. You're a single woman who is a mother now." He winked. "Let's put some respect on Alaunzo's name." He chuckled with food in his mouth.

Nye froze, hands immersed in the sink. Her eyes bore into him as she spat, "Alaunzo Pierce..."

Huhn?

I blinked after Zo replied, "Yes, ma'am?"

"Eat your food."

"Yes, ma'am."

That universal Black momma's command of the reigns would never not be effective. I actually felt bad for the kid. His confidence needed to be preserved.

"You never answered about last night," I probed while cutting into my pancakes.

"Oh!" He bit into a slice of bacon. "It was alright. We went to a bowling alley. Then to one of the cheerleaders' house. Her parents are out of town." He shrugged. "I stayed for a couple of hours, then peace'd it up with everybody and left. Plus, Gena called me anyway. My head wasn't even in it."

"What did she call for?" The irritation in Nye's question couldn't be missed.

"Nothing, Ma. Just to chill."

"And what're your plans today?"

"I'm actually going down to visit Pop Pierce later."

"Really? For what?"

"There's a rattling sound underneath the hood of the *Explorer*. He wants to take a look at it. Said if it's something he can't fix, he has a friend who can."

"That truck's pretty old. You should consider getting something newer, at least," I advised. He damn sure could afford it.

"I'll see. No rush for me, though. I like having a piece of history with me. It makes me feel like less of a guest out here."

I nodded, chowing down. The unexpected food was pretty good.

"Let me know if I can help in any way."

"What're your plans for the day?"

"Well..." I chewed. "First thing's first: I need to attack this laundry."

"Oh, happy day," he droned, sympathizing.

"Right." I scoffed. "Then I wanna spend a few hours with my guitars. Got a few things bouncing in my head and I need to get them off my chest. I have somewhere to be tonight, so I plan to lay low until then."

"Man, I still can't believe you're a musician. Moms told me, but I guess I'll have to see it to really get it."

"I can take care of your laundry."

My head swiveled to Nye, standing next to the island with a fist propped on her hip.

"That won't be necessary." I declined.

"It's okay. I know you had a long week and went to bed with another headache. Go. Do something you enjoy to help balance work. Zo, don't leave that plate on the table. The dishwasher's awaiting." Then she was out of the kitchen, completely bypassing her conversation with me.

I shook my head. "Some things never change."

"With Nyedeera Taylor?" Zo's eyes lit brightly. "Pray tell."

I shook my head, taking a deep breath. "How 'bout I ride with you up to my parents', get this truck looked at, then you bring me back here so I can get a session in and be ready to swing out tonight?"

His head fell to the side and a slick smile spread on his face. "So when you say swing, what exactly does that entail. What are you into?"

My eyes fell shut as I laughed my ass off. I had to get used to Nye's kid—even if that meant battling my trust issues for her against appreciating his charm and wit.

"We can talk—around—that on the way to Upper Freehold. Your food'll get cold."

The house was quiet when I returned home later that night. After hanging my coat in the closet near the garage door, I sauntered into the kitchen for a bottle of water and noticed the plate of food on the counter. A sticky note was stuck to the plastic dome covering it. *Just in case* was the message. Scoffing, I washed my hands in the kitchen sink, then grabbed the aluminum foil to wrap the plate. I plucked a sauteed string bean before folding the foil and placing it in the fridge. Room temperature, but crispy and garlicky with a lemony twist.

As I tramped up the stairs, I doubted Nye was asleep. Instead of heading straight into my bedroom, I made a beeline down the hall in the opposite direction.

After two knocks, I heard, "Come in." Nye was stretched out in bed, watching her laptop. She hit pause and managed a faint smile. "Good to see you looking…better. Needless to ask if you enjoyed yourself."

My brow furrowed. "I don't follow."

"That headache you came home with last night. It didn't exactly go away this morning. I'm assuming you live with them. They chronic?"

"For a few years now. Just started out of nowhere."

"Orgasms and things of that nature help some people cope. It can take the edge off, unless they're severe like migraines or sinus headaches."

Was she telling me she knew I had sex tonight? While she'd be correct, there was something weird in sharing that with her. I didn't know this woman.

But I did…

Even in Nye feeling as though she could take on such a conversation, it reminded me of the forceful nature I knew her to have when we were kids.

My lids squinted even more and I rolled my eyes to the side of the room. "Okay. Thanks for that?"

Nye shrugged with humbled confidence. "It's the least I can do. Observing the man you've become is quite fascinating, knowing my son resembles you in more than one way."

Which was why I was here. Exhaling, I hung my head. "Feel like I owe you an apology."

"For what?"

"For the unkind way I spoke to you last night."

She shrugged. "It's your truth. I deserve worse."

"You're Zo's mother. I have to do better."

"Better at what?"

"Controlling my confusion. Accepting your decision."

She sat up in the bed, adjusting the blanket over her lower body. "What are you confused about?"

"It's really not something I want to get into because it takes a while for me to properly articulate my feelings."

"So you've talked to someone?"

I guessed that was a fair assessment. "I have. My pastor, who's a therapist…and a friend." I nodded, eyes on my shoes. "This has been the most unexpected…phenomenon of my life. The last thing I would have ever guessed would happen."

"I'm sorry."

"And when you say shit like that…" I caught myself. "It's hard to find any authenticity in it. It's been twenty-two years. You can't be sorry for twenty-two years."

She nodded, eyes going below on the bed. "Do you want me to go?"

There wasn't an ounce of a damsel in distress in that question. Nye was looking for a solution.

"I want to do right by Zo. The fucked up thing about this whole situation is it would be an easier adjustment period if he wasn't such a cool kid. It would have been a simple signing of the check and giving him my number in case he wanted to say hello from time-to-time. But with Zo…"

"Hello is as natural as breathing, and the thought of saying goodbye is a nightmare." She shook her head. "It's not even an option. I understand." Her head nodded softly. There it was. She'd articulated my feelings in less words than I was able to over the phone with Ezra a while back. "He's finding his way in all of this, too. I'm afraid that in me connecting you two when I did, I overwhelmed him. Not only was he in the process of transferring, I don't think Zo's properly grieved his best friend. He was the apple of my father's eye. Zo loved him."

"And what about you?"

"What about me?"

"You've been here with Zo and back and forth to Arizona, checking in on your home and mother. Have you grieved your father?"

By the way her chest jolted, it was clear Nye's lungs hiccupped. "My father didn't believe in grieving. He'd proven that to me long ago, over and over and over again. I think enduring his unyielding…coldness weakened me."

"Sorry to hear you two never resolved your issues."

"Yeah. Me, too." She chewed on her lip. "Have you and your father?"

"What do you mean?"

"I remember him giving you flak about your career options. He didn't approve of your music, but wasn't sold on you going pro either."

"When the time came, I did what I thought was best for me. I've been doing it ever since."

Her chin lifted. "Forcing him to respect you?"

"I…" I considered that for a moment. "I don't think he truly respected me until he had to depend on me. When my father got sick a few years ago, he was the most vulnerable he'd been in his adult years: financially, health-wise, too. I stepped up and did what I had to do. I didn't even think: I performed."

"Has he thanked you?"

I snorted. "Officially, nah. It's all good, though. My mother has expressed her gratitude enough for the both of them."

I watched her swallow. "You're a good man, Launz."

My neck twisted as I stood in the doorframe. "Why do you keep saying that?"

"Because it's what I know—what I've always known."

"And since when did you really know me?"

Nye giggled softly. "You know Zo says you're not shy."

"I'm not."

She emitted gently, "I don't know why I can't accept that."

"Maybe for the same reason I can't accept you being weak." I recalled her father being controlling and a hard man. But weakening Nye? "I think anyone believing that would be initiating their downfall. I'm sure your man knows that."

She scoffed, shaking her head. "Don't believe everything Zo tells you."

My forehead tightened as I turned to leave the room. "I'll try to keep that in mind."

I swiveled in the chair and stretched my legs out on the desk. "What does your mom have to say about all of this?"

Zo grunted. "She isn't saying much at all and, to be real, it's all good. It's something I have to do on my own."

My eyes brushed against the freshly painted walls of my assigned office in *Kings* nation. Slowly, my plaques were being hung. My desk was still yet half-empty, too. I mostly made calls from here, opting to meet with the staff in conference rooms, more often than not.

"Zo, if this is what you want, I'll support you. I can have Monica send you a list of realtors who have rental listings. I guess it's up to you to decide where you want her."

"I know!" he groaned, clearly conflicted by this life-changing, impending event. "I want her close to me because, *duh*! Not having her close would defeat the purpose. But to be honest, since I've been here, I've been hanging out with you and the fam. I don't even go to my local grocery store. I go to yours or my mother brings me food. Grammy Jo sends me home with food and goods every time I go down there."

I nodded. "Decisions. Decisions. Decisions of an up and coming man."

"Tell me about it." He sighed.

A tap at my door had my head snapping up from typing a text

message to Monica about helping to find Gena a place. Trent Bailey gave a nod while tipping his fitted. He wore jeans, sneakers, and a navy blue leather bomber with a gold chain, waiting to be invited in.

"Zo, I have a visitor. I'm sending Monica a text now. She'll be hitting you up soon."

"When are you coming back to Jersey? Tomorrow? Maybe we can talk about it more."

I waved Trent inside.

"Tonight, actually," I answered. "I'm leaving after practice."

"Oh. Okay. I'll stop by in the morning."

"Looking forward to it."

"Alright. Bye."

"Later." I placed the office receiver back on its base, disconnecting the call. My eyes were on TB when I murmured, "What a surprise."

He scoffed. "I forgot to clean my locker for the season. Came back to get my things. I hear you're holding your practices again this week."

"I like to consider them as the team's voluntary practice. We're all putting in the work, getting to know each other." I sat on the ledge of my desk facing him. "I'm actually about to get out there now. They're locking and loading as we speak."

"Maybe I'll come out there to see what it's like."

"To practice?"

Trent shook his head. "Just to peep what my guys are doing."

"Respectfully, I can't allow you to do that. What we're doing out there is more than plays and routes: we're getting to know each other. It's a vibe. You coming out there can shift our progress."

"How you figure?"

"Because those guys are volunteering their time for the betterment of the team. You, declining my invitations, have essentially said you don't want to be a part of this process. I know it and they know it each time they show up and their captain isn't here with them."

"Damn, Pierce. It ain't like I'm gonna ensue a riot or anything."

"You wouldn't have to with words." I reached back for my phone when it vibrated.

Monica: *His momma cool with all this?*

I typed back quickly.

Me: That has nothing to do with the request I've given you.

I had no time for Monica's bullshit. Sometimes I allowed her to cross the line of being family; others, I didn't.

Peering up from my phone, I invited Trent to continue the conversation. After a beat, he did. "I don't know how I feel about you telling me I'm not invited on my practice field." He scratched inside his beard to his chin.

"The practice field is for committed players of this team. I would love to have you out there—your commitment. I'm still trying to gain your trust, TB."

Becoming visibly irritated, Trent backed up and dropped into one of the seats in front of the desk. "Who are you, Coach Pierce—nah. Fuck that. Who are you, Alaunzo Pierce? Why should I trust you after being got by the two before you?"

"I'm a God-fearing Black man who loves his family and football. I receive from the same spiritual leader as you."

"Yeah. You say that and so does Bishop E, but I ain't never fellowshipped with you before, so it's real hard to force a connection."

"I've been a member of *Redeeming Souls* for the better part of ten years. I've even played for them on the choir's album a few years back. I've played in the sanctuary countless times, just haven't been regular because of my job."

"I work, too, and I'm there a lot. So is Amare's wife, Parker."

I scoffed, "Because the commute from here to Harlem is a hike, but possible if you're committed to the ministry. I've been on the West Coast working. That commitment isn't feasible."

"You keep using that word! What's up with that?"

"Because it's one I know you're well versed with. It's what Bishop Carmichael says of you. It's what your wife tells the world when she posts about you—which is rare because she honors your privacy. It's what America has seen of you over the years."

"You've been following my wife on social media?"

I raised my palm in the air. "Bruh, I've trolled more than your wife, and not just you. I've made it my business, since getting hired, to find out as much as I can about most of the roster. I can assure you, I don't have an interest in your wife outside of her influence over you."

"And you're not married. Right?"

"Does that make me less qualified for the job?"

"No, but it can be a sign of your instability or inability to focus and make decisions for the greater good."

I shook my head, peering Trent dead in the face. I would not be punked or feel I had to prove my character to any man. "Bailey, I'm a forty-three-year-old man. No, I'm not as old as Lou or Nealson, but I'm also no kid. I'm happily single and won't apologize for it. I don't pay for ass and I don't sling my dick immorally. I don't have to. I'm good getting what I need the organic way. Now, all of this can only be proven with time. I can't offer much more than that."

"I'm sorry." His head swung left to right. "I can't trust so easily."

"Nah, TB. You *can* trust easily; you've been betrayed by the organization and your previous coaches and therefore, I'm the one paying for it."

"You don't know me, man—"

"And in many respects, it's a logical repercussion," I spoke over him. "I'm willing to prove to you I've got what it takes to lead this team to the playoffs and a *Super Bowl.* But what I can't do is continue to compromise my authoritative role on this team in your eyes and beg you to stay. I may not know you, but I'm a tenured coach and the fuck good at what I do."

Nodding, Trent stood from the chair. "I don't doubt your claims. I just need time to figure out if I want to trust them."

He was turning for the door when I shared, "Nah, bruh. You need time to see if you're going to recommit. And I'll have to wait for it to happen, but until then, I'm gonna need you to not 'peek' in on what we're trying to grow here. If you have any questions, I'm here: morning, noon, and night. You've been provided all of my contact information."

Trent nodded again before leaving my office. I took a deep breath when I knew I was alone. I needed that cat, I really did. But I would only coach one way: mine. Either Trent was all in or he wasn't. It just sucked that I had to wait to find out if one of the most talented QBs of all time would grace my roster in the upcoming season.

When I turned from the hall in the rear of the house into the kitchen, I sighed, "*The fuck yessss...*"

There it was, incongruously anticipated. A plate of food under a dome plate covering. I had no idea what was beneath, yet was filled with gratitude on sight. Stopping on the way home from Connecticut was an option, but I craved something homecooked.

I dropped my duffle bags outside the kitchen and crossed the room for the sink to wash my hands. Spoiled. Was I getting used to having a homecooked meal when home? I didn't think it was something I needed. Typically, when I craved it, I'd either ask Monica to whip up something or go home for my mother's never-failing skills. But today, after observing, coaching the staff and team, and staying behind after the voluntary practice session for questions from everyone, all I wanted was a good meal from my kitchen and my bed.

She left another sticky note with the same message: *Just in case.* Meatloaf, mashed potatoes, gravy, and string beans. Simple and savory. I nuked it in the microwave, then sat down at my quiet kitchen table and enjoyed Nye's culinary work in silence. So many thoughts raced in my mind as I chewed and inhaled. Rut Amare's point about selling the double move and slowing down to get open in Trent Bailey's absence. He had a point, and his needs had to be expressively considered and supported before he lost faith in his coaching team. Of course, that would be addressed if TB would simply make a call on returning. After he popped up in my office today, I had no idea which direction dude was leaning. No way would I call Ezra for more assistance. I had to do this independent of him at this point, and so should Trent.

Before I knew it, the plate was cleaned and I dumped everything in the dishwasher. On my way to the side of the kitchen I entered, while grabbing a toothpick, I heard humming on the opposite end. I'd just left from that side and hadn't heard anything while eating. Crossing the room, I sauntered into the family room where I saw Nye on the floor, leaning against the coffee table on her laptop. Her head bobbed, clueing me in on her listening to music as she typed away. She wore an oversized sweatshirt and short biker shorts with some sort of fluffy booties. The woman was definitely cozy here.

"Hey," I called out to her moderately.

When she didn't answer, I decided against touching via a simple tap and, instead, traversed the room until I was in her peripheral.

Nye's eyes quickly shifted at the notice of my appearance, then she slowly rolled them up to me and leaped from the floor. "Shit!" Her palm hit her chest. She snatched out an *AirPod*. "You scared the living shit out of me!"

I chuckled. "Sorry. You were quiet as a mouse until you tried to sing.

Her head pushed back slightly and Nye blinked hard. "No headache tonight. Yaaaaay!"

Not wanting to give thought to a headache, I ignored the observation. "What're you listening to?"

Still gathering her bearings from what I could guess, Nye didn't speak. She pulled out the other *AirPod* then tapped her laptop. The first line of The System's "*Don't Disturb This Groove*" bellowed from the speaker.

My brows lifted as my head bobbed to beat.

Old school...

"You know, it wasn't until I started using Zo's *Tidal* account that I realized I'd never heard the opening of this song. Listen." She rewound it to the beginning and we listened together. "Isn't that a guitar?"

"Electric," I confirmed.

Nye scoffed, eyes scurrying away. She then paused the track. "You know, I find myself listening for guitars in just about every song I hear."

"Do you now?" She nodded, but her regard remained on the laptop. Here was reserved Nyedeera. At least I could identify her moods. "What are you working on?"

Her eyes widened, processing my question. "Oh." She began tabbing her screens. "A write-up for work, writing my letter of resignation, looking for apartments, and preparing for an interview tomorrow."

"Damn. All that?"

"I'm great at multitasking." She flashed a charming smile.

"Quitting your job, huhn?"

"Yeah," she sighed. "I've finally decided. I don't want to return to Arizona to live. Visiting my mom is easy, but leaving Zo isn't." She rolled her eyes and murmured, "Especially when he's so intent on bringing his lil' girlfriend out here."

That reminded me of his visit in the morning. And *that* reminded me of my agenda tonight. I'd eaten, and now, it was time for bed.

"I hear you," I tried closing the conversation. "Nothing wrong with change, I guess, especially when it's regarding your child. Not that I know much about that either." When she giggled, rolling her eyes, I knew my obligatory conversation with her had been completed successfully. "I'm tired as hell. Gonna turn in."

When I ambled toward the opening of the room, Nye announced, "Hey, I can do that for you tonight. Zo dropped off his load last night and I figured I'd wait."

My eyes dropped to my luggage. "I'll get it sorted for you."

As I made my way to the foyer for the staircase, I realized how easy it was to acquiesce to that. This would be the second week in a row she'd done my laundry. Maybe I was okay with it because I'd had housekeepers in the past, some of whose names I could recount.

Shit. I didn't know and was too damn tired to try and extrapolate it.

Hours later, lost to the midnight, I tossed and turned in my bed. My mind wouldn't fully rest; dreams of plays and people on the practice field continued to play and my dick was halfway awake from her scent. After I'd showered and crawled into bed, I was immediately awash with a soft, clean floral aroma. I knew right away, Nye had been sleeping in my bed since I'd been in Connecticut this week.

Again, my mind was over-capacity and body too fatigued to react to it. But apparently, my cock did. It had been triggered while I struggled to sleep through it. That was until I rolled from my back onto my side, sliding my left arm beneath a pillow and hitting a small apparatus, causing it to shift. That woke me completely out of my sleep. Lifting from the mattress, I tossed the pillows to the side until my blurred vision picked up a purple dick.

What the fuck...

When I lifted it in the air, my brain jolted. A vibrator! A thick ass, rubber vibrator. My eyes rolled to the ceiling and I dropped back onto the mattress. This was way more than I bargained for. She was doing too much, had assumed more liberty than appropriate in my house.

You're fucking killing me, Nyedeera!

~TWELVE

PRESENT DAY

I WATCHED GEORGE WRIGHT'S MEN WORK IN the back yard. On one side, a couple of them were laying stones, sectioning off a garden. On the other, trees were being planted. As disarrayed its current state, it was all coming along.

"AP!" I heard shouted from behind me.

I knew it was Zo right away. "Out back!"

Seconds later, he stopped beside me, observing the labor. "I saw the blueprints for this. Nice, man."

"Thanks." I turned and greeted him with a dap. "What time's your first class?"

"Twelve-ten."

"Then let's get to it." I turned back for the French doors leading to the family room. "Let's kick it in my office. You mind if I smoke?"

"Not at all," he answered, trailing behind me.

Once we made it inside, I plucked a stogie from the humidifier, a cutter, and a lighter.

"Have you eaten?"

We were sauntering into my office when he answered, "I grabbed something on the way down."

Zo plopped himself onto the sofa near the door and I opened the windows before grabbing an ashtray. Then I pulled up a seat and laid out all my tools before me.

"So, let's politic." I snipped the cap of the cigar. "What's on your heart, young man?"

Zo snorted. "You know, to say I'm your only child, you sure have a natural way of making a kid feel important."

I froze while picking up my lighter. His grandfather came to mind. Zo had him to confide in regarding coming of age matters.

Reclining in my chair, I reminded him, "I'm a career-long coach. Been in the game for over twenty years. Of course, I know how to nurture and mentor young Black men—any race, actually." When Zo's eyes fell and he nodded in what appeared to be agreement, I thought to amend, "I would hope when it comes to the fruit of my loins, there'd be some kind of inherent ease. At least, that's what I feel when kicking it with you." I lit my *Macanudo Gold*, taking my time to rotate it, inhaling to create a steady burn. "Tell me, young king." I blew out the first smoke, relaxing into the chair almost immediately. "What are we doing about Ms. Gena?"

"Well, I want her to come out here. That's for sure."

"And this was your idea?"

"Both."

"Who initiated the decision?"

"I guess I did. It was something that crossed my mind before I flew out here, but I never made the call until a few weeks after landing and seeing how lonely she was. I was dealing with my Gramps being gone, making sure I submitted the right paperwork to *Rutgers*, then my mom going through with telling you about me. It was too much to make a call on at the time for me."

"So, you knew she was pregnant before coming to Jersey?" He nodded. "How far along is she?"

"Four months, I think?"

Four fucking months?

I couldn't react the way I wanted. Zo didn't need to be embarrassed. So, instead, I took a long pull from my stogie.

Letting the fumes go, I asked, "Does her family know? Her parents?"

He nodded. "She told them last month. Things ain't too cool over there."

"They're disappointed?"

"I think more than that, they're upset that she wants to come here. She'll be dropping out of school to have a baby." Zo buried his face in his arms. "It's so fucked up, man. We didn't plan for it to go down like this."

"Zo, as ugly and damning as this seems, having a baby earlier than you planned isn't the end of the world. And it's definitely not a dooming prospect for you and Gena, considering you'll have the support of your family."

He lifted his head to peer up at me. "My mom doesn't even know. She's gonna kill my ass. And if I ever wanted her to like Gena again after going around her in February and having her stay here, I can forget about that after telling her about the baby."

"It'll all work out. I promise you that. I can't speak for Nye, but I can say I'll hold you down on this. Be anything you three need. I'm sure my family will, too."

Zo nodded again, appearing to thankfully believe me. "Monica already hit me with a few rental agencies. She said she'll help me get through to the good ones with my budget."

"I don't think you'll have to worry about putting her in anything shitty." I'd just given him more than enough to move his girl out here.

"I'm not touching that child support money. At least, not if I don't have to. Gena's got a few dollars saved and I'm expecting the money from my grandfather's will. I'll get a job this summer, too. No. I'm not blowing your money on my mistake. I'm gonna step up."

I took another drag from my cigar and exhaled a cloud of smoke. "Tell me about her."

"Gena?"

"Yeah." I scoffed. "How did you meet?"

"Oh!" Zo laughed. "Junior high. She was the first student I met in the school. The guidance counselor assigned her to be my orientation buddy—is what they used to call them. She was…nothing to stare at. Brown skin, big kinky ponytails, and braces were all I remembered, but freshman year in high school…" Zo blew out a libidinous breath while rubbing his thighs. My head flew back as I chuckled. I knew that feeling. Still had them when encountering a fine ass woman. He laughed at himself, too. "Man! No more kinky ponytails. Now, her natural hair is pressed out and down her back. I see more of that bronzed brown skin and those teeth are the perfect size in relation to her lips. And her boobs! My god, man!" He fell to the side, giggling like a high schooler.

"So, you're a tit man?"

Zo shot up. "Why? What type are you?" I shrugged, not anticipating that question. "You like big asses?"

I flicked the excess ashes of the cigar into a tray. "I like meat." I tossed my head in a shrug. "But I like confidence, too. I guess it's a combo thing for me. I like something to hold, but I need some mental stimulation to…be stimulated all over."

Slowly and with wide eyes, Zo's head bounced up and down. It was comical how confused he was. "Okay…" His lips pursed. "I thought this was the time you'd give me a pointer—or two—on how to please a lady."

"Is that what your grandfather did?"

As stoic as my expression, I hated that I got such negative vibes from a deceased man. Maybe it was because since I knew of his existence, stories about him weren't so positive. Or perhaps there was a sting of jealousy at him raising my son without me knowing. I didn't know and tried to manage it.

"Nah." Zo laughed. "Gramps told me to kiss them good and let them know I'm a man. What that meant, I didn't know, but dude was consistent with that message."

Interesting...

I considered my approach as I heaved in more of the *Macanudo.* When I let it go, I shifted weight from hip to hip, licking my lips. "In my experience, kissing well is golden, but making a woman feel like a woman should always be the intent and pleasure."

The muscles in his face dropped. "What do you mean?"

"It means, son, that whether you're fuckin' or making love, your satisfaction should always come from her pleasure."

"But..." he hesitated. "You can't please each woman the same way."

"Which is where the fun kicks in."

"How?" His arms swung into the air.

"By getting to know them. After a few years of searching...exploring, you have a few tricks in your bag. Sometimes, it's a matter of trial and error." I tossed my chin in a shrug. "Sensual exploration."

Sitting back on the sofa, Zo appeared deflated. "Damn," he whispered.

"What's the problem?"

"I came here feeling clueless as a soon-to-be father. And after this short conversation, I feel like my stroke game is trash." Zo shook his head.

And that was true and fucking sad at the same damn time. I knew shit about parenting.

"Zo, man, I'm sorry. I haven't even begun to learn what it takes in the father department."

"But you're doing something." He nodded, convinced.

"How do you mean?"

"I told you, you needed to communicate with my mother. You went from not talking to her to letting her stay at your place without a complaint. That's meant a lot. For real. You seem to be this calm... boss. If I can get those two attributes, I'll be grateful. You know?"

Is that what I'm doing?

Here I was, ready to have a prickling conversation with Nye today when she got in from her job interview because I didn't want to fuck up her vibe about masturbating in my bed beforehand. Conniving, deceitful, sneaky, and bewildering. Nye was a web I was too damn old to find myself entoiled by. Her mendacious tentacles were far-reaching for me, too. Zo may have been a spitting image of me, but he inherited his mother's charm, something that caused me to pause each time my heart opened to him. The kid was charismatic and articulately expressive. Was he smooth-tongued like his mother? I mean… How was I really to know?

But still…

I took a deep breath, reaching over to dump more ashes. "How can I support you on this, Zo?"

The kid shrugged, mouth twisting as he hung his head. "Just keep being you. I 'on't know if Gena's the one I'll marry, but I can't have my baby grow up not knowing me or not…really knowing me. I know what that…"

When he hesitated, I jumped in. "Say no more. I'm with you. One hundred percent."

Then Zo's head lifted and eyes appeared again. "Already, I feel like I have family out here. Like you're my…"

Twisting the *Macanudo* between my index and thumb as my body tensed all over, I hid my emotions behind a simple nod.

Hours later, Zo had left to make his class, and George Wright and his landscaping crew had gone for the day. I sat in the family room, blindly flipping through pages of the Bible. My intent was to read the book of Matthew, and specifically for the story of Peter walking on the water. As many times as I'd read the parable, I came looking for more of Peter's perspective tonight. As I waited for her to get in, I wondered what type of confidence Peter had walked in before Jesus. Was he gullible? Was he a follower? Was he weak?

Why in the hell was that dude the only of the disciples stepping out of that boat onto the water? Was he *that* type of cat?

The follower.

Or the bold one, giving in to no fear.

Because right now, in my life, I once again felt like a Peter that night in the boat. My life was stable. Familiar. Without any agent of change.

Until Nyedeera Taylor.

While in this instance—or that of twenty-two years ago—she wasn't Jesus, both times, she came with something my dumb ass couldn't resist. The first was her aggressive charm. This time, it was my son. And my son was about to be a father. I wanted to be a part of it all, so if I had to get off the boat to see this thing through, I would. While Nye was far from Jesus, she had the ability to compel me to her.

The door off the garage opened and I closed the Good Book, placing it back on the bookshelf. I paced into the foyer to meet her in the hall. The moment she noticed me, her eyes burst wide and Nye's steps halted.

"Hey..."

"Hey," I parroted. "How did today go?"

"Oh," she chirped. Her eyes bounced around. "Tiresome?"

"That's too bad." I sidled against the wall. "I'm hungry."

Her lips stretched back, exposing her teeth. "You want me to cook? It's almost seven o'clock."

I scoffed. "Nah. I actually wanted your company. Since there's a mild temperature out, I'm going to a spot I like a couple of blocks away. You wanna come?"

"Uhhh..." She glanced down at her dress suit: a skirt and matching cropped jacket, silk blouse, and heels. "Yeah. I guess. I'm too tired to change."

"You may wanna consider your shoes." I pushed off the wall. "We're walking." I headed toward the front foyer.

"I'll be fine," she informed behind me. "Seriously, if I don't move now, I won't be able to until tomorrow morning."

I held the door open for her, swinging my arm like a gentleman, assisting her out. When she sauntered past, a waft of that soft, clean floral aroma hit me. I wanted to grunt my fucking annoyance of it, but remembered the greater good as I locked up behind us.

Checking in on her across the table, I noticed Nye's jaw worked so hard her lips protruded. She took another gargantuan bite into her burger and her downdrawn lips drooped even more, and I was reminded of her pronounced cupid's bow. Well, actually, I was reminded of it in Chesney's office back in January, but was so disgusted by the sight of her, I didn't dwell on it. Avoiding her until February when she had dinner with Zo and me at *DiFillippo's* helped with me not truly observing her features.

Tonight, as we dined on a white tablecloth outside on the sidewalk beneath an umbrella, Nye appeared famished, reminding me of my condition last night when I returned home from Connecticut. I inhaled my food and counted down the minutes until I reached my bed.

When she took another big bite of her burger, I realized she'd stopped talking for a couple of minutes.

"Good?"

Her dark eyes shot up to me and I noticed another feature I'd forgotten. The mole next to her nose and the one near her mouth. They gave her such a mature edge when I met her, but now they both appeared larger, oddly working for her. Her hair in the mild breeze was long and her curls loose around her shoulders. Then Nye nodded.

Chewing, she shared, "I don't think I knew this place was here. I gotta come back. Maybe bring Zo."

I wanted to get back to our conversation. "So, your mom's upset."

"Oh. Yeah." She chomped around her food. "I can't believe how she flipped once I told her I quit. I thought she'd be cool with it. She even told me since Zo and I've been out here to take all the time I needed to figure myself out. And now..." She swung her free hand out.

"Has your former employer replied to your letter of resignation?"

Nye downed the last of her second cocktail, her favorite mixture of lemon juice and vodka, then shook her head.

"I swear it felt like seventy seconds after I'd hit 'send' this morning in my car, that I'd gotten a call back from the vice president of operations, who's nothing more than a damn glorified secretary at the firm."

"What did he say?"

"He asked what they could offer me to stay." She flagged down a passing waitress. "I told him it wasn't about the money. Tod thinks I'm holding a grudge against the firm for hiring him after me at a significantly higher pay rate, then having me train him."

"But he's a glorified secretary."

She tossed her arm in the air. "Exactly!"

"Can I help you?" the waitress asked.

"Another." Nye pointed to her empty glass.

"Okay. I'll get that ready for you." She regarded me. "And what about you? How's the cutlet?"

"Good, as always," I murmured. "I'm fine. Thanks."

"Okay. Be right back."

"So, what's next?" I asked as an elderly couple with a leashed poodle strolled past, gazing at our plates.

One of the drawbacks of dining outside on a small suburban town block was the close proximity to pedestrians. But considering the temperature reached seventy-two degrees today, I had to take advantage of the weather.

"Zo didn't tell you?" I shook my head. "I'm thinking about teaching."

My eyes went wild as I grunted, "Teaching? Who?"

"College level." When I sat back, letting go of a light chuckle, she demanded, "What?"

"I can't see you teaching. You seem too..."

"What?"

"You seem too liberal. Too carefree to teach young minds to color between the lines."

Her eyes rose to meet mine with a soft gaze. "You don't know the adult me, Launz."

Ignoring that, my attention fell to my plate and I cut off a piece of the chicken. "What does your man have to say about you relocating?"

She slammed her head into her palm. "Shoot! He's here in the North East and wants to meet up before he leaves tomorrow. I'm so not in the mood."

Nye's drink was delivered to her as she finished the last of her burger. A dollop of ketchup mixed with mayonnaise was plastered on the corner of her mouth as she thanked the bartender.

Instinctively, I reached over with my napkin and wiped it off as she was bringing the drink to her mouth. Nye leaped in her chair, surprised by my proximity.

"Oh!" she chirped, then slowly leaned into my reach.

I tried not disturbing her lipstick much beyond what her ravishing of her burger did. Women hated that shit and I knew it.

Nye gulped down a bit of her drink, and I'd decided I'd had enough of my food.

"You good?" I asked, motioning her plate still with fries. "You want dessert?"

"What I need far surpasses dessert," Nye made clear before whipping her neck to get an errant lock of hair out of her face.

I had no idea what that meant other than she didn't want dessert. I got the attention of our waitress, who was inside the restaurant. When she arrived, I requested, "Check please, Amy."

"Oh, sure! No dessert?"

"Nah. We're good for the night."

While she printed out the tab, I finished my drink while answering texts. Nye people-watched and did the same as me.

"Here you go," Amy returned, almost startling me, I was so lost in multiple conversations.

"I can get that," Nye blurted as I dug into my pocket for my wallet.

"You'll do no such thing." I peeled off a few bills and placed them over the bill. "Good night, Amy."

"Oh, thanks!" She smiled as I stood from the table.

"Oh, shoot!" Nye shrilled, standing. She grabbed the table for assistance.

I leaped her way, taking her at the arm. "You okay?"

"You alright?" Amy asked at the same time.

Nye giggled. "Good thing no one's driving." Then her brows furrowed. "I'm fine! Let's go before I have to pee."

I scoffed, sidling up to her. Hesitantly, I took her at the arm and led her out of the gated dining area. The ambiance of Moorestown was nostalgic and picturesque. So many had the same idea I had to get out and take advantage of the break in the weather. April was always unpredictable weather-wise. Between the lights of the shop and the vibes of the residents socializing and my back yard being landscaped, I was looking forward to warmer temperatures.

"This is so cute," Nye remarked, eyes going all around to the ice cream shop, dogs on a leash, and even a saxophonist playing tunes.

"Yeah," I exhaled. "Only thing missing is melanin."

"This is true." She giggled. "Have you ever been to *Blackwood*?"

"Several times a year. Have a few friends who live out there."

"That's where I'm considering going. Professional, Black, progressive community. I mean, who wouldn't want to live there?"

"I remember the first time I visited, I left saying I'd move there when I married and settled down to have kids."

"Really? Not here? Moorestown has been voted the best place to live in the state several times over the years."

"You've done some homework."

She winked. "Most of my work is research. I find shit out."

I snorted, shaking my head. "Yeah, but I'd never raise my kids in a predominately white school district. And I'd only do chiefly Black if it was *Blackwood*. They're properly funded and its residents lord over the school system. They've got that shit down to a T."

"Yeah. I heard," she shared less spiritedly as we turned the corner. "I guess I never considered that. We always moved when my father got transferred. I didn't have any say in terms of his assignments. I was so used to surviving any social circle encountered as a kid, I figured he'd do the same."

I glanced down at her. "Did he?"

"Zo?" she giggled. "He did. My boy gave me very few problems. He developed a fan club at each stop."

"Like you?"

That was supposed to stay in my head.

Nye's head swung up to me, long lashes batting as her eyes beamed. "I wish. I wasn't liked in many of the places I grew up in. In my high school yearbook, I was voted most resilient. Most resilient!" She barked in amusement.

"Was your sister the same? And didn't you have a brother?"

"I do have a brother. No, my sister, Jenise, isn't like me. Neither are like me. My brother was laid back. He didn't give much in terms of conversation. My sis—" Nye broke her stride and immediately, I stopped. "Ooh!" she chirped.

That's when I realized she'd twisted her ankle.

"You okay?"

"Yeah. Tipsy in heels isn't always ideal when trying to keep the same pace as a taller man."

"Oh. My bad. We're halfway there. Take your time." My phone rang as she wiggled her foot. "Hey, lady."

"Hey!" she breathed into the line. "Change of plans."

"Oh, yeah?" I asked, eyeing Nye whose face tightened as though in pain.

"Yup. I'm actually going to drive to your place. I didn't book a room. I got a call from my assistant. A client of ours called with an emergency up in Manhattan. I reserved a room and will drive up that way once we're done."

My eyes bounced from a tree off the sidewalk to Nye, who was smiling at the houses. "Okay. That's fine, but I have company over and I have to drive up to Connecticut early tomorrow for a few meetings. So, I won't be able to host you... too late."

"Oh." Sandra droned, catching my drift. "Okay. Then I'll see what I can find in Philly?"

A hotel room…

I preferred my own bed to many of them.

Nye was gazing my way, eyes lit with amusement. She could hear Sandra on the other line.

"Let's see how the evening goes."

"Okay. See you soon."

"Cool."

"Hot date?" Nye teased.

"Just a private art viewing."

"Where?"

"Philly?"

"With Camay?"

"No." I shook my head. "A friend of mine by the name of Sandra."

"Ohhhh…" she emphasized softly, yet dramatically. "What would Camay say?"

"I guess you'd have to ask Camay." I flashed my eyes wild to humor her.

It worked. Nye's hair dropped behind her shoulders as she howled femininely into the night air. "Are you a player, Alaunzo Pierce?"

"I am most certainly not. I'm a single man, Ms. Taylor."

"A healthy one."

"Thank God."

"You have all these women, who I'm sure want to be number one."

"But I don't have one who wants to take care of all of me."

All the humor drained from her face. "And what does that entail?"

I resumed our strolling. "Everything important to me. And beyond my health and possibly my life. Can she take the things I've built alone and what we build collectively to continue to grow and nurture when I can't due to illness or even more, my untimely death? If not, let's just share what's fun."

"What's fun?"

"Sharing time when it's mutually convenient. I'm a simple man; I don't ask for much. I have my own. It may not be much, but I take care of myself—with the administrative assistance of my older sister."

What I thought was a soft-handed joke on myself didn't catch on with Nye. Her face was hard as though lost in translation.

"I never thought about that. A man wanting a woman who could love everything about him beyond sickness and health. But isn't that the same as loving you?"

"Nah. Marriage is an exclusive commitment. It goes beyond emotion. Loving and liking can be transient, compared to steadfastness."

"Are you capable of that?"

I squinted. "I don't think I have a choice now that I'm a father."

"Oh!" she tweeted again, stopping.

"You're gonna break your ankle."

Nye's head rocked left to right. "I've got to pee."

"That bad?" She nodded. I glanced around. "We're basically a block away from the house. Can't you make it?"

"Not if I keep moving."

"Nyedeera, you can't urinate on a residential block."

"I don't *want* to," she warned by way of a cry.

Oh, shit!

The woman made me nervous. I believed Nye to do all the crazy shit unimaginable, and squatting for a piss in the middle of suburbia USA was one of those things.

"What can I do to help you—not pee! What can I do to get you to not do it?"

"I don't know!" she cried. "I was doing good distracting myself with us talking, but the more I walk, the more it wants to come out."

"Damn," I grunted. "It was those cocktails."

"You're judging me again!"

I shook my head, then an idea came. "If I let you climb on my back, would that help?"

"I don't know." She performed the pee dance, looking crazy as hell in a sexy skirt suit.

"Let's try. I don't want you looking crazy in front of these white folks." I stepped closer to her and squatted, giving her my back. "Let your legs hang."

Quickly getting the idea, Nye threw her arms over my shoulder, where I grasped her soft hands and heaved her over my shoulders. The first thing that hit me was her clean floral scent. Then it was the soft tissue of her breasts against my back. I stood straight and began a power walk like my life depended on it.

"They're all white?"

"Mostly."

"That doesn't bother you?"

"Again. Without kids, I'm good."

"Are they good to you?"

"When I see them, I guess."

"So, what are you and Sandra gonna do after the art show? A little congressing?"

My brows met as I carried her toward the corner of my street. "What?"

"Some copula?" She snorted and cracked the fuck up.

"The hell?"

"You...know!" Nye couldn't breathe, she laughed so hard.

"Look, girl! Don't pee on my back."

"Okay!" she howled in laughter. "Okay! But are you gonna beat the cakes? Hide the sausage? You gonna intercorpse?"

I stumbled, laughing at that one. "You need to stop before you pee!"

"Okay, but wait!" She teetered. "You're gonna serve each other horizontal refreshments?" Her face collapsed against my head.

I stopped. "Nye, where the fuck did you get those from?"

The sound of sirens stole my attention. A cop car pulled up, flashing and all.

"Oh, shit," Nye breathed near my ear.

"Pierce, is that you?" he chirped, head out of the window, gawking at us.

"Oh, hey, Tod." I acknowledged with a nod. "How are you tonight?"

"I guess I'm wondering why you're barreled over, walking with a young lady on your back." He tried not to laugh as he followed aside us at a slow speed.

"She's not all that young, Tod."

"Yeah? You wanna let her tell me that?"

"How young do you want me to be?" Nye fired off.

I rolled my eyes. "Tod, this is the mother of my child. Nyedeera. She's been staying with me."

"You've got a kid, Pierce? Why am I just learning this?"

"Long story?" I droned.

"Is it his business?" Nye asked lowly. Then she hiked her volume when she demanded, "I don't have to expect this type of inquiry for my son when he's visiting, do I?"

Tod's goofy ass bellied out a chuckle. His thick mustache covered his top lip. "Well, hot damn, Pierce, you got a firecracker in this one!"

I shook my head. "Yup. A lawyer, too."

"Oooh!" He flashed his eyes wide, finding that funny, too.

"Yup. And one who doesn't like Tods with chestnut hair and long mustaches!" Nye was on one.

That made Tod cackle even harder. "Okay, Pierce. I see you've got your hands full. I'll send a unit over to do a wellness check in the morning."

I laughed at that with him. Tod took off, hooting all the way down the block.

"Your friend?"

"Friend? No. But someone I have a good rapport with."

"I hope him and all his friends will soon have a 'good rapport' with the other Alaunzo Pierce," she hissed.

The other...

That's when the weight of her giving our son my namesake hit me. To go through such lengths, only to keep him from me was baffling. I walked us to my front door where I let her down so I could fetch my key. I barely had the door open before Nye gusted past me and clomped her way down the foyer to the powder room.

And just like that, her impressionable energy was gone. I stood in her wake, her unique scent all over, haunting me.

~THIRTEEN

PRESENT DAY

"This is a really nice neighborhood," Sandra observed out loud as we drew closer to my house. "Lots of families. Right?"

I nodded, feeling something familiar about that observation. I enjoyed art viewing. The event took place in the Rittenhouse Square section of Philly. A mutual friend of ours hosted. It was an intimate group of people and I enjoyed the pieces as much as I did the energy of the room.

"Shit. I've got to use the little girls' room before I hit this road, Launz."

That was definitely something I'd heard earlier when nearing my home. I didn't answer as I turned onto my block, thinking about this ride I'd take in the morning. Thankfully, I thought to get a driver to assist with the commute. It was one of the perks of being a coach for the *Kings*. I could get so much done if I didn't drive.

I pulled into the driveway and tapped the button for the garage door to open.

"I'm kind of feeling a way about not being able to stay over." Sandra's hand glided over my thigh. I scoffed. "I've been looking forward to tonight."

"I'm sorry, sweetheart. I should have mentioned it sooner. So much shit has been on my plate lately, it's hard to keep up."

I pulled into the garage and parked the truck.

"Sounds like I need to get on Monica for not doing her job satisfactorily," she trilled in jest.

Scoffing, I smiled, turning to her. Sandra was a beautiful woman. Warm chocolate skin, dainty though a robust woman. Her confidence won me over without fail since the first time we met. She was full-figured, and I enjoyed every inch of her eighteen/twenty size. I'd been with several BBWs and the best were the ones who owned their full figure. Sandra knew her features and how to maximize on them. As a successful interior decorator with natural beauty, she worked rooms with her aura and size.

In sudden and temporary regret myself, I reached over and pulled her into a kiss.

"Mmmmm..." she hummed, hand inching up to my crotch.

Before it went further than my dick could bear, I pulled from her soft lips and murmured, "Let's get you relieved so you can be up for this ride up to the City."

As I turned to leave the truck, Sandra asked, "You sure we can't sneak in a quickie? It's almost two in the morning; your guests should be asleep. And even if they aren't, they're not staying in your room."

Chuckling, I closed the door and murmured, "You have no idea, and neither do I."

Smelling Nye's scent and softness on my back a few hours ago put me in a headspace I'd rather stay out of with her.

I helped Sandra out of the truck. Holding her hand, we walked to the door and I keyed us in. Once inside, she reached up for another kiss as we sauntered down the hallway. I had no idea how we ended up in the kitchen, likely because the light was on in there.

"See," Sandra whined, twisting her softness around me to be in my arms fully. "Quiet. Good houseguests are sleeping houseguests."

That tickled me and she broke into laughter, too. Somehow, my eyes rolled up from her at a motion in my peripheral.

My face dropped when I saw Nye at the table dipping tea bags into a huge clear mug. Two things came to mind: I'd never used the mugs my mother gifted me when I bought this place. The other thought was more of a question. *When did Nye's ass get that big?*

Sensing the tensing of my body, Sandra turned, following my line of sight. Nye stood there, deadpanned, twirling the strings of the tea bags. Her tight, flawless skin covered by a cropped gray, short-sleeved sweater covering only her breasts and shoulders. The matching shorts bore her ass cheeks beneath. Oh, and socks. Long knee-length socks with a messy ponytail.

She didn't speak, but eventually moved to the trash can to dump the bags. While taking a sip with her eyes still glued to Sandra and me, Nye toed out of the kitchen via the opposite end. The fat of her ass! It joggled with a piece of the shorts wedged between her cheeks.

My fucking…

Sandra whisked around into my chest, eyes wild. "Who the fuck is that?" she whispered, face tight.

I heard his heavy footsteps nearing my bedroom. While I wasn't nervous, I hoped to be ready for what was coming. Once opened, the doorjamb was filled with his lengthy frame.

"Nye…"

"Alaunzo?" I lay beneath the comforter on my side with my laptop across from me and tea in my hand.

"I don't play games."

"They're rather childish for me."

"And I won't be taken advantage of in my home or be embarrassed in front of my guests."

"Which guests?" I kept my volume low and as calm as his. "Them or me?"

"Neither. So, if you have another motive other than Zo for being here, I'd respect you more if you're upfront with it rather than being conniving."

Damn…

I was offended. "What other motive would I have?"

He cocked his head to the side and squinted. "With you, I never knew."

"You never asked either, if I recall."

"Maybe because I could never trust you to be honest."

"The only time in our lives I'd ever given you a reason to not trust me is when I left. Before then, if you lacked trust, it was because of my forwardness, my Nye-ness." It took time for me to learn this about myself. "I can't help who I am, but I do understand how my actions may be misinterpreted by others. If you were one of those people, I deeply apologize. But I can't change who I am."

His spine straightened in the doorway. "And just who are you?"

I shrugged, feeling weaker than I let on. "Nyedeera. Just Nyedeera."

"And who the hell is she?"

"With you? Unpredictable," I answered honestly. "and apparently territorial."

"I'm not yours."

"Right. You're Zo's dad, who performs tricks."

His eyes dropped, recalling his slipup with me about his dating life. Launz snorted, yanking the ends of his beard. "I'm not a kid, Nye. Apparently, I have one now to concentrate on, though."

"And neither am I a kid." I closed the laptop. "I'm sorry you haven't noticed." All he ever acknowledged was the old me.

"I guess I will when you show me that." Launz turned to leave.

"Can I ask a favor?"

He peered at me over his shoulder before shifting to face me again. "You're leaving in the morning for Connecticut?" He nodded, confirming. "Can I bum a ride with you? My friend wants to meet near the airport for coffee."

"Your man?"

"His name is Ernie."

His eyes bounced around as though he was considering it. Seconds felt like stretched minutes. "What time?"

"His flight leaves at five-twenty."

"I got a driver for the day. I guess I can make it happen."

"Oh, goodie." I supplied a tight grin. "Then maybe you can finally get to know the adult Nye."

"Oh, goodie," he mocked, then disappeared from the doorway.

So, this is what the League's like...

My eyes bounced all around Launz's expansive, high-rise office overseeing what he explained was the "practice" field. It looked like the big field to me, but what did I know? And what a view he had! Floor-to-ceiling windows illuminating every inch of it. The place was luxurious with modern décor; glamorous, high ceiling and full office furnishings. I wished Zo could see this.

"I'll take a look at them when they're sent over and get back to you with my recommendations," Launz assured someone over the phone while he sat behind his desk.

Though we hadn't been here long, he showed me around the *Kings'* front office. The place was huge and busy to say it was off-season.

A tap at the door had me turning from a few plaques on the wall. "Coach, they're ready for you," the young guy I met at the reception desk when we'd arrived informed Launz, keeping his voice low.

"I'll be right there, Devaughn," Launz replied. Devaughn was out as quickly as he'd appeared. "Mitch, I've gotta go. But send them over. I'll shoot 'em right back. Okay. Sounds good. Bye." He placed the phone on its base and rose from his seat.

"Time to earn your pay?" I asked more out of nervousness.

It was weird to be in his workspace, similar to how it felt being in his home the first few weeks.

"I guess so." He stopped in front of me, bringing a gust of his masculine and evocative fragrance. I'd been disturbed by it since sleeping in his bed. Underneath the earthy cologne was an aroma transporting me way back. *To my childhood.* "You're going to be good until it's time for you to go?" I nodded, following him into the hallway. "Okay. He'll drop you off and once I wrap up here, I'll come scoop you."

"Sounds adventurous," I squealed playfully aside him. "Will we get ice cream after if I behave?"

Launz rolled his eyes, trying to hide his amusement. Then I watched his attention divert. Ahead of us, a petite woman with beautiful hazel eyes approached.

"Hey," she greeted hesitantly, regard bouncing between Launz and me. "I didn't expect to see you today."

Launz stopped and so did I. "How are you, Jade?"

"I'm good." She smiled at me. "Hi. I'm Jade Bailey." She proffered her hand. "It's nice to meet you."

"Hey," I returned. "Nye."

Just when I was deciding how I'd play it, Jade's regard and the way she switched weight on her hips, signaling she was in no hurry to leave, mutely asked the magical question.

"Oh." Launz pivoted toward me. "Jade, Nye's the mother of my child."

Those irises lit with surprise, going from hazel to green. I didn't think I'd ever seen anything like it before. "I didn't—" she fumbled. "I didn't even know you had kids."

"Most don't, actually," Launz explained. "Nye, Jade is Trent Bailey's wife."

That's when my eyes went wild from discovery. "Oh! It's a pleasure to meet you. I hope you're enjoying your hubby during his time off."

That's when the vibe suspended. Jade's regard couldn't stay off of Launz, but not in a lecherous manner. Trust me: I'd seen that since we'd been here from several women. But Mrs. Bailey here seemed to be intrigued…or pleased.

"Coach!" Devaughn appeared behind Jade.

"On my way, Devaughn," Launz assured. "Well, it was good running into you, Jade. Unfortunately, it's on the way to a meeting—"

"I'm sorry." She sported a silly expression. "But Trent and I are having a dinner, inviting our couple-friends. I wish I'd known you had a family. I would have extended an invitation to you already… Nye, right?"

When it looked as though Launz was about to speak, possibly to correct, I clipped him. "Well, that's very nice of you. We'd love to come. Please, let me know if there's anything I can assist with. Launz has been dying to connect with the *Kings* family any way he can. We'll be there."

"Oh, great!" She didn't conceal her excitement. If Trent Bailey wanted to give Launz a hard time to the point of headaches, it was clear his wife was on a different wave.

"Good! I'll get your number from Coach's assistant?" I nodded, knowing damn well no one here had my number, not even Launz. "We're gonna get you plugged in, woman." She finally moved, sauntering between Launz and me.

"Looking forward to it." I turned to Launz, who didn't appear half as amused as me or nearly as elated as Trent's wife.

"Nye, this is work."

"And the *Kings* couldn't have selected a better head coach." I then whispered, "If being cool with his wife will leverage enough trust to get that dragon off your back, I'm down." I shrugged. "Go to your meeting. Looks like I'll be giving my number to your assistant, Devaughn."

He shook his head. "Devaughn is the receptionist. My assistant's name is Russell. Devaughn can help you locate him."

"Do you want my number?"

Launz stumbled. "Nye."

I rolled my eyes and laughed. "I'll just get yours from Zo and text you mine."

Winking, I stepped off toward the reception area to speak to Devaughn.

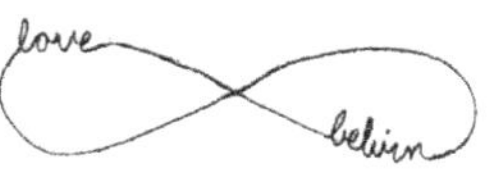

"Everybody seems to want a credit report. Neither one of us have any, though," Zo lamented in my ear.

"The two places you told me she liked wants one, too?"

"Yup. Monica tried to warn me about this." He groaned in my ear as I held the phone. "This shit seems so impossible!"

"What can I do to support you?"

"Actually...now that you mention it..." Zo dallied.

"What is it, Alaunzo?"

"My cousin, Lenora's, getting married in a few weeks."

"Okay...?" My attention went to the door of the café where a woman of Asian descent and a school-aged kid strolled out.

"And I want you to come."

My forehead wrinkled. "To a wedding?"

"Yeah," he exhaled into the phone. "I know it sounds weird. It's my mom's first cousin. But my cousins, my age, have had a few things to say about me not having a real father since we were younger. It's something I never liked. And as awful as it sounds, I wanna stunt on them a little. You know?"

That gave room for pause. It reminded me of this very complex, absolutely fucked up predicament we were in, Zo and me.

Abso-fucking-lutely...

"When is it, exactly?"

"The end of next month. Grams gave the specific date when she needed to RSVP for me last week. I can't remember but can get that to you ASAP."

"Wouldn't I need to RSVP?" When he didn't reply in sync with our previous rhythm, I called out, "Zo?"

"I kinda did already. You and Gena," his bass so soft, vulnerable.

I had zero interest in attending a wedding where I knew no one. Shit. I'd just done that in January and the only save for that event was a piece of American ass at a renowned European landmark.

"Don't leave me hanging, kid. If I'm expected, I'll come hold you down without a doubt. Send the info to Monica and I'll be there."

"Fuck," he breathed, sounding relieved. The expression twisted my gut. "Thanks for this. You have no idea what it means, man."

When the door to the restaurant opened again with random patrons exiting, I thought to ask, "How do you think your mother will feel about this?"

"Oh! I haven't told her yet. I spoke to my Grams about it and she told me to shoot my shot."

My lips protruded. *Really?*

"Interesting..."

"Oh, hey! That's Coach Gilchrist calling me. He wants to meet up tonight to talk about one of the trainers he thinks I'll work well with. By the way, he told me to tell you what's up and congrats."

The door to the coffee shop opened again, and this time a familiar frame with hair winding over her shoulders exited first. After her was an average height cat. He wore a fitted cap, but not in youthful fashion. He was clearly a middle-aged man. Suit jacket with jeans and shoes.

"Give him my regards. I'll hit you later."

"Okay. Bye."

"Bye, Zo."

I dropped the phone and glanced up. Ol' boy took Nye by the top of her ass and pulled her into himself. Hand splayed with possession, he cued her. With ease, she tilted her head and met him in a kiss.

Damn...

Seeing Nye so tempered and cooperative was a sight. I snickered to myself as my phone chirped with a text from my assistant.

Russell: ***just got a call from Alphonsos. arriving in less than two hours***

I dropped the phone as the driver was getting out of the front seat. Nye was approaching the truck. He opened the door across from me for her. A clean, floral zephyr drifted into the truck.

"Hey," she greeted noncommittal, fingering her dark tresses as she adjusted into the backseat across from me.

"Are you in any rush to get back to Jersey?"

"My sister's in Philly and wants to link up, but I told her I didn't know what time I'd be back in town. Why?"

"Apparently, a shitload of my furniture is being delivered today. My assistant got the heads up just a couple of hours ago and can't be there to receive it. It should only be a couple hours and then we'll hit the road."

"Oh." She readjusted her body in the seat. "That's fine. My child is grown and I'm unemployed. No work in the morning." Nye winked less spiritedly, then went to her phone.

I nodded to the driver, prompting him to pull off.

"So.." I breathed, feeling restless and underwhelmed at the same time. "How was your playdate with your man?"

"Oh," she chirped again. "I was a well-behaved little girl, daddy. What's my reward?"

That quip shocked the shit out of me and I tossed my head back, laughing my ass off. Leave it to Nye to consistently throw me askew with her wit.

"Here you go," he murmured, handing me one of the bags as he brisked through the kitchen.

"Mmmm..." I hummed in anticipation, placing it on the counter to dig through it. "I'm starving. Hope this place is good."

"I've had it before. No complaints."

As we pulled out the contents of the bag across from each other, I observed out loud, "Chinese recipes from a Japanese restaurant."

Launz shrugged, hiding his irritation. "Works for me."

We unpacked paper plates and utensils. We even ordered beverages from the Japanese restaurant nearest his place here in Connecticut. Similar to Jersey, Launz had a standalone, one-family property in a suburban neighborhood. According to him, there were a few Black families here. When we arrived two hours ago, he showed me around. The place was sparsely furnished, which was why we were there.

Launz had sofas in his living room, but only two tables. He didn't even have the rug beneath what furniture was there. However, he had a savvy stereo with speakers planted throughout the house. *Of course!* The man loved music. The first thing he did when we arrived was power it on. So making that a priority made sense to me. His kitchen dining set was here, but no plates.

"I think these'll help." He handed me metal serving spoons as I began opening the food containers.

How timely...

There were utensils, but no plates or drinkware. The house had four bedrooms, only one of which had a bed. A long and impossibly wide bed without a headboard, but mounted with a bountiful comforter and countless pillows sat in the middle of the room. Beside it was a folding table holding random items.

"You mind fixing mine, too?" Launz asked, sauntering out of the kitchen. "Yeah, Russell," he began another call with his assistant.

Oh...

That felt domesticated. It wasn't a problem for me, though. Today felt strange enough as it was. Seeing Ernie had totally thrown me off-kilter. Then being here at Launz's place longer than either one of us anticipated was another unexpected event. The delivery should have happened over an hour ago. When the day grew longer, Launz dismissed the driver for the day as he'd been on shift since early this morning to drive into Jersey to pick us up. Launz would have to call the contracted company to request another driver and car when the furniture finally arrived. Thank goodness I thought to bring my laptop and chargers with me for the ride.

When my phone vibrated in front of me and Ernie's name appeared, I ignored it. That sent my perturbation to a new level.

"You got anything to drink here?"

When I heard Launz speaking in the next room, I was reminded of his call. So agitated, I'd forgotten that quickly.

Seconds later, he reappeared. "The iced tea you ordered from the restaurant isn't correct?"

"I was referring to something stronger." I supplied a dejected grin.

"Oh." His dark irises circled. "Shit," he whispered. "The only thing I've got here is *Mauve*."

"What? *Mauve* and no wine for you?" Even I knew from this short time, Launz was a vino man.

"Yeah. It was a part of a welcoming gift from Eli Richardson."

"I guess it'll have to do."

Launz snorted. "Since when does *Mauve* just have to do?" He left out and returned mumbling, "I know you get down with vodka, but *Mauve* ain't nothing to sneeze at."

He was certainly right. The brandy line was top shelf but, as he said, vodka was my jam.

"And that's the limited edition!"

Launz observed the bottle. "Richardson's no novice. I wouldn't expect anything less from him."

"And you haven't cracked that baby open yet? That was made during World War I."

He shrugged. "You want some? It's the least I can do for having you up here so long."

"You'll have one with me?" When he hesitated, studying the bottle, I pushed. "C'mon!"

Launz peered around the room. "No glasses—oh, wait." He ambled out of the kitchen again and returned with shot glasses. "These came in the package with the liquor."

"Well, aren't they coming in handy? Pour us some!"

Launz peeled the foil and went about opening the bottle. He poured two glasses after rinsing them.

He handed me a shot glass. Even they were fancy, beautifully designed with dual tigers and bold calligraphy. "Ready?" I asked.

"What are we? Back in college, excited about one-and-a-half ounces of brown juice?"

"I'm excited about—" I struggled to think of something—anything. "I'm excited to be alive and drinking limited edition *Mauve*!" Launz's brows met. "And what about you?"

"I'm excited about eating." He raised his glass.

"Woohoo!"

We met in the air on a clink. Launz eyed me suspiciously as I tossed my head back to down the strong oaky, citrus notes. He was just seconds after me, making less of a face than me when swallowing. I finished with our plates, and Launz and I settled in the living room to eat. Sitting on the plush leather sofa, we dug into our food, allowing the sounds of chewing to compete with the music. When I came up for air, I found myself gazing around. The virtual emptiness of the place brought a question to mind.

"You've never toured with any of the musicians you've recorded with?"

He shook his head, licking those tan lips. "I did a leg of an American tour with Brielle when her lead touring guitarist had to have surgery on his knee. I hated that shit."

"Why?"

"Honestly? I don't like staying in hotel rooms like that. The short stays for months on end. It's enough to have to do it for football about eleven times a year. Then if I want to do any personal travel—but, at least, that would be a longer stay. Touring is different. You can easily be in a different room every night sometimes. That's not for me." His words were definitive.

"I guess I never viewed it that way. Do you travel often?"

"I do when I can, I guess. My friends are always having events all over the place, so I tab those into traveling."

"What about vacationing?"

"I guess it can be all the same for me."

"You go alone?"

"Do you vacation alone?"

I laughed. "Never."

"And *who* do you go with? Because I'm guessing that's what you're hinting at."

My eyes ballooned as I chewed. "Not really. When I go away, it's—well, obviously—with Zo or my girlfriends." I shrugged with my head. "Once in a while—"

"With Ernie?"

That made me laugh again. "No! Well... Kinda. Yeah."

Launz's head popped back and he smirked. "You sure?"

I rolled my eyes. "That's a loaded answer. For which, I need another shot. And so do you! Come on."

Slowly, he placed his food down and refreshed our glasses. After downing it, Launz took long gulps of his water.

"You ready to stabilize that answer?"

I couldn't help with the giggles. This was so embarrassing. "So a few years ago, about a year after I met him, Ernie asked to take me away. I kept blowing him off until I couldn't. So he booked a trip to Aruba..." I sat with my eyes wide and mouth open.

"And?"

"And was sure to include a suite for my girlfriends." I cringed.

Launz blinked deeply, those long dark lashes clapping. "The fuck?"

Regret washed over me. "I know!"

"He let you bring your friends?" The blinking wouldn't stop, and all I could think of was encouraging his thoughts of me being the worst kind of woman.

I rolled my eyes, falling back into the sofa with one hand tightly securing the paper plate. The other attempted to cover my face.

"He wanted to go away with me. Ernie has always said he wants to make me happy—even though we're not exactly together."

"So, a man who tells you he wants to make you happy and go away with you ends up footing an Aruban vacation for you and your girls? That's what makes you happy?"

"It's what made me feel safe agreeing to go away with him. If it makes me look any less horrible, I told him not to do it. It was his idea after I told him I wanted to go away with my girls." I opened one eye to peer over to him.

Launz dropped his plate on the coffee table. "That's a lot of bread."

"Ernie's an investment broker. He's been at it for a while." My voice shrank when I shared, "He's an older man."

"I could tell that from what little I saw of him earlier."

I sat up. "You saw him?"

He jerked a shoulder. "When he walked you out." My eyes squeezed closed. "Nye, if he's your man, what's the problem with—"

"He's not my man! Okay?" The squeal in my claim annoyed the hell out of me.

"Okay. Then what is he?"

"He's a friend." Launz scoffed. "A very good friend!" I amended.

His palms rose in the air. "Hey… No judgment here. Just empathizing with the man is all."

"Oh, like you haven't done anything extraordinary for pussy."

This time, Launz's eyes flashed wild. "Is that what he did it for? A piece of ass?"

I shook my head, exhaling. We didn't have sex in Aruba. "No. Not exactly."

"Wait. I'm so confused here."

"Let's change the subject."

"Oh! Is that all I have to say when you pry about the women in my life, when I bring them home for you to give us a show of your ass cheeks, or worse: me finding your vibrator in my bed?"

Bile shot to my throat and I fought to keep it down. My breathing grew shallow to make that happen. "*I*—uhhh…" Breathe! "I didn't mean to."

"Didn't mean to what?" his tone even, volume low. "Masturbate in my bed or leave your tool behind that aided you doing it?"

"I'm sorry, Launz."

Instead of acknowledging me, he picked up his plate and returned to eating. I tried, but no longer tasted anything. For me, it was a distraction from how crappy I felt.

"So, he spent all that dough and still no ass?" He resurrected the topic.

"For more details, you'll have to take another shot with me. I need it to help loosen up and vomit my shit."

On a deep inhale, Launz reached over and poured us each another shot. We swallowed them back at the same time.

When his dark, piercing eyes met me, there was a softness to his insistent inquiry. "What did he get out of 'making you happy' by way of tricking on your girlfriends?"

"A hand job," I whispered, eyes wide.

For a while, Launz seemed to be stunned into silence. That was until he uttered, "Is that what this is? Is that what I am to you now—back then? A goddamn trick?"

~FOURTEEN

PRESENT DAY

"WHOA! THAT'S PRETTY LOW, LAUNZ!"

I think the shit hurt my feelings.

Launz cocked his head to the side and raised his forehead, voice controlled when he uttered, "Is it?"

"It *is*, coming from someone who claims to perform tricks for the women in his life."

"It's not the same as being taken advantage of by someone who wants nothing more from you than you *can* give them."

He had a point. Sex was typically the commodity and could be an even exchange for consensual parties. But that's only if both are interested.

"I'm not sexually attracted to him—per se," I tried to qualify. "Ernie's sweet and thoughtful, but he's never given me husband or family vibes."

Launz chuckled. "So you think he's ugly, but find his money attractive? His adulation fuels you?"

"No! God, no!" Yes, I enjoyed the flattery, but… "Ernie isn't ugly at all. In fact, he's a rather handsome man."

"But you're not attracted to him?"

Launz was mellow, too smooth with his temperament in spite of his opposition. It felt as though he enjoyed pushing my buttons. Still, I was convinced of his convictions. The man was condemning me with unflappable charm.

"Those are not mutually exclusive situations. There are women who I believe are absolutely beautiful, but I have no romantic interest in them. Ernie and I have been good to each other."

"On his dime with no ass." He nodded his understanding.

This conversation began to grate on my nerves. "Launz, I'm no broke bitch or damsel in distress. I have my own career, one that affords me a comfortable lifestyle I can maintain without a man. Ernie has his agenda that I'm not necessarily with."

"But you won't let him go, and stick with handjobs instead."

This was all wrong. "I didn't say that."

"Then what do you do to pay rent for space on that man's schedule?" He leaned over, placing his elbows on his knees. "All working wealthy men have one thing in common: a shortage of hours in a day. If he's making time for you, the least you could do is be real with him." He shrugged coolly. "Honesty should be easier to pursue than sex. But I see you don't do either."

"I never said that," I hissed.

"Then tell me, Nye." He sat back in his chair adjacent to me, and rested the back of his head on threaded fingers. The knotted bulges in his arms had me ripping my eyes away. "What makes you worthy of a man's time?"

"Can we drop this?" I whined, leaning back on the sofa again.

There was a relieving pause of words. Xscape's "*Softest Place on Earth*" flowed throughout the house. I caught Launz's fingers flickering in the same fashion they did when he played the guitar, though I was sure he had no idea he was doing it. We caught eyes at some point, and I laughed when rolling mine away. His smirk didn't go unnoticed.

"I'm curious about this because I need to know how my son's been influenced over the years. Does he believe reciprocity of a mutual agreement isn't possible? Is that why he's moving Gena out here?"

My head flew to him. "That's a sore spot and you know it."

"It can be for me as well, if it's true."

"What exactly are you asking?"

"Who are you fucking? If it's not the man who spends money on you, then who the hell is it?"

"I'm going to need another shot for that. And you know the drill: I'm not doing it alone. Transparency ain't a fun place to be alone."

This time, I reached for the bottle of *Mauve* and refilled our glasses. I noticed Launz hesitating after I took my swig. Finally, he complied.

When he placed the glass down, stretching his mouth from the burn, Launz groused, "That will be my last."

I gasped. "Why?"

"Too much of that shit makes me nasty." His tongue darted from his mouth, quickly swiping his lower lip.

"What? Brandy?"

"Nah." He snorted, relaxing back into his seat. "*Mauve*."

"But you had it that night at *DiFillippo's* with Zo and me."

"Two glasses with ice. And that was only because I had some place to be later that night. It wasn't random at all."

Oh…

"Well, that's some female shit. I thought a little liquor only made us horny."

Launz stretched his legs, widening his groin. His hands threaded again, head resting against them. "And here you are, privy to my little secret. Now it's time to reciprocate. Tell me a dirty little secret."

My face wrinkled. "This can get ugly."

"Oh, let's not let it."

"I need alcohol for this type of transparency, and you're saying you have an adverse reaction to the only alcohol we have available. We need to introduce a new penalty."

He raised a brow. "What do you have in mind?"

"For every dose of confidence we need, a shot must be ingested. For those questions we refuse to answer—for whatever reason—we…" My eyes circled around the half-furnished space. Then when the idea came, I returned to him. "Strip. Take off a layer of clothing."

Launz's inspective gaze went from his shirt to his jeans. Then it searched me head to toe. I wore a dress. I'd kicked off my boots and cropped denim jacket when it was clear we'd be here a while and ordered food.

I was screwed. And tipsy at this point. Launz and I weren't close to eating half the food on our plates.

"This setup sounds very Nye'ish—at least, what I recall of her. But I'm game." He gestured with his hand for me to go.

Sighing my fate away, I began, "I've had my encounters here and there over the years. Sex for me hasn't always been…consistent because it hasn't always been…great. The best part of it is having control and it always being on my terms. Preconceived expectations, yet the most pleasurable outcomes."

"For who?"

"For them—him." I tossed my arms in the air. "You have so many women in your life. Even Zo mentioned the few who stopped over while Gena was in town."

"I need to speak to my son about pass protection."

I had no idea what that meant. "I'm guessing that's a football term."

"He needs to learn how to protect his quarterback is all."

"Okay, but that doesn't answer my question."

"You never asked one."

"How many of them are you fucking?"

"If you've been to my home, it's only because we've entered a point of intimacy that allows you access to it."

"So, all of them?" I began to do the math in my head, remembering his distaste for hotel rooms. "Do they all know?"

"They all know I'm single, yes. They know I'm available to them, yes. Do they know each other? No."

"Don't be cynical." I rolled my eyes.

"I'm just being thorough with my answer. What about you? How many men have you been intimate with at a time?"

I went for the *Mauve,* pouring myself a shot and downing it. "Two."

His eyes widened as his head swung back. "Big girl. Did they know?" I shook my head. "Was Ernie one of them?"

Rolling my eyes, I admitted, "He was, but you have to remember: with Ernie, I don't get sexually stimulated. I provide him with it. At the time, I ran across a guy who I found sexually attractive and was lucky enough to have chemistry with him."

"Sexual chemistry?" I nodded. "What does that entail for you?"

I couldn't look at him. This was getting too personal. I didn't even talk to my girlfriends about this shit.

"Have you ever had more than one woman—at the same time?"

Launz's eyes lit ablaze. "Are you into that?"

My face tightened. "No. I'm not talking about me. It's your turn. Have you?"

"Sure, I have." His tone was soft.

My eyes rolled up to him. "How many?"

His smirk was the most cunning I'd ever seen of him. "Three. But I've since decided two is my preference. You can't tell me you haven't considered it." His face opened further and I could see more of his teeth beyond his beard.

"I've been asked to and, yes, I considered it. I was told it would be all about him, but I declined."

As I curled my legs beneath me, "*Where I Wanna Be*" began to flow. I couldn't quickly recall the artist, but definitely associated the conviction.

"Seems you don't like putting in much work: you may actually enjoy it."

"How can you make that assumption?"

"What?"

"That I don't want to put in any work for sex."

He shrugged so adorably. "Reasonable deduction. Handjobs are not an act of intimacy."

I cringed. His words had power.

"You're misinformed, but okay."

Launz snorted, head bounced back slightly. "Answer my question."

"What?" my tone defensive.

"What does sexual chemistry entail for you? How do you satisfy a man?"

"How do I answer that?"

He shrugged as his tongue rolled over the corner of his mouth. "Honestly." I reached for the brandy— "Don't you dare take another shot. You're the mother of my child and as much as I have my issues with you, I can't have you shit-faced on my watch."

My clit contracted and I felt shame. Launz and my days of anything remotely sexual had expired years ago.

"I feel like I'm out here alone, so I need the courage."

Wordlessly and slowly, Launz reached for the bottle and made himself another serving. He didn't hesitate throwing it back. Then he tossed his chin, prompting me to continue.

Donnell Jones! How could I forget his name?

I felt the swirl in my head. I was definitely tipsy. Who grew up in the early two-thousands and forgot Donnell Jones? Or this song?

That's when I decided I couldn't answer the question. Doing it would bare too much of me. Launz may have been more attentive to me tonight than he had since I'd stormed back into his life, but he still didn't trust me. The *Mauve* was providing a moment of reprieve.

So, I climbed from the couch and bent over for the hem of my dress. My body shivered as I pulled it over my thighs and stomach. When it was over my head, I fingered my curls in place. Then I pulled the wedgie from my butt cheeks before tossing the dress on the other side of the sofa. I sat down and was then finally able to look at Launz.

"You're a beautiful woman, Ms. Taylor."

I scoffed. "I do okay at my advanced age."

"You don't seem so convinced. It's probably the handjob flow that prevents you from feeling as good as you look when with a real man."

"Sayeth the guy with five to ten women in his bed."

He chuckled soundlessly as I sat with my chin resting in my palms over my lap. "I don't have many women in my bed at all," tone still agreeable to peace. Finesse. "It's too bad you couldn't define sexual chemistry. We could've shared knowledge."

"You giving me tips?" I spit in laughter.

He twisted his neck and lifted his brows, shrugging. "Perhaps."

"Then what's sexual chemistry for you?"

"Being able to identify in a woman a need I can fulfill and her agreeing that I may do just that."

I couldn't help but laugh again. "Really?" Sounded like bullshit.

"Really. It's that simple for me, yet not a simplistic task. I can't have that with every woman I encounter, which is why your idea of me having a bevy of women in my bed is fucking laughable."

"I'm selective about who I sleep with, too. Most women are."

"Then what's so funny when I explain how I am?"

"Because claiming to see a woman across the room and sniff out what she needs sexually is a bit far-reaching, Launz. I can't believe you're saying this."

"Why?"

"Because the Launz I knew would never. He'd just…" I shrugged.

"Let you decide handjobs would suffice?"

I had no idea why I found that funny. Actually, I did. "Oh, I gave you more than handjobs."

"You damn sure did."

"And you seemed quite satisfied to me."

"I was."

"Then…" I shrugged, not understanding why I was so uncomfortable with this topic. Disturbed and…aroused. "Okay. How do you determine what a woman needs sexually?"

"By listening, paying attention to what she says and what she doesn't." His lips pushed upward. "By observing her reactions to me and my body."

"Then what do you do?"

There was a spell of time before Launz's hand went to his waist and he unbuckled his belt. My throat dried and squeezed at the implication. Then he scooted up in his chair and pulled his sweater over his head. I could see the cashmere brush over his golden skin. What was odd was when he tossed it on top of my dress, I could see a piece of his undershirt inside of the sweater.

His body clothed was so damn deceptive. The skin on Launz's shaven chest and abdomen was smooth, but its surface cut and hilly. Dark nipples pebbled and down-turned on his swollen pecs. And when he reclined in his chair, the muscles of his ribcage bulged and his abs rippled, honey skin folding absent of fat beneath. Chest free of ink, but arms both full sleeves of artwork, far more than what he had when I was a kid.

I cleared my throat then whispered, "That was two pieces."

"I'm a little warm. Plus, I know there's another question coming I don't want to answer."

Launz fixed both of us fresh shots. He drank his right away. I stared inside the golden liquid for a spell. My pulse beat fast in my neck and nipples hardened, growing into tight buds beneath the lace of my bra.

"What's your..." I couldn't gather my words. Launz waited patiently with his head cocked to the side. So calm. "How do you know you're...doing it right?"

He took a deep breath, mouth twisted in contemplation. Launz then crooked his fingers. "Come here, Nye."

My lungs seized at the baritone and authority in his request. I had a moment to think, didn't feel an ounce of unease from it. *But still...* This was Zo's father. He was a life I negatively impacted. Then I had the nerve to come back and perceptively rub shit in his face again. Launz owed me nothing. In fact, I felt I should be protecting him. From me. He had a functional and, seemingly, satisfied life. I didn't want to detract from that any more than I had with Zo.

Finally, I tossed back the shot, feeling the scorch down my throat that couldn't rival the one in my core. Then I stood from the space I misted on the leather couch and toed over to his wide spread thighs. His aroma at this proximity sent me.

Launz's expression was placid as he brushed over my body with his eyes. His inked hand reached to finger his dark, thick beard. "Don't be so nervous."

I couldn't help it.

"You don't have to do *thi—*"

My head fell back when his lips met my stomach. The hairs of his face tickled my skin wickedly. When his big hands cupped the back of my thighs, a mewl left my throat. His tongue roved around my belly button. My bra was unclasped and breasts dropped heavily.

Heaving, I asked, "What would Camay think about you doing this?" A torture question I just *had* to busy myself with.

Cool air hit the side of my stomach where his tongue trailed. My eyes rolled to the back of my head. "She's too busy thinking about you thinking about me."

Intuitive woman she is…

His mouth lifted to the skin beneath my right nipple, and the sensations from such an undiscovered area scared the hell out of me. When his hand slipped beneath my panties, my knees buckled and I latched onto his shoulders. Launz's practiced fingers brushed over my swollenness, rolling the evidence of my arousal around at the same pace as his tongue on my right nipple and his thumb on my left.

Involuntarily, my hips rolled against his pressure. Dizzy pleasure swarmed my brain and the croons of Carl Thomas' *"Giving You All My Love"* was but a distant sound beneath the humming of my entire frame.

He pushed a finger inside me so smoothly. I never liked being fingered, feeling men believed pleasure could be derived from simply being stabbed vaginally. Launz's thrusts were soft at first, explorative rubs all around. When we caught a rhythm, I ground against his massage, bouncing in no time at all. Cleverly, he polished my clit with his thumb, building a storm in my groin. His fingers, thumbs, and mouth had created a powerful harmony.

The buildup was so powerful, I held onto his shoulders with my head tossed back, bracing myself. And to further influence my response to his touch, Launz lifted my right leg, placing the bottom of my foot on his knee. It was clever and manipulating, indeed, opening me to himself and forcing my vulnerability. I thrusted into his touch.

"There you go," he groaned, so encouraging. "Let me see."

I chased pleasure with jerky coordination in my spine and legs until it wrapped around me like a blanket and rained over me like a shower. I cried out in pleasure unlike any other time I recalled in my life. It had been so long since I'd been given an orgasm, life suddenly felt cruel. My chest jerked one way and hips another, but both into *him*.

My breathing was uncontrolled, riotous. I couldn't gather the control to peel myself from him. Neither did Launz rush me to. He remained still, applying reverential kisses to my belly. The act speared my chest. My stretch marks from carrying Zo were visible. That stabilized my spinning.

Launz, holding my body into place, rose from the chair until he towered me.

"You're beautiful, Nye. Thanks for that," he whispered so softly into my ear, his natural bass had almost disappeared. It was as though the intimate proximity was needed for such a private message.

Then his mouth reached my neck, tonguing me slowly. My eyes squeezed. I didn't want this to end, no matter how much I knew it should have never begun. Shakily, my fingers raked up his hard back to the kink of his head. I pulled his head to meet his face with my own. Launz's eyes opened lazily as he studied mine. Reaching from my toes, I lifted to capture his mouth.

Smoothly, he scraped his beard against my chin, then cheek. His mouth lifted to my ear again. "You can't kiss me with lips that touched another man's just a few hours ago."

My body tensed in rebuke. "I'm sorry."

"Don't be." Our eyes met again, his in…adulation. "You deserve the attention you received from us today."

I panicked. "Is that it?"

He smiled, eyes tight. Launz found humor in my…need. "I'm a generous man, Nye. But I've had premium cognac and can't promise more without..." He brushed his thickness against my stomach. I convulsed, eyes closing.

"Please tell me you have condoms."

With my head wedged in his big palms, Launz nibbled on my chin. "One."

I nodded, licking my dry lips. "Okay."

"Okay?"

I nodded again. He took me at the hips, prompting me to open for him. Launz reached down and grabbed me by the back of my thighs, hiking me in the air. I straddled him, wanting to kiss him so bad, but respecting his stance. I had kissed Ernie and had never regretted it more than I did tonight. We were moving and so horny, I needed to put my mouth somewhere, so I found his neck and licked.

His breaths grew affected by my touch and it thrilled me, spurring me to do it again. While taking the stairs, he managed my breast in his mouth and I arched into it, moaning unrepentantly. The sucking sounds drove me wild, igniting the roll of my hips. Jaheim followed us with each step. "*Long as I Live.*" I gripped the thick kinky twists on his head. How hadn't I told him the style worked so well on him? I admired grown man Launz. Unlike the adult Nye, he was stronger and better.

He mounted the bed with me clasped to his chest, laying me down gently. Then Launz's mouth and hands were all over my body. He caressed, licked, and strummed places as though I was his favorite instrument. His pace was controlled and consistent. He licked my inner thighs and even the bottom of my cheeks, but his mouth never touched my throbbing sex. I watched him apply the condom to his length I no longer held memory of.

Then Launz lifted from my shaky body, stretched out like a ragdoll beneath him. The second his hands reached his thick shaft, the speakers belted, "*I'm a player...*" The three words set the tone for the remainder of the evening for me.

When he turned me onto my side, straddled my leg and entered me, the lyrics played. I watched him thrust inside me, fitting himself comfortably until I felt him at the helm of my core. Launz wanted my attention all over him as his abs contracted, triceps flexed, and shoulders bulged with each roll of his pelvis. He lifted one leg over his shoulder and thumbed my clit so conversely until I convulsed in another orgasm. I cried out helplessly

"...so right now, I'm gonna play..."

The song was long over on the playlist, but now on rotation in my head. He turned me over onto my hands and knees. And—my god—his glide into my pussy had me deceptively feeling I could cum. Launz pounded into me, violating the fat of my hips and ass. He grabbed them at the sides while our flesh met together in consecutive slaps. I felt his thumb near my anus, pressing on the rim. It was a lude and delicious turn-on. God, I was so wet. With each impale, my clit swelled and pussy slushed. Getting lost in all the sensations, my eyes closed to a squeeze.

This is Launz.

Alaunzo Pierce from Rutgers.

I tried to process that because I'd always had a piece of him with me, his presence seemed like a lifetime ago.

And he wasn't all of this...

Launz pulled out of me and flipped me onto my back. Surprisingly, I scurried into participation, wanting him inside me again. He stretched my thighs further apart and plunged inside.

"Agh!" I cried from the force, opening my eyes to see the beauty of him.

Launz's chest glistened with sweat as it flexed when he trundled his hips. He reached over, cupping my breasts without losing stride. The tips of my fingers reached his abdomen, but I needed more of him to hold. The ride was bumpy as he filled me to the hilt. Launz's ropey thighs were spread wide as he rocked into me. His nostrils were flared and tongue peeked through his lips. I needed an anchor, a chaser from the animalistic view of him. Why couldn't he just kiss me?

"'Cause I'm a player..."

I grabbed my head, back arched over the pillowy mattress. Frustrated, I swept my hair into my face.

"Not now, Nye," he grunted, pulling my hands down.

Then he palmed my shoulders so close to my neck and began to thrust even harder. It felt good, unbelievably good. I lifted my legs higher and spread them wider. Launz was demanding and I was helpless. His hands at my neck and thumbs on my throat, I held my breath, enduring his plunges. That was until I felt a growing sensation in my core. It hit fast and hard as it culminated in an explosion.

"Oh, shit," I panted, using language never necessary during sex. "Oh, shit!" I wailed.

My breasts bounced, caressing the air as I imploded. Launz's breathing turned ragged behind mine as his hips worked impossibly faster. His grip around my neck tightened and I wasn't afraid. I watched through a sheet of my wild hair when his head tossed back, beard toward the ceiling. His impales suspended on a final thrust inside of me. I could feel the thickness of his cock pulse feverishly, similar to my walls around him. His grip loosened, to my regret, and Launz pulled out and rolled off of me.

"My fucking MILF," he wheezed into the air.

~FIFTEEN

PRESENT DAY

"*My fucking MILF*," slipped from my mind and I had no idea how I let it.

Under normal circumstances, I would've measured my words around her, but right now, I was too exhausted and unusually satiated to do the double-thinking typically required around Nye. I knew I'd be met with regret in the morning, but for now, I needed to rest.

And that's what I did. After pulling off the condom and tossing it in the trashcan, I found the remote for the stereo system on the table and powered off the music. Collapsing onto the bed and pulling her softness into my fold had never felt so welcoming.

The house phone blaring in my ear stirred me from a deep, restful sleep. I peeled my eyes open and peered around the room. Nye's hair covered her ruddy, bare back. Another ring ripped my attention from her.

I rolled over for the phone on the floor. "Hello?"

"Coach, *Alphonso's* outside."

I recognized Russell's voice, but… "Who?"

"The furniture people. They're outside. They've been out there for a while. I tried calling your cell several times, sir."

"Shit." I closed my eyes, recalling why I was here. "I'll be right down."

"Okay."

I hung up the phone and rolled off the bed. When I slid into my jeans, I felt the weight of my cell in the pocket. Rubbing my eyes, I made my way out of the room to the stairs. Then my thoughts turned to arranging transportation home. I pulled out my phone and tapped to the app needed to make those accommodations.

I was just at the point of selecting the type of vehicle when I made it to the front door. Coincidentally, that was also when I could smell the garlic and sesame oil from the takeout and realized I didn't throw out the food. There were two guys waiting on the porch, one sitting and the other leaning on a post.

"Morning," I greeted. "Even though I was expecting you yesterday evening."

"Sorry about that, Mr. Pierce. There was a huge mix-up in our system—"

"A mix-up?" As I heard the words shooting through the air like bullets, a sweep of air whipped past as did a cascade of white cotton. Nye's one hand was in the air, the other clasping a sheet wrapped around her naked body. "And you didn't think to communicate this right away? Do you know what a grave inconvenience your incompetent system caused?"

What the fuck?

"Hey... Again, I'm really sorry about earlier. I shouldn't have gotten involved."

I couldn't even look at her. My eyes closed and I took a deep breath. She'd already apologized twice, and I low key wondered if there was a double entendre to her sentiment. Either way, I didn't have time for the repetition.

Earlier, I contemplated driving us back down myself, but had follow-up work to do with the *Kings'* general manager, Rashad Williams, and the rest of the coaches for the draft. It was just a few days away and when I thought I'd be working on this last night at home, my plans were derailed, thanks to the incompetent furniture company. That gave me less time to do what needed to be done.

Then I turned her away. "Nye, it's fine. Completely fine. I told you that."

She murmured, "Then why do I feel this coldness emanating from you again."

"Again?" I whispered, keeping with a respectful tone.

She blinked, appearing to be thinking. "Well, I've felt it since January, and you warmed a little since letting me stay at your place. But now..." She twisted her neck, combing the back of her hair as though uncomfortable.

"Now what?"

She swallowed, licking her lips. Nye's face sobered. "Since last night. You feel colder now, and I wonder if it has anything to do with last night."

I honestly didn't feel up to this conversation. We were in the back of an SUV with a stranger transporting us. Though my patience was on the short side with this girl, I would not say anything publicly to possibly disrespect the mother of my child.

"Out of all the things that occurred yesterday possibly affecting my mood today, you think sex is one of them?" Nye shrugged, eyes bouncing around. "Last night was…fun. It was a moment, but nothing to upset me. Don't sweat it."

I kept my gaze on her, waiting for her to cue the conversation was over.

I knew it wasn't when her face tightened. "So, it was a moment?"

"Did I miss something?"

"Did you—" Nye snatched her eyes away and readjusted herself in her chair. "I thought, at the very least, it could have been an opportunity for you to see me as more than a boarder or someone you—"

"What? See you as someone trustworthy all of a sudden?"

"Excuse me?"

"Nye, last night was last night. It doesn't change anything for me. I'm not angry or regretful. I'm simply trying to get work done."

"No. You said you don't trust me, Launz."

"Have you given me a reason to?" My face tightened when I amended, "Ever?"

Her lips pushed out as her head jolted back and Nye nodded. "Okay…"

Okay. Now please let me get back to this email…

22 Years ago| New Jersey

"What is it, boy?" she playfully shouted. Her eyes roved around the back yard of the old three-story house. "I hope there ain't no dogs around here." I shook my head, trying not to laugh. In fact, I couldn't laugh if I wanted to. I

was nervous as hell, my stomach in fucking knots. "Launz, these bags are heavy!" She stomped her foot.

"Okay," I finally found the balls to speak again. Her irritation was warranted, especially due to the hour. The sun was down and the temperature had dropped. It was now or never. "Follow me." I moved around her for the stairs.

"Where are we, and will we get mugged?"

Ignoring her, I opened the door to the back porch of the house, which led to a wooden staircase. We traveled past the second-floor apartment and I could hear Nye's heavy breaths.

"You want me to carry those?" I asked, pausing for an answer.

"You can't!" she groused, not breaking stride.

Finally at our destination, I waited for her at the top of the stairs. I couldn't believe how fucking nervous I was. My mouth was dry and palms, filled with Wal-Mart bags, were seriously misty. Hoping the door was unlocked as I was told it would be, I managed to turn the knob. I let out a quiet sigh of relief when it didn't stop turning. Pushing the door open, I saw there was only one light on, a few feet away in the kitchen.

I was able to find another light switch to illuminate the room. The place seemed smaller than when I'd seen it last week during the day. Shit. I was so fucking nervous.

"C'mon inside," I waved her in.

Nye strolled in, eyes swinging left to right under her tight brow line. There wasn't much to see, which was one of many reasons why I was so nervous. After dumping the bags, I rounded her to close, then locked the door and took the bags she held. I waited and waited for a reaction, and I guess I got one when Nye didn't speak for a while.

Just as I was about to suggest we leave, she turned to me. "You didn't want to just get a room? I could have paid for it."

I scrubbed my head with my palms. "Just like I told you in Wal-Mart when you offered, I don't need you to pay for things."

She whipped her neck. "I work just like you do. In fact, I think I make more."

Shaking my head, I tried to explain, "That's not the point, Nye."

She kept inspecting each inch of the place, eyes roving over the walls, sink, broken door leading to the bathroom. "Tell me: what's the point of this place?"

I twisted my mouth, unable to look at her. "Your birthday gift."

"My birthday isn't until next week."

"The guy only starts leases on the first of the month."

Since it was clear I wouldn't get invited to the League *draft that happened last weekend, I knew I had to focus on my plan B. That left room to make this living together thing with Nye possible. I couldn't commit to still being roommates a year from now because it was still my goal to play pro ball. But I wouldn't tell her any of that, not wanting to kill her vibe. Right now, Nye was happy. When the girl smiled, I felt a little dizzy and when she was upset, my fucking chest squeezed. So, hell yeah: I was down with happy Nye.*

"Leases on the first of the—" Her mouth hung open and Nye twisted and turned her spine, taking in the studio apartment again. "You..." She took off into the kitchen, though it was hardly a distance from the living/bedroom. Nye touched the stove, then turned and slapped the countertop. She opened the fridge, then slammed it shut before squealing, "Oh, my god! Are you serious?"

Fuck...

The muscles in my face began to tic, something I ain't never felt before. "It was all I could afford. Nicer places require a credit check and bigger ones cost more money—"

She ran around the wall separating the two rooms and jumped on me. "I can't believe you did this! How much is it?"

"Five-fifty a month." My heart pounded. "Heat and hot water included. I should have asked you—"

"We'll find something better in less than a year." She kissed me, making the smacking sound. My grip on her ass loosened, I was so damn relieved. "I'll find a better job and we'll get something bigger."

"Before you're done with school?"

She nodded. "I don't know a lot about New Jersey, but I do know I don't wanna live in Trenton for long." My eyes dropped to where her boobs met my chest. "You did good, Launz! Really." She jumped off of me. "I can get us a bed this week. I think we can squeeze a full-size mattress in here." Nye strolled near the door. "I see there's only one closet, and that's here. We can get one of those portable closets. My mother got those for us at our last place."

I glanced around the place again, now feeling more confident in my decision. Nye wanted out of her pops' place. And I... I liked being with Nye. It was that simple for me.

"Hey," she called out, and I turned back to her. "We have our own place! Do you know what that makes me?"

My brows met. "Happy?"

She nodded, approaching me with heavy lids. "And horny."

When I opened the bathroom door, Nye was gazing out of the plastic, open blinds of the window. With just a sheet cupped to her naked breasts, she hadn't moved much from where I left her. Her thumb and index finger were rubbing together, reminding me of her booger-picking therapy. The only question was where were they landing because there was no napkin in sight. After tossing the damp towel over the door, I walked over to her, picking up my sweats on the way.

"You good?" She nodded, briefly looking my way. I crawled onto the pallet we made with the bed-in-a-bag we bought from Wal-Mart. "Then why do you look so sad?"

Her mouth twisted in a smirk. "Because I'm hungry." She giggled.

"Again?" When she nodded, I reminded her, "I told you to get something more than the loaded fries from B-Way Burger." We'd stopped there to eat before heading over to Wal-Mart earlier.

"But that's what I was craving all day. Ugh!" She scrubbed her face with her palms. "I hate when my period's due. I get all crazy."

I smiled. "I kinda like your crazy."

She tossed a pillow at me. I was able to duck it while laughing.

"Yeah. That's because I make you cum!"

"Noooo..." I playfully shook my head, huffing. "You make me cum when

your period is nowhere around. But your ass is crazy all the time." When I laughed this time, Nye's smile faded. "What?"

"I love when you do that."

"Do what?"

"Roll your eyes."

"I do not roll my eyes. That's the shit you crazy women do."

Shaking her head, there was a gleam of wonder in her eyes. "You, too. And I can't resist you when you do. I didn't think it was the most masculine thing either...until you." I didn't know what to say to that. Again, happy Nye was my favorite. If her thinking I rolled my eyes like a bitch made her happy, I wouldn't argue with her. "You really are unique. You know that?"

"I do."

She shoved me. "I'm serious! I can't believe you did all of this. Well, I couldn't believe you'd give me a ride home last October from Corey's, but you did."

I squinted one eye and twisted my neck. "I still think you finessed me."

"Couldn't have been that good of finessing, I let you jump my bones a few months later."

"Nah." I snorted, "You jumped my bone, Nye."

Her mouth twisted as though she was busted. "You're right. I think it's you that makes me crazy. You're like this big ball of light. And now that I know you, I can see so much farther for myself."

Damn...

That shit was deep.

"Can I be real with you?" I swallowed hard.

"You better be."

"I feel the same way about you." That shit sounds cheesy as hell. *At least, I could have come up with my own words. "I mean..." I shook my head. "Nye, you be having a nigga tongue-tied."*

"Awwww!" She leaned over and wrapped her arms around me. "I like that I have that effect on someone."

"Huhn? What sense does that make?"

She shrugged. "You're the first guy and possibly the only person who makes me feel...important."

"Well, I'm glad to hear that." I really was. It made me feel less like a

sucker for always going with what she said. Nye had been controlling my actions since asking me for a ride last fall. Lately, she'd been influencing my desires, too.

"Good." She nodded coolly, mocking me. "Because I think we're soulmates."

My eyes went wild. "Whe—" I choked on my spit. "What?"

She shook her head, this time rolling her *eyes. "Let's just change the subject." I knew I should have told her no and remained on topic, but once again, the girl took my damn tongue away. "How much was the deposit?"*

Oh...

"Because he doesn't run credit, his deposit fee was heavy."

"How much?"

"It's not a big deal. I gave him fifteen hundred dollars."

"Oh, my god!" She shifted as though to stand. "I can have half of that to you tomorrow!"

"Calm down, Nye. It ain't that big of a deal. You can make it up some place else. You just said you were getting the bed. Plus, my father gave me a few bucks." The words were painful because with them came the memory.

"For this?"

I nodded. "He tried to convince me not to do it."

She sucked in a breath. "You told him about me?"

I shook my head. "I just told him I was ready to be a man. I graduate in three weeks. He tried to give me options."

"What did he say?"

"It was more like take this money I was giving you for graduation and stay here until you're able to find a job—a real one that ain't got nothing to do with music or football—or take the money and don't come back." The shit had gotten tired to me by now.

He'd been against everything I loved since I could remember.

"I'm so sorry, Launz. I really am," she provided with tears in her throat. "I'm sure there are fathers who respect the individuality of their children. Some aren't bullies and get that we may not know it all, but we know what we want."

"And what do you want?" I studied the beautiful mole next to her mouth. She had two and I'd never considered them to be beauty marks, until her.

She turned to me and snorted, "I don't know!" Her infectious burst of laughter had me grabbing my stomach as I cracked up. Only Nye. *"I just know I don't want to be home anymore. I want out."*

Sobering, I nodded. I didn't fully appreciate what Nye faced at home, but I did know being away on campus for these past four years was the break I needed from my father.

"I know the timing sucks, but it's late. I gotta get you home before your old man clocks out of work." She rolled her eyes and they soon glistened from tears. I reached for the back of her head. "Hey... Don't do that. We're gonna get through this. We made our first move—a big one!" I whispered more passionately than I thought I was capable. "Take your time, but you can tell them you're leaving." When I saw the first tear fall, I felt my heart shear. I kissed her, fortifying myself more than anything. "We're adults. We're about to do adult things. We're good...friends and have each other. We'll win."

Just when I was going to cut this sappy conversation, Nye turned to me with squinted eyes. "You're not trying to lock me down into a relationship, are you?" Huhn? *"Like... Some guys try to circumvent their way into a girl's heart. You're shy, Launz, and may not know how to be direct. I like you, but I ain't girlfriend material. Okay?"*

I shook my head, not wanting to go there with Nye. "Come on, girl. You gotta go."

The sound of her snickering annoyed me. Everything wasn't a damn joke.

Or was it with her?

My damn stomach feels queasy as hell...

I watched them. There were about six. They all had uniforms on looking more like painters' costumes. But the back of them had the same Sams' Moving Co. *logo. A moving company?*

It had been nine days since I dropped her off. Nine days since we agreed to furnish our new place. She hadn't been at Corey's, *abandoning her shifts. Ms. Cheryl posted for a new wait position the second day of her no-show. I'd been to the* BCCC *campus twice, even asked a few people had they seen her around. No one knew who in the hell I was referring to, which was understandable. It's not like it was a residential school and she lived on campus where folks would know her for sure.*

I'd been to the corner where I dropped her off for seven months, the place only a couple of blocks from her house. My expectation was to see her with another dude, but there was no action at the late hour at all. Finally, I came to her house. She let me drop her off in front of here nine *days ago. I saw when she toed around to the side of the house, sneaking into the window. The night I thought was the beginning of my adult life.*

Now, I see men carrying sofas and lamps from the house.

She never mentioned moving.

I'd been played. Nye had lied.

My gut told me to never trust the girl. She was too aggressive, too smooth with it. I knew it!

"I like you, but I ain't girlfriend material. Okay?"

I unlatched and pushed the door to my truck open with a shoulder. Before I could move my leg to step out, a wave of nausea hit and bile shot from my stomach and straight to the ground. It wouldn't stop. My stomach churned and twisted until it was empty, and even after, the dry heaves wouldn't stop.

The shit hurt.

"You okay, son?" I heard cried over my head.

It was hard to straighten upright.

"You need help, kid?" Another asked.

All the waiting for her to finish her shift. The rides with long talks about me and why I was so shy. All the fucking—the exploring. The hanging out mostly at night and not on the weekends. The jokes...they were on me. Her wanting to leave her father's house...didn't include me. What a fucking sucker I'd been.

With my damn stomach spinning and an unusual *throb inching up the back of my skull, I breathed, "Yeah. I'm good."*

I'm good…

~SIXTEEN

PRESENT DAY

"I'M SO TIRED," SHE SHRIEKED BEFORE A YAWN. "Well... Not tired. I just need to sit in one place for a few hours. I'm debating if I'm going to call Mommy and tell her I'll pick her up for breakfast. I kind of want to get down there to make sure Andrew's bag is how I left it for therapy."

Monica was rambling and I tuned her out. She wasn't tired, but I sure as hell was. We were on our way to my place from the airport. The draft was over and our picks were amenable, but nothing could replace the *Kings'* current QB. The QB who was still stalling his alignment to his team. I had so much shit to share and had been implementing it slowly, but surely. And it would be a smoother road if I had total commitment.

"Should we stop and get something to eat?" Monica broke through my reverie. "It's late?"

Without opening my eyes, I shook my head. It throbbed a bit, thankfully not too bad. Monica seemed restless, but I was decided. I wanted a hot meal and my bed to be fragrance-free. In other words, Nye's food, but no Nye. I hadn't seen her since I left for the draft four days ago. The timing had been perfect. We needed a breather after Connecticut. I'd heard a lot from Zo, though. He'd been planning a birthday party for his mother. I didn't want him spending a lot of money, so I offered my place. It was another complicated act on my part. Did I want Nye's people in my home? Hell no. But did I want to make life simpler for Zo? Without a doubt.

"Shit!" Monica swore as we turned onto my block. "I've got to meet Zo here tomorrow. I almost forgot!" I halfway paid attention. "You know…if that kid wasn't so damn cute and charming, I'd charge him for all the work I've been putting in for his ass."

I snorted.

Welcome to my world, big sis…

As the driver pulled into the driveway, I noticed a *Honda* sedan parked just beyond the front door. Monica tossed me a glance of curiosity before we left the car. I tipped the driver and picked up our bags from where they sat on the ground after he retrieved them from the trunk. It had taken her a few years, but I'd finally convinced my sister to pack light for short trips. It was such an easier task of transportation. We'd flown a lot over the years and not having to check luggage at the airport was the best deal for me. I managed our duffle bags while Monica fetched her keys to let us inside.

From the moment the door pushed open, I smelled garlic and herbs. My eyes closed, lashes fluttered as I trailed behind Monica, shutting the door.

The fuck yes…

She'd cooked.

Nye met us in the vestibule from the family room. Her chin was low and eyes timid. Then, rounding her, was another woman strolling into the foyer. Holding a wine glass, her gaze was more curious.

"Well, well, well…" Monica singsonged. "Who do we have here?"

Nye's attention was on me when she answered, "This is my big sister, Jenise." Her faced opened. "Welcome home, guys. It's good to have you back." Her tone was soft, eyes gentler on me.

It was hard to read Nye, but if I had to take a guess, I'd say she was nervous. But for what?

"Good to be back," Monica sighed. Then she nodded toward the woman whose inspection hadn't left me either. The muscles around her eyes were tight as though she was considering something. I didn't know her, even though I could now see the resemblance. This *was* Nye's sister. Oddly, it was good to know another side of her. Good to see she had a genesis of sorts. "Nice to meet you. I'm Monica, this big guy's big sister—and not just in size," she included her corny ass weight joke.

The women shook hands, requiring Jenise's attention to be off of me momentarily. It returned. "I can't believe how much my nephew favors you." Her tone was too close to seduction, forcefully familiar. To an unknowing woman, it was friendly. For a grown ass, single man like me with the experience of women I'd had, I knew it to be coquetry. "I would say it's nice to put a face to a name, but I'm especially familiar with the face…and the name." She extended her hand to me.

I didn't move, picking up sly-Nye vibes from her sister already.

"Oh!" Nye jumped into action. "I'll take care of these." She went for my identifiable duffle bags. I held them in the same hand and Monica's bag was in my other.

But I scooted back slightly, preventing her. "I'm good."

Nye chuckled coyishly, trying to rebound. "Of course, you are." Her smile was deep, shunning and trying to appeal to me. "You also have a bit of a headache." She stepped into me again, this time successfully taking the handles. "I'll take care of these. There's food in the kitchen. Why don't you go shower, then eat?"

"Shit," Monica grunted, one brow peaked. "What about me? I just got off the road, too!"

Nye's laughter turned more confident when she turned to my sister. "There's more than enough for you, Monica. I can warm you up a plate if you want."

"I 'on't know," Monica pressed her. "I know I don't pay the bills around here, but big sister's lives do matter. Ain't that right?" She winked at Jenise before grabbing her bag from me and taking off for her room.

Nye laughed, Jenise chuckled, and I did neither.

When Nye turned to me again, she forged a smile. Her voice low, she offered, "Shower, then eat. Maybe we can talk a little before you go to bed?"

I studied her dark eyes for seconds long. Too tired to codify, I dropped it.

Offering my hand, I tried to perk up. "Sorry about that, Jenise. It's been a long day. It's good to meet more of Zo's family. Hope to chat more in the future." She readily shook my hand.

Then she blurted, "Hang on." She squinted. "You do look familiar. Do you know Angie—yeah! Angie Moore, program director from *Arizona State*. You two hung out a lot."

"Yeah. Ang is my girl." *I don't remember you, though.*

Unless she fucked with Ang.

"Have you seen her lately?"

"I ran into her a few months ago at an awards dinner. Yeah."

"Oh..." There was an elongated break in conversation as Jenise appeared to be "reading" me.

I didn't like it and it was awkward having Nye between us, visibly out of character with her silence.

"Well," I began. "Like I said: it's been a long day of traveling for me."

"Oh, of course!" "I totally understand. I have an early flight in the morning. Perhaps another time."

And at that point, I had no more words. I needed some time alone. I gave them both a nod and took off for the staircase.

He appeared in the doorway of the family room holding a glass of his favorite wine I was sure to pour. The space between his brows was still pinched and his head leaned a bit. His belly filled out in his shirt a bit; unlike women with flat bellies, fit men's tended to be swollen and cut. Launz's fit belly would protrude slightly after a hearty meal. It was cute.

Exhaling, I smiled, sitting up on the floor. "I see you enjoyed the chicken. Your headache is still alive and well."

"Nothing a full night in my bed won't take care of."

I nodded. "Monica left for your parents' not long after my sister. She mentioned something about Andrew's bag for therapy." He nodded. I gestured with my head to the pallet I made on the floor for him. "Have a seat. I'd like to show you something."

And hopefully talk.

I was surprised when he didn't hesitate. Launz placed his glass on the coffee table and crawled onto the blankets. He murmured, "This brings back a stark memory." When he settled, crossing his legs, he flashed an insincere smile.

Ignoring the jab, though understanding full well what he may have been referring to, I took a deep breath. "So… These headaches. How long have you been getting them?"

He swiped his face with his palms. "Most of my adult years, I guess."

"You don't remember when?"

Launz combed his beard as he considered the question. "Maybe after college? I don't quite recall, specifically."

"Hmmmm… And they're not migraines. Right?"

"Nah. No migraines or sinus pain. I went to see a doc about them after the first year or so and was told they were headaches that could be treated with over-the-counter meds. I try avoiding pills when I can."

"Which seems to be often, by my estimation."

"It's been a stressful time."

I nodded. "I'd like to try something with you. Have you ever done wax play?"

He grinned and frowned at the same time. "As in BDSM?"

I shrugged. "It's used for that purpose more often than not, but it can be therapeutic, helping you to relax." I stood to get my tools I'd laid aside earlier, behind the chair. Bringing them back over to the pallet, I placed the candles, lighter, and baby oil next to the cup of water I'd already prepared. "In the throes of a headache, adding another sensation to compete with it can sometimes remove it all together."

I squatted next to him. Launz's gaze dropped to my breasts in a tank. Expressionless, he asked, "So, I'm trading one pain for another?" Then his eyes raked up to me.

"No. The wax isn't supposed to be painful—though you may believe it is if you're highly sensitive. In some cases, it can be particularly remedial. You can focus on breathing, sensory awareness, and/or control-relinquishing."

"Relinquishing control is a hard limit for me."

I sighed. "I know. You have trust issues."

"No." He shook his head. "I don't trust you."

Oh...

Rebounding quickly, I nodded with pouted lips. "I deserve that bit of truth."

"Truth is not the thing you deserve from me, actually, Nye." Our eyes locked, warring without words.

No matter how cold *to me* Launz was, I had to remember how we got here. The man I met over twenty years ago gave little resistance to my many requests. Not only was he agreeable, he was gentle, even in the discomfit I caused him. So, yes; I would forge ahead, bob and weave all his vile missiles. I was tired, though.

I nodded again. "Would you want to try?"

After a spell of time, I saw when he exhaled through his nostrils and rolled his eyes. "What do I have to do?" His voice, however, was more amenable.

"First, take off your shirt. Then lay on your stomach. We'll start on your back."

As he pulled his shirt over his head, Launz echoed, "Start?"

"Meaning tonight. If you don't like it, we won't do it again. If you think it works and would rather not do it with me, I can help you find a practitioner you can explore other body parts with."

He lay on his stomach without another word of protest. When I thought to put music on, I quickly decided not to. I needed to hear any evidence of significant pain or discomfort. After lighting the candle, I lathered baby oil in my hands.

"This is for cleanup purposes and so the peeling process won't be painful when we're done."

Using narrow, then broad strokes, I rubbed the oil into the grooves of his back. Gosh, he was so wide and hard. Touring it this way made me appreciate just how omniscient God was in his creation of mankind. It also appeared Launz took good care of each muscle available to him in his back.

"My sister was smitten with you. She thinks you're very handsome...which is odd, considering how much Zo resembles you." I chuckled to myself. "She said she's surprised you and I ever had a thing."

"Why?" he mumbled, face buried in the crux of his folded arm.

I shrugged, though he couldn't see me. "Because you have a job in the *League* with famous people—and you're good-looking, I guess."

"You guess?"

I rolled my eyes, face burning from fighting my smile. "I told her you're not famous and not even close to the type who wants to be. Told her how you made it clear to me you weren't rich."

"I'm not."

I rolled my eyes.

Wealth is subjective...

Launz may not have been rich, but he wasn't exactly middle-class either. I didn't make that argument to him because I didn't care. That was his business. It just hurt that he wanted to downplay his earnings because, as he said, he didn't trust me. I didn't need his money. I'd done well on my own.

Moving lower, I squeezed more oil to cover his waist, all the way down to the top of his glutes. "I thought she was going to jump you. I could tell she finds you very attractive."

"That's weird."

"Why?"

"Because you do, too. I'm kind of worn goods for the Taylor family."

I was glad he thought so. My mind was still off-kilter since Connecticut last week. I couldn't believe how much I enjoyed Launz. Still stuck on the Launz I knew back then blowing my mind with orgasms now.

And he didn't even go down on me...

That nipped at me, too, but it was a moot issue at this point. I was sure I couldn't have Launz again like that for another twenty years.

"Okay," I spoke low and calm. "I'm going to start with the candle now. If it's too intense, simply say stop and I won't go any further. I have water to cool the burn."

When he nodded his understanding, I reached for the candle, bringing it high above his back before tilting it ever so slightly. When the first of the wax met his skin, Launz's spine straightened. It was an unfair view of masculinity I had to helplessly endure. The second drop had the grooves in his back deepen more.

"Are we okay?"

"*Ye*—yes," he enunciated.

"More. Okay?"

Launz nodded and I poured more, causing little splashing. I created a thin trail to the right of his spine, beginning at his shoulder, ending at his trunk. I blew down toward his back to chase the heat of the wax. Then I repeated that same motion on the left side.

"You good?"

With flared nostrils, he hummed, "Mmmmhmmm..."

I dripped from his neck all the way down to the start of the crack of his ass. My eyes closed in torture watching him fight to not wiggle so much.

"You still okay?"

His head bobbed again. That's when I took my time and addressed his shoulders and the wings of his back. The more I poured, the less he reacted. Even the last drip was only met with a slight twitching. I killed the flame and put it back on the table. Then I blew on the most recent waxing drips, encouraging them to cool.

"You still there?" I asked softly.

"Hm." The dissonance in his throaty croak and body language would have been comical if I wasn't preoccupied with his discomfort.

I was able to get most of the wax from his skin, thanks to the baby oil pre-treatment. Using a plastic card, I removed the stubborn areas. It was an intimate act of hearing each other breathe and feeling him squirm. By the time I applied aloe vera and vitamin E oil, my mind was fortifying to share the matters that broke my heart.

"Okay. I'm done," I informed softly. Launz took his time lifting from the blankets. At first, he appeared disoriented. Then when he turned over and I caught sight of his erection, I understood. Candle waxing could be an aphrodisiac. But that wasn't my purpose tonight. I had truly been curious to learn if it could help with his headaches. "How are you feeling—other than..."

Launz scooted up near the sofa for a throw pillow, covering his excitement. "My headache left when you started on the middle of my back."

I sighed, eyes closing. "Good." It had worked! "I ran the course of your spine. It's a lengthy area."

"The shit worked," he murmured, much to himself, and nodded.

"I need to talk to you."

"Was this foreplay?"

I shook my head. "It's delayed information." Launz tossed his hand in the air, gesturing for me to go. "It was never my intent to leave Jersey when I did. Do you remember I told you my father was in the *Marine Corps*?"

"I do."

"I also told you we traveled a lot. I've lived in several countries and have been exposed to more cultures than I can recall from time to time. I learned when I was young—really young, exactly what my father's specialty was. He was reassigned way too frequently for him to simply be responsible for weapons and the logistics concerning them. I actually snuck out one night when we were stationed in Japan, and followed my father on foot to a meeting he'd been awakened in the middle of the night for."

I took a deep breath. "He beat a man with the buckle end of a belt until he fell unconscious. This was his job. It was what he did in each city and country we relocated to. He was a breaker. When men entering training for the *Marines* had difficulties assimilating to the mentality of the organization, Gunnery Sergeant Preston Taylor was the talent to acclimate them. It was the psychological portion of the training, yes. But it could get really ugly, like it did this one night.

"My father was called in because an 'unruly' new recruit was having a meltdown. Apparently, Gunnery Sergeant Preston Taylor thought the appropriate measure was to beat this guy with a belt until he passed out." My regard lifted to him. "Something clicked for me that night. My father didn't strike us regularly, but when he did, it was brutal. I saw him hit my mother a handful of times by the time I was in middle school.

"The one who caught it the worst from Gunnery Sergeant Preston Taylor was his junior. He'd ride my brother so bad, Jenise and I would cry for him. His beatings were longer and more brutal, requiring splints and even a cast once. We all have experienced the violent wrath of Gunnery Sergeant Preston Taylor. It was so irregular, but looming so the fear never died. He didn't want it to.

"That was the man who raised my brother, sister, and me. It was the man my mother remained married to until he died four months ago. It was the man I followed from state to state, until he left."

"That doesn't explain why you left and didn't even tell me you were pregnant."

"I didn't know I was pregnant until the night you dropped me off. Unbeknownst to me, my father didn't work that night. Out of all the nights his schedule didn't change in those seven months I'd known you, it had that day. He even figured out it wasn't the first time I'd snuck out, but wasn't accurate on how many times —thankfully."

I shook my head. "Anyway. Jenise is two years older than me. Back then, she was enrolled in *Seton Hall.* She was forced to drive back and forth each day for class that year, all because as a freshman, she got pregnant by a guy she was hardly 'dating.' And when Gunnery Sergeant Preston Taylor found out, he flipped on her so bad, my mother had to take her to the hospital for stitches in her lips. My nephew, Leon, was born with a gamut of health issues…severe retardation, immobility. My father arranged for him to receive care and residency in D.C."

Biting my lip, I confessed, "I always wondered if my father's beatings on Jenise caused harm to her baby." These were hard events to revisit, but I did. "The night you dropped me off, my father was waiting for me. He humiliated and bullied me. The man had a pregnancy test waiting. That wasn't shocking, though. I'd taken more of those kits before actually having any type of sex than I have since giving birth. When he made me take the test, I was fine, confident he'd get over my mishap once this was over. But when that thing read 'positive,' his slaps and swings on me didn't land as hard because shock coated me."

"I don't remember not using a condom."

"We did twice. It wasn't planned. Once in a hotel room where you wanted a round two, and another time in your truck." I winked, though feeling all the lows of pain in that moment. "They were both random, but one was successful. Anyway," I breathed. "My father was the most controlling person I've ever known. He knew we were being transferred and waited to tell us. We left two days later, didn't even pack up the house. My mother didn't even know we were due to move until that night we learned I was pregnant. Gunnery Sergeant Preston Taylor had already had a selfish plan of uprooting us again without notification."

"Again, why didn't you call when the smoke cleared?" His head bobbed and eyes pleaded with me.

I nodded, knowing I had more to share. "My father threatened you."

"There was nothing that man could do to me, Nye. Come on!"

Nodding again, I argued, "I thought he could."

"What?"

"He said he could've pressed charges for statutory rape."

"How?"

My breathing turned shallow. "Sex with a minor."

"You were nineteen, about to be twenty the next week."

I couldn't catch the cry shooting from my belly. "I lied. I was seventeen when I met you, Launz."

"Seventee—" he attempted to repeat. "You were in college." I shook my head. "But you had a job at *Corey's*. You couldn't have gotten a job there as a minor. You served alcohol."

Sobbing uncontrollably, I tried to explain, "I was hired as kitchen help. To clean. There was no extensive background check. I knew how to get fake IDs being a Marine kid. I knew…" I tried to breathe. "I knew how to get into parties and get jobs in high school. *Corey's* was the last one."

"Because you turned eighteen the next week," he accurately surmised.

Taking deep breaths, I tried controlling my diaphragm. I hated crying. It was something I avoided as much as I could.

Exhaling, Launz's eyes drifted blindly across the room as he shook his head. "Damn. This…" He blinked hard. "You could've called at some point, Nye."

"I wanted to. I really did. But so much time had passed that I thought you wouldn't have…"

"I would have believed you." His brows were tight, eyes angry.

"The statute…" I tried again, "of limitations. My father meant every word, and stupidly, I believed him. I struggled so bad—"

"That monster raised my boy, Nye!"

"He never…hurt…him! I…swear!"

"How do you know?"

"Because he loved...that boy more than he loved his own *chil*—children, Launz." I wiped my face. "He's never laid a finger on...Zo. He hated when I...gave him little thigh-pops as a *tod*—toddler. The man adored that boy. It was something none of us saw coming."

"And you never thought of me? My feelings?"

I shook my head. *Almost every day...* "I never forgot about you. I knew I pushed you into everything. I knew although we weren't a couple, I made you spend copious amounts of time with me. I knew I seduced you, Launz. I knew you didn't trust me. I felt like I'd already taken..." I felt like shit admitting this stuff out loud.

"Taken advantage of me?" He glared my way. "You did. Over and over again. You still are. In his wake, your father has, too. He took my son from me. I would have stood tall. My family would have adjusted. Hell, my mother has converted my old room into something she hopes Zo would feel comfortable staying in. That's how tall we all would have all stood."

His parents...

I sniffled. "I really thought what bonded us was our fathers."

"How?"

"When you used to tell me how he gave you a hard time about your career choices. How you said he didn't respect you as a man. I thought he was—"

"A monster like Preston Taylor?" *My God!* I choked on tears. He used that word again. It was the same one Jenise used to describe our father recently. "My father is a lot of things, but abusive has never been one. He would have never overstepped or omitted. Nah. Preston encroached on love. He kept my son away from me. My father would have never stooped so low."

I nodded, eyes stinging. "I'm glad to know that."

Launz snatched himself from the floor and grabbed his t-shirt. Just as he was about to cross the threshold of the room, I called, "Launz..." When he turned to me, I swiped the faucet of tears running down my face. "I'm so sorry. I apologize for my contribution in this. Gunnery Sergeant Preston Taylor was a challenging man, but one good thing he gave us was an introduction to the Lord. I've prayed for you every day. It's been a ritual since I was seventeen and heartbroken. I prayed for you to live a long life filled with love and rich opportunities." My eyes fell away when I could no longer fight the impending sob. "And I won't stop."

"And while I appreciate that—I really do, because I'm a follower of Christ as well—it doesn't absolve you of your lies before I even laid a hand on you." He shook his head, eyes rolling. "You're a lawyer. What about the statute of limitations? What about you simply explaining if he tried to press charges against me that you manipulated your way into my life?"

That hurt.

"I did consider it. For years, I believed in New Jersey, my father could have pursued you criminally and civilly. I had no idea the age of consent was sixteen here. He lied, Launz. My father threatened me and I believed his every word."

"This is a lot of shit to digest for me."

"I know. While you were away working, I put in an application for a development in Somerset. It's not too far from Zo. You can have your home back."

"My home back?" he scoffed. "You think you moving out is going to be me resuming a life I once knew? Nye, I've got a whole fucking grown ass son running around here. He's an adult! I've missed his birth, the years where you 'popped his little thigh,' his first step, first day of school, first time on a bike, first crush, first kiss, first football game, first fuck, first job...graduations—everything! You think you leaving my home is going to bring all that shit back?" His laughter was derisive. "Your supreme gift of manipulation can't fix the fucked-up-ness you caused in my life."

My heart twisted. "I found a boy I really liked and wanted to—"

"You found a man!" he shouted. "I've been a grown ass, able to legally drink, vote, and fuck man since you met me."

While that was true, Launz never seemed over my head maturation-wise. We fit and eased into a sexual relationship seamlessly.

I dropped it. It wasn't my plan to argue with Launz tonight. I only wanted to finally give him my side of the story. It was overdue. I'd been wanting to tell him when he'd learned about Zo, but Launz left no room for it. I'd been tolerated here in his home, not welcomed. Then we slept together last week. That was unexpected. I didn't think he found me attractive—trust me, I tested the waters the night he brought his date home. After sleeping with him, I knew the air needed to be cleared—or our past addressed.

The pain I sat in as he left the family room was scorching. Imagine going your whole life not fitting. Growing up as an outlier in each country, state, and neighborhood you lived in. I wasn't accepted at home or in schools. The first time in my life I felt a sliver of control—of being alive—was the second night I showed up to work the kitchen at *Corey's*. Usually, it would have taken weeks for me to work out the nervousness of being found out I was underaged.

Not here in New Jersey. That anxiety was overshadowed by the butterscotch-hued, skinny guy who carried a guitar case and very few words. I watched him for weeks, looking for an opportunity to say something to him. And I wasn't the only one crushing on Launz. I heard the waitresses fawn over him. When I overheard how Launz turned one down while washing down the cutting boards, my pussy cried. Nothing like that had ever happened to me before. So, when I got the opportunity to "fill" in for Lisa, I prepared to shoot my shot and I was determined not to miss.

Launz was perfect. His temperament inspired me in so many ways. I pushed him on everything: spending time together, taking me everywhere he hung out, and making me a woman. That was a feat. I watched porn clips for weeks, practicing on my mother's cucumbers before Launz even touched me. I was ready when he finally did—although it had taken months. It was worth the wait. He turned out to be the best I'd ever had, not that I'd had many.

Those were inarguably the best seven months of my life. Each day was adventurous and rewarding with him. Launz gave me courage to break from my father's spell of control by way of fear. He was what I needed to know my life belonged to me and not Gunnery Sergeant Preston Taylor. Until…

It did.

I cried myself to sleep on the couch, there in Launz's family room. I only knew because at some point in the night, I felt my body dipping successively and heard hard steps. I smelled him, too. Launz had carried me from the sofa up to my bed. He spread a blanket over me and squeezed my hand before leaving me to rest.

~SEVENTEEN

PRESENT DAY

Dumping the ashtray, I cringed from the disturbing odor of burnt cigar butts. As much as I enjoyed the aroma of them when lit—especially mixed with the delicious fragrance of Launz—when they were done, the smell was miserably pungent. He'd let the tray mount before discarding its contents. Once in a while, I'd come back here in his yard and clean up behind him.

Straightening my spine to tie the bag, I glanced around the yard. It was coming along beautifully. Most of it was done. The bricks of the fountain were drying today, the gold mulch around the trees and flower beds brought a welcoming sense of summer to mind. The rock LED lights trimming the garden beds and the new cemented walkways gave the space commercial appeal. What an investment! I wondered how much this set Launz back. Then I recalled him saying he bought the property cheap.

Smart guy...

As I sat down on the patio chair, I hummed peacefully. My life was a damn shitshow. I'd never been so unstable or clueless. It made me wonder if my father influenced the stability in my world. I'd never projected under his leadership, I always... adjusted. Now, there were no guidelines. In this chapter of my life, I had no parameters, no staples to provide stability. There was just... I gazed into the moving blue sky, the exact demonstration of my future.

"Beautiful, isn't it?"

Her soft tone startled the shit out of me, but I wouldn't dare let her know. It may have been her plan to rattle me.

"Camay," I greeted, sitting up as she pulled off gardening gloves. "I didn't know you were here."

"You seem quite comfy. Cozy, too." Her eyes fell to my bare legs in short denim shorts, *Ugg* boots, and an old *Asé Garb* hoodie.

"Isn't that the only way?"

Camay's reply was an inscrutable smile as she peered around the yard. "You know, I told him to go with *PAMAPIC* flat, solar ground LED lights, but he went with the rock one instead. I *did* push for the pink weigela blooms to cut the monotony of the green shrubs and apparently, he listened to *something* I advised."

"Teamwork makes the dream work. Right?"

I could feel her eyes on me, but refused to look her way.

"So, I heard you fly in and out to check in on your mother. How is she? She isn't ill, is she?"

"Oh, no. My mother is healthy. Vibrant and full of life." I still wouldn't engage her with my eyes, pretending to be aloof with her inquisitive presence.

"Oh. So, you're not in a rush to get back to her?"

"I don't live with my mother. No, I don't have a need to 'tend' to her, if that's what you mean."

"Okay." She implemented an insincere chuckle. "I just figured you've been out here for a few months now and would need to resume some sort of responsibility. How's Zo settling at school?"

That's when I did glance her way, making it clear, "My son's settled and has adjusted exceptionally well. Launz and I have seen to it."

"Oh. That's good. I'm happy to hear." She giggled again, then took a break to think of her next line of inquiry. "Launz keeps telling me how good of a kid he is. I know this has been a lot on him, and all. You know?"

"I do. And he's been great, expanding his family and claiming his birthright."

She stumbled at that. I knew it for sure the second I turned her way when she hadn't replied right away. Camay's cinnamon face was long, then she attempted to rebound quickly with a smile. "How did you two meet?"

"Launz and me?" She nodded. I had no desire to answer this or any question like it. Still tender from my conversation with him two nights ago, God only knew what he'd shared with Camay about me. "He gigged at a restaurant I used to waitress at." I colored the truth a bit but didn't lie. This was none of her business.

"Oh!" she chirped again. "I bet he was a cutie." Camay romanticized my story *for herself.*

"Oh, you have no idea."

"I do. He's a very handsome man."

"He's a delicious man—no disrespect," I tried for decorum. "But he was an especially captivating kid back then. Talented and smart, too. How did you two meet?"

She sucked in a breath, surprised by *my* inquiry. "Oh, Alaunzo and I met at an affair. I work for a non-profit stroke organization dedicated to Black lives. We raise money for research and provide education to that targeted audience. We have wealthy donors. Our organization was able to get Alaunzo there. You may not know his father suffered a stroke a few years back. It created, for him and his family, a need for resources.

"There's the big stroke org, but we do the work for Black people, so our resources are specific to them. He showed to a fundraising event one year then volunteered for the board the next. We worked together and the rest is history."

My head jerked back and I frowned playfully. "What? No sparks. No triple take when he walked through the doors of the event in an expensive ass Italian suit?"

This time, when Camay laughed, it was a true nervous chortle. "Well, yes. I was attracted to him right away. And you may or may not know this, but because Alaunzo is so darn serious all the time, I didn't know how to approach him. So I was happy when he asked me to dinner after one board meeting. I didn't know what to do with myself. I told him to give me a minute and I went to the bathroom to call my momma. She said, 'Girl, if you don't carry them hips out with that handsome young man!' And that sealed the deal for me." Camay giggled in a girly way.

He asked her out. What if I'd have waited for him to approach me at *Corey's*? I doubted he would. Was that Launz's preference? To be the hunter? My aggression would have never allowed him the opportunity.

"Sweet," I replied, struggling with my own insecurities of Launz's perception of me.

"That's what my mom says about us. She's crazy about the man, always wanting to fix his plate and pour his wine. She's so cute."

"Does she live with you?"

Something dark washed over Camay's face at that question. "I live with—we live together. It's her place, but I help out with bills."

"Oh! Interesting. So, when you cook for Launz, your mother's there enjoying the festivities. Cute is right!" I mustered as much of my acting skills as possible to omit the shade in that one—because it was shady as hell.

"Not exactly, but she's my world."

"Cute."

"When's the next time you'll be visiting your mom?"

"Ummm..." I hadn't been expecting that question. "I haven't even thought of it. I've got a few interviews set up over the next week."

"Mother's Day's coming up."

"I know. My birthday's the day after."

"Really?" Her eyes grew large. "Mine's the day before. On Saturday."

This Saturday…

"Oh, nice. Taurus gang." I pumped my fist, an act of forced commonality. The only thing Camay and I had in common was a dick we enjoyed—at least, I did. "Any special plans?"

"Well…" she sang, shoulders lifting to meet her ears. "We have a tradition. Alaunzo takes me to one of my favorite restaurants that's actually inside of a resort. We stay overnight, dancing to live music. So fun."

My eyes widened as I struggled to think of a response. "Sounds like it." Then I thought. "You know what would really spice up the night?"

"What's that?"

"*Mauve*. Make sure he has a few thumbs of it. That premium brandy will dull the strongest of inhibitions." I winked.

Camay blinked with an empty smile on her face for a spell, likely processing my suggestion. "Well," she suddenly trilled. "I hope you do something fun for yours." She stood from the arm of the wooden chair. "I'm going to get back to these rose bushes before I get too hungry. I skipped lunch today. I guess I've been on the move."

"Do you want to go in and get a snack?" Camay's eyes blossomed and she looked toward the house. "No. He's not home: I don't want to be rude. I'll be fine."

"Oh," I croaked. "Okay." Then I turned back toward the garden.

Weird girls...

Maybe Launz's type is weirdo.

"So, imagine my surprise when I finally call, all to hear my Grammy ain't home, but out with her *boyfriend*," Zo teased.

That charm tickled my parents equally. "I guess I was out with my boyfriend, huhn?" my mom remarked.

"Yeah," he pushed. "You out gallivanting with your boo-thang while I'm on campus craving banana muffins and collard greens."

My parents couldn't stop laughing. At that moment, I just so happened to catch eyes with Jenise. She was speaking to a guest at one of the tables and glanced up. I really wished I hadn't. I'd been trying to avoid her since being out here.

"Awwww, baby!" Mom cried. "But Monica didn't tell you we were in Harlem, supporting your father?"

Zo pivoted, gazing my way. "No."

Mom shared, "He had a live show at his church."

"You know he plays for that big-time church over there," Dad added.

"Oh!" Zo chirped. "Yeah. You did tell me about playing for your church. I didn't know you played last night."

"My bad." I patted my chest. "I know you have finals and ain't wanna distract you."

"Bro!" he declared so passionately. "I would've come. No stress at all!"

"I know, man. I know. There are other opportunities."

"Like when? I know things are gonna be picking up in Connecticut soon."

"Aren't you recording again soon?" Mom asked, trying to assist.

Monica kept our mother abreast of her life. Perhaps because Mom was Andrew's primary caretaker, she did, or because that's what daughters did with their mothers. Either way, a significant portion of

Monica's life included me. Therefore, my mother was well-versed with my schedule.

"Yup. Monday—*but...*" I quickly recalled his mother's birthday being that day just as Jenise sidled up to our small group. "I know you're taking your mother out for her birthday."

"Depending on the time, I can do both." I appreciated Zo's determination. "When and where?"

"That big ol' star," Dad playfully whispered. "Ragee."

Shock could be detected in Zo's body language right away. "Oh, damn—I mean, dang!" he corrected himself. "I'll be there!"

Chuckling, I shared, "I'll have Monica send you the information."

"That's what's up!" His beam was inspiring.

"Zo, you ordered both the ribs and the pork shoulder?" Monica shouted, stepping onto the deck with large serving dishes in either hand. "Boy, I told you one or the other. We ain't got that many people for all this food!"

"Oh, shoot!" Zo jumped into action, scurrying over to Monica.

My parents and I laughed, watching him try to sweet-talk her when taking a dish from Monica.

"We're gonna get a seat," my mother informed. "Someone said she'll be here soon."

"Maybe over there by that fountain." Dad pointed out into the yard.

As they took off, Jenise slid in front of me, obstructing my view. "It's really nice of you to do this."

"I don't think I've done anything. This was Zo's idea. You helped him out."

"Yes, along with your sister. But none of this would be possible without you offering your home. It's quite lovely, by the way."

I did offer to have Zo do Nye's surprise birthday party here today. He seemed determined to celebrate her and since there wouldn't be a lot of people in attendance, it didn't make sense for him to have to pay for a facility. George Wright and his men cleared out two days ago, completing their work. The property looked amazing and spring was upon us, making it only right to show off the landscaping.

"I appreciate that. But it was no feat supporting Zo."

"Does that mean you don't support Nye?"

Excuse me?

I owed no one an explanation regarding Nyedeera. This was not a conversation I cared to have with anyone, especially her sister.

I smiled at Jenise. "I'm not sure how to answer that. My son wanted to do something special for his mother's birthday, and I supported him on it. No different than you did by getting her friends out here for the occasion."

From what I'd heard, the four girlfriends in attendance flew in from Arizona. Some brought their significant others. Unfortunately, Nye's mother opted not to come out due to a conflicting doctor's appointment.

"Just what *do* you think of my sister? I've been wondering this for some time now. I've tried to glean information from her, but Nye's not said much."

"Shhhhhhhh!" Someone hushed over the yard. "They're here!"

Nye had arrived. She left for the airport hours ago to pick up her girlfriend who wanted to come out here to "check on" Nye and celebrate her birthday. That's how they got her out of the house. Only they gave her a time for the woman's flight that was embellished by two hours. So, I had no idea of the temperament we'd be receiving from Nye.

My phone vibrated and I saw Camay had texted me.

CJ: *I'll be ready by six. Which room did you reserve tonight?*

I glanced up from my phone and finally replied to Jenise, "I guess that's because there isn't much to say. Excuse me." I took off to address Camay's text.

As I typed, a resounding, "*Surprise!*" had me peering up. Nye's whole frame appeared tense, eyes wild, and mouth hung low. She wore short jean shorts, exposing her long, toned thighs, a collared shirt half-tucked into the waist of her shorts, Chucks, and a sloppy ponytail at the top of her head.

She observed the gargantuan periwinkle balloons boasting "Happy birthday Nye" and ivory ones in the shape of the numbers three and nine to represent her age. She looked at the flowered arc Monica was able to pull off. Behind it was a black backdrop cloth with *Nye's Last Dirty Thirty* in gold letters. The setup was superb and fitting for a woman who was loved and honored. I respected Zo for that—though he had lots of damn help from Monica.

Then Nye found me. She flashed an unbridled smile, struggling to not stare at me too long. That's when she began recognizing her guests. There were no more than twenty of us out here, so it was inevitable that it would happen. One by one, she hugged them and screamed their names. Then Zo came into her view, and the way they looked at each other then jumped into an embrace where he swung her around was of absolute adoration. I believed she *knew* the party was Zo's idea.

"Alright! Alright!" Jenise commanded the attention of the crowd. "She needs to get right. We were able to surprise the woman who can't be outsmarted. Now, let us allow her to change into something more appropriate for the occasion."

The small crowd responded with their disappointment and happiness collectively. Zo made a small path for her to get through for the house. I was up on the deck where the buffet table sat. As Nye walked up the stairs her eyes slowly roved up to me. She stopped at my side.

"Thanks for this."

"This was all your son's idea."

She nodded, eyes still gleaming. "But you're here. I know you have a special birthday to celebrate today."

My head pushed back. "Do you now?"

She smiled beautifully as she nodded. "Live band, good food, and a nice suite."

"She told you that?"

Nye nodded again. "When she was over tending to your rose bushes a few days ago. How did the recording go?"

"It was a success. My pastor was elated, so…" I bobbed my head on either side, hating how her sister was in earshot, visibly peering in on us. "You left your booger napkin in my room again."

Nye's eyes flashed wide but her grin never faltered. "If you leave your door open tonight, I can leave a little something more. But I understand you have overnight plans."

My forehead shot up at that proposition as Nye started for the house.

"And there you have it." Zo presented the original card to his grandparents.

"Oh, dear!" Launz's mother cried.

They cheered, marveled by his age-old card tricks.

"He did that?" Launz's dad asked as he cackled, blown away.

I laughed myself, more at Zo's determination to keep my father's card tricks alive but deep inside, I was kicking myself for my inappropriate behavior earlier. I couldn't believe how I propositioned Launz the way I did. A few days ago, he'd basically told me he didn't trust me, didn't want to, and never would again in life. But today, in the height of my astonishment of being honored, I tell the man I want to fuck him.

This was insane. I'd been praying. A lot. I prayed for direction and to resume my normal self. That was the thing, my life had not been anything I recognized since my father's last days in hospice when I finally decided to contact Launz. Being out here didn't help. I'd basically been on vacation for four months—though not emotionally. Emotionally and mentally, I'd been compromised.

Even earlier: after flirting with Launz—something I did not expect to do—I changed into a floral, short-sleeve mini dress. I was out here in less than five minutes and had to bite the bullet: I met Launz's parents. It was an incredibly nerve-racking performance of integrity. I had to employ it as Mr. and Mrs. Pierce graciously asked several questions about me, circumventing the most important one. Why had I kept Zo a secret. I wondered if Launz had told them. They didn't give any clues to knowing. I walked away with my head held high, but felt so hollow inside.

Seeing my girlfriends, Rhea, Cynthia, Loretta, and Patricia took me by total surprise. Rhea, Cynthia, and Loretta brought their husbands while Patricia decided to be a rebel and leave hers behind. I was beyond thrilled to see their faces. Apparently, Jenise provided hotel information close to Launz's place. See. *Vacation*. Today, I'd seen the familiar faces of women I'd known for years, but in a new place. A newly renovated Moorestown, New Jersey back yard. The place looked amazing! The flowers and balloons, soft feminine colors, and even the smallest thoughtful details all swelled my heart.

"Okay. One more. Only one because pretty soon, Pop Pierce here is going to know all my secrets!"

As his grandparents tittered, Jenise pulled at me. "Yeah, you do that. I'm going to steal your mother away for a moment."

We walked a few feet near the punch table, by the fountain. I turned to her with curious eyes.

"What's up?"

"He left."

I glanced around the expansive and gorgeously landscaped yard. "Who?"

"Zo's father. That's who."

Oh… "He had a…date."

"See! I knew you weren't doing it right with him."

"I beg your pardon. Doing what right?"

"Him. Your ass needs to be doing him."

"Why?"

"Because he's a high-class man who is single and fine as fuck. Do you even know his estimated value?"

"No. And I don't care. I need to know mine since I quit my job." I rolled my eyes for light distraction, not wanting to take on this discussion with my sister.

Besides, Launz came to and stayed at this shindig longer than I would have ever guessed. He even brought his parents—well, Zo may have invited them, but Launz didn't veto the idea.

"The man signed with the *Kings* in January for a whopping $7.3M annually with a $750K in incentives. Do you know what that's for?" I shook my head, confused about why this was her business. "Bonuses if he takes the team to the *Playoffs*, *Super Bowl*, and/or wins coach of the year."

"Jenise, that's none of my business, and I don't know how it's yours either."

"Because you are my sister and are entitled to this..." She swung her arm, gesturing the property. "...and more. He owes you."

That's when my frequent companion, guilt, resumed its weight on my shoulders, its dreadful presence looming over my head like a dark cloud.

"Launz doesn't owe me a dime. Whatever missed monetary contributions necessary have been worked out between him and Zo. Jenise, I don't care about that man's wallet. You know I've never been interested in men that way. I pay my own bills. If I want, I have to work toward getting it."

"You feminists crack me the hell up thinking you're less of a woman because you let a man treat you like a lady. I've been warning you about that since Ernie began sniffing around your ass. Wake up, Nye: you have access to a wealthy, good-looking single man! And guess where he is? On a date with a woman willing to give him what you won't."

"And what's that?"

Her eyes swept me from head to toe. "A lot of ego-stroking and a little ass—well," She retracted. "Alaunzo—"

"Launz," I corrected.

"Launz..." She rolled her eyes. "Is in his early forties, so he'd likely want a lot of pussy in the beginning, but then the frequency will fade out. It ain't that hard, Nye."

I snorted, shaking my head as I snickered at her. My sister had a knack for giving unsolicited and unproven advice about men. And it was mostly about men of power. She didn't believe they could be single or faithful, so in other words, they were whorish creatures. I believed her low expectation of men came from her experiences with our father. He may not have been rich, but was powerful and forthcoming with his desires. He'd also cheated on our mother, at least twice. Add that to his waspish temperament and you'd know from where Jenise's unfounded arguments and viewpoints were derived.

"What's so damn funny?"

"The fact that I'm not you. I don't pursue men based on their most recent tax returns. Also, I'm not looking for a man. I have greater priorities."

"Like what?"

"Like my son!"

Jenise's face tightened, gaze going behind me. "Looks like Zo's well-liked. And you know what? It appears you are, too. You just can't see past your feminist ways to recognize it."

"What are you talking about?"

"The man wants you."

What?

I scoffed again, "Are you crazy?"

"You know I'm not."

"So why would you say that?"

"Girl, the man couldn't keep his eyes off of you. From the minute you walked into the yard to his last gaze on your ass when you went inside to change. The whole time you two were out here, *Launz* was stealing gapes your way. This is why I don't understand why you won't just play nice." She winked. "You may just like it."

"Like what?"

"His dick game." Her brows shot up as Zo joined us, hooking his arm around her shoulder.

"What're you two Taylor sisters up to over here?"

My mouth twisted as I looked Jenise dead in her eyes. "Your aunt's being nasty while I'm fighting for integrity."

Zo laughed. "Sometimes, integrity is overrated. Be nasty for once in your life, Mom. Oh, wait! You *were* nasty only once in your life. I'm proof of that." He waggled his brows before walking off, humored by his little corny ass joke.

Jenise thought it was funny, too, as she howled. "I love that kid."

I rolled my eyes, turning away. "I've got guests to tend to."

While I was far from innocent, I wasn't in the business of using people. Neither was I with a lot of men, evident in the fact of Zo's statement about me being "nasty for once." But the indisputable truth was I didn't know what I wanted. I enjoyed being here in Jersey and close to Zo. I'd come to love this home. Monica and I got along well. And Launz… The explosion of our history scorched my soul. Yet strangely enough, I wanted him physically. I'd been craving the passion he paid my body back in Connecticut. The way I responded to the man had been unprecedented, and I wanted to explore it over again.

I exhaled, now pretending to be making a fuss over the dessert table. None of that mattered right now. We were still celebrating my birthday. Besides, Launz would be having a romantic night with one of his associates.

Not that I really cared.

Yes, you do!

I'd just fallen asleep a little after two in the morning.

Jenise got bored sometime after our tête-à-tête and decided to leave. I was convinced her ennui was caused by Launz's absence and that of talk of him. The party eventually transitioned into the house once the night air had chilled. Rhea, Cynthia, Loretta, and their husbands left around midnight. Monica tried to stay to clean up, but I had no parts of it. I knew she had to get home to her son, Andrew. The Pierces left earlier to relieve his companion for the day. After expressing my abundant gratitude to her, I assisted Monica to her car, sending food for the Pierces.

Patricia stayed back when everyone left. We finished a bottle of *Château Blevin* Launz had stored as she told me her husband, Derrick's, desire to have his aging mother live with them. I missioned my mind and heart to be available to her grievances. It wasn't hard after knowing her for years. She was a passionate woman, working as a paralegal for *Klein and Schmitts,* the firm I'd recently resigned from.

While I didn't think it was a difficult feat for her to, at least, try in the name of her marriage, I listened and wholeheartedly offered my support to her. Marriage, I could have only imagined, was a game of submission and grace. She seemed tired and a bit intoxicated by the time we were ending our girl time chat, so I insisted she stayed in one of the guest bedrooms on the third floor.

Once I had her settled, I cleaned up what was left over from the party, which wasn't much. Zo cleaned a lot before he crashed in the basement. It was fully finished with a pull-out sofa and entertainment system. No way did I want the kid to leave after all the work he'd put in. Then I learned he'd packed an overnight bag. The boy thought he was slick. Tomorrow was Mother's Day and he was determined to double-dip on the celebration. Sometimes, I felt I didn't deserve such a thoughtful human being.

Once I was satisfied with the house being restored, I slowly climbed the stairs and showered before crawling into my bed. Strangely enough, I wasn't as exhausted as I should have been. My mind replayed the birthday celebration I felt I didn't deserve either. With all the energy of the day, I found it hard to settle down. But I did eventually, at just before two in the morning. So when I heard the security system disarmed and deep steps climbing the staircase, my eyes flashed open.

He's home?

It was Launz. I knew the weight of his footsteps, though surprised by his presence *in his own home* at this hour. He was supposed to be out with Camay. They were supposed to be celebrating her birthday *—overnight!* I drew in a shaky breath, then swallowed involuntarily past a sudden lump in my throat. A surge of heat flashed between my thighs. My heart pounded almost louder than my clitoris. As he climbed the last few steps, I was on an elusive edge.

Then I waited. I waited for his decision. To see if he took my foolish proposition seriously. Seconds felt like long hours as I listened for the sound of his doors to close. A few times, I confused my blaring pulse for the sound of it. So, I had to get up and see. I'd lost my mind. Again, for Launz, I'd lost my mind. What was it about this man that made me forfeit my dignity for him each and every time?

It was open.

Oh, my god!

A wave of excitement had me gripping the doorframe as I peered around it. I felt lightheaded, yet a surge of arousal settled in my groin. Irrationally needy, I toed down the hall, not hearing anything other than the blood rushing through my ears. I made it to his room and Launz was nowhere in sight. Turning, I closed and locked the French doors. Seconds later, sounds of his shower cracked the air.

~EIGHTEEN

PRESENT DAY

I SAUNTERED OUT OF THE MISTY BATHROOM anticipating my bed. Loud fears and stressors competed with my exhaustion. The new draftees, the new nutritional programs all the players had received customized plans for by now, and their reactions. All of that and more would have to give me a reprieve until after a solid six hours. Then I'd be able to think with a clear mind.

Out of nowhere, my dick throbbed. That shit was the last inconvenience I needed. I canceled any plans of a relief for tonight a few short hours ago. Another impasse I'd have to resolve, and soon. My footsteps halted as her scent grew imminent.

How did I miss…

When I came in, I ambled straight into the closet to dump my pockets and strip, then continued into the shower. I'd only turned on the lights in the bathroom. Had she been sleeping in my bed again? In the dark of the room, her silhouette on my bed became clear.

"Girl," I more or less groaned than chastised. "This setup is too porn'ish." I was ass-naked.

"Or maybe those nasty romance novels my mom used to sneak and read," she jested softly.

Damn.

I couldn't get rid of her. And not just physically either. Nye's presence—her aura—was haunting. Not only was the woman smart and calculating, she was strong and resilient. I couldn't stop thinking about her. Couldn't erase the imprint of her poised, feminine posture, her unfailing and cunning smirk, the sounds of her cries when I pounded into her. *That* wasn't the prepared and scheming Nyedeera. I'd given this and her lots of thought lately. That night in Connecticut was her being led and not leading. I liked that Nyedeera.

But I liked this Nye *sometimes*, too...

"Are you always this aggressive with men?" I asked, pulling back the comforter to get in bed.

My dick was fully erect now, forcing me to lay on my back. Nye crawled over me, pulling the blanket down, revealing my need. Of her.

"Once, when I was seventeen then again at twenty." She lowered her head to my throbbing cock. "But the second time was forced." Her soft warm hands gathered me. "Nothing organic like the first." She winked. "Who so happens to be my third, too."

Then her head dipped and soft lips kissed me. She did it once more while stroking me. When her tongue encircled my head, I was in pain, so fucking aroused. The woman had this unique, innate talent at disarming and ensnaring me with little effort. I was uncomfortable with it from the moment I met her at *Corey's* and despised it now, realizing that after how she left me with a secret child, she could still dismantle my fears and insecurities in the heat of my bed.

The softness and warmth of her wet mouth had my head spinning in pleasure, but I fought for lucidity.

"What's organic?" I whispered, inadvertently giving away the efficacy of the spell she had me under.

Her jaw tightened and she bobbed a few times before releasing me on a pop. "What I've felt about you since September of nineteen ninety-nine."

Nye ran her tongue over the ridges of my dick while ringing the head with pressure.

I licked my lips. "The first time I saw you was in October."

Nye's torso raised fully and she stood on her knees. She kept one hand on my cock as she arranged her knees on either side of my thighs, straddling me.

"But the first time I laid eyes on you…" She strained, trying to slide down onto me. Once she was about halfway seated, she breathed, "… was in September. The finest thing I'd ever seen." Nye bounced on me, flexing the walls of her pussy to fit me in. "Until I gave birth to my child."

My child…

Her hands found their way to my abs for an anchor and she rocked her hips, squeezing her heat over me. She set her rhythm and I relaxed into it, watching her focus. Other than her being the initiator most times, I didn't remember much about sex with Nye back then. Hell, I didn't even recall not using a—

"Nye…" I reached up to her flapping breast, squeezing her nipple.

"Hmmm?" She bit her lip.

"I don't fuck without condoms," I whispered gently. "Do you?"

Her spine curled, lost in pleasure I was proud to give, and Nye couldn't speak right away. "It's not something I've done in a while."

"Go without condoms?"

She shook her head, hips thrusting faster, hands shifting up to my chest. "This."

She was coming already and damn, was Nye fucking beautiful. Face stricken with unrelenting pleasure, body tensed to endure it, I enjoyed this space with her. Nye wasn't ahead, she was hanging on. To me. Absent was the clever smirk, witty phrases, and inexplicable energy from her. She clenched her fists with the cords of her neck strained, eyes closed, and lips unsealed while succumbing to pleasure.

I reached up and tongued her neck, tasting that soft, clean floral aroma against the beat of her pulse. Her body rocked against mine, tits rubbed against my chest. Her hands reached up to my head, gripping my twists at the root. The ache felt good, and Nye's excited pussy was even better.

Her expressive breaths pushed into my ear as I squeezed her ass cheeks, pulling her into me. The only woman I'd occasionally go without a rubber with was Camay. She was one of a few women I knew who fucked me exclusively, and I had a faith in her unshared with any other woman. Something I compromised for this woman.

If I were smart, I'd tell Nye to leave. I'd have a man-to-man with my son and explain the conflict of his mother staying at my place. He'd have to understand how much their presence had disrupted my world, and after just four months of me conceding to accepting only him. Zo was a man who would soon be a father; he'd have to respect it. On the same token, I had to be prepared to accept if he didn't—

In a flash, her arms around me tightened as her pelvis pulled back and shook. Nye's open mouth met my shoulder, her teeth sharp and lips softer than pillows in their wake. Her entire body convulsed uncontrollably over me, teeth chattering as she exploded. Nye may have been on top of me, but I was topping her. In that moment, a revelation fell upon me. Nye had the same needs as any other woman in my bed. She wanted to be tended to, adored, revered, and seen.

Nye hadn't been seen before I met her. She apparently wasn't tended to much now. The question at hand was if I wanted to be the man to see, address, and tend to her.

Before I could think any further, my body was prepared to release. Nye's sinuous movements for this stretch of time could no longer be endured—especially without a condom. I buried my face in her neck as I let one off, blasting into her tight pussy, pulling her into me by the fat of her hips. Height, weight, agility: Nye's body was, for sure, the perfect fit. She kept plunging down onto me and I assisted her until I lifted her from my throbbing cock midway to let my cum, mixed with hers, drip from her pussy.

Nye's tight eyes opened.

"You feel that?" I asked.

Biting her lip, she nodded, not seeming to be confused by what it was. I let her down to rest on my deflating dick as we caught our breaths.

"You—" She licked her lips, silently giggling. "Your body."

I glanced down the small portion of it I could see with her obstructing the view. "I like it just fine."

Her smile faded. "Me, too."

I bit her chin, then kissed it sweetly. "Good."

"You still refuse to kiss me?" Though I knew it was a sincere question, she giggled through it.

I slapped her ass. "I'm just realizing you weren't sleeping in my room."

As she lifted and swept her thigh from over me, Nye asked, "What?"

"Your gifts. I still see the balloon."

As she asked, "What balloon?" I reached over and turned on the lamp on the nightstand. "Oh!" She blinked fast, adjusting to the light. "The bag says *Happy Birthday Day*, but the balloon over the other gift bag says *Happy Mother's Day*."

Nye looked confused; she held a sheet to her breasts and finger-combed hair from her face.

"That's because today's Mother's Day, Nyedeera."

She turned to me with a shame-faced smirk. I enjoyed that over her typical clever beam any day.

Now cleaned of our intimate, liquid formula, Nye sat at the bottom of the bed opening her birthday gift. She pulled the tissue paper out and wrapped inside was her gift.

She turned to me. "A *Connecticut Kings* tee—whoa!" Her eyes grew wide. "A cropped tee?"

I tossed my chin toward her. "Your belly ring bone is cute."

She glanced down, sucking in a breath. "You like my piercing, Pierce?" I snorted. "You did it again."

"What?"

"Rolled your eyes."

"I'll try not to do it again."

"Nah. I like it. Remember?"

I watched her trade the long t-shirt for the new cropped one. Nye's body was still youthful at thirty-nine. Other than the ring of stretch marks around her belly button, her body held no proof of having ever carried a baby.

When she turned to me with it on, I murmured, "Glad I successfully guessed your size."

Laughing, Nye turned and grabbed the other gift bag. This one was bigger. She lifted a box from inside and unraveled the deep purple ribbon. Then she lifted the lid.

"*Crystal K.*" She turned to me with big eyes. When I gave her nothing, Nye pulled out the fluffy robe and matching slippers. A card slipped out. She opened the flap. "A gift card to *Crystal K*'s? Like… Is this real?" I shrugged. "This is the largest Black-owned spa resort in the country. It's exclusive…full-service…expensive as hell, too. I've been eyeing this place since I came out here. There's day counseling, yoga, meditation rooms there, and hotel stay. I just couldn't commit to the price tag. How did you…"

Rubbing my eyes, I reminded her, "I perform tricks, Nye: I'm good for a thoughtful gift or two." I gazed up at her and winked.

She was crestfallen instantly, shoulders dropping as she exhaled. "It was her birthday. What happened with Camay?"

Shit…

"It's late. Too late for heavy conversation."

She gathered everything and placed her gifts neatly on the floor near the doors. Then Nye went to the top of the bed, forcing me to turn around. "Yeah, but… What we just did—again—and without condoms…" Her face fell into her palms. When she lifted, I could see the tears pool, but Nye swallowed them back. "I've not been perfect, but I swear I'm more responsible than when you last knew me. I have no words for what we just did. I can't sincerely apologize for it either. I just want to not be your enemy."

"Is that it?"

She paid a moment to consider it. "No. It's not. I want to be in your life. I want to be someone you trust. As corny as it sounds, because of Zo, I want to develop a bond with you."

"Because of Zo?"

"I understand it has to be."

"I can't tell, if you're sneaking in my bed at night, Nye." I cracked a smile to soften the blow.

Nye didn't participate in my humor. "I know," her voice cracked as she buried her face.

"Are you crying?"

She kept her face buried but shook her head. Then she came up for air and her eyes found me. "I like having sex with you."

"I'll accept your compliment."

She shook her head. "But I know we're cooking up a disaster by doing this."

Nye was right. "I'm struggling to see you as this new person," I admitted.

She nodded, seemingly owning her shit. "But you feel it."

"What do you mean?"

"When we're...intimate, I feel you open to me. You're even way better at it than you were back then." I shook my head and Nye's volume increased. "Your intimacy with me is better because you didn't trust me back then. You can't tell me any different, Launz."

"I fuck you better because I'm a grown ass man who knows how to please a grown ass woman. I still don't trust you."

Pursing her lips, Nye hung her head. She took her time to softly ask, "Then why are you here with me instead of celebrating one of your many 'friends' birthday?"

I pulled in a deep breath for that loaded question. "Because of your conversation with her."

"What exactly did she say transpired in that conversation?"

Oh, now we're in our esquire mien...

I played along.

"Hmmmm… I think it all got fucked up when she said you mentioned giving me *Mauve*."

"What was wrong with that?"

"The fact that I laughed my ass off."

Nye blinked deeply. "Why? What was so funny?"

"Maybe the fact that I'd never told her."

Her mouth collapsed. "I didn't consider that. I mean, yes. I was being an asshole…because I was feeling insecure after my conversation with you about who I was back then. I didn't know if you'd shared that with her. But I didn't think…"

I didn't want to hear it. Nye was being Nye when speaking to Camay. That, I was convinced of.

I shook my head, deading her bullshit before I got roped into her spell. "Whatever transpired in that conversation has made her uneasy about our arrangement here. She wants me to do what is probably the smartest and most responsible deed."

"Which is?"

"Ask the mother of my child to find another place to stay until she figures out where she wants to land."

"So, she broke up with you?"

"So, she thinks."

"And what does that mean?"

"It means that while Camay and I are not in an exclusive relationship, I will give her space on this call she's made."

"And what if she doesn't change her mind?"

"Then I'll have to accept her decision. I respect her. A lot. I don't want to force a woman to stay with me. Ever. It's by and large the exact reason I'm happily single."

Nye whispered, "Why do you think a woman would leave you?"

I was done with this conversation and knew my next words could unnecessarily extend it or shut it down.

Fuck it.

I decided on honesty. "Because the first 'woman' I laid it all down for like a fucking fool did."

Nye's eyes closed to a squeeze and this time, tears did fall down her face before she covered it with her hands. "I'm so sorry."

Yup.

So you've said…

Get up…

My eyes fluttered open and I could feel the light crust around them. Then I smelt him. His strong, yet resting heartbeat was beneath my head. We'd finally fallen asleep, but only a few hours ago. He held me. Launz pulled me into his arms a few hours ago and offered a period of reprieve. No fighting. No judgment. No accusations of me being manipulative. Just the peace of silence and acceptance.

But now I had to go. Not only did I have an unsuspecting guest upstairs, but Zo was here as well. The last thing I wanted him to discover his father and I having been intimate. I slipped from his thick arm and chest and stepped into my slippers. When I made it to the doors, I peered out first and listened for sounds of anyone being awake. Then I tiptoed down the long hall, bypassing the spiral staircase, and dipped into my room.

Feeling fuzzy, I sat on the bench at the foot of the bed. I was physically tired and incredibly emotionally exhausted. That's when it hit me: I was crazy about the man. I was at it again. I allowed my mind to work overtime, trying to melt into Launz Pierce's body and live there. With him. I was aware of how irrational that expectation was, but now I owned it. I wanted him to see me, accept me, and want to be with me.

A knock at the door had my pulse racing immediately.

"Come in," I announced with a dry throat.

"Hey, Ma…" Zo strolled in casually, then stopped suddenly. "You okay?"

"Why?" I covered my dry, swollen mouth. "What's wrong?"

"You've got…tear tracks?"

My eyes widened. "Oh." I wiped my face. Shit. *No!* The last thing I wanted was Zo getting wind of my "mess" with his father. It was embarrassing no matter how strong my feelings for the man were. "All that celebrating, I guess."

He gave a spiritless, "Oh." Zo's brows were knitted, expressing his caution. "Ummm… Ms. Patricia is up and needs to get back to her hotel. I can swing her over there real quick, if you want."

"Oh!" I leaped over the bench. "I can take her."

"No worries. It's Mother's Day," he reminded me.

It is…

"That's nice of you, Zo." I hated to smile, looking so dry *and* crusty first thing in the morning. I stood and headed toward the door. "Let me wash my face and brush my teeth so I can tell her goodbye. Two minutes."

Two hours later, I was dressed for the day and cleaning the kitchen from the breakfast I insisted on making Zo and his father. It was my way of saying thanks for the party yesterday. I had lots of trash to organize and needed to go through the house again to be sure I'd picked up all the cups from last night.

As I walked into the kitchen, I heard Launz commenting, "Oh, that's dope."

"What is?" I asked absentmindedly.

They'd been chatting for a while, Launz finishing his post-breakfast coffee.

"The restaurant I'm taking you to tomorrow for your actual birthday."

Helplessly, I smiled. Zo had always been generous with me on my birthday. His gifts got more extravagant when he began working and earning money. I fought with him when he'd do too much, but hated breaking his spirit at the same time. He was a thoughtful kid and I appreciated that about him.

"Wanna go one-on-one before we head up to Upper Freehold?" Zo asked. "I've been eyeing that dusty basketball court out there."

Launz smiled, head shook coolly. "You don't want this work, kid."

"I'mma go grab my kicks." Zo stood. "I'll grab your old man knee pads while I'm at it."

I rolled my eyes and laughed quietly while setting the dishwasher.

"Boy, you 'bout to catch your first spanking from this old man," Launz threatened as Zo left the kitchen.

I wiped down the counter when I felt him near. Launz poured out the rest of his coffee and placed the mug in the sink.

"I'm on birth control," I murmured, but loud enough for him to hear.

Then I turned to look at him. Half of Launz's face was lifted in a smirk. "Well, I figured as much with the gusto you had last night when climbing on top of me." His smile widened and I saw the adorable crinkles in the sides of his eyes.

As much as I wanted to share in his humor, I was so torn. "Zo."

Launz's index finger slowly swiped at my exposed belly in my crop top hoodie. "What about him?" He smelled dangerously good and the shit annoyed me.

"He's not going to be happy if he finds out."

Launz's eyes rolled above my head then lobbed back and forth. He whispered, "I hadn't considered that."

I figured it was because he never considered me. Launz, like me, had no intention of becoming intimate again. But the reality was that we had.

"I think you should go get ready. It'll be time for you two to head over to your mother's soon."

"And you're sure you don't want to come?" The sincerity in his eyes twisted my heart.

I shook my head. "I need to call my mother and get some sleep. I have a *Zoom* interview in the morning and a hot date tomorrow night." I winked, dismissing him.

Launz nodded, then left. I was finishing with the kitchen when Zo came back in.

"Yo, I just got a text from Lenny Jr. about the wedding."

"Oh, yeah?" I rang out the dish rag over the sink. I'd forgotten that 'thing' was this month. That reminded me of Jade Bailey. "What about it?"

"He said he heard about me bringing my pops." Zo's tenor was drenched in such excitement.

I steeled over the sink. "Bringing who?"

"I told Grams. I didn't tell you? He's coming."

My eyes closed as my forehead stretched. "You can't just invite random people to a wedding, Zo. Those RSVPs were due a while ago."

"I know. Grams hit me up, asking if I wanted to bring Gena." *Gena?* "I asked if I could bring my father. She said since Gramps won't be here to go anymore and Uncle Junior said he can't make it, we were down two people in our family on the original invitation, so it could work."

Shit. "Zo!" I groaned.

"What's wrong with that?"

"Maybe the fact that the three of us are working things out as best we can and are still in a sensitive spot."

"How? We're good. You two are finally getting along. He and I hit it off from the door. Why can't we all just be a family?"

"Because it takes time, Zo. More than four months."

He flashed the same charming grin I had to endure from his father just seconds before he came back in here. "I think we're good. In fact, we're better. We're bomb right now. Don't worry, Mom. We're fine."

Ignoring his ignorant yet innocent assurances, I moved on. "Hey…"

"The semester's done next week. Are you going back out West... staying here?" I stood straight to look his way.

Zo scratched his head.

"Ready?" a thick tone asked.

Zo jumped into action and caught the basketball Launz tossed. It happened so fast, it startled me.

"I stay ready," Zo declared while laughing and tossed the ball back at him.

"Launz, I forgot to mention to you, Jade Bailey texted me with an invitation to their home."

"When?"

"Yesterday. A few hours after you left."

His forehead lifted. "Interesting. Good and interesting. Was the invitation just for you?"

I shook my head. "Next weekend. She mentioned their anniversary. She definitely mentioned having another couple over, too."

Zo laughed. Hard. "Oh, shit," he cried.

"Mouth, Alaunzo Pierce!" I warned.

It made Launz smirk. "Let's see who's laughing in a few." Then he headed for the door at the side of the house, his face screwed with confusion.

I followed his line of sight and caught Camay's short auburn tresses blowing in the mild wind. She was picking through a shed box on the side of the house. Too distracted by his phone, Zo didn't catch it.

That's when my wits snapped into action. "Boy, get off that phone and help me put this trash out on the curb for tomorrow."

I'd done it only once before. It was typically something Launz did. But when he wasn't in town, either Monica or his part time housekeeper took care of it. I made quick work of pulling the bag out of the trash in the kitchen and tying it before handing it off to Zo.

"Here." I had to speak louder than the voices he could possibly hear outside. "And put down that phone for a minute or two, would you!"

"Be right back!" Zo thought he was yelling out the open window to Launz.

He followed me to the garage door at the back of the house. I had him toss the bag into one of the bins before we pulled the three of them from the garage, all the way to the corner. When I saw the minivan parked but running at the curb, I hoped Zo wouldn't ask.

"Over here," I pointed to the right of the bin I'd brought out. Just as Zo pulled around me, the driver's door of the minivan opened. I tried to ignore the elderly woman stepping out by assisting Zo with one of his bins. "Okay. Good job. Let's go."

I turned quickly back for the house to inspire Zo's actions. He eventually followed me after noticing her. Zo's face screwed, then he looked my way.

"Who that?"

I shrugged, trying to forge a smile. Then I felt a sharp thwack at the center of my back. I leaped around and caught a hairbrush falling to the ground.

"What the hell?" Zo mumbled.

"Was that necessary?" I asked the woman who was hardly five feet tall with spectacles, chubby cheeks, and a silver gray chignon bun on top of her head.

"You slut! Didn't your mother teach you anything?" her raspy tenor shouted.

"Excuse me, lady?" Zo turned to her. She gasped when recognizing him, I figured because of his heavy resemblance to Launz. "Did you just throw that at my mother?"

Her mouth fell to the ground.

I took him at his arms, pushing him toward the house. "Zo, it's okay. Let's go back inside."

"But she just threw that hard brush—lady, what's wrong with you?"

"Zo!" I pushed harder. "It's okay, baby. I'm okay. It's just a big misunderstanding!"

"A misunder—" Zo wouldn't drop it. "I heard that sound. That was hard, Ma!"

I shook my head. "It's fine. She's an older woman, Zo. Leave it be."

"Not the way I should leave your little rump be, missy! Control your boy!"

Zo spun around and scoffed. "What?" His eyes wide with shock-humor.

If I wasn't so anxious about it all or hadn't figured out in my mind that Camay ran home last night and shared her breakup with her mother, I would have laughed.

Just as I'd gotten him facing and moving up the driveway and toward the house again, the woman continued. "That's right. Play dumb, you little wench! Home-wrecker! Scallywag heifer!"

"Mom!" Zo barked while laughing.

"I know! I know!" I continued to push him.

To my right, in my peripheral, I saw Launz edging out from the other side of the property. His pace was quick and on his heels was Camay. He assessed Zo and me as we were reaching the garage doors, then his attention went to the old woman.

"Momma!" Camay cried, running out to her mother with gardening tools in her hands. "I told you to stay in the van!"

I shook my head while guiding my son away from the drama that was my life.

~NINETEEN

PRESENT DAY

I RETURNED HOME COMPLETELY SPENT, though my mind wouldn't stop. What should have been a typical amenable holiday turned out being one that was a particular pain in my ass. I was restless and annoyed as fuck at my pounding head. Before I could decide on how I would end my day, I needed to check in with Nye.

The light was on in the family room and I could hear the television going. When I made it to the doorway, Nye's anxious regard was on me. She lay on her side with one leg crossed over the other in a tank and biker shorts. The top of her hair was in a ponytail and the bottom flowed over her shoulders. She was beautiful, the object of my torment as of late. I didn't know whether to fuck and hold onto her for dear life or to toss her out of my home and life for good. The prior was a frightening prospect; the latter was impossible.

"You okay?"

I noticed the napkin with small balls of matter scattered on top. Smiling, I sauntered to the single sofa and dumped my weighted body. "I'm good."

"You're smiling, so I guess you're not too worked up. I saw the clip."

"Which clip would that be?" I sat back, exhaling.

"The one of your quarterback in that interview with Ebonee Williams, admitting he's considering leaving the *Kings*."

I scoffed, rubbing the bridge of my nose with my eyes closed.

That would be the pain in my ass…

"Oh, that clip?" My question was more of a statement.

"What is up with that guy? He's really carrying his emotions into this upcoming season? Is he always this sensitive, or has he reserved all his bitchiness for you?"

"Trenton Bailey is a solid dude who has been burnt by my predecessors. He's also—quiet as it's kept—been abandoned by his parents to varying degrees. What I'm catching is simply the result him—"

"Not being able to trust easily."

My lids detached and I found Nye's starkly serious expression.

"Of sorts, yes."

"None of that has anything to do with you." I chuckled. "What's so funny?" she demanded.

"Camay and another one of my lady friends whom I thought I'd come to trust have said the same thing."

"What?"

"That the fact that I can't trust a woman enough to be monogamous has had nothing to do with them." In no mood for a "deep" conversation, I smiled for good measure.

Nye's eyes fell. "Oh."

Dismissing the souring moment, I explained, "If Trent's talent didn't supersede his current state of insecurity, I wouldn't give a fuck." My eyes landed on her again. "You know?"

"But because you believe in him and his contribution, he causes you headaches every time you see his hesitance."

There was no need for me to deny it. Nye had seen me stressed over this very subject a number of times.

"Anyway." Enough of my work shit. "How are you? I asked Zo to text and check in."

"Which time?" she hissed, rolling her eyes. "The boy's called and texted virtually every ten minutes since you guys left for your parents' this afternoon.

"He didn't like leaving you. It is Mother's Day, after all."

"Yeah. But I'd been given the most thoughtful, and possibly undeserved party yesterday. Thanks again, by the way. And we're going out to a very expensive restaurant tomorrow in North Jersey for my actual birthday. I could sit tight alone in between. I called my mom, practiced some yoga poses, and even read my Bible today. I was fine."

"And about earlier?"

"Oh." Nye's brows rose. "You mean with your main squeeze, Camay's, mother?" Her lips pushed upturned. "I've got bigger, more pressing issues than one of my baby daddy's lovers running off crying to her mother about why he's not putting me out. That place I told you I put an application in just had a major fire near the unit I was looking to rent out. The damage is astronomical. They have no idea when it will be repaired and ready to rent again." She shook her head. "It was so cute. The perfect size for me and Zo—when he isn't here or God knows where when school's out."

"Don't worry about moving out, Nye." I groaned, eyes closed as I breathed through the rolling aches. "It'll happen when it happens."

"And what about your personal life?"

"It'll happen."

"What if I don't want it to continue as it's been?"

My lids blinked open. She rolled her eyes up as though her words slipped instead of being confessed. Me not having a personal life? What the hell did that mean? That was like asking me not to study the game of football, to not breathe.

Damn...

Another roll of pain spiked in my forehead.

"I'm going to bed." The words left my mouth, but I didn't budge.

"Stay right there. Let me get my kit," she informed softly.

Shit…

The wax was hot as fuck—well, maybe spicy. I didn't feel like I was being burned. It felt like small needles zipping in random directions. The heat lasted seconds long, but the sensation from the suspense of when she'd drip next was some other shit. Then when her cool breath chased the heat, my dick swelled. My heart pace quickened and I fucking shivered at her ministrations. That headache? It was gone within the first five minutes. I wouldn't have believed it if she hadn't done this "wax therapy" on me twice. The first time could have been a fluke. Where did she learn this from?

That was another conundrum about the mother of my son: I didn't know much about her. Nye *wasn't* the same girl I knew. She was now an accomplished woman who seemed to run from the confidence I once knew her to stand on. She'd been attentive, supportive, and a great mother—God, she was a present mom, something I adored—yet she was fireless. *Well, a little.* There was that stunt she pulled in her panty shorts when Sandra was over. Or her sleeping in my room. Then there was her vibrator in my bed. Those incidences were performed by the Nye I knew.

Who was *this* Nye?

"All done," she murmured. "How are you feeling?"

Engulfed in that soft, clean floral aroma of hers, I felt deluded in comfort and arousal. So, I simply hummed and attempted to nod against my folded arms. Even the sensation of her peeling the dried wax from my back aroused me. I couldn't do it, though. Fucking Nye had to stop. She was right earlier, our son could possibly be fucked up by this. It wasn't like we were working on something substantial. I wasn't that type of man. I enjoyed being single.

"All done," her voice so soft.

I turned from my stomach to my ass, leaning back on my arms. "You get off on this?"

"Waxing? I like helping."

"Is it what you do with Ernie?"

Her eyes dropped and Nye busied herself with cleaning up. "I only want to help, Launz."

"I won't judge. I'm just curious."

She paused, then gazed my way. Nye was hesitant when she answered, "Ernie has anxiety issues. He gets stressed and overworked. This helps him to calm his body so his mind can extrapolate."

"Is he like this after?" I motioned to my erection with my eyes.

Nye followed my line of sight. She turned away, licking her lips. "I'm not trying to manipulate you here. I just wanted to help."

"Hey…" My head rolled over my shoulders. "I'm not mad at all. It's an arousing practice. My question is do you get aroused? Is this where you give Ernie a hand job?"

Her eyes squinted, but I didn't care. I wanted to know. "Launz."

"No judgment."

"Launz, please."

"Please, what?"

"I'm not answering anything about what I do with Ernie."

"Then answer if you're aroused right now like I am."

She closed her eyes, shaking her head. "I'm never not aroused when I touch you, Launz," she whispered. "I just don't do the candle waxing to manipulate you into sex."

"So, you don't want me now?" My voice dipped. Nye shook her head, but I knew she was lying. Then I thought to prove to her she was only fooling herself. I left the floor and began removing my socks, jeans, then boxers, all while I looked at her. She pretended to halfway watch while placing the cap back on to the baby oil. "Are you turned on now?"

I clasped my hands behind me as I peered down on her. Nye's mouth fell completely open so fast that she caught it and licked her lips. Her eyes at the head of my cock, standing in the air. The electric atmosphere turned heavy with anticipation.

"Why are you doing this to me?" she whispered.

I bent over just slightly to get into her line of sight. "Which one of us are you talking to?" Her eyes bounced up to meet mine. "Ah! So, I wasn't included in that conversation?"

I watched her lick her lips again and swallow. "Who's the manipulative one now?" Her voice low, throaty.

I chuckled. "Come here, Nye."

Instinctively, she walked over to me on her knees. Nye didn't need the formal request. She never took her eyes off my dick as she met it hands first. Her tongue circled the head as her hands massaged the shaft. And goddamn. The woman was stunningly gorgeous with her mouth wrapped around me. In no time, I was once again "behind" Nye. She mentioned being good at hand jobs, but adding her mouth took her skills to executive level.

She stroked with her hands until she took over with her mouth alone. My head dropped behind my shoulders a few times from the skilled pressure of her lips, jaw, and tongue. Shit. Impressed was an understatement. It took months to teach head to a new lover. And while I could offer Nye a tip or two about the sounds I enjoyed hearing when being blown, she definitely had a beautiful technique.

And she didn't tire. Nye gave me eye contact while she bobbed over me rhythmically while using the tip of her tongue to rub the underside of my head. The shit drove me crazy and by the way her eyes were fixated on me, Nyedeera knew. I could come now, though I didn't want to. I wanted this to last forever. But another side of me, the insatiable alpha in me, wanted the branding of her mouth. I wanted to see my shit dripping from her lips and chin.

The thought propelled my thighs apart. I moved an errant lock of hair from her face as I watched her head bobble and eyes tear. Then the pads of my feet heated.

"*Ahhhhh…*" pushed from my belly.

Seconds later, I was jutted into her mouth as I stared at her, expressionless. Then that one time she pulled back before pushing in, my creaminess was lathered over my shaft. Nye still didn't stop. She kept sucking, just switching up the pressure as my hips jolted. My cum spilled from her lips and down her chin.

But I didn't give it all to her. I pulled back and reached down to pull her tank over her head. Next, I had her stand so I could remove her biker shorts. Nye wasn't wearing panties and I was in agreement. I sat on the comforter she set up for my candle waxing and invited her to straddle me. Nye did, taking me in as she sank down. I wasn't fully erect, but knew I would be again when she started to move. Her strokes were shallow at first then she sped up, I could tell ready to cum.

I sat back on my arms. "Lean back. I wanna see us."

Nye slowed to obey. While straddling me on her knees, she leaned back so I could see her bikini waxed pussy. My cum mixed with her excitement had me thickening again. Her clit was swollen and exposed, and I was slightly embarrassed by the fact that I hadn't tasted it yet. I thumbed it, familiarizing myself with her. Nye's thrust turned wild when I did, reminding me she was ready to cum.

"You ready?" She nodded, biting her lips together with squeezed eyes. "One promise."

"Okay," she panted, eyes still closed.

"Don't hold back on me."

Nye nodded and I pressed into her even more while driving into her wet, snug pussy. It was so needy, so eager. Her breasts were wild and loud as she danced on me.

"Oh!" she cried, neck long, hair sweeping over my legs. I rubbed faster and faster, and Nye fucked me harder and harder, chasing her impending orgasm. I loved this. "Launz!" her plea helpless. The shit excited the fuck out of me.

"Let's cum together." I was ready.

Seeing her lithesome body rocking over me, taking my dick as I rubbed her clit was a sight I could get addicted to.

Nye's ass slapped my thighs while her pussy eagerly met my thumb strokes. Head hung back, she cried out loud and hard. And I exploded inside of her.

Again.

Fuck.

"Here you are, sir."

I glanced up from my phone to see the waiter hand my son the leather check holder.

"Thanks, man." Zo received it and peered inside.

"Did I bankrupt you?" I asked while trolling Jade Bailey's social media uselessly.

She didn't post many pictures of her family, mostly birthday shoutouts for her children and a few—and I mean *a scarce few*—usies of her and Trent. He, on the other hand, posted candid pictures of her a little more frequently, but nothing sickening. I had never been in a serious relationship, especially during the social media era, so I didn't have a working practice of how frequently posting of a significant other was. Either way, I didn't pick up what I was hoping to. I wanted to know more about her, and you couldn't glean much from her pages because Jade rarely posted.

"You're a cheap date," Zo returned.

I peered up at him with furrowed brows. "Compared to who?" He snickered, pulling out his wallet. "I know you're not comparing me to Gena."

"Why you been acting like you don't like my girl no more?"

While Zo smiled, I could see the sadness in his eyes. I tapped out of *Instagram* and pulled in a deep breath, sitting back in my seat. The restaurant was quaint and sparsely filled for a Monday. It felt quiet enough to address the elephant in the room for Zo and me.

"You know I've always liked Gena, Zo."

The humor dropped from my baby's face. "Then why you been tripping on her like this?"

"Because I'm a mother who has just a few months left of guidance with you and I hate that I'm spending them telling you to not be tied down in a relationship at *this* point in your life."

"This point? You wanted Gena and me to break up?"

"No. I guess what I mean is you've moved all the way out here and I would have respected your relationship more if she'd—you two—would have given you more time to get settled here. You've just met your father and you're still acclimating to his family. All the while, attending a new school with new coaches and teammates, all of whom you have yet to meet. That takes time."

"That's where I don't agree with you. When you meet good people and you're a good person yourself, it don't take a long while to vibe." He shrugged. "You just do, Mom. I've been vibing with everybody out here. What's wrong with Gena getting a new start, too?"

"Maybe the fact that it isn't authentic if she's just following you. I've been meaning to call her mother to see what she thinks of all of this. I, personally, would want my daughter to maintain some independence. You two have been going hard for so long. What's wrong with just letting it breathe?"

"Can I ask you a personal question and you not take it the wrong way?"

"You know you can ask me anything, Zo. If it's inappropriate, I have no problem telling you that."

"Have you ever been in love?"

I blinked hard at that question. "Okay." I sat up in my seat. *I'll go this way with it.* "Mr. Ernie proposed to me."

"What?" His eyes ballooned. I nodded. "When?"

"A couple of weeks ago."

Zo's beam was wide, then his brows met. "But wait! Ain't he supposed to come to me first? Like… Gramps ain't here no more. I'm the next in line."

I rolled my eyes, finding that sincere question cute and funny. "You have a point, sir. But I went up to see him in Connecticut where he was closing on a deal and, to my surprise, he popped the question."

"Where's the ring?"

"He wants to go together for me to pick it out."

His head reared, and Zo couldn't stop blinking. "Whoa! So, y'all getting married?"

I shook my head, smile fading. "I don't know. My point in bringing it up is to show you how, at my age, I was able to get a degree, go to law school, pass the bar, get a sustainable job, and buy a home, all the while being a mom. Some would say the only thing missing from my life is a man." Shrugging, I continued, "I beg to differ, but *if* I wanted that last piece to make my life—quote unquote—whole, I have that option. I haven't missed out on anything being single. I've worked hard and can now focus on companionship." I flashed a smile and winked, lying my ass off to my son.

My words weren't false exactly, but they were misleading. I used to want to be married with kids. I wanted to be in love. The problem was becoming a single mother and traveling every couple of years, chasing after my father's career. It didn't make for sustainable relationships. It took years to develop the courage to leave his control and put my life back in order. That began with introducing Zo to his father.

That's all it was supposed to have been; about those two. Then I slept with Launz and discovered a fleeting piece of my womanhood. I had to have him again, although *I knew* it wasn't right. Last night, the man came in my mouth and inside my core, something only *he'd* done before when we—*I* was a kid. I felt things and had done things never explored. The way he made me cum by his thumb and dick disturbed my soul. I still didn't know if I came from my clit or deep inside my vagina. Launz was in both places *and* my head. The way I didn't have to think when with him intimately. I just…followed and obeyed him.

No wonder why he has a harem of women…

Feeling emboldened by that experience, as I lay on his chest in the family room last night, fighting sleep, I demanded, "*If you're going to be with me raw dog, you have to be monogamous…to me.*"

Launz didn't reply. But I woke up this morning in my bed.

Without him. Maybe I was in over my head. I shouldn't have given him the ultimatum. Perhaps he enjoyed variety similar to how it had never bothered me that I was single. Until I intersected with Alaunzo Pierce again earlier this year.

"Hey," Zo burst my introspective bubble. "How about we go check in on ya baby daddy."

I was confused. "Monica said he'd be recording this week again."

"Yeah. He had a session last week with his choir. I missed it because he didn't want me to slack on my finals. But you know how dope that would have been for me. It was at his church. Pop and Grammy Pierce were there." *Pop? Grammy?* "You know Gramps would've been in his element. He loved gospel music."

He did, and it annoyed me…

I hated the pride of the memory in my child's smile.

"Zo, maybe I should sit this one out. Let Launz work without me being around."

"Nah, Ma. It's cool. I told him I'd pop in either today or tomorrow. We should go. I won't even tell you who he's recording with."

"You said his church."

Zo shook his head, placing his debit card inside the bill jacket. "That was last week. Let me surprise you." He winked. "It's still your birthday, girl."

I sat back, exhaling.

This couldn't be a good idea…

We walked into a nondescript building in Montclair. The sign above the entrance said *Checkerboard*. There was a small lobby area painted an awful glossy red. A few people were standing around talking to each other or on their phones. I followed Zo to a door with a sign attached that read, *"Closed Session,"* wondering if I should have come along. The other half of me was glad I did because this place seemed shady.

That was until we entered what looked like a lounge with a stage. The checkerboard flooring was stark against the leather chairs, giving the place a vibe. The tables were too small for it to be a restaurant, though I smelled food. Attending the bar was a man and woman in black vests with white collared shirts rolled up at the sleeves. Tables were sparsely vacant. The stage was practically filled with musicians engaging their instruments and background singers behind microphones.

Just when I noticed the one holding the guitar by its neck, I was bumped into.

"Ah, man," the tall, good-looking, beefy guy murmured, his hand going to my arm. He smelled like heaven. "I apologize." He held his phone in the air. "When the wife texts, my attention is gone." He scoffed while walking away as I nodded like an idiot.

"Oh, shit!" Zo whispered, bouncing on his toes. "That's him!"

It is…

"Zo, you sure it's okay for us to be here?"

"Yeah, Ma," he assured while his eyes ate up the whole room. "I told him."

"Did he tell you he was recording with Ragee?" I couldn't believe the words falling from my lips.

Yes, I knew Launz was an accomplished guitarist. The plaques in his little home studio told that story. But being here and seeing this side of him made me feel like an interloper.

"Yup." He turned to me cheesing. "That's your birthday surprise. They're recording for his upcoming album."

I looked past Zo's towering frame and saw Ragee—or Raj, as some referred to him as—chatting with the background singers. He was in all-black, filling out his jeans and button-up shirt I noticed was undone at his chest. He looked like a damn model. I was a huge fan of the man for years. Zo knew this. While I'd always considered him good-looking, in person, that nigga was *faahn*!

"What up doe!" Zo charged excitedly.

I didn't see Launz approaching, but damn sure smelled his delicious cologne. His hair was freshly cut at the sides, coiled twists touched up and wild. Launz, too, was dressed in all-black. He looked grown and stately. Tempting and forbidden.

"You made it," Launz noted, smile just as wide as Zo's.

"Ah, man! You know I did. Mom's acting scared," Zo rattled on.

That's when Launz acknowledged me. "The birthday girl is here."

"Yup. And this is my treat, so don't take credit for it," Zo joked.

Launz's smile stirred my groin. "Wouldn't even think of it."

"I know that's your baby's moms and all, but I'm the man on this day."

"How was dinner?"

"It was straight. I got that Chilean sea bass you recommended. Melted like butter in my mouth. Mom got the big scallops. Them joints looked juicy!"

Zo, shut up, boy!

My child was really feeling himself as he soaked in the room.

Launz nodded, slanted eyes on me as he smiled. "Would you like a drink?

"Nah, I'm driving," Zo answered.

"I would hope so because of the special occasion. I was actually asking the birthday girl here."

I grinned goofily. "I don't think we're going to stay long. I see you're working. Don't want to intrude."

Any more than I have already in your life…

"Damn!" a husky timber breathed into the microphone. "Just when I thought we were ready, somebody wanders off." Ragee covered his eyes from the bright stage lights as he peered into the room.

"Coach Strings!" someone shouted as the rest on stage laughed.

"Coach Strings?" I parroted, surprised by the moniker.

"Because I can coach you on thrumming strings or…other things." Launz made a show of wiggling his fingers in the air. My groin churned at the fact. He then pivoted and returned, "I'm chatting with my son!" Launz shouted back.

"Yo, that's him?" Ragee's deep timbre rasped. Then were the

rumbles from people on the stage and a few on the floor. But did Ragee ask was that him—as in he knew of Zo? "Come here, young king."

A few people abandoned their places on stage to peer down at Zo.

"You told him about Zo?" I whispered to Launz.

His brows met and he smirked coolly. "He's my son."

"I know. I just—"

"Goddamn, he looks just like you, Coach!" Ragee roared, " I knew it when I ran into him at the crib!"

"Damn sure do!" someone agreed.

Then my child started running his mouth. "Yeah. It's my moms' birthday. I wanted to support the old man and surprise her."

"That's your mom?" Raj asked, still kneeling over at the tip of the stage.

"Yeah." Zo pointed my way, beaming brightly.

This kid…

"I'm so sorry," I whispered to Launz while shrinking.

Launz chuckled.

"Man! I thought she was one of Reggie's PYTs when I bumped into her," Ragee shared. "That's you, Coach?"

"Used to be," Zo answered.

"Shut up, Zo!" I cried, dropping my head.

Launz's laughter deepened. It was clear he enjoyed my son's loquaciousness.

"She's a queeeeeeen to-*who* meeeee!" he sang, remixing the famous *Coming to America* skit.

The room ate it up. It even inspired Ragee and the background singers to perform a rendition of Happy Birthday. Zo's expression was priceless as he looked on.

"Thank you," was all I could say when they finished. I waved Zo over to me when he was done with his usie picture with Ragee. Then I advised Launz, "You need to go."

"You sure I can't get you a drink?"

"I'm sure. But thanks."

As Launz took the stage, Zo and I found a vacant table.

"This is so cool!" Zo cheerily shared while tapping through his phone. "Wait till I tell Gena!"

"So, what're we gonna start with?" Ragee asked the stage. There were a few shrugs. "Let's do something to warm up."

While a few words were exchanged, a melody sounded. Launz strummed his guitar with quieted expertise. It reminded me of those days at *Corey's* when the band would give him the bridge and he'd play in lead. His eyes were closed, almost to a squeeze, bottom lip fastened between his teeth. He played long enough to get Ragee's attention, but the sequence wasn't familiar to me. The others visibly leaned forward to follow him. The chord arrangement was heavy, dramatic.

The pianist was the first to follow, playing along. Next was the organist, and the drummer was soon after.

When Ragee caught on, his big body leaped to the microphone and crooned, "I'm a playaaaaa. Girl, I thought you knew..."

My jaw dropped behind my closed mouth. It was the 112 song that had begun to haunt me. I'd heard *"Player"* countless times, especially after its release in the early two-thousands. It was a good track. Introspective, raw, honest, and authentically bold. It was clear. Settling down was not a present destination for the author, or now performer as Ragee's robust vocals delivered the message effortlessly. He sang the song with as much conviction as he did his own. Wasn't he married?

Launz isn't...

And that's when it dawned on me. The lyrics. They were him. Launz selecting this song was him responding to my demands of sexual exclusivity last night. He was saying he didn't want to forego condoms because he enjoyed being with other women.

Respectfully.

My heart rented.

Shit...

~TWENTY

PRESENT DAY

"Wow! Five years of Black marriage is a beautiful accomplishment," Nye commented over the Bailey dinner table. "Are you planning a celebration?"

Trent looked to Jade for her answer. "Yeah. We're going to Japan with Stenton and Zoey—" Jade dropped her face on the upper side of her hand. "I hate to feel I'm name-dropping with people I've just met. I'm sorry."

"No." Nye laughed along with Jade and Ezra's wife, Lex. "Don't worry. I guess that is weird for you, though. It's totally fine. I'm actually having my own experience with Launz's breadth of friends myself. Where exactly in Japan, Trent?"

I knew the move. Nye was pushing Trent into the conversation. He'd been polite since we arrived at his home for dinner along with the Carmichaels, but he'd been noticeably reticent. It was rude as hell, an energy I wasn't accustomed to getting from my players. I'd been beyond patient with Bailey. At this point, I'd begun giving up any hope of him being on the roster this season.

"Uhhh..." He scratched inside his beard. "Okinawa. I'm always mispronouncing it."

"Oh! Okinawa. You said it correctly. Lots of rain in May and June, but gorgeous, nonetheless. Are you taking the kids?" Her eyes directly on him.

"Yeah. We're gonna make it a family thing." Trent tossed his chin toward me. "Speaking of: I didn't know you had a kid."

"Launz has always held a distinct quiescence to his robust energy."

Ezra came through with the diversion on the Zo topic. He knew the full story and understood the sensitivity of sharing it with Trent at this time. I'd always thanked God for that man. He was the first pastor I ever saw myself being led by since leaving my parents' church. My faith walk would be directionless without one Bishop Ezra Carmichael. We didn't speak often, but he'd always availed himself to me as a friend and spiritual leader. And for that, he'd forever have my support. I never charged my church to play or record. It was my act of worship to give freely.

"Yup," Nye agreed. "He's shy."

Low key annoyed, I snorted, "I am not."

I'm just not talkative like you and Zo...

"We worked in the same restaurant—well, I worked there as an employee, Launz played there with the band some nights—and I was there for a whole month before he even looked at me," Nye painfully shared. "And that was when I aggressively pushed him to give me a ride home."

Ezra blinked as his wife laughed. Nye shook her head as she continued to eat. She opted not to drink tonight, which was strange, I guessed. I honestly didn't know her social practices.

Jade giggled. "Oh, my god! That makes me think of Trent when we first met. He would hardly look my way. It drove me crazy."

Lex howled out, "And in his pants! Poor TB!"

Trent dropped his head, markedly embarrassed, but found the humor in the moment as well as he laughed. Trent Bailey having to be aggressively pursued sexually? That was funny as hell until I remembered it to be my experience with Nye.

Wow…

My phone vibrated in my pocket again when I thought I'd powered it off earlier. The deluge of texts and calls from my agent, friends, and Monica, drove me crazy. I'd heard. *Yes. I knew!* And right now, I just wanted to get through with this useless dinner so I could endure the aches rolling in my cranium while I revamped my offensive platoon.

"Check out the aquarium there, not that you need kids for that," Nye shared while staring up at the chandelier, playing with her fingers. Oddly, the innocuous act was damn attractive to me. "I love aquariums. Also, the historic *Shurijo* castle is an attraction. Nothing that ever tickled my fancy, but folks rave about that. You guys are probably already going to do the beaches and see some of the islands—"

"You've been there before?" Jade asked.

"Not to all of them, no. But I think I really liked—or my mother often took us to Zamani Island for scuba diving—or was it Kouri? It's been so long ago, I can't say with certainty."

"Your family traveled extensively?" Ezra asked.

"Mmmm…" Nye nodded while swallowing a sip of water. "Not so much recreationally. My father's a Marine—was a Marine."

"When did he die?"

Lex snorted, "What makes you think he's passed away, E? The man could have retired."

As Ezra gazed at Nye, he rasped, "Because Marines never retire. They despise the term. Once a Marine, always a Marine until your last breath."

Visibly uneasy, Nye coughed into her hand. "This is true." She grabbed her glass of water. "You're a Marine?"

"No," Ezra answered, combing his beard with his fingers. "When did he transition?"

"At the top of the year. January."

"Oh, I'm sorry to hear that," Jade interjected. "Just when we thought we were over with twenty-twenty *and* Trump. That's awful."

With a stretched forehead, Nye shook her head. "It's totally fine." In her uneasy state, she peered my way. It was clear for support, so I flashed her a smile, understanding the complexities of the subject.

"So," I broke the awkward air. "July for the big release date, huhn?"

Ezra, understanding the question, nodded. "Yes, sir. And I do believe the world is in for a treat with this new body of work."

"The worship experience was truly amazing," I admitted, still in awe of the recording concert we did at *Redeeming Souls for Abundant Living in Christ* a couple of weeks back. "It was lit."

Lex nodded, agreeing with me.

"Off the chain," Trent commented.

"You went?" Jade asked as though she was shocked.

"Had to. It was my first time actually seeing Coach in the building."

Here he goes with the subliminal shots...

"I've never seen you in the sanctuary either," I argued coolly.

"That's because, Trent, you're primarily up in the balcony and Launz is down somewhere near the stage, whether he's playing or not."

"Zo said your parents had a great time." Nye smiled my way. "I'm looking forward to checking out the church someday. Maybe the next time you play?"

I nodded, not having a problem with that.

"So, how long have you two known each other?" Trent's brows met as he sat back in his seat. "You look pretty young," he referred to Nye.

He was with the shits, I knew.

Nye glanced my way, grin playing at her face. "We were kids. Launz was a senior at *Rutgers* and I was...nowhere near graduation." She giggled.

"That long, huhn?"

Nye nodded. "And yet, not long enough." Her charm was fading. Something was going on inside of her I couldn't decipher.

"Do you want more children, Nye?" Jade asked buoyantly.

Nye's face brightened and contorted at the same time. "I don't think so. My baby's grown. If I were to have more, I would have wanted them raised together."

Trent's head whipped to me. "And what about you, Coach? You want more kids?"

The room went silent for a while. I couldn't do it. Fuck that. I would not let him treat me like a pandering pussy. I didn't feel obligated to discuss my personal life with players. That was something done in bonding, not on demand.

With my head toward the table as I sat back with one hand at the base of my wine glass, I murmured, "I don't understand the nature of your question."

Trent scoffed. "I'm just trying to get to know you."

I lifted my head. "You're not. Let's at least be honest here."

The tension in the room was now suffocating, but I would survive it. I would leave this house with my dignity even if it included a major fucking headache.

"Okay." He nodded. "Like I told you, I don't know you. My wife thought to have you and Ms. Nye here over to make that happen."

"Bailey, I've interviewed—and quite successfully—for the role of your coach. I'm not about to do it again with the captain of the team who can't make up his damn mind about a job he's getting paid to do and the game he claims to be passionate about."

"I'm just making sure history isn't repeating itself because, according to the blogs, it damn sure seems to be." His nostril flared.

And there it was. He'd gotten wind of the story about Tynisha Lang and me back in January. I had no idea how the shit leaked, but someone took a picture of Tynisha and me at the door of my hotel room, kissing while I keyed us in.

Monica sent me the link on the drive up here and the first thing I thought about was Zo seeing the grainy pictures. Not my mother or father; my son. What does he think of me now? Is he disappointed?

Embarrassed? His coaches at *Rutgers* would know. I knew them all, though I hadn't been in contact with them out of respect to Zo, needing him to make a name for himself. This shit reflected on him now. I asked Monica to contact Chesney for options, possibly cease and desist orders. This "meeting" was in the way of me following up on it.

"Trent, maybe we shouldn't," Lex suggested softly.

"Now, I don't mean any disrespect." He shrugged. "It's already out there. A man has to be accountable for his actions."

"It's not our business, baby." Jade patted his hand.

"She's married to my friend!" Trent shouted my way. "You ain't got no respect for marriage, Coach?"

Lex snickered. "He's—*they're both* for the streets, Trent!"

Jade broke into a silent laughter, trying to hide her face.

"Beloved!" Ezra warned his wife.

"I'm sorry, but—" She tried managing her laughter. "Everybody know!" That made Jade laugh out loud and unabashedly, tears at the corner of her eyes. When Ezra's narrowed gaze wouldn't let up, Lex relented. "Alright! Alright!" She straightened in her chair as though in an effort to calm down.

"Jade, this ain't funny!" Trent attempted to compose his wife. "And marriage aside: Ms. Nye, you seem like a real nice woman. How does this make you feel?"

I jumped to my feet. "Don't ask my—"

Nye was aside me, grabbing a fist planted on the table. "It's okay, Launz. We can leave now." She then turned to Trent, who slowly stood with his chin toward the air. Jade followed, extending an arm of comfort over his abdomen. "To answer your question, Trent: Launz doesn't owe you that explanation. We're all aware of the pictures. But he doesn't owe anyone an answer to his time with Tynisha, not even me. And yes, he should still be respected as your coach and our friend." She pushed me to turn away from the table.

I struggled with being led by a woman. This was between two men and I had to set a boundary for Trent, whether he'd return this season or not. But there was that fucking superpower Nye held over me. It was no less potent than when she was seventeen years old and I was a goddamn grown ass man being finessed. The woman's aura was strong and mien powerful against my willpower. Between her insistence, my headache, and the need to move on from this night, I conceded and left the dining room. Nye's hand was cupped by my own when she stopped and turned.

"You can't lead with mistrust when getting to know someone, Bailey. A true connection happens when you trust *yourself* to being open and honest to the process of getting one." Her voice was filled with conviction and motherly wisdom. And I don't mean mother in a literal sense: I mean nurturer of a village. Of my child. "Good night," she bade the room and we promenaded, hand-in-hand, down the hallway to the front door.

The rain hadn't let up a bit, and I was grateful when Nye didn't flinch. We traveled down the pebbled driveway in front of the mansion, past the stone pillar. I felt betrayed and led on by Trent. If he knew this before sitting the mother of my child and me at his table, I wish he would have kept it a buck and canceled at the last minute.

The water beat down on us as a sensation swelled my chest that I refused to acknowledge. She was in step with me. She didn't bolt or take Trent's invitation to condemn me. Nye knew about the story and hadn't shown an ounce of jealousy or resentment after I all but told her I had no interest in being monogamous for her. She still cooked my meals, washed my clothes, participated in conversations with me, continued with the candle waxing when needed, and even fucked me properly.

And I haven't even—

I stopped, yanked her little body back in her heels, and grabbed Nye to me. Pulling her up my body to meet my mouth, I kissed her. Hard and with violent lust I'd never expressed with a woman, I took her tongue and lips. It was smooth, eager. When I felt her hands at my hair, grabbing patches in evident appreciation, I melted into her. My balls jounced and knees went fucking weak at the taste of her. Even in the rain, I could taste that clean floral fragrance. The scent of her hair products melting into the mix. Her natural body odor, it all intoxicated me, truncating my existence to what I'd been fighting against. Falling for this girl who was now a bona fide woman.

I welcomed her thighs snaking up my legs and folding around my waist. Rain pelting over us, I wanted to taste Nye more than I wanted to breathe. Covering. That's what the woman had just given me in there. In front of my pastor and first lady. Against a colleague, she covered me in a way Monica hadn't even done, and I knew it was because I'd never yielded to her. Nye *forced* me to yield…and I didn't like it.

Not wanting to let her go, I walked us the rest of the way to my *Wrangler.* I opened the passenger door to put her inside, where we finally disconnected. When Nye was in the passenger seat soaked from the rain, I couldn't walk away. We were both out of breath and shivering. Nye's eyes were heavy, lips swollen and trembling. She was gorgeous, even completely drenched. The mole near her mouth stark and beautiful.

Nye's eyes closed, chest heaved. Then she peered my way again and I took her at the sides of her face and tasted her mouth all over again. She squeezed the sides of my shirt at the waist, holding onto me. She tasted of safety and promise, something I hadn't had in so long. I wanted to drown in her, but decided to let her go at some point so we could breathe. Finally, I closed the door and crossed the truck for the driver's side. A shadow down near the stone column at the entrance of the house caught my attention.

Trent stepped out beneath the attached carport, gaping my way without apology. I had no words for him, so I slid inside the truck and we took off for South Jersey.

He parked at the entrance of the house, so we tumbled in through the front door. My heart trembled and body was on fire. The close to two-hour drive had felt like an eternity to process the fact that Launz had kissed me. In the mouth, he'd kissed me. It had only taken him close to a month. We'd had sex several times, but until tonight, I didn't have the benefit of his oral pleasure. And, shit, had I been missing out. This was possibly worse than waiting on him to finally have sex with me twenty-two years ago.

The agony of patience.

And now, back in Moorestown, I didn't know what we'd do, but I knew I wouldn't be sleeping alone. I wanted to be with him. Even if we'd spent the whole night kissing, I'd take that act of intimacy with him and wear it like a badge of honor. So, with weighted wet clothes, I headed straight to the stairs, staring behind to watch his actions. Launz's eyes didn't leave mine as he locked the door then took two steps at a time to reach me.

"Mmmmm…" I fell into him as he kissed me from behind.

His tongue in my mouth felt as needy as my heart for him lately. His hands were on my jacket, peeling it from my shoulders and arms. My soaked blouse was next, then my panties and jeans as I kicked off my shoes. Launz removed my bra and my groin churned. Tossing it, the bra plodded down the stairs, as did the rest of my discarded clothing. He lifted my wet hair from my shoulders to tongue the back of my neck. I fisted his thighs behind me.

Launz had been different. His touch was now more aggressive and his tongue moved with evidentiary mastery. I shivered as his mouth moved down my back, his tongue tracing my spine. He bit into my damp ass, nudging me to bend over. When my palms gripped the ledge of a step, my back bowed at the feel of his tongue coursing the fold of my cheeks. With natural ease or plain old horniness, my spine arched even more and hips spread to open for him.

His mouth went to work, licking between my folds as I struggled to keep my head up. The tip of his tongue reached my pounding clit, where he licked and licked. Warming began in my core and grew hot. Helpless tremors prickled my thighs as I stood on my toes. I was on a hysterical edge, afraid to let it go.

What happened at the Baileys? Was it him feeling sorry for me when my father was brought up? Or was it my words to Trent himself about his regard for Launz? Whatever it was, something had changed and I was afraid to let it all go for a man who stripped me bare emotionally. As I danced into his face, I was terrified at the prospect of falling for a man who didn't trust me.

But as soon as a stinging smack to my right cheek ignited a smarting sensation and Launz croaked, "Come now," quickly before returning to my swollenness, I shuttered.

Ass jerking in the air, standing on my palms and big toes with seized lungs, I exploded. Convulsing, I couldn't think of anything. Launz abolished all of my resistance, rendering me a sobbing fool.

This is so not Nye...

Back in his bed, cupped by his whole frame, my thoughts about tonight still wouldn't form into words. My fears were still suspended as we lay in the dark. He'd made love to me. We made it to his shower where Launz took me again, but not just with his hands, dick, and sexual adeptness. His mouth was all over me, giving the illusion of complete openness.

"I'm leaving tomorrow," I whispered.

His arms, chest, and legs tensed around me, and for seconds long, I didn't think he'd speak.

"Why?"

"I'm going to see my mother."

"For how long?"

"Just for a few days. She has a couple of doctor's appointments scheduled I'd like to attend with her. Then I'll fly with her down to the wedding."

There was another long pause before he asked throatily, "You're just now telling me?"

My eyes widened in the dark. "I haven't seen a lot of you. You've been recording for a few weeks now."

"But you knew I'd be recording."

His body around me still hadn't relaxed.

"Launz, you're leaving for Connecticut soon, too," I tried to keep with the low, intimate tone. "Is there a problem with me leaving, too?"

His heat left as Launz lifted from around me, turning over to his other side. The last words he murmured were less confounding than his sudden mood switch. "I'll let you answer that."

What. The. Hell?

I jogged down the stairs, ready for a cup of coffee and a stogie to prepare for a Zoom call with Chesney then my offensive line. That was until I stopped at my wet jacket and Nye's entire ensemble, including her heels.

Shit…

I began gathering it all, wondering if I should toss them all in the washer and start a load or be smart and stow everything for Nye to decide how she wanted them sorted. *She may want to have this blouse dry cleaned...* I held it in the air, feeling confident about that call.

A clearing of the throat broke my thoughts. Monica stood just outside of the family room with a mug in her slippers. Her mouth was twisted and eyes hard on me.

My brows met. "What time did you get in this morning?"

"I didn't. And let me tell you something: I don't care what game you play with Nye—add her to the birthday list of the rest of them for me to send shit to—but you better keep one person in mind. Zo is a good kid and from what I've seen, he don't play about his momma. So, you think about that the next time you get selfish and irresponsible with her again."

"It's not like that, Nick."

"Yeah. Yeah. It never is the morning after. But by noon, you'll be able to admit the truth. And that is, at best, the most you can give her is a tad bit more than you did Tynisha Lang."

I shook my head. "It's not like that." Then I nodded. "Yeah, Nye and I have some complicated, possibly foul shit between us on the surface. But she's not someone being tossed away or added to the list I give you for gifts."

"Okay," she warned, turning away. "Well, you better let your son know about all of the 'respect' *and dick* you've got for his momma. Remember, he's out of school now and could have been here last night instead of at Mommy's and Daddy's."

Tell him what?

I took a deep breath, frustrated so soon into my day. I couldn't explain to Zo what I didn't understand myself.

"And it looks like the house in Connecticut is fully ready for move-in," Monica shared over Zo's speakerphone. "This morning, all the

beverages and non-perishables were delivered and Russell put them all away."

"That's good," I replied as we pulled into the resort where Nye's cousin's wedding was taking place in Virginia.

"Oh! Speaking of which," she chirped. "Zo, Gena's belongings were delivered about thirty minutes after you guys left for the airport. What time is her flight arriving down there?"

Zo hit me with puppy eyes. "Tonight."

"Okay. What about your mother and grandmother?" Monica asked.

"In a few hours," he shared, wary eyes back on me.

I scoffed, shaking my head. He'd been sulking since we left Jersey a few hours ago. We flew down this afternoon for the matrimonial festivities and the whole while, Zo lamented.

"Okay, baby," Monica continued, "Well, the last thing on my list is the suite has been secured, Launz."

"Nice," I remarked, grateful Zo didn't react to that *seemingly* bland information, though for me, it wasn't at all. "I'll hit you later about that meeting with Whitaker. I'm waiting to hear back from Miles Brown for his availability."

"Sounds good. Alright," Monica let out a deep breath. "I'll be down at Mommy and Daddy's this weekend. We're taking Andrew to the park tomorrow. The weather's supposed to be nice."

"Give the homie a pound for me," Zo requested.

I was happy to see the faint sign of happiness on his face when thinking about my nephew. His cousin.

"Will do, baby. Bye."

"Later," I bade.

Zo disconnected the call and turned to me as we sat in the back of the *E-Class*. "So, what if she tells me I have to go back to Arizona?"

"Who? Your mother?"

"Yeah!"

I laughed. "She's not going to tell you that."

"But if she does, could you at least mail all my things, and Gena's, back to Arizona?"

"Zo…" I shook my head as the car came to a stop in front of the resort. "Nye knows your girlfriend is coming to stay with you. That's the biggest detail of this whole plan as it is."

"Yeah! But the fact that I don't have a place for us to stay kills the whole plan. Besides that, man, it's been hard not having her to bounce ideas off of. I'm used to her handling everything. She's my best friend, man. Do you understand how stressful it's been not having superwoman in on one of the biggest moves of your life?"

"You could have just told her."

Zo's head shook with adamance. "Oh, hell no. Then she would've pressed me again about why it's so important to not have Gena out here. Then I would've gotten diarrhea of the mouth and told her she's pregnant. Then I wouldn't have to worry about you sending my shit back to the West Coast. I would've just hoped you paid for my funeral…and Gena's."

When his door was opened by the driver, I smirked at Zo, placing a hand at his shoulder. "Just tell her. Don't bring any emotion into it when you do: truth needs none with women. So, don't get choked up when you do what needs to be done." Zo nodded, likely trying to convince himself. "C'mon. This old man needs a nap before meeting your family tonight."

I was honestly in no mood to meet anyone. Didn't want to see anyone—*but Nye…*

Zo scooted out of the back seat and I followed from my side when the door was opened for me. "That's because you had to keep up with me this morning in the gym," he joked.

I laughed, not giving into his competitive personality. "We good?" I bumped fists with the driver.

"Very good, Mr. Pierce." The chauffeur nodded. "Thanks for your generosity. And good luck this season, sir!"

"Thank you." I waved, taking off.

I followed our baggage being pulled on a luggage cart by a bellhop into the cool lobby. There were people moving about, even several at a barroom adjacent to the front desk area. I went straight to an available attendee to check in. While I shared my identification and confirmed the accommodations, I could hear Zo speaking to people he knew.

"And the rental?" I inquired about.

"Yes, sir," he assured. "It's all ready for Mr. Taylor."

Zo needed to go pick up his mother and grandmother soon. Then he had to turn back around and get Gena from the same airport a couple of hours later. I needed to crash. It had felt like a long day already. Last night, Zo and I stayed out late, playing cards with a few of my friends in Philly. Then we worked out this morning before my barber came through to get my hair right and hook Zo up, too. That left us minutes to leave out for the airport.

He'd been a fun companion, I had to admit. Since Zo wrapped up the semester, he'd been spending his time between my parents' and my place. Nye had been in Arizona with her mother for close to a week now. I hated how much her absence had been a thing for me. We'd spoken just about every day either with Zo in the mix or separately. As much as I didn't like her being away, the time had given me an opportunity to reflect on a lot of things.

There were small fires between Nye, me, and Zo. The pregnancy, Zo's future, Nye's future, and my relationship with the both of them. I'd thought a lot about it over the past few days, prayed a lot on it, too. I'd just hoped all would work out without anyone getting hurt or feeling betrayed. Either way, I knew my actions as the man of this trio had to start with Nye.

"*Oh*, that's him?" I heard the stunning wonderment in a woman's voice.

I closed up my registration as a guest then turned, seeing Zo speaking with a few people.

With all expectant and amazed regards on me, I grinned and bore the mundane formalities. Placing my wallet inside my messenger bag, I extended my hand to the man first.

"Launz Pierce."

"Yo, man!" he croaked. "I know you. *How*—! Ah, man! It's an honor."

Zo explained, "This is Mick, the future groom."

"I appreciate that, my guy. Congratulations. Glad to be here." I nodded then moved on to the woman. "And you are?"

She didn't speak at first, still swallowing my presence.

"This is Lenora," Zo explained. "The bride."

"The woman of the weekend. Happy to be a part of your special day."

Her eyes swung between Zo and me. "Oh, my—" So stumped, it seemed, she laughed—at herself. "Where's Nye?"

"She'll be here soon," Nye's sister, Jenise, offered, appearing out of nowhere. She applied a warm angling of her head and smiled. "Zo, you should be picking them up soon. Correct?"

"Oh. Hey, auntie!" He greeted her with a hug and kiss, which Jenise reciprocated.

"Hi, Launz," Jenise greeted me.

"Jenise," I returned. "Good to see you again."

I hated this. The way the woman looked at me was as though I was on an auction block.

"I'm sure Nye's looking forward to seeing you." She smiled in a way that brought the Nye I used to know to mind.

Jenise was being messy. But damn, if only what she said was true.

Zo laughed. "You funny, Auntie!"

With her eyes on all parties, Lenora giggled, too. She was lost, trying to distinguish the truth and the joke. Had Nye told her sister about us? I honestly didn't know and wouldn't slip in front of Zo.

"Oh! Because I was about to ask, 'Ain't Nye single?' Last I knew she was," Lenora commented. "She's too damn determined to prove women don't need a man for companionship to get one. Feminists stay mad, cold, and lonely."

Oh…

"There's nothing mad, cold, or lonely about my sister, sweetheart." Then Jenise's beam turned dark on her cousin. "She's educated, has tenure in an industry that will always thrive, and a handsome face—" She pinched Zo's cheek. "—like this. What reason would she have to be mad, cold, or lonely?"

"Well," Lenora faced me. "if you're single, I have a sister who's known to be the prettiest Taylor." She laughed. "My husband-to-be here doesn't agree, but that's been the consensus—Oh!" she chirped. "Here's Latanya now."

I didn't want to meet more family. Not now. I needed a quick nap and a candle wax session to get my head right. Not this. Not strangers I don't care to see or know—

Damn!

A beautifully dark skinned shortie strutted to our small gathering in gold biker shorts and a matching tank top, leaving nothing to inquire of her curves. Her hair was big and kinky, styled into a fluffy flow. The curve in her hips mixed with the small space between her thighs reminded me of Salena, my sienna Caribbean beauty, who I'd just had a difficult conversation with a few days ago about ending our friendship. I explained it was because of some personal shit in my life needing to take precedence.

That was enough. Before 'Latanya' even made it to our group, I announced, "I hate to do this, but I've got to go. I have a call in five minutes I need to take upstairs. It was nice meeting you two. Congrats again." I handed over the rental and suite key to Zo. "Here you go. I'll hit you later."

Zo snickered. "Alright, man. Wish me luck," he called behind me.

"You don't need luck," I shouted back as I grabbed our luggage cart, not wanting to wait for assistance. "You're a Pierce; favor is already flowing through your veins."

I caught one of the elevators just in time. It was occupied by an older woman of Asian descent. I selected my floor and waited for the doors to close. As they did, Latanya's curvy figure appeared, ass could be seen from the side as she talked to her sister. Just before the doors met, she winked and tossed her chin forward. To me?

A sputter of laughter shot from behind me. I turned to the elder woman with gray streaks. "Looks like she wanted to trade places with me."

A part of me wished, and the other didn't. My last hookup at a hotel for a wedding ended up biting me in the ass. The bloggers were still yapping about that shit. Ebonee Williams did a "special" segment on it last week. D.J. Paulie D and Ruby Voodoo of the syndicated Power 105.1 morning radio show had their own just yesterday. The shit annoyed the fuck out of me. Fuck what the knowledge did to Trent Bailey. It required a long conversation between Zo and me, where the kid assured me he was okay with it. I lowkey believed Zo was impressed by my single life. And while *that* may have been true and a save, it made me secretly wonder if the story about Tynisha Lang and me was the reason Nye split town without much notice.

My hand went to my head where a tightening began in my skull.

Yup.

I needed a nap.

~TWENTY-ONE

PRESENT DAY

"He's a very handsome man." My mother grinned coyly while swaying from side to side unrhythmically to the music.

"Mmmmhmmmm," I returned the same energy.

She wasn't being forward and I wasn't in the best mood.

Lenora and Mick's reception was in full swing in the plush banquet hall of the resort. The music was lively as the guests danced and the food was tasteless. That was likely due to my sour mood rather than the work of the facility. There had to be over two hundred people in attendance, bearing witness to the two exchanging their vows. Now they were all celebrating. I said they because I could think of a thousand other places I'd rather be, including fighting a kangaroo. The only reason I was at Lenora's wedding was to accompany my mother. If Gunnery Sergeant Preston

Taylor were still alive, he would have attended with my mother instead.

Zo and Gena were on the dance floor. She wore a frumpy pant suit and heels, refusing to remove her jacket, though I know she had to be hot in this Virginia heat. Zo looked happy. *Oh, to be young and complicated-less again*. But my life's complexities had already begun at their age.

"And not because Zo looks so much like him," my mother continued with her musing.

I turned her way, then followed her line of vision to the bar. Launz was there with Mick and his friends, holding court. They'd been riding his dick since I arrived last night with Mommy. From the moment we arrived, relatives were asking about my mother's grieving and Zo. They were sure to mention meeting or hearing his father was at the resort. Some even shared they knew he was a big-time coach for the *Connecticut Kings*.

Last night, at the rehearsal dinner where everyone was oddly invited, aunts, uncles, cousins, and family-friends alike all had comments to make about Zo's father coming to the wedding. The shit was embarrassing. The discovery of Nye's son's father resurfaced burning curiosities of his identity that took years to go dormant in my family.

He'd been distant. Still. It started when I told him I was going out to visit my mother. He'd closed up on me…again. And not that he'd ever opened to me. Launz just tolerated me, similar to the way he did more than twenty years ago. I was lucky to be irritated enough by his multi-million dollar quarterback in said quarterback's home, telling him in not so indirect terms he was foul for treating Launz the way he'd been. That earned me his mouth—on mine and other sacred parts of my anatomy. But open? No. Launz hadn't opened to me at all.

All week at my mother's, I struggled privately with my direction in life even more than I had before sleeping with Launz. I came to the conclusion it was time for me to let Zo go and be an adult. Consequently, it would be freeing his father as well. Launz and I had no future. Hell. I couldn't even see myself in anything more with the man other than his sheets on occasion. I would never reduce myself to being one of many to him. I'd felt Ernie entertained other women over the years, and no, we were not an official couple. However, I never felt like a member of an ensemble. He'd given me lead. I'd been thinking a lot about his proposal in Connecticut, too. The whole thing with him was vexing.

But what irritated me was the tumbler of brown juice Launz held tonight at the bar. *Mauve*. Why was he drinking *Mauve*? What was he thinking? Where was he emotionally? Had I missed the latest news about Trent Bailey? Couldn't have. It was now a pastime for me to drop in on sports news for updates. Nothing had been reported. And it wasn't like I could've dropped by his suite last night because Zo and Gena were staying in one of the two bedrooms Monica reserved for them. I didn't exactly think calling would be a great idea either. How much could he say in front of them?

And now, looking at him, the "shy guy" at the bar, socializing with strangers, I felt...jealous.

"Alright everyone," the host announced. "We've seen the groom take the garter, now it's time to find out who the next bride will be!"

"You should go." My mother laughed.

"Never." I rolled my eyes. She cackled even louder. "You'll have better luck with Jenise."

"Hell no!" Jenise dropped down into Zo's vacant seat next to me. "These bitches will never get the satisfaction."

My mother giggled again. "Where's Oliver?"

"The little boys' room," Jenise answered. "It was time for me to rest these dogs."

I glanced down at her five-inch, blue crystal-embellished *Aquazzura* sandals. Then I glanced down to my sandals, grateful for sticking with four-inch heels. She'd brought a date this weekend. Oliver. He was one of many for her in terms of associates. She rotated them based on need. My sister was a practicing attorney herself in entertainment law and did well. She'd been married twice and engaged to a third man a couple of years ago. Jenise had her own way of going about companionship and I stayed out of it. But I knew she wouldn't come to Lenora's wedding without a plus one. Lenora and her sister would, once again, judge Gunnery Sergeant Preston Taylor's daughters for similar reasons to why he condemned us: we were unruly and driven by the wrong type of success. *Whatever that meant.*

I observed for the next few minutes as the single women excitedly gathered on the dance floor, giddy with anticipation of being marked "the next." They screamed, pushed, and jumped in the air like silly girls. I snickered when my cousin, Latanya, won.

"Hell," Jenise hissed. "I'll be married before that woman."

"Oh, behave, young lady!" my mother chided.

We continued to watch as they moved on to throwing the garter. The guys were more reluctant to participate than the women were. *Pathetic hopeless romantics.* The host had to push men onto the floor. When he went for Zo, my body tensed.

"He better not," I grated, mouth tight.

Although I didn't believe in this tradition of garter-throwing, Zo and I were already in a sensitive place about his insistence on having Gena stay with him here out on the East Coast. This wedding began that journey for them.

His little big ass better not try to take it too far…

Zo thought wisely and expressively declined. But his father didn't when the host pleaded with him. I bit the inside of my cheek when Launz stood in the small crowd of men, looking unfairly dapper in a black suit tailored to his fit body, crisp white dress shirt, and printed bowtie. He wore the goddamn ensemble so well, blending the grittiness of his tightly coiled natural hair to the urbane suit. Launz's posture told of his worldliness, his ability to suit the occasion—literally and figuratively.

The garter was sent into the air and without moving an inch like a few of the others, the damn thing landed on his thumb. A choir of women went up, expressing either disappointment or excitement. I couldn't tell which one.

"Oh, hell no!" Jenise hissed.

A minute or two later, I figured out why. A chair was placed in the center of the dance floor for Latanya. Launz had to put the garter…up her leg…onto her thigh! My cousin sat, twitching in the chair with anticipation. And so many women were up near her for the show.

Oh, shit…

Launz preferred dark skinned women. *Natural women.* Not only did he tell me this when I met him, but many of the few I'd seen in person and in pictures he had stowed throughout his home checked both boxes. Latanya fit his type.

I'm light skinned with natural pressed out hair—at least!

"Lenora tried to 'introduce' her to him yesterday," Jenise leaned over and whispered loudly to me. "I told you to lock his ass down. A man like that shouldn't be single. He's too fine and too damn paid."

I rolled my eyes hard. She was crazy and that made me crazier in my insecure state. Jenise didn't even know Launz's occupation until a few months back, let alone that we'd been sleeping together. It was a good thing I didn't confide in my sister. I'd been proven to be a fool right here, right now if I did.

And to add insult to injury, the deejay switched songs, I guessed, to spice up the moment. Of the gazillion tracks he could have played, he went with 112. My eyes closed slowly to a squeeze. Yup. The song that had been haunting me since the first time I'd slept with Launz in Connecticut, *"Player."*

Launz made a show of removing his jacket and handing it off to my son. *My son.* His two-step toward Latanya annoyingly made me tingle. What was he doing? Was I not right here? No, we were not together, and even if we'd never slept together recently, he was still my son's father, which coincidentally was why he was here.

And Zo? He cracked the hell up, holding Gena just off the dance floor. She apparently found humor in this, too, tittering right along. Launz took a knee at Latanya's chocolate legs slathered in oil. Her dress was so tight, she had to constantly pull it down or else her pussy would be exposed.

To Launz…

Ears ringing, muscles wound tight, and blazing blood shooting through my veins, I felt ill. This was too much, and yet there was nothing I could do, but watch.

"Drink this," Jenise ordered discreetly.

She'd put a shot down on the table. I turned and saw her date, Oliver. He must have brought it for her. I felt no need to question it. Instead, I snatched the glass into the air and gulped it all back.

"Another one," I demanded, tapping the table.

"On it!" Jenise dashed away.

"Nye!" my mother giggled. "You can't be upset, honey. It's harmless fun. That's all."

I wanted to explain to my mother there was nothing harmless or fun about my heart being exposed out there on that dance floor. This. This was what heartbreak and betrayal felt like.

Before I knew it, Jenise had returned with another shot. I was able to get that down faster than the first.

"Another?" Jenise perceptively asked and I nodded, consenting while going for my phone.

"Slow down, Nyedeera," my mother warned.

Ignoring her, I shot off a text message.

Me: We've never discussed prenups.

"See. It's over," my mother continued. "And everyone's laughing."

Seconds ago they were oooh'ing and ahhhh'ing salaciously. There's a difference, Ma!

Ernie Witherspoon: *Because you haven't given me much of your time. We can discuss that. Anything to make you comfortable.*

Finally, I braved a glance over my shoulders and saw people dancing as they were before the garter shit began. Then I pivoted in my seat in search of Launz. Corner to corner of the room, I couldn't find him *or* LaTanya. I didn't even see Gena and Zo.

Oh, no!

I stood to leave. "I need some air, Ma."

"Don't worry. I can get back upstairs alone, Nye. Just gather yourself." She was annoyed and I was livid.

On my way to the door, I passed Jenise, who lifted the shot into the air. Without a break in our strides, I retrieved it from her hand, tossed it back, and left it on a table before exiting the room. My search began there in the hallway. That led me out into the large lobby. Next,

I thought to try the suite Launz shared with Zo and Gena. My heart thundered on the elevator ride up. If Latanya's ass was in that suite, fucking or not, I would claw her eyes out.

When I made it to the floor, Gena and Zo were just letting themselves inside the suite.

"Hey!" I managed a smile. "I was looking for you two. You just up and left. Your dad, too. Everything okay?" The lies poured effortlessly.

"Oh, nah." Zo let Gena inside. "She has to pee. I don't think he's in here. The place is dark."

"You mind if I use the room phone to call Jenise? I think she left with a headache."

"C'mon." He waved me inside.

I checked my vibrating phone.

Ernie Witherspoon: ***You there sweetheart?***

I rolled my eyes, deciding to ignore him. The suite was huge compared to my double queen standard room with Mommy. Zo turned on a few lights for me. Both bedroom doors were open.

"This your room?" I asked.

When Zo nodded, I made a dash for the other. Inside, the comforter and sheets were scruffy, but no signs of Launz. After pretending to make a call, I left out, prepared for a mission.

He had Mauve!

"Alright, baby." I zipped past him. "I'm going out for drinks. Check in on Grams. Okay?"

"I got you!" he shouted behind me.

My first thought was to head back down to the lobby then the banquet room before flipping the resort upside down. Then, while at the elevator, I thought to send a warning shot.

Me: Where are you? And I'm warning you both now I'M PRETTY FUCKING VIOLENT!!!!!!

Crossing my arms, I tapped my feet while waiting for the elevator to arrive.

I leaped with murderous excitement when the bell tolled. Coincidentally, my phone vibrated in my hand at the same time.

Alaunzo: ***East tower. 16th floor. Suite A.***

My head snapped back.

"Oh, you're honest, honest!" I hissed to myself.

I was currently in the west tower. I'd have to cross over and take a different elevator system for that suite.

I did.

Less than ten minutes later, I was knocking on the door of suite A on the sixteenth floor of the east tower. Impatiently, I knocked hard again then squatted to remove my sandals. Before I could make it to the second foot, the door opened. Launz held his phone with his bowtie unraveled and the buttons of his shirt undone and pulled from his trousers. I rushed inside, looking for Latanya. She'd gone way too far. Back in the day, Jenise cussed her out a few times for trying to talk to the same guys she did in the summers. I didn't play those games, and she'd learn tonight.

I searched the bedroom then bathroom, the living room then the kitchen, and finally the powder room. That's when I turned to find Launz near the door holding my sandal in one hand and his phone in the other. He tapped it and seconds later, "*Player*" crooned through the speakers of the living room. My heart ripped in my chest.

Launz tossed my shoe to the side and seductively sauntered toward me. My eyes closed at his persuasive aroma. He pulled me into his hard chest, one hand at the small of my back and the other pushing up my skull through my loose hair. His mouth lay against my ear and I could hear his breaths. When his teeth grazed my lobe, I shivered pathetically.

"Why are you doing this to me? Why do you enjoy punishing me?"

His hand was at the back of my gown, zipper going south. Seconds later, the dress was pooled at my feet, and I was down to just a thong. With his virile strength, Launz gripped me at the ass and pushed me up his body, my chest rubbing against his until my breasts reached above his broad shoulders. He buried his face in my bosom, inhaling audibly. Then he bit my right breast, causing my chest to cave and I shivered. His lips swept against the pounding of my heart to my left nipple, where he licked then sucked. My hands went to the high top textured structure of his coiled hair where I gripped. He nipped at that breast, then went to lick and suck the right.

"I miss these," he shared thickly. My head rolled back. "I miss *you,* Nye."

His virility was in his voice, his scent, his strength. Launz sat me on the dining room table at an angle, forcing my knees into the air. My lungs disappeared when he cupped my face with his big hands and kissed me. His lips were soft, tongue expressive and hands greedily holding me in place. I was so turned on, I could feel the heat emanating from my sex as he rested between my thighs.

His mouth left mine and traveled down my chest to my belly button. He yanked at the bone ring with his teeth while pulling my thong down and over my legs. I reached back, gripping the table with my palms. Launz's mouth landed on my open sex. His tongue spread wide as he licked me. He was inside then lashing on my clit as I watched. And just as I grabbed his hair, prepared to explode, he pulled back.

He lifted me from the table and carried me into the bedroom where he lay me on the bed. I watched Launz remove his clothes.

"You're not playing fair and you know it."

"Thank the *Mauve* later."

When he was down to nothing but a standing cock, and thick and heavy swinging balls, he reached over, pushing my arms out above my head. My thighs opened in anticipation of his hips, my pussy prepared excitedly for his girth and breadth. Launz sank into me without guidance of his hands or mind. He watched me take him, feeding himself to me like a thick cobra.

"I'm jealous," I whispered, choking back a cry, tipping my vulnerability. My eyes fluttered open.

"And *that's* my safe space with you."

His fists were planted in my palms, reminding me of his distrust. But Launz wasn't wearing a condom.

"That's unfair."

His tongue flicked out, swiping my bottom lip. "It's the game you set long ago."

"I felt betrayed watching you with my cousin. That's gotta be what heartbreak feels like."

Launz pulled out of me and arranged me onto my belly. He plunged into my core, immediately meeting a sweet spot my spine curled to. My face into the mattress, he pounded me hard with precision until my belly warmed and I exploded.

As I mewled into the comforter, he grunted in my ear, "Heartbreak is a girl you were crazy about disappearing out of nowhere, causing you to never trust again. Betrayal is her coming back with a gift she'd been holding out on for over two decades."

While in the throes of a powerful orgasm, those words haunted me. I felt debased and revered all at once. Was *this* manipulation or Launz's method of honesty. He lifted me to my knees, thrusting with abandon. In no time, I was lost to it, relinquishing to the pleasure. Like it or not, Launz was an incredible lover, consistent with passion and results.

When he pushed me down and rolled me over to my side, entering me that way, I recalled. *Mauve*. He'd been drinking it all night, revving up his sex drive. I enjoyed every second of it and took each thrust while watching his thick, tanned and lubricated cock disappear into me rhythmically.

"*Ahhh*!" I moaned, rolling my hips. "*Launzzzz...*"

He groaned against my pussy, coming in my hand. Launz had gone a long while before reaching an orgasm, and his first was alongside my third. I sat on his face while reaching back, fisting him to a creamy mess.

Struggling to catch my breath, I crawled off of him and toed into the bathroom on shaky legs. I washed my hands and found a washcloth to do the same for my tender sex. He entered behind me and meandered to the shower to turn it on. Launz was over the toilet, urinating as I toed out. I thought to find my gown to get dressed, but was too spent to get the heavy thing on. I needed a few more minutes. Then my thoughts went to my mother.

I reached for the phone to call our room.

"Hello?" she answered.

"Hey," I struggled for normalcy. "You okay, Mommy?"

"First Zo, coming here *and* calling. Now you. Chile, I'm more than thirty years older than you and you asking if *I'm* alright? You're disturbing my sleep. Are you okay?"

"Sorry. Yes, ma'am. I'll be in soon."

"Then I'll see you then."

"Okay—" She hung up the phone. "Okaaaaaaay…" I breathed out loud.

I was spent myself, emotionally and physically. And I felt stuck. Too tired to get dressed to leave, yet not comfortable enough to climb into this bed. I couldn't even if I wanted to. I couldn't just show up to our room in the morning. What if Zo was out looking for me? I lay my shoulder against the headboard and closed my eyes just to relax. I heard the shower eventually turn off, then the sink start.

The next thing I knew, Launz was in front of me, pulling the comforter down to tuck me into the bed. I must have fallen asleep.

"No," I whispered. "I can't stay. My mother."

He slid into bed behind me and kissed my shoulder, smelling of mint. "I can't stay either. I have Zo and Gena to think about. I'm surprised he hasn't called yet. Either way, you and I need time alone. Now that we've gotten physically reacquainted, we need to talk."

Panic rang through my belly. "About what?"

"About us." He kissed my cheek this time, freshly perfumed beard tickling my sensitive skin. "I've missed you."

"So you've shown."

I heard his laughter begin at the thundering of his chest first. "Yes, but not just for that. I didn't like you being away, and I knew I wouldn't when you told me you were going."

I steeled against him. "I don't know how to respond to that."

"I understand. It's unreasonable. I totally understand how a lot of my shit has been unreasonable toward you, especially as it concerns your absence from my life and your return with Zo."

"I don't understand."

There was a slight spell of time before he spoke. "I never acknowledged your trauma." I believed Launz waited for me to speak, but I had no words, so he continued. "I listened to your story of being manipulated by your father to leave town and never contact me about my child, and made the whole thing about me."

My eyes closed. "Because you were the victim, Launz. I get that."

"And what *I* now get is so were you. As difficult as it is to reconcile, I have to remember you were a seventeen-year-old child. By the way, that significant fact grates at my fucking balls. I let a seventeen-year-old kid finesse me."

He made it sound so trivial. If I wasn't so tender over the whole ordeal, I would have laughed. "I'm sorry."

"I believe you are. I can see in the way you walk around with your shoulders caved in—but before I get into that, I need to acknowledge your abuse. I remember you showed to *Corey's* with the bruised arm. I thought it was extreme, but didn't know it was *that*. No, he had no business laying a finger on you, but in my mind, you were so formidable, Nye. I didn't think you'd take anybody's shit. I'm sorry for the caricature I created for you in my mind. Your father was abusive—"

"It wasn't a regular occurrence—"

"And not just physically," he spoke over my excuse, not allowing me to finish. "You've explained how much of a monster he was, and if I can be honest, my dirty fantasies include him being alive."

"I'm fine, Launz. Really."

"It's not just about you. It's about Zo and me. He raised my boy,

Nye! Not only did he deny me my child, but encroached on love like I told you. Not only the potential you and I had, but what I should have had with Zo. He impeded on my future as a man…to you and Zo."

The first hot, errant tear slipped and I quickly swiped it away. "How do we move on from it? I hate it here. I need to move on."

Another kiss from him on my head warmed me more than I was willing to admit. This was hard. "That brings me back to the weight you've been carrying. Your light has been dimmed. I don't know for how long or what did it, but since you've been back into my world, I can sense your shrinking."

I sniffled. "I *could* be a new person, Launz. I'm thirty-nine now."

"No, baby. I've heard it from Zo in so many ways. And you said it yourself when you told me about your father's encroachment. You need to be healed. So do I, and so does Zo."

I turned over beneath the covers to face him. This sounded impossible. "So what do you propose?"

"I spoke to my pastor and a couple of my friends—"

"Really?"

His nodded as his eyes assessed me softly. "I'm over forty, beautiful. Grown men talk. I've never pretended to be perfect or have all the answers." He kissed my forehead this time. "Anyway. I think counseling would do us well as a family."

My head jerked back. "A family?"

Launz nodded again. "Whether you and I continue exploring each other or not, we're a family. Zo needs help adjusting to having a father as much as I do having a son. You need help with that weight you carry because of it all. I can't stay stuck, Nye. I have a job that requires the best of me. Until my personal life is addressed, I can't give what's best to anyone else. Hate it or love it, you're my family."

I didn't understand. "You think we should…like be a couple?" My eyes narrowed.

Launz's expression matched mine. "I think we shouldn't put the cart before the horse. I'm pretty fucked up and won't pretend I want a relationship overnight. But I'll give you monogamy."

Sucking in a breath, I asked, "Really?"

"Only because your pussy's good and your mind—when you resume its original state—will keep me on edge. I'm sure, and I'm fucking petrified."

"I'm not a heartbreaker," I whispered in total truth. "I'm not like that."

"Then we'll have to see what you are, but first, some counseling to help us sort shit. In the meantime, I don't want you rushing to move out. In time, we'll decide if *we* need that. And I want you to have access to the house in Connecticut, too." My eyes grew as big as saucers. "Again, let's take it day by day, but seeing that you're the mother of my child—"

"And my pussy's allegedly so good..."

Closing his eyes, Launz inhaled deeply. "That part. Especially that part." He nodded, then his eyes were on me again. "I want to give you access to what I have. To me."

Immediately, I saw many nose-picking sessions in my very near private time. Launz's direction overwhelmed me.

I closed my eyes, lips twisting. "I see the *Mauve* has left your system." I was definitely sober. "And we don't have a lot of time in the suite you booked for my cousin."

Launz snorted, "Is that what you think this was?" I nodded. "This entire resort is to capacity. It cost me a many of beans to get this for us before I even checked in. Thank Monica and her persuasive skills."

I crawled down his body, watching his expression turn from humor to sensual curiosity.

"You can thank me soon enough."

I reached his resting dick and licked it. Soon enough, he became alive in my mouth. Launz was rather thick, not too long, and beautifully bronzed and veiny. I lost my cool when his tongue pushed from his lips in expressed ecstasy and he bit his lip. That simple act was all I needed to feel emboldened. And by the lustful gleam in Launz's expression, he appreciated it.

The man was nasty, and I believed it was beyond the *Mauve*. I'd been missing out on this undeniable chemistry and a level of sensuality I didn't know existed all these years. The old Launz could only please me with his mouth. Real adult Launz did it with his mouth, cock, hands, and mind.

Now, I wanted to show him what I could do.

When the bell of the elevator tolled and the doors parted, Launz was leaning into the corner. His heavy eyes swept over to me. Regretfully, we had to part ways. I was soiled, emotionally wrung out, and tender in all of my private parts. A wild thought had me smiling his way.

"What?"

"I feel like a teenager all over again."

Launz pushed up to put a leg in the opening of the elevator. "How so?"

"I had the time of my life—"

"The fuck of your life," he challenged.

My grin deepened. "Yeah. That. But I couldn't stay like an adult. I did it in secret because no one can know, not even my mother. Now, I'm sneaking back into her space, hoping not to get caught showering off my dirty little secret."

Launz snorted then leaned into me. "In due time, Taylor." He kissed me sweetly before I stepped off the elevator and toed barefoot down the hall to my room.

~TWENTY-TWO

PRESENT DAY

Lord, be with us…

I knocked on the door feeling the tension shooting from Zo and Gena behind me. Instead of acknowledging it, I kept my focus ahead.

Nye's mother opened the door. She saw me first then the anxious kids.

"Oh, hey." She smiled. "Good morning."

"Good morning, Mrs. Taylor," I greeted her as she moved aside to let us in.

"I know Zo called and said he was stopping by before we went down for breakfast, but I didn't know I'd see you all." Her voice was sweet and cherubic.

The room was small. Two beds, a desk, chair, and patio. So, there was no place to sit.

"It was lovely meeting you last night," I offered Mrs. Taylor. "I wish we had more time for a proper conversation."

"Oh, I understand." She smiled, sitting on one of the beds. "I'm just happy he's happy."

She patted a sulking Zo on his ass lovingly as I sent a text.

Me: Nothing has changed between us. I meant every word I said last night and more.

"Mom's in the bathroom?" Zo mumbled to his grandmother.

"Yeah. She should be coming out soon."

The door to the bathroom opened slowly. Nye stepped out in denim short, shorts and a tank. As she peered into her phone, she used a towel to dry the ends of her hair and all I envisioned was her being in my suite, waking from a night in my bed. Teenage vibes was right. The secret shit wasn't my thing. Nonetheless, the curiosity in Nye's wide eyes when her regard lifted from her phone brought me back to the here and now.

"Good morning, Nye," I offered.

"Hey. Good morning," she replied warily, regard bouncing around everyone in the room. "Mommy said Zo was coming down before we went to breakfast…" she prompted an explanation.

"Yeah," I took the bait. "Why don't you have a seat." I pointed to the bed.

"I'd rather not," her tone was curt, distrusting.

I nodded, understanding her fiery nature. "Okay. I know you and your mom are checking out in a few hours, and Zo brought to my attention this morning how he has yet to have a needed conversation with you."

"About what?" she asked him.

Zo's head was already low. He dropped his eyes, too.

I took a deep breath, pushing through. "Ummm… I know you'll be returning to Jersey in a couple of days and want you to know Zo and Gena will be staying with us. Indefinitely."

Her brows met and she peered over to Gena then Zo. "Indefinitely? I don't understand."

When Zo didn't speak up, I forged ahead. "You know Zo's been looking for a place to rent for Gena. In New Jersey, the market's challenging. I decided last week to invite her to stay with us in Moorestown."

"Oh." I could read the confusion on her face. Nye didn't fully get it. "You couldn't tell me?" she asked Zo, practically pleading with him to speak. The kid was no help. She looked to Gena, who stood far away, near the patio door, her hands clasped at her pelvis. "Do your parents know about you moving in with a virtual stranger? Because Zo is going back to school in the fall. He'll be living on campus because of the demanding football program he's enrolled in."

"They do, actually," I explained. "I've spoken with both Michael and Kim and assured them Gena will be in good hands. That you and I both will take care of her."

Nye's head whipped my way. "Who said all of that?"

I lowered my chin, issuing her a leveling gaze. "I did."

"Look, Ma," Zo finally decided to arrive to this conversation. "I know you won't be around long—with being engaged to Ernie and all—but Gena and I are grown. We don't need much. Just time to get on our feet."

What the fuck?

"I never said we were engaged, Zo!" Nye charged defensively. "I said he proposed." *What?* She wouldn't even look at me. "Secondly, why are *we* committing to long term care? You two are still young. Why are you making such a drastic decision?"

I cleared my throat, an act of nervousness, I guessed. "Because Alaunzo and Gena are expecting, Nye." With my eyes pinned to her, I dropped my chin.

"Expecting what?" Nye's gaze shot around to everyone in the room.

Her mother sat stoic and speechless. Gena then pulled up her oversized *BSU* hoodie and exposed her very much protruded belly. *Damn...* I hadn't even realized she was so progressed. She'd been doing quite a job at obscuring it.

"Oh, my God!" Nye cried, covering her mouth.

I wanted nothing more than to hold her, but knew it would send a conflicting message, especially now that *we all* knew she was proposed to. For what seemed like forever, silence swelled the room. Nye didn't move and neither did anyone else. I knew what betrayal felt like, this situation hitting close to home. Finding out your lineage is being extended during not so great circumstances could truly be a blessing. Like in this case of learning we were going to be grandparents.

Just as it could have for me if I knew Zo was on the way or that he even existed.

With that, my job was done. Nye and her mother needed breakfast before they left for the airport. And Zo needed to face the music.

"Gena, how about we go grab a bite while Zo speaks to his mom and grandmom?"

She nodded, eyes going to Zo whose face was toward the floor. "Okay."

I directed her out of the room. When the door closed, I finally felt the weight of fear, disappointment, and pain all happening back in that room.

"She's gonna kill him," Gena whispered. "As big as you are, I still thought she was going to kill you, too."

"So did I," I admitted.

I did what I had to do for my son without regret. But at this point, I had to let Zo be a man and sit in his shit, and let Nye be a mom and sort through it.

The door slammed shut, marking the absence of Launz. I didn't know if that meant more to me or Zo. Because immediately, he fell into my lap sobbing.

"I'm so sorry, Mom! I didn't mean it. I swear, I've been responsible. I slipped up and it won't happen again. I'm sorry!"

I took him at the back of his head and pulled his brawny shoulders into an embrace. Catching eyes with my mother, I caught the tears flowing down her face. This was a grace I wasn't bestowed by Gunnery Sergeant Preston Taylor. While I was confident he would have supported Zo if he were still here, I knew this was not the acceptance I received when he was nothing more than a bean in my young belly.

"We'll get through this, son," I murmured over his head. "I promise we will."

"She said she liked him," Nye shared.

"What does *like* mean?"

"I don't know how Gena means it, but Black women have to feel comfortable with their medical practitioners. We have to be confident that our voice is heard. I tried gauging that from her."

"And what did she say?" I stopped tapping on the mouse, cleaning out my inbox.

Her voice dropped an octave. "That he was nice."

My head fell toward my lap as I sat behind my desk and I laughed silently. Nye was on her bullshit. "Did you articulate that to her?"

It had been a couple of weeks since Lenora's wedding in Virginia, which meant a couple of weeks of adjustments. Gena and Zo were in a bedroom on the third floor of my home. They were settling in as much as they could under the heavy circumstance.

Nye was accepting of Gena's pregnancy, but wasn't quite over the betrayal of it. She didn't like the idea of becoming a grandmother at her age. Still, she'd taken Gena out shopping for maternity clothes and even bought her books on pregnancy and caring for babies. We bought Gena a car, too. Nye insisted on going half, not wanting me to bear the cost alone for some crazy reason. We were also able to come to an agreement that Gena wouldn't be concerned about a job until after the baby was born.

"I guess," Nye hissed. "I'm just glad we found a doctor out here, and so soon. She's due September twenty-ninth, by the way."

My brows shot up. "Damn. Does she know if it's a girl or a boy?"

"These kids want suspense instead of smart planning. Gena told the doctor she didn't want to know."

That was a downer.

"Damn."

A knock at my open door got my attention. It was my cornerback, Ambrose McNeil. I waved him inside and pointed to one of the seats across from my desk.

"Right! These kids are different," Nye groaned.

"That, they are," I replied more or less about what was before me. "I gotta go. My appointment just arrived."

"Okay. Before you do: I want my mother to come out."

"Okay." My chin dipped. "When?"

"I don't know. She's saying she's fine and busy, but I don't like her out there alone. It's been five months since my father, and I hate that I left..."

I understood.

"You don't want her out there alone so much. I'm okay with whatever you decide, Nye. Do what you need to do."

There was a slight pause before she murmured, "Thanks."

"Later."

"Later."

Placing the phone on the receiver, I gazed over to Ambrose McNeil, who some referred to as Mosquito on the field, while taking a deep breath. "Do you even dress out, bro?" I tried using terms this generation did, which was one of the benefits of having Zo around. I learned the latest dialect.

He squirmed in his seat, clearly uncomfortable, understanding yet not appreciating the joke in my question. He even swiped his face with a palm as though sweating.

Grabbing my cell, I scrolled down the post written to rip his ass to shreds, realizing this was my first one-on-one with Ambrose. "Wow." I chuckled. "She really lit y'all up. Huhn?"

I'd been working my way down the roster, but had started with the guys who showed to my voluntary practices in April. Today, I needed to speak with my cornerback whose name had been in the media for some messy shit that had nothing to do with the game.

Mosquito here was a guest on a *SportsOne Network* sponsored podcast known for being more salacious than journalistic. The conversation turned controversial when tennis star, Teagan Tolliver, was mentioned regarding a twerking video on social media alongside Vanity, the rapper. Degrading and misogynistic locker room rhetoric was exchanged about Teagan. And so she replied in a post annihilating Ambrose in response.

Shit...

While Ambrose was a guest on the show, he didn't contribute to the debasement. However, he was present for a conversation on the problematic ass, mid-grade podcast as were two other players, Kyle and JR. I had meetings with them scheduled as well. This would be the lighter one because Ambrose wasn't the offender. I was sure his public relations team and agent had already lit into his ass, but I'd be remiss as this team's leader if I didn't express my condemnation for it, too. I hated seeing the discomfit in Ambrose's demeanor, especially with my recent public blunder with Alston's wife. Nonetheless, I had to do what I had to do.

"You want to know the very first thing I was told about you, McNeil?" I asked while tossing my cell onto the desk. "I was told you were…untouchable. That your place was indefinitely assured on this team because of your last name."

Brose shook his head. "I don't need anything handed to me. I'm not just here for…show. I'm willing to work *and* earn my place."

Examining his words, I tried smiling to disarm his defensiveness. "You know… I'm glad to hear that because I told Eli that same thing." When I registered the shock on his face, I nodded. "Yes, Eli." Then I asked, "You're Amos McNeil's kid, right?"

Brose blinked successively, giving away how fast his mind was working. "Yes, but I don't bank on that. "I'm here because I want to play, and because I'm damn good at it. I don't need favors."

"Relax, kid." I found humor in his alarm. "I've heard from your coach and trainers. You're fast as hell and fucking obstructive to the opposing team." Hence the moniker, Mosquito. "I'm telling you what I know, not what I think—as of now." He took a deep breath, mind visibly working in overdrive. Bringing up Amos may have been a trigger for him. Ambrose wasn't a rookie. He had history in the *League*, so I only wanted to focus on his output and nothing else. It would benefit me none if he were here for political reasons rather than that of his raw talent. Each player had a story, is what I learned over the years. They had to be addressed by their uniqueness if I wanted to optimize on their contribution. "Remind me what happened to you."

Brose's eyes snapped back up to me. "I…took a bad hit. A really bad hit. Ended up with a torn hamstring in the shuffle. It took me a while to fully recover from it."

I nodded, now recalling it all. According to the reports, Ambrose had "never quite recovered."

"How much was your bounty?" I fingered my beard as my memory returned. "Do you know?"

His forehead stretched. "Nah, it was never confirmed that it was on purpose."

I scoffed. "Sure. But we know what we know. Right? The opposing team's worst nightmare takes what was intended to be a career-ending hit. *We know*. Maybe not outside of this room, but *we know*."

Ambrose shook his head. "I don't know. I didn't want to end up ready to kill a motherfucker, so I had to tell myself to let it go."

I nodded. *Alright...* "Good. Because really, it doesn't matter. All of that is over as far as I'm concerned. And I'm glad to hear you're not dwelling on it. That lets me know you're living in the here and now, and you're ready to be a part of this team, which is what I need. I need people who are committed to *this* team. To this season. To showing up."

I hoped he processed my words judiciously. I needed everyone's all. Fuck everything that took place before I came aboard. I needed everyone's focus here and now.

"That's all I want to do," Ambrose declared with conviction. "All I want to do is work. I'm not really here for anything else."

"Then I need you to do a better job of showing it, because interviews with these messy ass gossip shows, and shit? That ain't it. If you want to look at ass, look at ass. If you don't want to look at ass, don't look at ass. Appreciate the free show, or don't. Either way, that ain't the shit I want to hear you talking about on the internet—not even being adjacent to the conversation. As my sister would say, *'that's women's business.'* And this team doesn't need you in that.

"I would say be more selective about the mediums you chose to interface with, but honestly, I'd rather you not. You've got a damn good PR team to sort that shit for you. Utilize them. No matter what part of the season we are in, you represent this team. And you know what getting on the internet to speculate about women's right to twerk or whatever the fuck makes you look like?" Thinking about Nye's feministic take on this drove me to be completely real with him. "Like you don't have shit better to do. And if you don't have shit better than that to do, you might have to find a different job."

"I was not talking about that woman," he hissed, hands slashing the air for emphasis.

I couldn't help but laugh because I knew he wasn't. I watched the stupid ass podcast. But still…

"And you see how that didn't make one shred of a difference. Right? Because you were associating yourself with muthafuckas who don't have anything better to do. JR? He may not even be on my team this season, and yet his words have a two-time world tennis champion who makes enough on a win to buy both of your contracts on your neck." I stopped. Taking a deep breath, I caught the coachable moment I almost missed.

"Look, McNeil. I'm not about to highbrow you simply because I'm your coach. Shit. Everybody who cares to know—and some who don't—knows about who I fucked recently." His eyes rolled away when processing the pictures of Tynisha Lang and me in Paris. "Yup. Everyone. But not because I put it out there. Because some fucked up individual did. Our situations are different, but as a coach, I want to foster an environment of transparency. And this is my truth: it doesn't feel good having my name out in the public for anything other than what I do professionally. That's close to the statement you made on the podcast. I get it.

"Once your shit is out there, you're at the mercy of the court of public opinion. That ain't no shit I signed up for. It doesn't make me any money, neither does it serve my family. I've learned from what I did and will move differently going forward. So to you I say: make better decisions. Your coaches say you've been looking good out there. They say you're performing better than you did coming off your draft. That's the kind of news I want to see attached to your name. Not this other shit."

"Yessir." He gave a noble neck bow. "You don't have to worry about it anymore."

And I did the same, gesturing the conclusion of this meeting. Without further rebuttal, Ambrose left my office. I went tapping the speakerphone to call Zo. That's when I saw Ambrose dapping it up with none other than Trent Bailey. Before I could think to hang up, Zo answered.

"Whadup," he panted.

"Just wanted to check in and see how the training is coming along."

"Hard as fuck. 'Bout to start a new circuit now. Feel like I'm gonna die."

"You're supposed to be near death right now. When that sensation subsides, you know you've moved up to the next level. But training is never easy and rarely fun, kid." I hired a trainer to get Zo football ready for his official training season. My guy was good. My son…not so great. His numbers needed to improve if he wanted a career in the *League*. I didn't want him sitting on the *Scarlet Knights'* bench if he aspired to be an integral component of the team. "You wanna be broken in for those voluntary trainings next week."

"Yes, sir," he wheezed. "I will."

"Alright. That's what I need to hear. I'll hit you later."

"And Senior?" He'd been referring to me as his senior lately.

I believed it to be endearing *because he'd had my name?*

"Yeah, Zo?"

"I appreciate everything, man." Zo's vulnerability had my eyes shooting up to Trent. This was a private moment I didn't want to share with anyone who didn't respect me. "I know I haven't told you, but I'm grateful for the way you've held me down, sir."

Needing to end the call, I nodded. "It's been an honor. Without a doubt."

"Alright. Later."

"Later."

Pulling in a cleansing breath from what was an emotional tug at my heart, I gave the visitor my attention while disconnecting the call.

"Come in." Trent sauntered in and took the seat McNeil made vacant. "How can I help you?"

He inhaled deeply. "By accepting my apology."

"For?"

Trent nodded as though fortifying himself. "For the shit I've been slinging your way all this time." When I didn't comment, he continued. "I was wrong. I'm sure you know I've been in my feelings about the direction in leadership of my team. Been feeling like the front office ain't been protecting us with the last shoddy hiring they did of

Nealson." He shook his head, exhaling with his eyes cast somewhere on my desk. "I don't know, man. I'm still salty as hell about having yet another new coach. Feel like it's making my team and me vulnerable as hell." Then his gaze swept up to me. "Either way, none of that was on you. It's between me and the bigwigs, and I've rightfully expressed my grievances to them. I gave my ultimatum, too."

"Which is?"

"Which is if we don't, at least, make it to the *NFC Championship*, I'm done." I nodded. "Look, Pierce, I'm going to give it my all, as I always do. But I need to be reminded of the spirit of winning for this team. I need to make moves, not promises. This ain't personal."

"Neither do I believe it is. It didn't get personal until you put a microscope over my life. I tried doing the dance for your good graces." I shook my head. "I don't like that shit, neither am I going to tolerate it. I've only asked one thing of you and, of me, you ask for a camera in my fucking bedroom. That ain't me, man."

"I wasn't expecting all of that, but I understand you." He paused, face tightening. "Then again, I guess I have had a bit of insight into your bedroom."

"Not by having knowledge of the Tynisha Lang incident. That was a one-time occurrence in a distant land where I didn't even know her full name."

Trent blinked hard. "She hit you with the short name?"

I nodded. "The nickname. But my dumb ass didn't think to get more."

"No judgment here. Been there, done that. I remember when names weren't important, only the rubbers."

My head continued to bob in agreement. "I don't do married women. One of my limits. Young, too. It's not my practice to fuck anything under twenty-eight—not that I need to share that with you. Because it's neither my practice to discuss my personal life, something I believe you understand."

"I do, but that's not what I was referring to when I said I may have had insight. I was talking about Nye."

What?

Defensively, the beast in me rose protectively at her name from his mouth.

"What about her?"

"She reminds me of someone dear." He sat back and plucked at his beard. My brows lifted and neck twisted to invite him to share more. "She seems solid. Like a lioness protecting her cubs. I know that kind of love, man." I could have explained it wasn't love, only Nyedeera's innate nature to be outspoken. *She's a lawyer for god's sake.* I didn't, though, because it wasn't necessary. "Prophetically?" he asked, sitting up in his chair.

Understanding his request to go beneath the surface of general conversation, I nodded. "Please."

"We don't appreciate the role of partnership in our women anymore. For some men—me formerly—it's about what satisfies us. We only set out to exchange gratification with parameters benefitting us only. Women, for ages—particularly our Black sisters—have seen this game for so long, they're playing right alongside. *Or* are they playing against us. Either way, there's a division amongst us. A war that doesn't edify unity.

"I didn't get married until I found that one who could define the role of partnership in terms I understood. She was fly, her package wasn't pretty, but her potential was clear and her output set the table for my life." He shook his head, smirking. "I ain't mean to get deep. My point is, I sense that protective nature in Nye. It was only a flash, but it's what too many Black men don't have because they don't understand as protectors, we need protecting, too. We, Black men, in America war damn near every day. More often than not, we survive. We endure. But there come those times when we're weak or weakened and the only advocate available to us is the one we need: our partners."

I nodded, trying to absorb several of his points.

"I'm more of a success as Jade's husband than I was as happy, single ass TB. I'm better to her than I was any to woman I'd had before her because all of my passion goes just to her. And when all that energy—transient lust and desire—was rerouted into one direction, I could customize it for her to bring out the best *in* her. I peep-Tom'd y'all in front of my crib that night. In the rain. You kissed and held that woman like you were receiving an energy from her you needed to recover from what I'd given you inside.

"I've seen you around enough to have peeped your mannerisms and temperament. All that quieted tension you lead with. That no-nonsense coaching you do. That unshakable and unruffled persona under pressure? All that shit was dead that night in the rain when you withdrew your needed strength from her." He gave an emphasized neck bow. "That's the power of a Black woman in an exclusive partnership."

Trent stood from the chair. "That's the commitment you asked of me. It's what I came to assure you, you have. I'm locked in and will be front and center at the voluntary practice tomorrow morning. Right now, I need to run a few errands to open up this apartment."

"Is your family with you?"

"Nah. They don't technically come until the season starts, and not fulltime even then. For the next few months, I'm up here on my own. Jade's official season is over, but her time never expires." He winked. "She pops in at her leisure and stays as long as she needs me."

I laughed quietly, leaning back in my chair. "Well, I'm glad to have you back. I'd be grateful to implement some burning ideas on a team as talented as the *Kings*."

"I hope no more are like that nutritional program." Trent dropped his face into his hands.

"Oh, you don't like it?" I played coy.

"Who the hell does? I looked at my regimen and wanted to throw that shit back where it came from." He chuckled. "But Jade passed it along to my chef out here. I start on Monday."

I nodded. "Looking forward to the transformation, man."

"I'm looking forward to winning the *Super Bowl* again, but we'll have to see." He turned back to amend, "And work."

Shit…

I sighed internally as he left my office. It felt damn good to not be stuck with a headache after a conversation with TB.

~TWENTY-THREE

PRESENT DAY

I WALKED FROM THE HOUSE TO THE GARAGE where Launz was sitting on the back of his pickup. *The* pickup he drove when I met him. I discovered he had it, though covered with a blanket, when he let me borrow his *Audi* last winter. It brought back beautiful memories of innocence. Tonight, he was sitting on the back of it, gazing at nothing more than the stars over his property.

"Here." I handed him a slice of cake on a small plastic plate, then hopped up on the tailgate next to him. I was unbelievably excited about digging into the custom-made *Magnolia Belle Bakery* cake I had sent up from Virginia. It was my mom's favorite bakery, and that woman never got it wrong when it came to sweets. I loved the bakery myself and thought to order Launz's Father's Day cake when we made a stop there on the way to the airport last month when leaving Lenora's horrible wedding. "Have you enjoyed your first Father's Day?"

We'd made a big deal out of it. I made a feast of a breakfast. Zo took his father to the *Moorestown Creek Country Club*. Launz was a member there, but he wasn't expecting to see a few of his friends and a new—and expensive—set of clubs awaiting him. After, Zo and Launz traveled up to Launz's parents' to celebrate with his father. I sent gifts, though not ready to be a part of the family yet. I'd still been struggling with insecurities deriving from my guilt. When Zo and Launz were done, they returned to the house to shower before we all, including Gena, took Launz to dinner, showering him with gifts and words of appreciation. One of my gifts was having this pickup truck rebuilt and cleaned. It had been a task of sneaking in repair guys while Launz was away in Connecticut, but I'd gotten it done.

Now, we were having his cake. We were—*finally*—alone, enjoying the truck.

"I think so," he mumbled, using his fork to cut into the slice of cake.

"What do you mean?"

Launz shrugged. "I guess I've got to get used to all the attention."

"It is Father's Day. All the attention should be on you."

"You didn't have all this last month on Mother's Day," he countered.

And that's when I got it. "I never felt like I deserved a big to-do on Mother's Day. We've always made my mother the focal point."

"But you've been a good mother to Zo. I can tell by the way he regards you," he mumbled, big shoulders hunched over. "This is really good, by the way. Not too sweet and really moist."

"Then the cake and I almost got something in common." I winked at him. Launz's response was the rolling of his eyes. That reminded me of something. "Launz..."

"Yup." He pushed a piece of cake into his mouth, his gaze into the stars.

"I could have contacted you about Zo before I did." He turned to me and I couldn't muster the courage to look at him quite yet. "I didn't know until I *really* got to college that my father had lied to me when we left Jersey. The legal age of sexual consent is sixteen. But at seventeen..."

"You were a child who believed your all-knowing father."

I nodded, enduring the burn from tears trying to sprout. My father made me weak and I hated it. I learned in therapy last week that the reason I'd never been interested in a full-fledged relationship was because I never saw a strong woman in one. We'd moved around too much in my childhood for me to witness a tenured, healthy, lasting marriage. And it wasn't something my parents had.

So, admittedly, I tried to stay a leg up on men I encountered. For me, dating had been about anything but companionship and mutual exchange. Even that was laughable, considering I'd not had much good sex until Launz this year. So that meant, I'd had no noble use of men. So soon, the therapist had gotten me to see the long road of healing ahead of me. She even recommended I end my sexual relationship with Launz until I was ready to properly give us a meaningful label.

I'm still working on that shit...

"Yeah, but..." I exhaled, a familiar ache flashing in my stomach. "I could have reached out then or the next year...or the following. I just didn't have the courage. I didn't think it would be fair to you, and at that time, I didn't know what was going on in your life. I just knew you'd be married and working on babies with your wife."

"Why?"

I shrugged. "Because in my eyes, you were good. You were husband material."

"You wanted to marry me, Nyedeera—"

"No!" I yelped. "I didn't say that!"

"I'm just teasing you. Don't overkill my ego." When Launz rolled his eyes again, my heart melted. "Say no more. I hear you. I'm moving past that. Nothing we can do to change anything."

I pulled in a breath. "You really mean that?"

"No, but I'm working on it."

When he didn't laugh, I got really concerned. "Hey..." I shoulder-bumped him. "What's going on?"

Launz shook his head, going for the last of his cake. That reminded me I hadn't started my own.

"Nothing important."

"Okay. Let me be the judge of that."

I heard him exhale. "We've gotta tell Zo."

I forked a piece of the cake, impatient for the bliss of it hitting my tongue. "Mmmhmmm."

"I'm serious, Nye," he repeated, this time looking my way. "We've got to tell Zo."

Finally, I gave him my attention. "I know we do. Why are you putting emphasis on it now, at nine at night?"

"Because I want to flip you onto your knees here on the back of the truck and fuck you without worrying about him coming out here catching me, then feeling betrayed."

My jaw dropped and I lowered the plate to my lap. "Launz…"

His eyes closed. "I know. It sounds extreme, but I'm not good at discretion when it comes to sex and affection. I want those things with you, and don't want to ruin my relationship with my adult son while doing it."

My pulse raced and throat went dry. "I turned Ernie down and told him I'm seeing someone."

"And? What does that have to do with what's happening in my home?"

I took a deep breath. "I understand your logic. Try to understand mine. We're progressing. We're making room for each other, Launz."

"Yeah, but I'm a dog without a leash, Nye. Right now, my son's my leash."

I turned back around to the bed of the truck. "You know why I rebuilt the engine?" Launz shook his head. "Because I think Zo was conceived in here."

He met me with a tight gape. "What?"

Smiling, I nodded. "Mmmhmmm. We were careful with condoms except for that one night—it was actually twice, but the one time—when you drove me to that park. Where was it?" I tried thinking. "It was a Sunday night, after *Corey's,* and it had a movie theater…"

Launz's gaze lifted as he considered it. Then he turned to me. "Branchbrook?" His brows were knitted, but he smiled.

"Is that the name? There was some old ass Batman movie playing."

"The one with Jack Nicholson as the joker."

"Oh! Right! That *was* him." I laughed. "I probably would've known for sure if I was watching the movie."

"*I* tried watching it." He scoffed, shaking his head.

"You were ignoring me."

"Hate to break the news to you, but at the movies, people tend to..." He nodded. "watch the movie."

I leaned into him. "Until I put my hands down your jeans."

"I don't recall that, but I do remember the weather being mild."

"Mmmhmmm." I nodded, agreeing. "Because it was April and there were a few days of mild temperatures, just like it was a couple of months ago."

"But we were hot as hell under the one blanket I miraculously had in here."

"Because we had to be discreet with our boning." I winked while laughing. Then I sobered. "I've always believed that's where we conceived my baby boy. Our baby boy." When Launz didn't reply, I began devouring my cake. It was delicious. Yellow cake with cream cheese, crushed pineapples, and coconut. She managed a firm frosting to case the cake for the inscription. Then a thought occurred, one that made my groin warm. I elbowed him. "Today's Sunday." My eyes narrowed and I whispered, "You think they still play movies?"

Launz dumped his empty plate behind him and dug out his phone. As he looked it up, I finished my slice, wishing I'd cut a bigger piece like I had for Launz.

Suddenly, he jumped off the tailgate and grabbed his plate.

When he headed toward the house, I asked, "Where are you going?"

"To get a couple of blankets and tell Zo and Gena you want me to run you to a few stores in my truck."

Oh, my god...

A balloon of excitement burst in my belly, heating me all over. Would I have sex in public at thirty-nine years old?

Heck yeah!

"Oh, hell no!"

"What the hell?"

"What?"

They all yelled at the same damn time. I stood there mortified. This was entirely too much, and I'd had enough for the night.

"Where the hell did that statistic come from, Jenise?"

I watched my unrecognizable sister shrug before taking a sip of her cocktail. "Which one?"

"Let's see..." I tapped my chin. "Start with the statement about most married men cheating."

"Oh, *heeeell* yeah," Lex's neck-rolled as she emphasized the word.

Elle, leaning against the counter, shook her head. Tori McNabb, the boxer, peered at Jenise with her arms crossed over her chest, and Jade stood with one fist propped on her hip, waiting for her response.

"I read it in an article," Jenise weakly answered. "Besides, do I really have to provide empirical data to grown ass, allegedly successful women?"

"You do!" Jade shouted.

"Why?"

"Because you're a lawyer," Lex, who I'd met months ago, answered. "And even my two-degreed ass don't walk around wearing an air of authority when I speak. Quantify it. You can't use terms like most, many, or all without backing it up with numbers."

"To make you feel better about your husband, who looks nothing like a pastor, by the way. So you know what that means."

"What?" Lex asked, shifting closer.

"He has a bevy of women at his feet."

Lex's eyes narrowed. "Are you implying my husband has cheated on me?"

Jenise rolled her eyes. "Can we stop this? Can we be true, thirty-plus-year-old women and get real here? Your husbands are all celebrities, or work closely with them. Even your hubby, Lex, is a celebrity in the walls of his church. If you think they have not sampled outside the crotch of your panties, you're delusional. It's in men's nature to have more than one lover, particularly Black men! Back before our people were enslaved, we had kingdoms governed by men in legal, polygamous relationships." She curled her lips to the side in a shrug. "Inherently generous with the peen."

That's it!

The kitchen went up again as I went for my purse on the back of the chair at the table. The girls were sounding off while I headed out.

"Nye!" Jenise cried out to me. "Where are you going?

"I'm not staying here in this cesspool of false statements and toxic jargon. I've got better shit to do like prepare for my grandchild."

"Why are you yelling?"

"Because it's disgusting to see you being a guest yourself at a 'friend's' girlfriend gathering on your pompous, false narratives shit. I don't even know who you are. But let's not forget, Zo's father is Jade's husband's coach. *And* I just learned tonight he's good friends with Tori's husband. I don't want to be a part of anything that jeopardizes those relationships."

Jenise scoffed. "We're all grown women here. It's what we do."

Speaking over the other women, my neck snapped back and I asked, "You're telling me you get pretty, come here, get drunk, and insult every woman in the room about what you perceive to be their baggage?" I snorted, "Oh, girlfriend, I don't know about you, but I'm still working through my bag, trying to remove all the trash. That ain't a community act."

"My thing is," Elle Hunter, the head of a public relations company, interjected. "Who are you to determine what our baggage is?"

"Period!" Jade banged her fist on the counter.

She seemed violent, and I couldn't blame her. My sister, Jenise, invited me over to a girls' gathering in North Jersey. When I asked who'd be in attendance, she said just a few of her "new friends." She had already been in the area, so I agreed to drive up and meet here here. And from the time I arrived I'd seen a side of my sister I never knew existed. She was judgmental, highfalutin, and all around toxic! I couldn't believe the rhetoric she spewed about relationships and her low view of women—Black women. And I wasn't alone. These women were offended, too. And Jade, the only I'd semi-known, had been so worked up, I feared she may hit my sister. That Lex, too. Preacher's wife or not, the woman went hard for Harlem.

"Let's not do that, Jade." Jenise's voice was deceptively low. It was a part of her characterization tonight. She presented as disarming while insulting the room. "You live in a mansion in Alpine. Don't start acting like a stoop-sitter from Camden. And besides: you did good. Single mothers aren't desirable to Black men."

My neck twisted and head fell to the side. "Don't you have a son, making you a single mother?" I asked. "And haven't you been married twice since having him? How dare you!"

Lex's eyes went wild. Elle's mouth dropped. Tori's head flew backward.

"The fuck?" Jade demanded.

Jenise rolled her eyes. "Yes, I am a mother. My situation is unique, though. It has never been an expectation of mine to have my child taken care of. That's never the case for this generation of women who can barely scrape together two pennies to pay the portion of rent the government isn't covering. They want to be all in a man's face and don't spend quality time with their kids—"

"When was the last time you spent ten minutes with Leon? Have you even visited him this year?"

When I saw the blood drain from Jenise's face, it dawned on me: *she forgets her own baggage. Scratch that. She sees my nephew as baggage!* That's when I finally walked out.

"Nye, no!" Jade called behind me.

"I'm fine," I assured without looking back. "I'll text you when I get in. Sorry, ladies."

I made it out of the house, down the driveway, and to my car when the click clacks of her heels drew closer. "Nye, wait!" After opening the door, I looked Jenise's way. "What was that?" she panted, out of breath from the jog.

"That's what I wanna know—no! Actually, I want to know exactly who the hell are you? I didn't even recognize you in there!"

"It's just girl talk."

"No! It's you belittling other women. I always knew you were a know-it-all and judgmental, but never did I know you were a bully!"

Neither did I know these women weren't friends of Jenise. My sister, being an entertainment attorney, ran in the same circles as Elle, the public relations guru. From what I gathered since arriving, Jenise had been invited to their private get-togethers a few times on Elle's grace. Imagine my shock when I showed up and saw Jade was here with *her* friends, *not* Jenise's. And based on her bullyish antics, these women would never be friends with my sister.

"I am no bully, Nye! You know me."

"I thought I did. But one thing's for damn sure: you're broken. Just like me. The difference is I don't target women to take my insecurities out on."

"First of all, I'm not broken and neither are you. We are successful, educated women who have traveled the world and made something of ourselves. Shit. We've overcome a lot and just because I recognize it and have an opinion of the lazies of the world, doesn't make me judgmental. Secondly, I don't target anyone."

"You do, even if you don't see it. Just like I've avoided relationships because I didn't see how growing up with a monster for a father didn't leave much hope for connecting with a real man emotionally. And we're all broken: you, me, and Junior. Your disconnections are worse than mine. You two have become disjointed with blood. You don't even see Leon regularly. I guess Gunnery Sergeant Preston Taylor was right when he said Zo and I have seen him more than you have."

"Gunnery Sergeant Preston Taylor didn't know what the hell he was talking about. He had no idea of how I spent my time since leaving his house. He wanted me to take care of a child with more illnesses than I could name. He didn't want me to have a life. He wanted me to be like—"

I nodded. "Like me and pick up and follow behind him every transfer he had?" My eyes went out into the distance as I swallowed that truth. "I did. And maybe that was wrong for me." Jenise scoffed, agreeing. Still, I continued, "But it was the sacrifice I made for Zo. He needed a father figure and I was too cowardly to finally clue his real father in on the boys' existence. We're all scarred from the coldness of that man. Broken."

Jenise shook her head, adamantly dismissing me. "Nope. Then speak for yourself."

"Oh, *we* are. I've been in therapy, Jenise. And *really* getting open and honest about…me."

"So that's where this broken narrative is coming from." She tossed her hands in the air while nodding her understanding. "There it is!"

"Think about it: Junior…" I thought of my brother every now and again, but had always respected his lead and reason for keeping a distance. "He never comes around. He showed to Gunnery Sergeant Preston Taylor's funeral and left immediately after the burial. He kept in touch with our parents less than you. The man wants no part of his childhood."

"Well," she murmured, scratching the back of her head. "Everybody ain't strong like you, able to look a monster in its eye over and over again." She shook her head.

"Then don't fake the courage of staring a woman down and degrading her." I moved to get inside the car.

"Wait." I saw the alarm in her eyes. "How are you? How's Zo and Gena? The baby?"

I took a deep breath, considering her question. "I was with Gena at her appointment yesterday. The baby's healthy and growing. Zo's been busy. He's back in school and on campus. Football season starts soon, so he's locked in. The crazy kid's planning to do their baby shower in Arizona in a week—or so he thinks because it's what his aunt, Monica, and I have been doing."

"Oh, right! The baby's due next month?"

I nodded, cringing at Gena being so close to the no-flying period of pregnancy. I'd just booked all of our flights and hated the quick turnaround time for the trip. I'd planned on hanging around at my mother's to ship the gifts back to Jersey. But Gena, Zo, and Launz all had to fly right back out: Gena because she was so advanced in her pregnancy, Zo because of school, and Launz for work. It was what it was. The sweet part about the mayhem was Launz's parents' determination to support Zo by flying out to the shower.

"Yup. We're all ready for *me* to be a grandmother. And I've been helping Zo plan his father's birthday party." I twisted my mouth, nodding.

"Zo has always been the best celebrator. Remember that year I flew in for your birthday, and when we got back in late from that lounge, he had slippers, perfume, nail polish, and flowers laid out on your bed to surprise you?"

I did recall. Zo had a talent at thoughtful gifting. "He's so sweet, but I hate that he takes on so much. I've been forceful in assisting because his father's birthday is a couple of weeks before the baby's due. The kid is nuts."

"And what about you? You've mentioned everybody but yourself."

"I'm healing, Jenise. I'm healing and happy about it." Between keeping up with Gena to make sure she wasn't lonely or didn't have any needs in Zo's absence, keeping up with Zo now that he was heavily training, life had become a non-stop task.

"What about work? The last we spoke, you said you were going to teach at the college level."

Nodding, I shared, "I got an offer at *Stockton University*, but they want to pay pennies for my tenure."

"So, wait!" Her head fell to the side. "You're staying in Jersey?"

"My child and grandchild will be here." I shrugged.

"But you're going to continue to stay at the house?" I pulled in a deep breath and nodded. Jenise walked around my opened door and crossed her arms as she leaned into the car next to me. "You're fucking him."

"I have my own room where I'm totally comfortable for now."

"You're not denying it." There was a stretch of time as I gazed into the night air. "Would he?"

"Would he what?"

"Would your baby daddy deny he's fucking you?"

That stumped me. I didn't know. It was completely lost upon me how Launz referenced me. Since Lenora's wedding, we'd agreed to monogamy, something I had no reason to believe he had failed me at. Launz and I had been secretly dating and sexing—a lot. With heavy discretion, we did couple's therapy and made love every chance we could.

All summer, the man had shown me a tender side of him that never failed to blow my mind. Sometimes, I'd sneak up to Connecticut and he'd have a day out on a boat planned. His chef would cook us up delicious meals. We'd swim in the pool in the backyard of his house with candles lining the deck. Yet, suddenly Jenise's question didn't sit well with me. We caught movies in his local neighborhood up there where we didn't have to duck and hide from Zo. And thank goodness, coaching in the *League* wasn't the same as being a player, and especially a franchise player.

Once, last month, we were invited out to dinner with Trent and Jade and Wil Cunningham and her husband, Ramsey Bishop, a running back on the team. Because Jade was split between being at home with the kids and had to be home the next afternoon for their son's game, she invited me to ride up with her. So I packed a bag and met her in Alpine. Then we drove up to Connecticut. We waited for Launz and Trent at the front office while they finished up a meeting with a few of the staff and players. Jade and I had too much time on our hands and decided to have a drink at the bistro the *Kings* have on their property.

One drink turned into three and by the time we made it through dinner with the group, we were two sheets to the wind leaving the restaurant. I was the only rookie of the crew because I didn't realize paparazzi was outside waiting for pictures until it was almost too late. Launz threw a jacket over my entire torso, blinding me. My drunk ass was barreled over with my steps being led by Launz. It was a sight and comical a few days later when he and I were able to laugh about it. The paps were there for Trent, Wil, and Ramsey. Launz and I were casualties who feared our son finding out about our torrid summer affair.

That experience was daunting, but I'd been having the time of my life with Launz—and Zo, and even Gena. That made Jenise's question viable in my mind. Who was I to Launz?

Okay. And who is he to you?

What did I want to be?

I turned to smile at my sister before tossing my purse into the car. "I think you need to go in there and apologize to your 'friends.' I'm going home now. If you continue with holier-than-thou rhetoric, Lex is going to beat your ass then pray for you after. And Jade is going to help her, but not with the prayers."

I hopped into the car and watched my sister step away before pulling off. My mind wouldn't abandon thoughts of my new life and fragmented family. Then a memory of a call Launz received last week from Sandra, his plus-size model chick, came into mind. She was alarmed by my voice on the other end when I answered, and that annoyed me. It made me question why she had still been calling Launz. So I asked him. He readily admitted he'd forgotten to tell her that he was in a "relationship" and could no longer be friends with her. That annoyed me even more, although I believed him when he said he'd make Sandra aware right away.

One of the issues we'd discussed in couples therapy was titles. Launz and I had equally preferred staying away from them. He had his reasons and I had mine. The one common cause of our preference was Zo. He still didn't know about us. Our therapist pinned that for a future tackle.

Would your baby daddy deny he's fucking you?

Jenise's question echoing in my head infuriated me. Now on the *Parkway,* I fished out my phone and tapped until I got to his number.

"Yeah, babe?" he answered briskly, yet softening it for me.

I could tell he was busy. Launz was away for training camp. I didn't care. What I needed wouldn't take any amount of time to settle.

Or would it?

"From here on out, I'm your..." I licked my lips, peering into my rearview mirror to switch lanes. "girl. Starting today, you tell people, I'm your..."

Why was this so hard? I was stupid. Totally. And too damn old to feel uncomfortable with something as simple as having a boyfriend. But the word couldn't roll from my tongue. It felt awkward. I was Zo's mother. I'd never had men around him because I'd never had a boyfriend. Even Ernie had never been comfortable in my home. That was Zo's place and it wasn't until he'd gotten older that I'd allowed him to know there was an Ernie.

"Girlfriend," his thick cords snapped me from my thoughts.

"Yup." I nodded in the dark of the car. "That's it."

"I haven't had one of those in so long, you know?"

"Welp." I shrugged as though he could see me. "You've got one now. So, get used to telling people—except for Zo."

I could hear his soft chuckle. "Okay. Well, while I'm busy telling people—except for Zo—why don't you get used to the idea of being one?"

I nodded, lips pressed together. "I can do that."

"Good." He took a deep breath. "So can I. But I've got to go. I've got six people here in the room with me wildly flummoxed by what's being said on your end of the call."

I recoiled. "Oh, no!"

"Oh, yes...girlfriend." He laughed and I could hear the chortles of others in the back. "Later, babe."

I squealed his popular closing line, "Later."

~TWENTY-FOUR

PRESENT DAY

I SIGHED THOUGH MY WHOLE BODY WAS COILED tightly in angst.

At least we've got them pinned deep, so the game is going into overtime, at worst.

Observing the field fixedly, I couldn't believe how that was the case twenty-three seconds ago. *But now?* The ball was on the fifty-yard line with twenty seconds remaining, which meant the *Steelers* only needed about fifteen yards to be in their kicker's field goal range.

My ears were ringing as I clenched the railing in a suite at *Hotep Black Financial Bank Arena* in Connecticut. It was the home of the *Kings*, but this wasn't my—or Launz's—assigned suite. Security had come to where my mother and I were, watching the *Kings* take on the *Pittsburgh Steelers*, telling me Launz had requested we were taken to a different suite to meet someone. The *Kings* were in the lead and my blood pressure was normal, so I had no problem switching views.

Imagine my surprise when I learned the suite that we'd been escorted to belonged to none other than the world heavyweight champion herself, Tori McNabb, and her husband, Ashton. Launz had told me he was friends with Ashton and wanted me to meet him, but their schedules hadn't permitted. But today, my mother meeting Tori McNabb was the real treat. I had to keep reminding myself of Launz's connections. I just hoped Tori didn't think of my sister when chatting with my mother today.

That damn Jenise…

My mother loved Tori McNabb, too, so after the introductions, I left those two to chat while I followed the game. This was my third *Kings'* game this season, which meant it was my third time seeing Launz in action as a coach. It was quite an experience. I'd learned the game of football from supporting Zo since he was in middle school, so I understood it from a player's perspective. But now, I viewed the game through new lenses because Launz was a force on the field.

His temperament was always controlled…until an unlikely victory was secured. He paced, communicated discreetly, and even performed hand signals that would snap an animated Rut Amare out of a fit of rage or prompt aggression in Ramsey Bishop. His indecipherable expression remained stoic, but his presence was powerful on the field.

It gave me insight on who my "boyfriend" was. The man was far from shy. Launz was reserved and selective with his energy. He was a coherent spectator in an often chaotic world, taking in more than he put out. And, God, was he so damn sexy out there!

But the sexy leader was now going to have to trust his defense. He needed to forget about that prevent bullshit. Now was time to tighten up on the outside receivers to stop the out and ups. I was unable to read Launz's lips as he chewed out his defense after being forced to call the team's final timeout. I didn't fully understand his ranting, but his frustration with the play of the defense over the last twenty-three seconds was made clear by his pacing and tight movements.

"*No headaches today. Please…*" I whispered a prayer his way.

It was a stressful time, even off the green. Last week, we were able to successfully pull off Launz's birthday party, even with his and Zo's impossible schedules. Last night, my mother and I attended Zo's home game then woke up early to support his father today. *My man.* We left Gena behind to rest. Her due date was in less than two weeks, and some of us doubted her making it. I was sure with the way I was displaying my tension, curled over the railing, that poor girl would've absorbed my stress.

I watched the defense trot back out onto the field and into their various positions.

My eyes stretched wide, and at the same time, Ashton croaked, "Pierce, please tell me you're not about to play it safe!"

"Right." I swallowed hard.

He'd echoed my fear.

Roethlisberger lined up in the shotgun and peered over the defense's coverage before calling out the signals. Just as the ball was snapped, Tyler Hill took two steps up toward the receiver to tighten the coverage. Ashton joined me, leaning toward the field in disbelief. Launz had decided to risk it all and play bump and run!

"Oh, my…" I murmured, torso slowly moving to the right, I was so engulfed.

Hill bumped Washington just enough to knock him off his route before Roethlisberger realized it, so he followed through with the called quick out. Hill stepped right into the path of the ball, picked it off, and headed straight toward the end zone with no one to impede his track there.

My arms shot into the air. "Yes! Oh, my God! Yeah, baby!"

Ashton's handclaps matched my excitement as he hooted, "Oh shit! Oh shit! Oh shit!"

Launz and the *Kings'* sideline exploded as Hill dove into the end zone untouched with three seconds remaining on the clock.

"Daaaaaamn, Hill!" Ashton cheered.

I was finally able to sit back down. Dramatically, I let my legs stretch out and flexed my arms wide. My mother and Tori were cracking the hell up at my "extra-ness" as if I had any claim to the *Kings'* victory.

But I'll be rewarding the man who does…

Her hips moved faster and the fat of her ass slapped lasciviously against my abs. The wavy ends of her dark tresses swung across her tapered waist, sometimes reaching the spread crack of her ass. And she danced on me. *Fuck!* Nye lifted higher, at times, giving me a view of where we met rhythmically, withholding nothing. She wanted me to see the straining of my cock, the flesh of her pussy, and the lubrication of her desire. The sight of her reverse cowgirl couldn't be more erotic.

"Ready?" she panted.

"Almost." I groaned, "Not yet."

How did she know this was what I'd needed? It had been mere weeks since the last time I'd had Nye. We were in touch daily, but often not together. She'd been stretched, trying to take care of Zo and Gena and, discreetly, me too. We were in therapy. Although most of my sessions were done virtually because of work, the guidance had been unbelievably good. Not only had I been learning to understand a lot about Nye, I'd been getting to know some shit about myself, too.

Maybe I was in love with Nye when she was seventeen. I hadn't been ready to claim that. Nonetheless, I had been captivated by her enough for her absence, in tandem with her alluring presence, to have done some damage. I may have been older than Nyedeera, but my maturation level and romantic experiences did not advance her—per the therapist—when our worlds collided. That meant whatever highs or lows I'd experienced in that brief duration of knowing her had made a significant impression on my psyche.

That may have been why I appreciated the laws of singlehood all these years. Over the summer, I learned monogamy wasn't a difficult feat for me; safety had been. I felt emotionally safe when I didn't have to invest too much of myself into one person. Being honest about my lack of desire to be with one woman at a time liberated me. Now that "nimble Nye" here had returned to my world, requesting monogamy, my freedom had to come from the safety of trusting her.

Had I fully? I was still working on it. Nye was still a transient soul from what I could gather. Her permanent address was still back in Arizona from when she transferred it from her sold home, and she still had no job. That wasn't the "stability" I preferred to feel safe in giving her my total trust not to up and go at any given moment. Zo still didn't know about us, something I had to explain to the few friends and associates of mine who knew about our secret affair. Nye and I were still creeping. So, yes. Although she'd been present to me lately and flexible with my demanding scheduling, I'd still been working on my safety issue.

"Oh, *shiiiii—*"

Nye pushed off my dick, backing her naked body down my body so that she sat on my face, and took me into her mouth. While fisting me artfully, she used her jaw, tongue, and lips to command my release. And I hungrily ate her pussy, propelling my explosive orgasm.

"*Ohhhhhhh!*" I cried uncharacteristically, yet not giving a shit. This was my time to emancipate my stress and frustrations from a week with mostly a bunch of testosterone-driven, aggressively virile players. "*Ahhhhh!*" I cooed, uncontrolled and unbothered.

I licked and sucked her wet swollenness while gripping her cheeks against my face. Nye knew when to let up on my tender dick, sitting up and riding my face. This was a different type of therapy. She knew. The woman knew how to blow my mind.

I'd once heard Trent Bailey getting clowned in the locker room for regularly having hickeys on his thighs. He unrepentantly shrugged it off, explaining coolly how his wife giving him concentrated kisses in his groin area made him cum quick. Well, Nye knew her fucking me hard then jacking me off in her mouth while letting me eat her pussy extended my orgasms made them much more intense.

By the time Nye was dancing in a fit of an orgasm, my dick was swelling again as she descended on it, taking me into her mouth all over again. The woman had become more than my girlfriend. Ms. Taylor had been my muse. Over dinner tonight, when I'd made it back to the house, Nye told her mother she'd been healing.

She was right. Nye had been healing me, too.

I sauntered into the kitchen on a mission. Launz would be leaving this morning for Atlanta for the *Kings'* next game and I wanted to fix him breakfast before he did. My mother sat at the table quietly having her morning coffee. She'd been doing this since I could remember, especially when Gunnery Sergeant Preston Taylor was either working during the morning hours or traveling for work. She taught us that when she was at the table alone with a mug, don't even speak to her unless someone was hurt, dead, or the house was on fire.

Well, it stuck. I let her be as I went about collecting pots and pans. Next, I went to the fridge, hoping Russell had fresh eggs, milk, and cheese stocked. I sighed with relief as I collected them all into my bosom and carried them to the counter near the stove. I returned to the fridge to check the expiration dates on the bacon and sausages. I'd seen them the last two times I was here in Connecticut visiting. *Hmmmm…* They were nearing their respective dates, so I decided to cook them both and throw the rest out.

"Nye…"

"Hmmmm?" I searched through the cabinet.

"Have you heard from more of the colleges you applied to for work?"

"Uhhhh…" I pushed through the bottles of seasonings, looking for cinnamon. "A few, yeah."

"When are you going to start?"

"Start what?"

"Work."

"Work where?"

"Oh, I don't know. At the highest bidder, I suppose?"

The sarcasm in her words made my forehead wrinkle. "I don't follow, Ma."

"Don't you need your own living space?"

"I'm not sure I've ever had my own space. When Zo came around, my space was his." I sighed. "And now with this baby coming, I don't know if I'll ever know what it's like to live alone without children."

"So, you'll be living with Launz and the kids?"

I turned to her. "I don't know. What made you ask that?"

She didn't answer right away, drinking from her mug instead. "Just curious."

"Why, Ma?"

"Because back in February, you were on a quest to find yourself. You didn't know where you wanted to plant your feet."

"Okay…"

She slowly turned to face me. "I heard that young man last night. His—" She cleared her throat. "—passionate howling woke me from my sleep. Now, I don't know what you did to him or what you're doing, but I want to tell you to be kind to yourself."

I was embarrassed. My mother heard Launz and me. How much had she heard? Not that it mattered. She'd heard.

"I don't know what to say, Mommy."

"You don't have to say anything. Just listen. Don't make an already complicated life even more complex." Her shoulders lifted, reaching her ears. "If you're happy with Launz, get comfortable there. If you want to see what it's like to have a strong partner, try it out. But don't make this process more difficult than it naturally is by overthinking the good things in it."

"We're...trying to figure things out. Our history together scarred him. I'm trying to..."

"Now, I know I'm no role model for marriage and happiness. My life with Preston wasn't great, and for *that* reason, I'm telling you to do something that'll make you happy. I'll tell you a secret. For years, I'd come up with things to do when I left your father. Year after year it was something new. I'd take up skating. Move to San Juan. One year, I decided to open an apple orchard. Then a few years back..." She chortled. "would you believe I considered acting? Hey, if these old people in Hollywood got their big break after going gray, I'd give it a shot."

I laughed at that. Sobering, I murmured, "I'm sorry you didn't pursue any of those things."

"Yeah. Me, too. I let fear hold me back, whether it was for you kids or Preston—even Zo when he came along. I was never kind to myself. You're better than me, Nyedeera. You're stronger, smarter,"—She winked—"and you're so independent. But you're not kind to yourself. Having a man can be more than about being dependent on him. It can be for the nourishment of your soul. It should be about balance and relief when life tries to knock you down." She smiled devilishly. "And from the sounds of whatever it was you were putting on that young man, I'm sure he wants to be kind to himself and have you, too."

"Mommy," I groaned into my hands.

Her girlish titter lightened my chest. "Honey, I've got three kids and ain't never hear that from your father when making y'all kid—"

"Ma!" I cried, hiding my entire face.

This is gross!

"Okay. Okay," her voice softened. "One last thing."

Peering through my fingers, I shrilled, "Okay..."

"Tell Zo." She nodded. "Yeah. He might get mad, but give the boy credit. He's done well with his father. He didn't balk then and I don't think he will now. You deserve to be romanced in public, not in the dark. Zo's love is happening in your face, no matter how premature it is. You deserve your loud love, too, Nyedeera." Then she turned around, going back to her mug.

And preferred morning silence.

I stepped out onto the deck holding my heart in the crux of my arm with my chest swelled with pride. It was really my ego, but either way, I felt accomplished. I'd changed a diaper for the fourth time. As she stared up at me, preparing to fall asleep again, I grinned so damn hard.

"How did it go?" Zo asked. The big ass smile on his face belied his low expectations of my work.

"Easy-peasy," I beamed. "Not an ounce of poop anywhere outside of the old diaper."

Gena gasped before giggling, "Good job, Poppy!"

"Oh, no you didn't, Alaundria Zoey!" Zo playfully scolded my dozing grandbaby.

Nye clapped, cheering me on as she laughed. She knew how much having this little girl around had rocketed me out into orbit. I'd only felt so responsible for and protective of a tiny blessing like this once before. That was with my nephew, Andrew. When we'd gotten a diagnosis on him, I knew it would be a financial challenge to keep him safe due to his compromised state. And with my grandbaby, Alaundria Zoey, who was loosely named after her dad and me, I had a second. The blessing was the princess was healthy by all accounts. Having her on earth these past four weeks had been a test of my focus.

I wasn't able to be present for Alaundria's birth because we played the *Titans*. But I flew out that night and headed straight to the hospital before she turned a day old. I couldn't stay long, but I remained by her side until Nye and Monica were pulling me out of Gena's hospital room because I had to get back to work. Needless to say, I was in love. Thank God for *FaceTime*, so I could see her practically at will. And when it came time for the *Kings'* bye week, I knew where I'd be until we had to report back for check-in. Home. With my family.

"Alright, gang. It's time for Poppy to smoke," I announced.

Nye hopped to her feet and began clearing the table. We'd eaten dinner out here on the deck. I had just finished up when Alaundria took a poop in her grandmother's arm. Gena assisted Nye and Zo ambled over to me to retrieve his princess. Our princess.

"Ma, you 'bout to be out here with him? I can't believe you be smoking cigars," he lowkey clowned her.

But why not. Nye and I smoked together all the time now. Had been practically since the spring. It was our bonding time when we'd puff, practice our breathing, and kick it about almost anything.

"Maybe I will," Nye murmured, playing distracted as she gathered the serving pans.

Her lying ass was running game. She knew she'd be right out here with me, just as she'd be sneaking into my bed by one in the morning —or maybe three when Princess Alaundria had begun to sleep a solid three hours, lessening the chance of her parents needing to leave their third-floor bedroom. I'd secretly been regretting giving them the third floor. The problem was one of the two bedrooms on the first floor was occupied, part time, by Monica. Zo and Gena needed a second room for Alaundria's nursery that had already been meticulously painted and decorated.

Still, late into the hours last night while angrily waiting on Nye's sneaky ass to creep into my bed, I considered moving Monica to the third floor and paying to redo the nursery on the first floor. But when Nye finally made it into my bed and I ran the idea past her, she reminded me of Monica's heavy weight and how challenging it would be for her to get up and down the stairs from the first to third floor. That shit had me vexed, even as I made love to Nye in the wee hours. It wasn't until then that I'd decided.

Zo was just about to walk into the house when I turned to him. "Zo, let Gena take the baby. I need to kick it with you for a minute." Nye's head swung up from the table. "You, too," I amended. "Zo and I will be down on the lawn when you're done here."

With pinched brows, she nodded and continued clearing the table.

"Hey," Nye greeted when arriving to us on the lawn. "Bro talk?" she joked.

"Always," Zo chuckled, then stood for her to sit.

I stood, too, grabbing my lighter now that I'd had my stogie cut since waiting on her to finish up in the kitchen.

"Have a seat," I pointed to my chair. Watching Nye take to my instruction without hesitation reminded me of how close we'd gotten, even with me being on the road. She'd softened so much, and I liked it. "Zo, you can take your seat, too. I have a few things to say, and I want you guys' utmost attention."

"A'ight, Coach!" he jeered.

"So, Zo, you know your mom has committed herself to therapy since the spring." He nodded, glancing over at her. "I want to share that I've been in therapy the same amount of time. We've actually been seeing the same practitioner, a seasoned professional recommended by a number of people in my circle."

"Yeah. I heard she's tight," he shared, looking his mother's way as Nye nodded.

"She's been really good. Her specialty is couple's counseling, but we've progressed enough in our therapy that she's offering to see you, too—once the season ends for you, of course."

Finally, Nye seemed to have relaxed. She had no idea what this talk was going to be about. I hadn't shared it with her. The therapist told us both I didn't have to when I was ready.

"Me, too?" His eyes bounced back and forth.

"You've been your mother's best friend for a number of years." I shrugged. "You've been becoming my favorite for months now—until Alaundria."

"Until Alaundria Zoey," he spoke at the same time as me.

That caused a chorus of laughter. I wouldn't be ashamed of my affection for that little girl.

"Plus," I continued. "you've undergone lots of changes in the past year alone. Being told about me, your grandfather's health taking a dive, him passing away, starting a new school and football program, meeting me, finding out you were going to be a father yourself, meeting new family, getting to know me, moving your girl across the country, living with her, and finally, having a baby." I was damn near out of breath from that list. It made clear how important this was. "So, yeah. The therapist is willing to bring you in to help us all...balance this family."

Zo shrugged. "Yeah. I guess. Anything can help. Right?" Then his gaze hit me. "I hope you don't think I'm not full circle on who you are to me."

"Oh, no." I shook my head. "We're good."

"Because I know it's been strange now with me calling you Senior. It's just that I didn't want to make anything weird for you by saying dad or pops. Seems so corny, but I know who I am to you. That's why I gave Alaundria your last name." Then his gaze hit Nye, who smiled almost sadly. "I've been thinking a lot about having my last name changed." He turned back to me. "To Pierce. Maybe switching my last and middle names to keep honoring my Gramps."

My chest tightened at the emotion lodged in his throat. I didn't want Zo torn over me. I was just grateful to have him. But don't get me wrong, I'd be happy out of my ass for my son to rightfully have my name. Of that, there was no doubt.

"That means a lot to hear you say, son." Now my fucking throat was closing on me as I peered blindly into the distance, fighting for focus. "It's gonna make what I'm about to share with you so..." I sucked in a breath. "Look. Man to man, I need to come clean with you about some real shit." I yanked at my beard. "It's going to sound really shady, but in due time, I hope you'll allow me to share my reasoning with you—or I can tonight."

Zo's brows narrowed and he searched his mother's face for an answer. "Y'all ain't thinking about breaking up the little family we managed to build in these few months. Right?" His heavy gaze met mine. "I mean, if she ain't here with us—with Gena and the baby..." His eyes grew wider. "I mean, no disrespect to Aunt Monica, but she ain't here often at all to replace my mom. She's either with you or down with Drew."

I shook my head. "I damn sure ain't telling your mother to leave—"

His head flew to Nye. "Then why do you think you gotta go?"

"Zo!"

"She's not going, son," I interjected, voice slightly hiked. "It's my hope to get her to stay as long as possible...for all of us." I took another deep breath and manned the fuck up. "Zo, your moms is my lady. We've been growing a friendship for months now and—"

"And y'all ain't tell me?" he yelped. His back fell into the chair. "Gena said this shit, yo. But I ain't believe her. When?"

I motioned to Nye with my eyes, prompting her to participate. This shit was harder than I thought. Zo was a good kid.

"Since the spring," Nye finally chimed in. "A little while after I started staying here."

"So, I caused this?" His scoff was bitter. "If y'all could find it in yourselves to kick something off now, why in the hell couldn't you do it twenty-one—twenty-two years ago and bypass my fucking L?"

"Alaunzo Pierce!"

"Easy," I warned. "Watch your mouth, Zo."

"I'm just saying. Alright. Y'all getting this therapy and I'm happy, but think about all the shit I've been through not fully knowing who I was? How much better would I be as a person, better as a football player? Why?" he posed to Nye. "Why did you wait all these years to do this? Why do that to him—" He pointed to me and my fucking stomach flipped like lightning. "—to me, Ma?"

Sucking in a deep breath when the first tear fell from Nye's face, I interrupted again. "I've said all I should say now. I'm going to head to the back of the yard for a smoke—I may walk around the block. Nye, I think it's time for you to talk to your son. Tell him who you are, about your trauma, and our encroachment on love." Her eyes closed as tears glistened on her cheeks. "Can you do that right now?"

When Nye nodded, I made a dash for the walkway, putting my back to them before my emotions fell down my face.

If he wasn't fucking dead already…

Epilogue

LAUNZ

"THANKS FOR YOUR TIME. GOD BLESS," WERE my last words to the press.

I stood as they shouted more questions in hopes of extending my time at the post-game press conference. The cameras flashed as I left the stage in search of Monica.

When I found her just outside the door of the room, she was typing into her phone. "We're all packed up and the captain just called. They're loading and gassing up."

I nodded as we headed toward the locker room. My gaze found the security escorting me at *SoFi Stadium* and he jumped into action, cutting ahead of us to follow him through a door. Moving swiftly, Monica finally caught on to the urgency and picked up her feet. Tailing behind the tall burly figure, we made a beeline for a secured door, separating us from the camera crew following behind.

"Well, damn!" Monica cried, looking behind at the closing door while lifting those small feet from the floor and moving.

They were only doing their jobs, but I was all talked out for the day. My expressions of the game and my team were given on the field when the commissioner handed off the trophy. I'd explained to my staff and players my actions whether we won *Super Bowl LVI* or not beforehand. Jade had already secured a yacht for TB and their family and friends. He'd be flying out of L.A. first thing in the morning. I heard Ramsey Bishop saying he'd stay in town for a few days, catch a couple of events, then fly out to Mexico with Wil and their baby. Rut Amare had his family out here for the game, staying in Orange County at Azmir's. They were flying home in the morning so Rut could celebrate in Connecticut then move the party train on down to Trenton.

Sloan mentioned her plans on the plane ride to Los Angeles. She and Nate Richardson had a suite in Napa Valley booked out for the week. Eli and Melody would spend a few days with the Jacobs before flying out to Croatia.

"Thanks," I murmured to the security when he opened the car door for Monica and me.

I slid him a four-figure tip for his cooperation. It wasn't until we'd pulled out of the lot that I reclined in the backseat, laying my head on the rest. Echoes of cheers and whistles still rang in my ears. The shit was surreal. Not that I had any complaints, it just wasn't exactly my time to decompress. But I was damn sure anxious.

"You sure you ain't wanna shower before flying out?" Monica asked with her face toward her phone. "Then again, I guess you can do it on the plane, right?"

Closing my eyes, I began to pray silently, giving thanks. The words felt stale, but I pushed through because it was my act of worship. I'd won the *Super Bowl* before. The *Seahawks* burst my cherry, but as the offensive coordinator. I was so stressed from having to leave my parents to finish out a job before taking an extended leave. I'd even gone to the National Championship twice as a head college coach and won. Those wins were followed by me whisking off the woman of my random selection to Greece and the other to *Marye Island*. Those were good times.

"Oh, *shi—*" Monica chirped, followed by a cry. "Awwww!" She pushed the face of her phone over to me. I snorted affectionately at the image, belly warming and unimaginable anticipation hiking. I closed my eyes again, now thinking about her. "Wait. Did you read the caption?"

Alaundria Zoey Pierce's grandmother and grandfather #OrWhateverTheKidsAreSayingNowADays #CK #WinningTeam #ConnecticutKings #CoachPierce #TeamPierce #YouOnlyHopeToLook-ThisGoodAsAPoppyAndMumMum

A bigger snort pushed from my nostrils as I tried to relax.

"Y'all so cute, Launz!" Monica complimented. "Let me send this to Mommy."

Taking a deep breath, I continued with silent prayer.

"Mr. Pierce," a soft, beseeching voice called me from my sleep. I opened my eyes to the flight attendant. "The captain just informed us of landing. Kindly buckle your seat—"

Before she could even finish her sentence, my hands moved to the strap.

"Damn!" Monica laughed. "Don't forget to wipe the drool, bro. Ain't that something Zo would say?"

As she entertained herself, I checked my phone. My notifications were going crazy. At some point during the flight, my friends, family, and even a number of "ex-friends" hit me up via text and/or social media. Oddly, nothing came from her, though I saw she tagged me in our usie picture from a couple of weeks ago. I decided to start with Trent Bailey's text. It was long and expressive, just like the guy himself. I took my time absorbing his humility and reflection on the season. We'd worked hard—busted our asses—but did it together. The whole organization rose to the occasion to bring the team to its rightful place as champions. I appreciated his acknowledgment of my contribution.

"Smooth landing, huhn?" Monica commented across from me, peering out of the window.

I sat back in my seat as the jet sped down the runway.

The sun was new when I made it inside the house. The place was quiet, smelling of food from the time I entered the back door. In the kitchen, there were loads of pans covered with aluminum foil laid out on the counters. When I made it to the foyer, an arrangement of balloons spelling out *CONGRATULATIONS* floated over the doorway. The thought warmed me as I hiked up the stairs with my duffle. One of my bedroom doors was open and I tossed my bag on the floor, near a wall before sauntering into the closet to strip for a shower.

The stream of hot water relaxed me, and I was just out of the ear-ringing phase from the stadium. I wasn't sleepy, yet not exactly ready for a run either. There were some things I needed to do before sleeping off the day that began over twenty-four hours ago.

After drying off and tossing on a pair of lounge pants, I remembered to charge my phone. As I powered it off first, I heard her. The soft, incoherent babbles fully articulate to me loosened my chest. Ambling from the closet and into the bedroom, the sight of the back of her head cracked my face into a smile.

Gena, holding her just outside the doors of my room, tried to get her attention. "Look who's home, mama!" she announced cheerily. It took several attempts, but finally, Alaundria's attention found me and her chubby arms flapped with excitement. "Yes! It's Poppy!"

"Thank you for this," I expressed, receiving my muffin.

"I knew you'd want to see her." Gena surmised correctly. "Congratulations, Coach."

I bowed at the neck while Alaundria rubbed her face excitedly into my bare chest. "Thank you."

Gena left us to it, and I turned around, going back into my bedroom.

"Hey, princess!" I murmured. "I've missed you so much. You know, life can be so boring without you with Poppy." I lay us out on the bed, placing her on my chest for tummy time where her little hands went straight for my beard.

This.

This is what was most important to me. It was *my* plan after winning or losing the *Super Bowl*. I'd done well this season by the *Kings* and simultaneously learned what was to be valued even more than my role with them. I was Dad and Poppy now. As her tiny palms smacked my chest while Alaundria caught me up on the happenings of the house, I knew I mattered more to four individuals under my roof than I did to an organization paying me millions for my craft. I understood variety didn't have to be with lovers. It could be with personalities under one roof. It could be with building my lineage.

My muffin and I talked for a while. I enjoyed my one-on-ones with her so much, time wasn't a factor in my mind. That was until the baby talked and stretched herself to sleep. Alaundria Zoey was even gorgeous during repose. Even with heavy eyes, I could gaze in her perfection all day.

A shift in weight on the mattress had my eyes flash wide open. Nye was over me, lifting the baby from my chest.

"She's spoiled at four months, solely at your hands," she whispered, more like hissed, leaving the bed.

I watched the wiggle in her ass beneath the silk of her short robe as she crossed the room to Zo waiting at the door. He smiled, winking my way.

"You know Queen Nye gotta be alpha around here when it comes to Big Alaunzo." He received my sleeping muffin from his mother. "Even when it comes to Alaundria Zoey."

I snorted, sitting up and scooting to the edge of the bed. "I don't remember falling asleep."

"You need that," Zo advised, adjusting the baby at his shoulder. "Good job, Pops. That work was epic."

I rubbed my sleepy face. "I appreciate you, son."

"A'ight. I'm going. Baby girl got first dibs on you; when Ms. Taylor's done, you won't be no good, I bet." He laughed, turning for the hall.

Nye's neck whipped to face him, her palm on her high hip. She rolled her eyes. "He needs to sleep restfully. Close the door behind you."

Shaking his head, Zo was sure to obey.

Squinting, I stretched my arms above my head. "How are you?"

"I could ask you the same thing. I see you didn't even shower before boarding the plane."

"You told me to come straight home."

"Take a breather. Celebrate with your team a little first."

I shook my head. "My leash was yanked."

Behind me, she mounted the bed and walked over to me on her knees. Without hesitation, she took me at the shoulders, her palms applying massage-level pressure. I relaxed into her touch, head rolling behind my shoulders.

Damn.

I missed her. Lately, I found myself always missing her.

"Even happy dogs need leashes." Her warm, soft lips grazed the skin of my neck. The feel of her silky tongue trailing from my shoulder to beneath my ear had my eyes closing and dick twitching.

"We don't like being away from our owners either."

She pulled my head back by my kinky twists and kissed me with more tongue than lips. This was nasty Nyedeera. I should have been expecting her. She hadn't had the best of me in weeks, thanks to my chaotic schedule. It was impossible for her to pop up in away cities and be secretly awaiting me in my hotel suites. Distance from me, I'd learned, didn't work for her. Her absence also made me realize how dependent I was upon her sneaky manipulation.

Felinely, she crawled around my sitting frame until she straddled me. Her mouth went to work on me again. Our tongues met, hers in hunger while my movements were lazy. I loved teasing her.

"I got the job," she whispered.

My eyes fluttered open and head eased back. "At *NYU*?"

She nodded, combing my beard with her fingers while stroking her spread hips over me.

"When did we discuss this?"

Her lips met mine. "When I told you about it."

"About applying."

"Same difference."

I tried focusing my heavy eyes with her so close. "Big difference."

She took me at the back of the head, dismissing my argument with a kiss. Her little hand pushed between us in search of my cock.

No.

I flipped her onto her back, deftly pushing her legs in the air. Leaning lazily on my side, I dipped my face in the apex of her thighs. Spreading my tongue, I brushed her valley with broad strokes. She hummed her appreciation. I kissed her lips and tongued deep inside of her before flicking her swollen clit with the tip of my tongue.

"*Ssssssluuuush...*" her cry incoherent, but understood.

Then I lifted, resting my head on her inner thigh. "I don't think that's what she told us."

With her eyes closed, Nye asked, "Who?"

"Belvin."

Her head swung up. "What about her?"

"You can't make decisions like that without consulting me. It's what we want to build toward. Right?"

Nye and I were still "dating." It was something we decided on, and equally preferred for people to not suggest we get married simply because of our history. We had a family together Nye and I were committed to strengthening. I made no secret of my desire to build a brand. That started with my family. My household.

"We are?"

"Have I done anything to make you feel less than equal or voiceless?"

She shook her head, eyes closing. Nye licked her lips. "No, baby."

"Then why do I feel left out of that decision?"

Rubbing her lips together, she reached down to finger my hair. "I'm in love with you," she whispered so low, I thought she was crying.

You've never told me thi—

My fucking lungs seized and eyes grew as wide as saucers. "What does that have to do with you taking the job?"

Nye's eyes squeezed closed. "My edge." She looked at me again and whispered, "I don't want to lose that with you. I know your insecurity is me leaving, but mine is becoming boring and predictable to you."

"You don't have to get a job in New York to keep me hungry." Bad choice of words likely because I was hungry for her, considering her juices were slathered over my mouth, nose, and beard.

Why were we arguing while my dick was hard?

"But I do have to get a life, Launz. You're on the road a lot. I'll just be teaching at the college level, a seasonal role similar to yours."

"But what about Zo…Gena and the baby?"

She shook her head. "What about you…and me? I've given Zo twenty-two years—more than that if I count my pregnancy. It's on him and Gena to give that to their child. What if I want a baby?"

My face opened wide. "You want more kids?"

Nye rolled her watering eyes and murmured, "Thank God I don't, based on your reaction."

"I'm not saying—" I took a deep breath, silenced by the turn this conversation had taken.

"I want to focus on me. I've been denied that for far too long. Launz, I've done right by Zo. He's grown. Focusing on me is doing what feeds my soul. That's you. So, hell yeah: I'm thinking of ways to enrich what we have here. I want to be selfish for once."

She was crying.

God, I hate when she cries...

Mentally rolling my eyes, I moved up the bed then pulled her on top of me. Similar to my muffin earlier, Nye was over me. This position for me gave them a moment of superiority over me. Nye needed control and I didn't mind giving her the position of caging me. That inferiority was my weakness. I wanted her stapled to me.

I watched her wipe her face dry with her hands, her nose reddened with emotion. Then Nye placed her hands on my chest. "I'm ready to be kind to myself, Launz."

"I want to be kind to you, too."

"Good. Because I didn't accept the job."

My face wrinkled. Nye's expression loosened into her signature cunning grin. She winked at me. Her tricky hands managed my half-mast erection.

"I don't get it."

Nye arranged me between her wet folds, rubbing us together.

"I applied to three schools in Connecticut." She reached down and kissed me, swallowing my confusion. Her pussy still roved over my cock, lubricating me.

"Nye..." I tried around her busy tongue.

She rolled her hips up until her cunt captured the head of me at her opening and I was inside of her. This felt like twenty-three years ago. Her adroit skills suppressing my good senses. The sounds of her wetness suctioning then releasing me weakened my fight. She was riding me, rolling her ass over me, and tonguing me down. Sinking, my one hand forked her scalp and the other gripped her at the side of her waist.

Would we marry? I didn't know. Would we be together forever? I hoped so. The prospect of seeing a collection of properly rolled boogers next to my bed had never seemed so appealing. Either way, Nyedeera Taylor would always be the first and possibly only woman to weaken my resolve by capturing my heart. It was hers to influence forever.

But...

I reared my head deeper into the pillows, separating from her just as my belly warmed from her passionate dance. "Connecticut." Seeing her only through my lashes, I groaned, "I'm good with that." I'd have her more to myself that way. She could come back to the house to check in when I was on the road and be back in Connecticut for work *and me* by the time I returned. "It sounds like a genius idea to me." I liked her selfishness already.

With eyes as low as mine, she beamed, stroking me a few times. "I know, which is why I lied about *NYU* first."

Wha—

I smacked her meaty left cheek hard. "I'm gonna spank your ass."

Nye managed to sober her giggles. "I'm looking forward to it. But let me let one off first. I've missed you, Launz."

And I made it happen.

Nye being kind to Nye was fine by me.

The End

###

IMAGERY

#PenningWithoutParameters

🩶 #ImGonnaMakeYouLoveMe 🩶

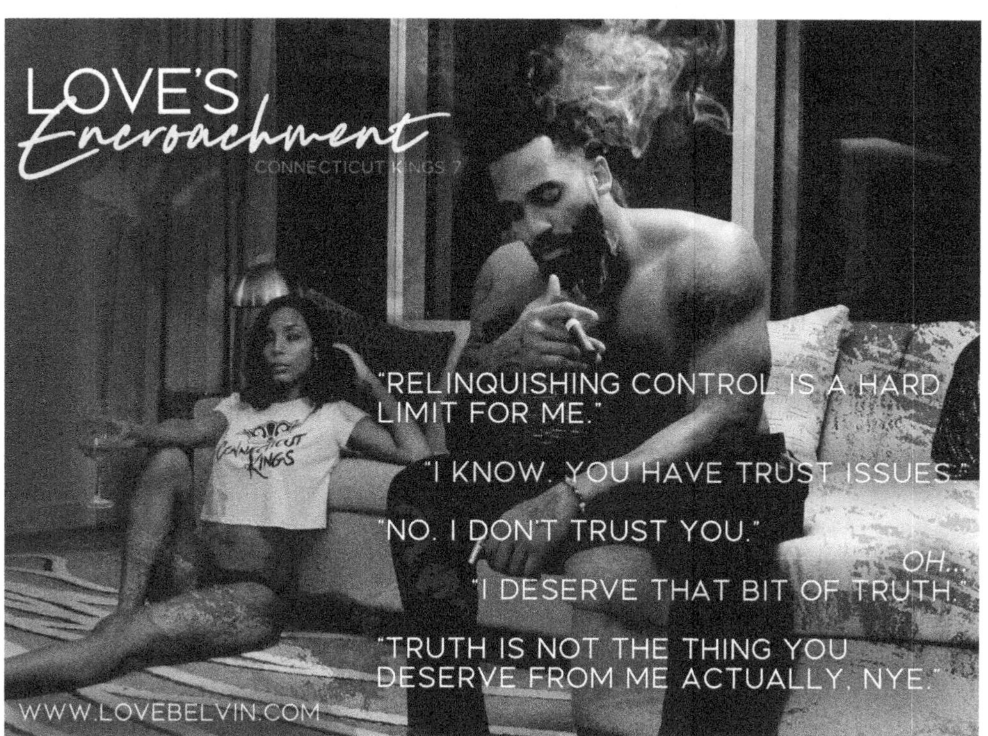

LOVE'S
Encroachment
CONNECTICUT KINGS 7
"RELINQUISHING CONTROL IS A HARD LIMIT FOR ME."
"I KNOW. YOU HAVE TRUST ISSUES."
"NO. I DON'T TRUST YOU."
OH...
"I DESERVE THAT BIT OF TRUTH."
"TRUTH IS NOT THE THING YOU DESERVE FROM ME ACTUALLY, NYE."
WWW.LOVEBELVIN.COM

~LOVE ACKNOWLEDGES

Visuals: **Indelible Images** – Mae, you were the consummate professional from start to finish. Thanks so much for your patience and diligence on this baby. I'm looking forward to many more bomb shoots with you! #GirlPower **Frank Trigg** – It was Launz at first sight for me. Thanks for lending your well-groomed image to this project. I mean… The cigars! Whoa! It was meant to be. LOL! I wish you nothing but success! Chunia – I appreciate you serving as visuals for my feisty Nye. Job well done. *FIRE!* My best to you in all your endeavors!

Beta Reader: — Yorubia, this will likely be your last gig with me because you're so annoying. So take your last bow. RME. Hope you got your stimulus check! LOL!

LBTR — Afi, Angela J.J., Artemysia, Ashley, Ayanna, Bonita, Brittany, Courtney, Danielle, Denise, DeVona, Diva Dee, Doris, Ericka M., Gail, Grace, Heather, Heidi, Hyacinth, Jasmine, Kamashia, Karmen, Katrina, Kendra, Kerry, Keyma, Kim, Kimmiko, Kita, Korei, Lafay, LaSonde, Linda R., Linda W., Malaika, Marshall, Michelle R.O., Michelle T., Mocha, Monique H., Monique N., Natoya, Nena, Nikki, Rakia, Quan, Regina, Richell, Rose, Roslyn, Samona, Sharon L., Sharon F.W., Shaun, Sophia, Stacey, Tanisha, Tara, Teresa, Terri G., Tesha, Tiffany, Tineka, Tonya, Tralaina, Vivian, Wendi, Yolanda P., Yolanda U., and Yorubia, I appreciate our connection. Never forget that. Love you guys FOR REAL. ***Jemeka*** & ***Rita***: It's been a rough season in our individual lives, and I appreciate how we've held on to each other through the storms. Love you ladies, dearly. Can't wait to hug you guys again!

Special thanks – Bailey West, thanks for your military knowledge and getting me right on the Gunnery Sergeant. My absolute best to you!

Christina C. Jones aka CCJ — You dat bomb chick! I'm so grateful for you. Thank you so much for the support you provided me during my low season. You're definitely holding me down. I appreciate you for supporting, empathizing, and chiding when I'm being "tough Love." Love you so much, girl!

Interior Artist: Cedeara Ardell McCollum — Thanks, baby girl, for the imagery you've designed for my books! Love you always!

Proof Reader: Tina V. Young — You're a beast and my secret weapon. Thanks so much for your constant dedication to #TeamLove. Thanks for those football plays and being sure I stuck with the CK structure. #SecretWeapon

Editors: Zakiya Walden of ***I've Got Something to Say!*** — I think you had too much fun with this project. I laughed while you fussed at everybody—me, Launz, Nye, Trent, Camay…everybody! LOL!

Santisha Taylor of ***AccuProse Editing Services*** — I failed again, and you've showed up again! LOL! One of these days, I'm going to make you proud. Teehee! I'm so grateful for your expertise and warm bedside manner!

MDT: Almost there!

Master, my ***Jireh***, my ***Rohi***, Ephesians 2:10 (NKJV) "For we are His workmanship, created in Christ Jesus for good works, which God prepared beforehand that we should walk in them." *May my steps always be ordered by You. Thank you, Father.*

~OTHER BOOKS BY LOVE BELVIN

Love's Improbable Possibility **series:**

Love Lost, Love UnExpected, Love UnCharted **&** ***Love Redeemed***

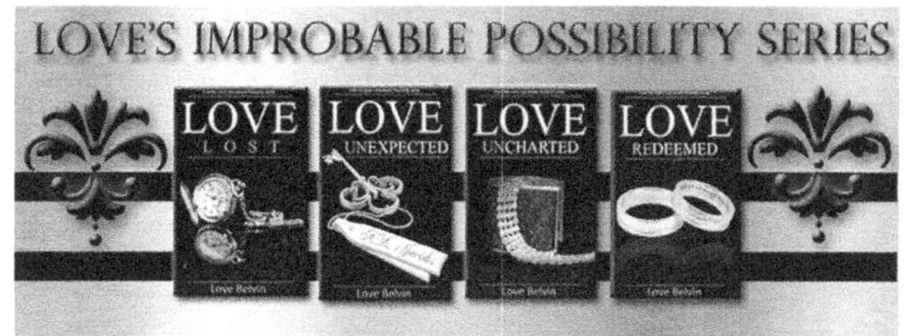

Waiting to Breathe **series:**

Love Delayed & Love Delivered

Love's Inconvenient Truth (Standalone)

***Love Unaccounted* series**:

In Covenant with Ezra, In Love with Ezra & Bonded with Ezra

The Connecticut Kings **series:**

Love in the Red Zone, *Love on the Highlight Reel, *Determining Possession, End Zone Love, Love's Ineligible Receiver, *Pass Interference, Love's Encroachment, & *Offensive Formations (*by Christina C. Jones)

Wayward Love series:

The Left of Love, The Low of Love & The Right of Love

Love in Rhythm & Blues series

The Rhythm of Blues & The Rhyme of Love

The Sadik series

He Who Is a Friend, He Who Is a Lover & He Who Is a Protector

The Muted Hopelessness series:

My Muted Love, Our Muted Recklessness, & Our Reckless Hope

The Prism series:

Mercy, Grace, & The Promise

Low Love, Low Fidelity (Standalone)

~EXTRA

You can find Love Belvin at www.LoveBelvin.com
Facebook @ Author - Love Belvin
Twitter @LoveBelvin
Goodreads: Love Belvin
and on Instagram @LoveBelvin

Join the #TeamLove mailing list on my website to keep up with the happenings!

Click here (with WiFi) to join!

Made in the USA
Coppell, TX
16 April 2024